Getting Home

For Some Dogs, It Just Isn't Easy

Written by Kimberly Manuelides

Edited by Lauren Lowther
Proofread by Jen Katz
Cover Art by Frankie Pardoe

A Story from 1st Ride Publishing

ISBN 978-1517590741

Dedication

This book is dedicated to every dog and every person who has ever struggled to find a place in this human's world and to those who have persevered and helped them.

To Colby, Sasha, Atari, Bonnie, and especially to Tim, without whom none would have made it.

Special Dedication

Sister Mary Sunshine, my Sasha, was my best friend. She was my plucky guide and companion of many years who always seemed to know when to push her head under my arm and demand a good scratch. Her sense of humor and her pure determination were an inspiration when times were tough and her judgment I learned to trust. Sister Mary Sunshine, my Sasha, recently crossed the Rainbow Bridge, but not before she shared her wisdom with those who earned her trust and affection.

Getting Home
For Some Dogs, It Just Isn't Easy

Written by Kimberly Manuelides

Other Books by 1ˢᵗ Ride Publishing:

Science Fiction / Adventure
The Champion of Clarendon Ditch Trilogy by Matt Galeone
The Champion of Clarendon Ditch: Book 1 –The Hatching (2012)
The Champion of Clarendon Ditch: Book 2 –The Alliance (2012)
The Champion of Clarendon Ditch: Book 3 –The Champion (2012)

The 15th Chair Trilogy by Matt Galeone
The 15ᵗʰ Chair: Book 1 - The Journey (2014)
The 15ᵗʰ Chair: Book 2 - The Return (coming 2016)

Dramatic Fiction
An Image of Us, Robert G. Edwards (2013)
Purple Meadow, Robert G. Edwards (2013)
Chasing the Surface, Robert G. Edwards (2014)
The Amalgamist, Cristel Orrand (2014)
Khayal, Cristel Orrand (2015)

Creative Non-Fiction
Into the Heat: Fighting Fires in Baltimore City, Ray Lockett (2015)

Horror
Withered Hosts, Scott Bisig (2014)

Books by 1ˢᵗ Ride Kids
The Special Beat of Ordinary Feet, Patricia Perrin (2013)
Sparky & Squeaker, Jen Katz (2013)
Willoughby's Whiskers, Patricia Perrin (2015)
Helping Hooves & Humongous Hearts, Beth Williams (2015)
Oberst & Valentine Find Their Human, Matt Galeone (2015)

For a current listing of 1ˢᵗ Ride Publishing's library of published works check our website at: http://1strideenterprises.com/books/

Prologue

"Whatever happens, don't get angry! Don't panic! Don't bite!" Mamma barked frantically at her son and daughter.

"But, Mamma, what's happening? Where are they taking us? What about you? What about you, Mamma? Where are you going? Mamma!!" Skeeter tried desperately to get back to her mother as the stranger was pulling her away.

"Don't worry about me, Skeeter! Just remember those words." They pulled her further down the aisle, away from her holding cell.

"But, Mamma! Come back!" cried Skeeter's brother, Mikey, desperately trying to get away and back to her. He struggled against the unsympathetic Impound Man who shoved him into a separate holding cell.

"Mikey, you too! Don't worry about me. It's too late for me. I'm done for. Protect your sister and remember what I told you!"

"Get in there, you!" Impound Man shoved Skeeter into her cell. "And stay there!" he said, giving her a swift kick in the chest. "You too, you lout," he said to Mikey, kicking him in the tail. The gates to their cells slammed shut.

Mamma was gone. Skeeter and Mikey stood alone in their cells, trembling. Skeeter paced around her cell frantically.

"Mikey, where's Mamma? What are they doing to her?" Skeeter barked back to her brother.

"I don't know, Skeet; I can't see her anymore," Mikey pushed his face into the wire of his cell, trying desperately to catch a glimpse of Mamma, but without any luck.

"But, Mikey! Why do we have to be apart? Mikey, where are you? I can't see you!"

"I'm over here, Skeet. Just down the aisle from you," he replied with his bravest bark.

Mikey and Skeeter both barked wildly, begging Impound Man to put them together, but to no avail. Mikey looked around at his cell. First House had been bad, chaotic, crowded, loud. This was worse: a tall chain link fence, a long strip of concrete. Only a small bowl of water in the corner. A padlocked gate. Nothing more. Not even a mat or blanket to keep him warm.

Other dogs, some of them big and menacing, others, like him, small and terrified, occupied the other cells. Some barked frantically for their owners to come get them. Others, like him, whined, paced, and cowered in a corner away from Impound Man, who also paced back and forth, up and down the aisle. Up and down, up and down, back and forth. As Impound Man paced, he struck the wire of the individual cages with a piece of hose, threatening any dog that got out of hand. Eventually, Mikey pulled himself into a tight ball, covered his ears, and cried. This was not how things were supposed to be. This was not what he had in mind days before when he'd organized their escape from the backyard.

Chapter 1

Two months later, a small, kind-looking lady came to the Impound. "They're down that way," gestured the Impound Man. Approaching Skeeter first, the lady entered the cell quietly and sat down at the gate. Skeeter was a little small for her breed, light, sleek. Built like a cheetah, thought the lady. "I bet you can really run, can't you girl?" the lady said looking at Skeeter appraisingly. "You've got a nice face, smart expression, I bet someone will be able to really work with you and turn things around for you. Just you wait and see."

"Mikey, what do I do?" Skeeter called out, pacing nervously around her cell, her long tail curled stiffly over her back.

"Remember what Mamma said, Skeet. Don't get angry. Don't panic. Don't bite. Maybe you'll be lucky and get out of here." Mikey had seen others get out, relieved to be claimed by their owners or even strangers with soft voices like the lady sitting in Skeeter's cell. So far though, their owner had not come for them. She had not even stopped in to check on them. Mikey and Skeeter had to contend with Impound Man on their own, and Impound Man had little regard for the feelings of dogs like them on the Impound's death row.

Skeeter paced some more, watching the woman on the floor.

"Come on, honey. It's alright. I'm here to take you and your brother out of here," she said, extending her hand encouragingly.

"Don't get angry, don't panic, don't bite," Skeeter repeated to herself as she approached the hand, head down and tail between her legs.

"There there, sweetie. It's okay. I won't hurt you." The lady scratched Skeeter's chin gently as she slipped a collar over her head and offered her a small piece of hot dog. "Come on, honey, let's get you and your brother out of this place."

The lady got up quietly and led the nervous Skeeter down the aisle to her brother's cell. "You'd think they would at least have put you guys next to each other," she muttered under her breath.

"Watch out for that one. He's aggressive," said Impound Man, pointing toward Mikey with the piece of hose he seemed to always have at the ready. The lady looked around her at the small, cramped runs, filled with terrified dogs, most of them, like Mikey and Skeeter, there because of their owner's ignorance. Impound Man, standing stiffly behind her, menacingly handled the hose.

"We'll be fine," said the lady, watching Mikey closely as she approached his cell. "Do you think you could hang on to Skeeter here for a minute while I get him?" Impound Man took Skeeter's leash and gave it a strong jerk. The lady shook her head and gritted her teeth. Best to hold her tongue until she got the two dogs out, she thought. "Hang in there guys, almost out," she said quietly as she entered Mikey's cell.

Mikey watched cautiously from his corner. His head was down, but his tail curled tightly over his back as he paced a tight circle. He eyed the lady suspiciously.

Skeeter called from across the aisle. "Mikey, she just got me out of my cell, Mikey. Maybe she's here to pick us up and take us out of here. Both of us Mikey, both of us. 'Member Mikey, 'member, 'member Mamma's words!"

"Shut up, you," growled the worker, giving her leash another jerk and stiffening his grip on the hose "just in case."

Mikey listened to his sister's words. Eyeing the lady entering his cell, Mikey repeated, "Don't get angry, don't panic, don't bite," over and over to himself.

"Come on fella. It's alright." The lady sat down in the cell with him. "You can come over here. I won't hurt you," she said, extending her hand softly and tossing a couple of pieces of hot dog his way.

Mikey cautiously approached. Was it possible he, too, was getting out? Most of the time, he'd observed, people only came for one dog. Could this lady seriously be coming for two? He took a deep breath and nervously began to pace the back wall, barking, head down, tail still arched over his back. His head pounded with buzzing and drumming. The sound of fear. The sound of his memories from the First House.

"It's okay. Take your time. We're getting you guys out of here, boy. It took some doing, but you and Skeeter are going far, far away from this place." The lady sat quietly on the floor of Mikey's cell, extending her hand encouragingly.

Mikey perked his ears. He *and* Skeeter? Both together, away? Mikey looked at the lady cautiously. She looked alright. She was quiet, small. She moved easily, with no sudden jerks. Her face looked kind and her eyes were soft. She didn't look anything like anyone he'd ever seen. That could be a good thing, he thought.

Mikey approached the lady cautiously and accepted the piece of hot dog from her outstretched hand. "There you go. See, it's okay. I got ya," said the lady as she gently slipped the collar over his head and gave his chin a gentle scratch.

Once outside his cell, Mikey saw his sister standing anxiously next to Impound Man. He resisted the urge to land a solid bite on the man as he handed Skeeter's leash over to the lady. Skeeter, on the other hand, focused only on her brother. She hadn't seen him in two months. "Hey, Mikey! We're going! We're going! Wow, you look awful. You really lost weight and your coat looks terrible," she exclaimed. Mikey gave his sister a good sniffing over, the buzzing in his head subsiding somewhat as he smelled her familiar breath.

"You don't look so great yourself, sis. But wow, it's great to see you again!"

Skeeter gave her brother a playful swat. "Where do ya think we're going, Mikey? Where? Do you know? Are we going home? I don't really want to go home but it would be way better than here, don't ya think?" Skeeter bounced as they exited the Impound.

"I dunno, Skeet, but wherever we're going, please let it be better than here." Mikey looked around, skeptically eyeing the large truck in front of him and imagining it full of dog crates and loud, angry people, like the last time when they'd been taken to the Impound.

"Ok, guys, you can have your reunion later. For now, let's get you into the truck and out of this horrible place," said the lady. She led the excited but nervous dogs out of the Impound and to the truck with the gentle driver who would haul the two dogs away to safety and, she hoped, recovery.

A dog breeder and trainer herself, the lady knew she had to try to rescue the dogs when the First Owner called her in a panic on the eve of her trial. It had been the dogs' trial, really. Too often loose. Too many nips. The last nip – of a child – required a couple of stitches. The townspeople were up in arms about the dogs and wanted their revenge. "I know I've allowed a terrible thing to happen," First Owner cried on the phone, barely coherently. "Can't you please come help? Testify? Anything? Can you find the two young ones a home? I'm afraid it's too late for their Mamma."

The lady didn't hesitate. As a breeder, she felt a duty to help out dogs in need whenever and however she could, even if it was just to get them out of their situation and on their way to a safer place.

The lady had been to the First House to evaluate the situation and then to the trial, where she implored the judge to spare the lives of all three dogs, only to learn that Mamma had been killed even before the trial began. What she saw and heard at the First House sickened and saddened her. They weren't bad people, but they had let the situation get out of control. Having worked with dogs all of her life, she knew that sometimes families found themselves in circumstances that had spiraled out of control, and their dogs often paid the price. What she had witnessed at Skeeter and Mikey's First House, however, was the worst she'd ever seen. A downed and useless fence; dog crates in rooms piled with boxes, newspapers, and toys; adolescent boys who themselves were traumatized and starved for attention. A widowed mother, exhausted, grieving, frustrated, lost. How could anyone function in an environment like that?

Shaking her head and fighting back tears, she looked at the two traumatized young dogs now huddling in their crates in the truck. She hoped that the kind shelter lady she'd found to take them in would be able to help them begin healing. She doubted that they'd ever be able to leave the shelter, though. Their trauma had been so great; they were likely to need special care for the rest of their lives. But maybe, just maybe, the right family would come along.

She closed the crate doors softly, gave each dog a kind scratch on the chin and turned to speak to the driver. "Careful with these guys, they've had a rough time. How long do you think the trip will be?"

The driver looked sadly at Mikey and Skeeter, already as far back in their crates as they could wedge themselves, and shook his head. "I can see that. The trip should be about ten hours. I'm going to drive them straight through so we don't have to worry about stops. Those mats and blankets in there should help make them comfortable."

The lady smiled gratefully. "Thanks, and thanks for volunteering to transport them."

"I'm heading that way anyway, it's no big deal."

Giving Skeeter and Mike one last look, the lady wished them good luck. She knew they'd need it.

The driver shut the truck door, and soon Skeeter and Mikey were fast asleep in the warmth and darkness of the cab, safely stowed behind the driver.

As the miles passed, Mikey would occasionally awaken and look across the crate at his sister, curled tightly on her blanket. He'd heard her cries at night at the Impound and knew she hadn't slept more than a minute at a time in the two months of their ordeal. He hadn't slept, either. Although he had no idea where they were going or what would happen next, the lady and the driver seemed different than Impound Man. Hopefully, he thought, wherever they were going, life would be better than it had been so far.

At dawn, the truck pulled down a long driveway and finally came to a stop. Mikey and Skeeter peered out of their crates and watched as the driver spoke with Shelter Lady. She radiated warmth, kindness, and energy. "Thanks for making the trip, Mac," she said to the driver. "Would you like a cup of coffee?"

"No thanks, Ma'am. I really need to get this rig into town. I'll just leave these two with you and be on my way."

"Did you have any trouble with them?" she asked, peering curiously into the truck at the two huddled dogs in their crates behind the seat.

"No, not really. They were a bit nervous to start, but they settled right in. Need help getting them out?"

"No thanks. We'll be fine," she said, quietly taking Mikey and Skeeter's leashes before opening their crates to let them out. "Come on guys, let's see how you do with the other dogs." Mikey and Skeeter looked around skeptically. The place was quiet. No screaming. No frantic barking. Just grass and a seemingly kind lady looking down at them softly.

Skeeter gave herself a big whole body shake. "Mikey," she said hopefully, "I think this might be better."

Mikey looked around dubiously, unwilling to commit. "We'll see, Skeet. We'll see."

Chapter 2

Don't get angry. Don't panic. Don't bite. After the truck driver had dropped them off with the Shelter Lady, it was easier to remember Mamma's words and to practice them than it had been at the Impound. Shelter Lady was kind. She gave them their space, time together, and a big, well fenced yard to burn off excess energy.

Except for the other Shelter Dogs, who barked as they played and romped in the yard, it was quiet. No cars, no banging, no shouting. Still, it was hard. After two months at the Shelter, the buzzing in Mikey's head had dulled from a loud thunder but it was still there.

He and Skeeter talked about it sometimes, but talking about the Before Time, the time before they came to live with Shelter Lady, was hard with the other Shelter Dogs around. Most of the other dogs hadn't been through what they'd been through. Most of the Shelter Dogs had not had a First House as chaotic as Skeeter and Mikey's First House had been. Most of the Shelter Dogs had not been at Impound, certainly not on Impound's Death Row. No, most of the other Shelter Dogs had lived in nice homes with nice people and had no idea why one day they'd been dropped off at the Shelter, sometimes by a crying family member, sometimes by a stranger who had picked them up after their family had mysteriously disappeared. Most of the other dogs had been promised Forever Homes and believed that a Forever Home was a good thing. They were the lucky ones. Their previous memories were a comfort to them as they waited.

These dogs talked for hours at a time about wonderful places with warm beds, kind people, and family adventures. Fools, thought Mikey. Homes were scary places. Why would anyone want to live in one, especially forever? If those places were so great, why were they here anyway? Why not stay with Shelter Lady, he wondered. It was quiet here and the yard was fenced. No loud kids, only a quiet one or two who helped Shelter Lady every now and again. No bikes, no banging on crates, just peace and other dogs and Skeeter. Skeeter was recovering well from the Before Time. She bounced and played with the other dogs, soaking in their tales of Forever Homes. Sometimes at night, before going to sleep, she would talk about their Forever Home.

"Mikey, when do you think we are going to Forever Home?" she'd ask. "And, Mikey, what d'ya think it looks like? What d'ya think it smells like? I bet it has a big yard and lots of room and the people are nice and we get to play all the time, and they'll play with us, real gentle-like. You know? And, and I bet it smells like food and grass! Oh, Mikey" she'd say wistfully, "Mikey, I wanna go to Forever Home." Oh, how she could go on. At least the other dogs gave her something to dream about instead of having nightmares about First House and Impound. Maybe, someday, for her, he thought.

At night, with his sister tucked in and warm by his side, Mikey's own thoughts ricocheted. One moment, his head would buzz, filled with the ghosts of the Before Times, Impound Man,

First Lady, First Lady's kids, Mamma. The next, he would recall the other dogs talking about Forever Home, and a tiny part of his mind allowed him, too, to yearn for that mythical place.

But, inevitably, his Before Time memories would come rushing back, and he was reminded that, for him, it was likely too late. He was too old, too damaged, too dangerous. At least, that was the consensus of the other shelter dogs as they all pondered their own fates.

"After two years old, dude, your socialization window is closed, closed, closed," said one dog.

"Yeah, and look at you. All you do is pace. No human's going to like that, man," said another.

"Seriously, and you ain't even friendly to nobody, no people, no dogs. You're just way too serious," complained still another.

Maybe they were right, he thought. But at least he'd gotten here. Here was better than there, better than the First House, definitely better than Impound.

But then, one Saturday evening, right after supper, two months after being dropped off at the shelter, Shelter Lady announced brightly, "Mikey, Skeeter, tomorrow might be your adoption day! And, if we're lucky, they'll take both of you. Just make sure you impress the old one when you meet her. Either way, when the people arrive, please, please, don't get angry, don't panic, and don't bite. Just keep it together, Mikey, and maybe you and Skeet will go home together."

Skeeter's ears pricked up when she heard Shelter Lady's words. She knew what "Adoption Day" meant. She'd seen other Shelter Dogs on their Adoption Days. "Did you hear that, Mikey? Adoption Day! And for both of us!" Skeeter bolted around the yard, running circles around her brother and Shelter Lady.

"I dunno, Skeet. Let's just play this one by ear, ok? We've never met these people and who knows, we may not like them. Why are you always in such a hurry to get away from here anyway?" Mikey grumbled, trying hard not to let Skeeter talk him into hoping for something he didn't think could happen.

"Oh, come on, Mikey. Don't be that way. We could like them and they could like us and we could go with them and then we'd all be happy," Skeeter coaxed still bouncing playfully around her brother.

Shelter Lady looked sadly at her friends, watching their conflicting expressions. Seeing the clouds crossing through Mikey's eyes as he watched his sister scampering around the yard, Shelter Lady gave him a soft scratch on the chin. "Come on, boy. Cheer up. These people have heard all about you and they really seem like they could handle that noggin of yours," she said gently. "Anyway, do your best tomorrow, ok?" Shelter Lady turned off the light and closed the door behind her. "Good night, guys. Sleep well."

That night, of course, neither dog slept. Instead, they curled up tightly next to each other, practiced Mamma's mantra and wished she was there to help them figure out what they should do. "Mikey, what if they don't like us? What if they only like one of us?" Skeeter fretted. "Do you think if we mess up, Shelter Lady will send us back? I don't want to go back, Mikey."

"She's not going to do that, Skeet. She never sends anybody back. Remember last week? It was supposed to be Bubba's day, but the people didn't like the way he looked and then he jumped on the little girl and knocked her over. Shelter Lady didn't send him back. Besides, don't worry, Skeet. No matter what, we'll be together," Mikey promised, putting on a brave face for his sister. "I'll protect you when the people get here. Just hold it together."

13

"How're you going to do that, Mikey?" Skeeter asked, putting her chin across his back, her eyes wide and blinking hard.

"Don't know yet, Skeet, but I've always done it so far. Somehow I'll just have to do what I've always done."

Indeed, Mikey had always tried to protect her. At their First House, Mikey had been the one to intercede when the family boys chased Skeeter around the house with skateboards, slingshots, and squirt guns, or terrorized her by banging on trash can lids. He'd interrupted the local town kids when they had trapped Skeeter in the alley behind their house, some of them on bicycles and skateboards, forcing her to run for her life. And, when the family kids had pounded on Skeeter's crate until she trembled and hid under her blanket, Mikey had pitched a fit, barking, grabbing and shaking his mat until it was torn to shreds, and slamming his head and paws into his crate door to draw attention away from her. Even here at the Shelter, Mikey was the one to intercede when his sister's constant playing and chatter annoyed the older dogs.

But at the Impound, it was Skeeter who had saved Mikey. Seconds before he had acted on the impulse to bite the hand that had been poking and prodding at him during his temperament test, Skeeter had implored from her cell, "Mikey, remember!" And he had. Thanks to Skeeter's intervention, his death sentence was commuted, and two days later, the kind lady and the truck driver had shown up.

Mikey curled up next to Skeeter and tried to think positive thoughts. Maybe, just maybe, tomorrow they'd both go "home," whatever that was.

Sunday morning finally broke. Adoption Day had arrived. Shelter Lady brought Mikey and Skeeter into the adoption room, where they found Shelter Man sitting at the table, slicing hot dogs. This must be a big day, thought Mikey. Usually Shelter Man stayed out of things, and Mikey liked it that way. Nothing wrong with him, but Mikey found human men to be scary, unpredictable. They were louder, they moved more abruptly, and they were moody. One minute they were gentle, the next they were pushing and pulling. Some of them, like Impound Man, kicked and punched.

Shelter Man had never done any of those things. He seemed alright, actually, but Mikey knew men to change abruptly and for no good reason. So, instead of giving Shelter Man a chance, Mikey kept his distance and made sure that Skeeter did as well, moving in front of her if she strayed too close. Seated, cutting hot dogs, at least Shelter Man was not causing trouble.

Shelter Lady, though, was nervous and decided it would be better for the dogs to meet the people separately. She, Mikey, and Skeeter went back to the kennel.

The other Shelter Dogs barked excitedly on their return. "This is your big day, guys! You could be going to Forever Home!"

"You've been here so long! Aren't you happy?" exclaimed one.

"Why would I be happy?" asked Mikey, sulking in his corner.

"Well, like I said, you could be going to Forever Home!" wagged the chatty one.

"Mmm. Maybe. I dunno. Forever Home might not be all it's cracked up to be," said Mikey.

Skeeter, however, was buoyed by the other dogs' enthusiasm. "But it might, Mikey, it might! And you and I could play, and sleep, together with our people and they'd be nice to us and give us treats and scratches and we could go places and …"

"Skeeter! Enough!" barked Mikey. "Let's just play it cool, alright? Don't get your hopes up."

Skeeter dropped her head and her tail drooped between her legs. "Okay, Mikey, but still, wouldn't it be nice?"

"Yeah, c'mon, Mikey, don't spoil it for Skeet. You don't know, this really could be her lucky day," said the chatty dog.

"Sure, but…"

Shelter Lady reentered the kennel and interrupted their conversation. Snapping a leash on Mikey, and giving him a scratch on the chin, she encouraged, "Come on, boy. Let's see how you do first. Just remember. Don't get angry, don't panic, and for God's sake, don't bite."

The buzzing in Mikey's head, never quite gone, grew louder. Entering the adoption room, Mikey's Before Time memories came flooding back: people poking, dragging, pushing, shoving, kicking. Cages, separation from Mamma, separation from Skeet. Cold concrete. Alone, other dogs hollering and clambering in the night. Mikey was scared. Strangers rarely brought good times. He didn't care what the Shelter Dogs said about Adoption Day and Forever Homes.

Best to be loud, he thought as he and Shelter Lady entered the room. Maybe the people would go away and leave Skeet and him with Shelter Lady and the Shelter Dogs. Mikey paced around the room and barked loudly, his tail curled tightly over his back, his face tight with tension.

"Just have a seat and ignore him, he'll calm down. Just give him a chance," Shelter Lady said nervously. The people were also nervous and stood watching Mikey pace and bark, pace and bark. "Please. Sit down," Shelter Lady said to them, gesturing at the table next to Shelter Man.

The people sat. Shelter Man pushed a pile of hot dogs toward each of them. "Just give him a piece when he comes over to you. Don't make a big fuss of it. It will help him calm down," Shelter Lady explained.

With the people seated, Mikey's buzzing eased. He took in his surroundings and noticed another dog in the room. A very old dog, judging by her looks. Almost completely white where she'd once been black and tan, just like him. Her tail was short, unlike his, which curled in a sweeping arc over his back when he was nervous or excited, but it wagged gently as she eyed him from across the room. He could tell from looking at her small compact body that she'd once been athletic, like him, but judging from the way her body sagged and her elbows bowed, he could see that had been a long time ago. Mostly though, the old dog looked sad and tired. Really sad. Really tired. "What's with you?" he asked, trotting over to her and giving her head a good sniff.

The old dog looked at him and returned the sniff. "It's been a long day already and I'm still stiff after a long drive yesterday. To top it off, we spent a God awful night in the tiniest, most disgusting hotel room I've ever been in. It was cramped and smelled. The beds were too soft. At least the pizza we had for dinner was good," she continued, continuing to sniff him head to tail, sizing him up.

Forgetting all about the humans, Mikey looked at the old one with wonder and asked, "Are they dropping you off here?" He'd seen some of the other shelter dogs get dropped off simply because their owners thought they were too old. Why else would this dog be here?

The old one looked at Mikey with a start and gave Mikey an indignant snort. "Heck no! We're here to take you home with us, *if* I approve."

Mikey gave a snort in response. *"You're* the one Shelter Lady says I have to impress?" Mikey exclaimed.

"I guess so. Don't see anyone else around here, do you?" replied the old one.

Mikey looked around nervously at the strange people. "What about them?" he asked.

"Well, sure, they have to approve, too, but I have the final say in whether you come home with us."

"Come with you? Home? What is home, anyway? D'you like it there? How long have you been there? Why did you drive so far and stay in a stinky hotel room? What is a hotel room, anyway?" Mikey's questions poured out in a torrent.

Sure, the other Shelter Dogs talked about these things, but here was a dog from the outside talking about home like it was a good thing. However, judging from her looks, she was having a rough time of it. As far as Mikey could see she could hardly move, and she looked really sad. Why would a dog that was as sad as this old dog be so emphatic about going back to her Home? It made no sense to him. Not to mention, according to the old one they'd had a bad night in a stinky, tiny hotel room. That sounded horrible, whatever it was!

The old one eased herself down onto the rug next to him. Home's where they are," she said, gesturing warmly toward the two people seated with Shelter Lady and Shelter Man. "I live with them. Why wouldn't I like it there? We go places, see things, eat pizza. The drive was bad and the room was cramped, but that wasn't their fault. They tried to make me comfortable." The old one got up stiffly walked up to the man and gave his hand a friendly nuzzle.

"But, homes are loud, scary places, with mean children and angry men," Mikey responded.

"Not my home," said the old one, gazing affectionately at the man seated at the table. "My house right now is quiet, too quiet, actually. I spend my day alone waiting for these people to come home. That's why we're here for you, so I don't have to be alone anymore," she said, looking at Mikey with a hint of kindness.

"So, why do you look so sad? And why are you alone so much? And how old are you, anyway? You look really old," asked Mikey, curiosity taking over his caution.

The old one chuckled. She liked Mikey's looks. He had physically recovered from his stay at the Impound. He'd put on weight. His coat was glossy. He was handsome and strong. He was mostly black, with brown points just above his eyes and muzzle; white socks and a splash of white on his chest. His eyes were bright. He held his tail in an arc over his back as he paced around the room athletically, with a vibrant bounce in his step. His bark was loud and commanding. But for the tail, he reminded the old one of her brother the first day they'd met so many years ago. Her brother's tail had been docked and he was broader, but the markings, the attitude, all remarkably similar. Holding his gaze appraisingly, the old one responded, "It's a long story, kid. If you come with us, maybe I'll tell you on the way home. What's your story, anyway? How did you end up here?" she asked, ignoring the question about her age.

"I dunno. If we come home with you, maybe I'll tell you." Mikey wasn't going to let the old one get one up on him.

"Wait a minute. Who's we?"

"Me and my sister, Skeeter, of course," said Mikey, now fully remembering the mission of the day. He brightened up at the thought of her and determined to put his best paw forward for both of their sakes. "Skeeter? She's the best! She's smart and she's funny. We help each other. She's amazing. Where she goes, I go; where I go, she goes. That's what I promised Mamma and what I promised her." Mikey gave the old one a full play bow as he spoke about his sister.

Noticing but deciding to ignore the bow, the old one paused her nudging of the man's hand and looked thoughtfully at Mikey. "Oh, that's right. I thought I'd heard there were two of you. When I just saw the one of you I thought maybe I'd misheard. My hearing isn't what it used to be, you know. Well, I guess you both better make a decent impression then," said the old one.

"But I still don't understand. Why should we want to come with you and those people? Why not just stay here?" Mikey asked, still skeptical of the whole Forever Home concept.

"That's up to you, kid. But this Skeeter you just told me about, don't you think she deserves a chance at a better life, better than hanging around with a bunch of silly shelter dogs? And look at you, you're a wreck. Nothing but pacing and barking for no apparent reason. What's wrong with you?"

The old one had a point. The Shelter Dogs had told tales of nights spent on sofas under blankets with their humans, taking trips with them to faraway places full of adventure. Forever Homes. But if those homes were so great, why did they end up here, he wondered? The old one told of long drives, hotel rooms, and pizza with these two people who she seemed to like. She actually looked at both men seated at the table without a trace of fear. She walked right up to the man she came with and, without any hesitation, demanded—and received—a piece of hot dog. Skeeter did deserve better than to spend her life in a shelter, even a nice one like this. She deserved a chance to curl up on a sofa with a human, her human. Maybe he deserved better, too.

Mikey stopped his pacing and looked at the people seated at the table. He noticed a small piece of hot dog extended his way from the lady. She looked nice, calm like the Shelter Lady, and the lady who took them away from the Impound. And the man, he didn't look too bad. He seemed tired and sad like the old one, but not menacing like Impound Man. He looked more like Shelter Man.

Holding his breath and remembering his mantra, he dropped his head, lowered his tail, and took a step forward toward the lady. She didn't flinch, but spoke to him softly. "C'mon fella. It's okay," she said extending her hand quietly and looking away. Not so bad, he thought.

So he tried. Mikey grabbed the hot dog quickly before the lady changed her mind, then darted to the other end of the room. Hmm. Hot dog good. Time to run around and make some more noise in case they got any ideas. Running around and making noise was just the thing to do at times like these, he thought. Burn off some energy. Release the tension. Make a show.

"Kid, you need to calm down," said the old one. If you keep it up, you won't get any more hot dogs. And they might not take you, either."

Good point, thought Mikey. He tried again. It wasn't so scary, really. The people seemed nice. She had a soft voice and a gentle face. The man stayed seated safely with Shelter Man and offered him a hot dog.

"What do you think, old girl?" said the man looking down kindly at the old dog next to him. "Do you think Mikey would be a good friend for you?"

The old one sat down next to the man and took her hot dog confidently from his outstretched hand. Things looked hopeful.

Mikey took another piece of hot dog from the lady and decided to sit down next to her.

Seeing Mikey relax a bit, Shelter Lady turned to the people, "so, now that he's settled down a bit, would you like to meet Skeeter?" she asked.

"Absolutely," said the lady, scratching Mikey's chin.

"What do you think, old girl? Do you like your new friend?" asked the man again, scratching the old one's ears and handing her another piece of hot dog.

Shelter Lady left the room, and a few moments later Skeeter came out, whirling and barking and making the biggest impression she could. Mikey's buzzing, which had subsided as he talked with the old one, grew louder again. Skeeter had buzzing too. Mikey could hear it by the tone and pace of her barking. He could see the panic in the whites of her eyes. Skeeter's buzzing saddened, frightened, and angered Mikey all at once. She was so young when the Before Time happened. Only one year old. Why did they have to treat her that way? He'd vowed then that he would protect her and never let that happen again. Never let anyone hit her or kick her or take her away like they'd taken Mamma. So far, he'd managed, but only just. They'd made it out, out of the First House, out of the Impound. What to do now?

Skeeter was scared, but she was determined to find Forever Home. She tried pushing her way past Mikey toward the lady seated at the table. Having completely forgotten that moments before he had been happily munching on hotdogs and considering the possibility of Forever Home, Mikey barked, "Just stay in the background, Skeet. Let me take the heat." He pushed his sister out of the way of the lady's outstretched hand.

"But I want to meet the people, Mikey. Why can't I meet the people? They look nice," Skeeter barked as Mikey pushed her away from the man as well.

"Don't you remember what happened last time? They acted nice at first, too. Remember? This could be just like that," said Mikey, frantically trying to keep up with Skeeter as she tried push her way around him to meet the people.

"Oh, c'mon, Mikey. That's not fair," whined Skeeter as she tried to make her way past her brother.

"No. Stay away from them, Skeet. It might be a trick." Mikey pushed her away from the lady's outstretched hand.

"But, Mikey! Let me meet the people!" Skeeter was determined.

"I said no, Skeet. Stay away."

It might have ended with an argument, but at that moment, Skeeter noticed the other dog in the room. The old one had managed to wedge herself next to the lady and was standing close to her for support. Distracted from her effort to meet the people, for the time being, Skeeter turned to her brother. "Hey, Mikey, who's the old one? Hey, old one, who are you? And how old are you anyway, you look … ancient!" Skeeter bounded over to the old one to give her a good sniff, almost knocking her over.

The old one, who had been watching the two youngsters with a mixture of amusement and alarm returned the sniff. "I'm Sasha, but my friends call me Sister Mary Sunshine. I'm fifteen," she said.

Skeeter and Mikey both stopped barking and gasped. "Fifteen!! I've never known anybody that old before. Wow! You must know everything!" Mikey exclaimed.

"You don't look so Sunshiny. Why do they call you that?" sassed Skeeter.

"Hey! Mind your manners, Skeet!" barked Mikey His head still buzzed loudly. What if Skeeter blew her – their – chance? What if this ancient Sister Mary Sunshine didn't like disrespectful young dogs?

"Kid, I told you that you need to calm down," said Sister Mary, looking directly at Mikey, who appeared to be losing his cool. "I don't mind the question. It's just what they call me, that's all. Skeeter, push your way through your brother and go make friends with the lady there. Don't let him hoard all of the attention. Go see what you and she think of each other. That lady and I have been friends for a long, long time. My bet is that you will get on with her just fine. Kid, you get out of your sister's way and go get some more hot dogs from the man, and let him give you a scratch. He doesn't bite. You can't keep pacing around him, constantly barking at him and snatching hot dogs. My bet is that you and he could be great friends if you got your head together."

Taking Sister Mary's advice, Skeeter shyly approached the lady. "Don't panic. Don't bite. Don't panic. Don't bite." She repeated to herself over and over.

"Go on, child, the lady won't hurt you, I promise," said Sister Mary, giving the scared young dog a nudge. Skeeter blinked hard and took a deep breath. This was her big chance at Forever Home. Slowly, slowly, stay low to the ground. Okay. Take the hot dog. Get a pet. Back away.

"Whew! I did it! Sister Mary, I did it! Mikey! I'm going to take a victory lap."

Skeeter tore around the room and then made another try with the lady. She got another hot dog. "Hey, Mikey, check me out! I got a hot dog too," barked Skeeter.

"I know! I got some more from both of them! And look, watch this, I've got my paws on her lap!" Mikey said. "I got a pat on the chin from the man and a hot dog and then a pat from the lady and a hot dog. I put my paws on her lap and she didn't even flinch. I'm going to try to put my face in her face and see what she does," enthused Mikey, now wagging his tail in huge circular arcs.

"Mikey, be careful! You know people don't like it when you put your face next to theirs!" Skeeter barked, alarmed at the risk her brother was taking.

"I know, Skeet, but there's only one way to find out if these humans are honest. You have to put your face right next to theirs and then see if they will look you in the eye."

Mikey was determined to test the lady. Putting his paws firmly in her lap, he leaned up to her face, took a good long sniff of her breath, and looked her right in the eye.

"Well, hey, there buddy!" the lady exclaimed, gently giving Mikey's belly a scratch. "What d'ya think? Want to come home with us?" she asked, returning his gaze with a smile.

"You did it; you did it, Mikey!" exclaimed Skeeter. "You looked right at her, and she looked right back and didn't even stiffen up or nothing! Let me try the lady! You go test the man. See what he does."

Mikey trotted over to the man and gave him a try just as he had tested the lady. "Nope, no flinching, and I got a hot dog!" said Mikey.

"Me too!" said Skeeter, hopping off the lady's lap. "Let me try the man." Skeeter was now thoroughly enjoying herself, convinced that Forever Home was just minutes away for both of them. "Look Mikey, he passed my test too!" Skeeter said brightly.

Sister Mary smiled as the lady scratched her ear. They looked like nice kids, she thought, a little rough around the edges, but overall, nice. At least they would dispel the awful gloom that had descended over her family in the past few months.

After an hour or more passed, Sister Mary grew tired and the people saw the need to go home. Decision time. "What do you think, Sister Mary?" asked the lady.

"They'll do. I can handle them," answered Sister Mary.

"What do you think?" asked the man, looking skeptically around the room at the two excited, nervous dogs and then at his old friend, Sister Mary, standing quietly next to him.

"I think we should take them both," said the lady, looking hopefully at her old friend, who seemed to have been cheered by the visit.

"Both?" asked the man skeptically.

"Both," answered the lady and Sister Mary.

"I'm not sure she can handle both; what if you could only choose one?" asked the man.

The decision was a tough one for them. Skeeter was a year and a half, a female, small and submissive, but clearly very active. Mikey was four, a male, clearly fearful, but holding it together. Sister Mary seemed to have taken a liking to them both.

"Best faces, children," coached Sister Mary, recognizing that her people were making their decision and wanting it to go well for her new friends. "If you guys want to stay together, you better make your best case to these people now. Look confident. Be friendly. Work the room," she urged giving Mikey a nudge toward the man.

Each dog tried, putting a head on a lap here, a nose under an arm there. Skeeter begged. Mikey pleaded, not really believing that the stories he'd heard of Forever Homes were true, especially not for him, but hoping for the best anyway. Even Sister Mary did her best to convince her friends that she could handle – they could handle – both young dogs. At one point, all three dogs lined up in front of the lady and implored simultaneously. Shelter Lady and the lady looked at each other and smiled.

"Hey, look, guys, they are really making their case," Shelter Lady said hopefully.

But, in the end, it was decided. Mikey would go with the people, but Skeeter would stay at the Shelter. The people were concerned that Sister Mary was just too frail to handle two young dogs. They'd decided to take Mikey on the theory it would be easier in the long run for Shelter Lady to find Skeeter a home. She was younger, and still in her socialization window. Given his size, history and age, Mikey would have a harder time finding a home if they left him, and the people thought they could handle him. In time, they hoped he could come around to being a confident and happy companion for Sister Mary. So, it would just be him. That would be the best for everyone, they thought.

"Ok, let's get him in the car. Say goodbye to each other, guys," said the Shelter Lady, clearly disappointed in their decision, but happy that Mikey was going to a home. Hearing their decision, however, Mikey's heart sank. Wow. What now, after all they'd been through together? Never see each other again? Never know what Skeeter was doing or what happened to her? Skeeter was the one who deserved a home, not him, he thought.

Forgetting his earlier boast about how he would make sure they stayed together, Mikey cried, "Skeeter, what should I do?" as the lady took his leash and headed for the door.

"Just go with the people, Mikey, I'll be fine. You can come back and get me later." Skeeter said.

Mikey was uncertain and tried to pull the lady back to her as Shelter Lady led Skeeter away toward the kennel. "Just go, Mikey, go!" Skeeter cried as she walked through the door, taking what she thought might be the last look she'd ever have of her brother.

Skeeter knew what the people knew. She'd heard the other shelter dogs say the same thing. Mikey had few shots at Forever Home. This was probably his best chance. Indeed, it might be his only chance. She owed him that much.

As Skeeter left the room, Sister Mary gave Skeeter a reassuring glance. "Don't you worry, child. If I know my lady, we'll get you out of here, too. Just let me work on them a little."

Saying goodbye, the lady gave Skeeter a scratch and a gentle tug on her ear. "Don't worry girl, everything will be alright. Hopefully, we'll come back for you, but it really is up to Sister Mary. Let's see how she does in the next few weeks with your brother." The lady knew the decision to take just one dog was the "right" decision, but in her heart she really wanted both dogs to be together, particularly after all they'd been through in their Before Time. The man paused too, and gave Skeeter a long look, his eyes deep and sad, but he said nothing.

"Don't worry, Skeet," said Shelter Lady as the car pulled out of the driveway. "Something tells me, you'll see your beloved Mikey again. We just have to be patient. They'll come back."

28

Chapter 3

The man scooped up Sister Mary and gently eased her into the back of the car. "There you go, girl. Get yourself situated," he said, helping Sister Mary settle in.

"Don't get angry, don't panic, don't bite, don't get angry, don't panic, don't bite," Mikey chanted as he jumped into the back of the car with Sister Mary. The space was small, but big enough for the two dogs to ride comfortably.

"What's that you're saying to yourself over and over anyway?" asked Sister Mary as she settled onto her mat.

"Oh, that," Mikey said sheepishly, "I didn't mean to say it out loud. Don't get angry, don't panic, don't bite. It's just something Mamma used to always tell me and Skeet, that's all."

"Wise dog, your Mamma," said Sister Mary kindly.

"Yeah, she always knew what to do and say, but then one day they took her away from us. Since then, we've kinda been on our own," said Mikey sadly as he looked around for a place to sit.

Sister Mary looked thoughtfully at the nervous young dog in front of her. She could see that he was struggling to hold himself together in the strange environment without his sister. "Don't worry, kid," she said encouragingly, "these are good folks. We'll help you sort things out."

The dogs' conversation was interrupted by the lady. "I'm riding with you guys back here," she announced, sliding her way quietly into the back of the car. "Move over Mikey. I'm not leaving my old friend back here with a strange dog, and besides, this way you and I can get to know one another on the ride home."

Adding a person to the small space was nerve-wracking, but Mikey appreciated the lady's sentiment. Standing up for friends and family made sense to him. It was what he'd always tried to do. So, Mikey held his nerve, didn't get angry, didn't panic, didn't bite, and moved over for the lady.

Sister Mary, who had already claimed her spot right on the big mat behind the man's seat, promptly fell asleep. The lady claimed her space too, also on the mat, next to Sister Mary. Maybe he could score some mat space too. Hmm, he thought, maybe he could find a spot between Sister Mary and the lady. That way he'd get more mat. Nobody seemed to mind. Cool. The buzzing faded. The drums in his head stopped beating. Maybe, just maybe, the Shelter Dogs were on to something about Forever Homes.

After a time, Sister Mary stirred. She raised her head and gave Mikey a long, appraising look. "So, kid. What's your story? You have the body of a four-year-old, but the face of a ten-year-old. You already have grey around your eyes and your whole face is creased. You look athletic enough to drive a herd of cattle, but you're afraid of your own shadow. How did you and Skeeter end up at Shelter Lady's house?" Sister Mary was not one to sugarcoat things.

"It's a long story," Mikey said, staring out the window, "I'd rather not talk about it right now. Can't we just hang out back here?"

"Sure, it's up to you, but I'm telling you, we are going to be in the back of this car a long time. Do you have any idea where you're going?"

"Of course I do!" Mikey turned from the window indignantly and put on his best confident face. "I'm going to Forever Home."

"Geez, kid. Sure, forever home, forever home, any idea where that is? Or even what it even means?"

"Well, sure. It's really, really far from the Before Time and it's where you stay forever, sit on the sofa, and eat pizza."

Sister Mary just about fell off the mat laughing, which was hard because she was already lying down. But then she looked at her new friend and saw the hurt and confusion in his face. Not just his eyes. His whole face. His whole body. He really didn't know. He'd obviously been through a lot, but none of his experiences had prepared him to do anything but yearn for a safe, quiet place and a piece of pizza. Maybe, she thought as she watched him monitoring the people in the car with her, maybe someday he'd get it.

Sister Mary remembered her own trip home. It had been a long time ago, so long she'd almost forgotten. Thirteen years, almost to the day. But, looking at Mikey, the hurt and confusion on his old/young face, riding in the back of the car with two strange people, she remembered that trip like it was yesterday.

Back then she'd been a Kennel Dog, a proud member of the House of Staufenfeld. She lived with her mamma, aunts, uncles and cousins in a nice kennel. It was grand. Lots of room to run and play. A nice place to sleep at night in the company of her family, and a nice lady who took care of everybody. Every day the nice lady would let them out in the yard and she and her kennel mates would run, up and down the hill, chasing each other, stealing toys from each other, and playing keep-away. Oh, how much fun they had as a family!

Her mamma had many puppies, and all of them – well, almost all of them, anyway, according to the rumors – were living happily with people around the country.

Sister Mary, though, had been special. She'd been selected to replace her mamma one day as the head of the House of Staufenfeld.

But, one day, life changed. The nice lady took her to the vet with tears in her eyes and told her it was not Sister Mary's fault. The lady had been put "out of business." After a brief tussle with some strange people, Sister Mary went to sleep for a little while and when she woke up she felt somehow different. Not bad, just different. Then, a trip to the pet store where she got a wash and a nail trim, and then a visit from some people, the same people who were with her now.

The people were strange then, awkward, overeager. So was Boyo. What a pompous, rude dog he had been when they first met! Boyo had announced himself as the head of the House of Something or Other. Sister Mary had been unimpressed, and haughtily introduced herself as the head of the House of Staufenfeld. But she had followed Boyo and jumped into the peoples' truck out of curiosity anyway and bam! The door closed, and there she was with Prince Boyo Something or Other for a miserable, three-hour ride away from home. She hadn't even gotten a chance to say goodbye to her family or the nice lady who'd taken care of her since birth. What would happen to her?

What would happen to the House of Staufenfeld? She'd fretted over these questions as the car sped away from her first home

That night, the people had made a big deal of giving her a mat and a place in their room, and Boyo had made a fuss about taking her around the house, showing her this toy and that toy. But what did she care about that? The room had been small and indoors. No fresh air. What about her pack? How would they manage without her?

She had spent the first five days trying to find a way out of that cage of a house, trying windows, walls, glass doors, with no success. Two months later, an opportunity had arisen. She had broken away from the man, pushed her way out the door, and run for it. Wouldn't her family, her real family, be surprised when she got back home, she had thought as she had sprinted down the street, leaving the man and Boyo far behind. But, twenty miles later, tired and sore from all her running, she started having second thoughts. It was dark, late, and she had been working up the nerve to run across a six-lane highway when a stranger slammed on his brakes and stopped his car right in front of her. The next day the stranger had returned her to the people's house, and the relief in their faces and tears in their eyes had changed her mind about them forever. Particularly the lady, Ruth, who had held Sister Mary that day in her arms until both of them had stopped shaking.

Pulling out of her reverie, Sister Mary looked again at her young friend. Her eyes softened and she decided to ease his mind if she could.

"So, kid, take a look around you and take it all in, alright? These people drove all day yesterday in this old car with this giant mat, and spent the night in a stinky hotel room, just to help you and your sister. And to find me a friend or two. This lady, here, she moved heaven and earth for you, even though she didn't know you, just because she heard about what happened to you guys. I was there when she read the news. You should have heard her explode. I mean, I've hardly ever heard her that upset."

"That man, there, he's tough, hard to read, but he's got a heart of gold and will stop the earth from spinning if it will keep you safe. Get to know him and he's sure to take you on some amazing adventures. So, relax, kid. Things are going to be better now. You'll figure out what Forever Home means. You'll know it when you feel it. You'll get it one of these days. But for now, just remember what your mamma told you and get some sleep. It's going to be a long ride."

Mikey looked carefully at Sister Mary, studying her face. He wanted to believe her, but could he? Was there really such a thing as Forever Home? Maybe. At fifteen, Sister Mary was the oldest dog he'd ever met. Her face was completely white, but she bore no creases around her face and her ears were soft, gentle. Her gait was unstable, but confident, and her eyes! Those eyes were the kindest eyes he'd ever seen. They could hold his gaze for, well, forever. Her eyes were happy, honest, and sparkled with good-natured mischief, despite their age.

Maybe she was right. Maybe things were going to be okay after all. Maybe he really was getting a Forever Home. So he took her advice for the second time that day. Mikey curled up between Sister Mary and the lady and, exhausted, put his head in the lady's lap and went to sleep. Just before drifting off, Mikey lifted his head one last time. "Sister Mary, what do you call these people anyway? Do they have names like we do?"

"Of course, they do, kid. The lady here is called Ruth, and the man is called Max."

"Ruth and Max, Ruth and Max. Ok," he yawned. "Talk with you later."

"Night, kid."

Miles stretched into more miles. Mikey slept the best sleep he'd ever slept, nestled safely on the mat between Sister Mary and Ruth. Every now and then, he'd wake, look out the window, and take in his surroundings. Ruth and Max seemed happy. They chatted quietly, the radio playing in the background. Ruth gave a soft scratch to Sister Mary, followed by a gentle belly rub, and then the same to Mikey. It was nice.

He decided to investigate Max, driving in the front. Flopping his paws over the back of the front seat, Mikey looked out the front window and at Max. Noticing Mikey's head next to his, Max grinned and reached into the bag next to him. "Hey, buddy, what's up? Want a French fry?"

"Do I want a French fry?!" thought Mikey. "I *love* French fries. Well, I've never actually had a French fry, but they smell amazing! Maybe this will work out after all."

Mikey chomped on a fry and then a chicken tender that Max gave him. And then another. Mikey looked out the front window for landmarks that could lead the way back to Skeeter, just in case, and then went back to sleep.

Many hours later, Ruth made an announcement. "We're going stopping at Mammaw and Pop Pop's! Pop Pop is cooking and making special treats for Mikey. They're dying to meet Mikey, and I could really use a break!"

Mikey looked at Sister Mary, alarmed. "Ok, Sister Mary, who's Mammaw, who's Pop Pop and what's the scoop on them?" he demanded nervously.

"Keep calm, kid. They're nice old people. We visit them a lot. My brother Boyo and I stayed with them sometimes when

Ruth and Max went away. From what I've heard other dogs tell, it beats the heck out of staying in a kennel. The food's always good. They have lots of space in their yard. You'll like them."

Skeptical but reassured, Mikey again checked the scenery out the front window and snuggled back down between Ruth and Sister Mary.

An hour or so later, they pulled into Mammaw's and Pop Pop's driveway. Sister Mary waited for Max to pick her up out of the car and gently steady her while she got her balance. Once she was out, Ruth let Mikey out and held onto his leash as everybody went inside. Sister Mary went first and immediately announced herself.

"Hello! Hello!" she barked brightly as she tottered into the room, greeting Pop Pop. "Hello! Hello!" Sister Mary greeted Mammaw and the rest of the room.

Smells overwhelmed Mikey at the door. Sniffing the air, Mikey could make out bacon, peanuts, and who knew what else? Whatever it was, Sister Mary was right, these people did like to eat some good stuff. Pop Pop was standing by the stove, leaning over a tray of something interesting. Mammaw was sitting at the table with some other lady. Worried that this might be some sort of setup, Mikey looked around at Sister Mary nervously.

"Sister Mary, who is that other person? You told me there would only be two other people here. Why is she here?"

"Oh, that's Ruth's sister Stuff. She's alright. I like her, too. She lives with L'il Bud and Sammy, Uncle Pete and Jake. You'll meet them soon enough."

Mikey was not yet sure whether he should trust Sister Mary and the people, but decided to try to make a good impression. "Don't get angry, don't panic, don't bite," Mikey whispered to himself as he entered the room.

Mikey tried to focus on the situation at hand. No anger, no panicking, no biting, he thought as he trotted around the room anxiously. "Hey, buddy, want some salami?" Sister Stuff held out her hand.

"Well, yeah, of course!" said Mikey as he approached her extended hand cautiously but hopefully.

"How about some pastrami?" Another hand, this one Max's, offering some pastrami. Not bad either.

"Want an oyster with bacon?" This one from Ruth. Wow! Sister Mary smiled and munched on the extra piece that Pop Pop dropped for her as he went by with a plate of goodies.

Plate after plate went by. Snacks were doled out by everyone. The people laughed, Sister Mary laughed. Mikey tried to take it all in and even laughed a little himself. After a while, Ruth and Max decided it was time to leave for home.

Back in the car, heading for his new home, for the first time in a long time, Mikey was hopeful. Except for worrying about Skeeter, things in his young life seemed to have taken a turn for the better. Maybe the shelter dogs had been wrong, he thought. Maybe he wasn't too old or too damaged for Forever Home. Even the buzzing from the Before Time had ebbed. He was glad for Sister Mary's company; she did seem to know a lot. And, Ruth's lap was a nice pillow for his tired head. It was too early to really get a read on Max yet, but Mikey was hopeful. Sister Mary, small and frail as she was, genuinely seemed to like and trust Max. Max did share his food, so he couldn't be all bad!

Chapter 4

Gnawing on the blanket Shelter Lady had given her when Mikey left, Skeeter looked at her new kennel-mate. "He'll come back for me. He promised. He always does," she said, eyes wide, trying to convey as much confidence as she possibly could.

"How can you be so sure?" said her kennel-mate.

"I just told you! He said he would and he always does!"

"No he didn't. I was listening. He just walked right out the door and never said a word, not even goodbye."

"That's not true, he tried to get back to me, but they pulled him away. Anyway, he said so before! And he always does! Besides, Sister Mary said so and the lady…"

"You don't know. You just don't know," barked Skeeter's kennel-mate. "Even if he wanted to, how do you think he'd find you? Do you have any idea where we are, how you got here, or even where he's going? And what about the lady anyway? You met her one time for half an hour. You don't know anything about her."

Skeeter thought hard. She was only fourteen months old when she had arrived at the Shelter. So much had happened before and after, she was still trying to sort it all out. Where was she and how had she gotten there? She remembered the drive from the Impound to Shelter Lady's. It had been long and cramped. "Don't worry, Skeet, just keep practicing Mamma's sentences and you'll be okay," Mikey had told her, trying to stay confident and upbeat for both his sister's sake and his own. They'd been in the back of a truck cab though, so neither dog really could see where they were going. Just lights and darkness, lights and darkness, as the driver drove on through the night.

Upon arriving at the Shelter they had heard the other dogs, just as they could at the Impound. The Shelter Dogs had sounded hopeful, however, not desperate like the dogs at the Impound. "Come on guys, here you go. Let's get you in and settled for the night." Shelter Lady had led them inside to a brightly lit room with a large kennel and mat with blankets at the end. "You guys bunk in here for the night. I think you'll sleep better together," she had said as she turned off the light and left the room. Still frightened but exhausted, both dogs had dropped on the mat together, snuggled under the blankets and drifted off to sleep.

In the weeks that followed, Skeeter had tried to forget what came before their shelter days. The Before Time was not worth remembering as far as she was concerned. Just a lot of yelling, barking, banging, teasing, chasing. Impound Man with his big boots and that piece of hose he carried, always aiming at her.

"Skeeter," her kennel mate interrupted her reverie. "Skeeter, how can you be sure that Mikey's coming back for you?" he demanded. Having no good answer to her kennel-mate's question, Skeeter shook her head and glared back at him. Mustering all the confidence and bravado she could, she barked back, "It's none of your business anyway. Mikey's going to Forever Home and then when it's time, he's coming back to get me. Besides, Shelter Lady told us we didn't have to worry about how we got here. Past is past and we're all going to Forever Home one day."

Skeeter's kennel-mate decided to leave her alone. He had worries of his own and besides, he hadn't meant to upset her. He was really hoping for an answer. Shrugging his shoulders, he dropped his tail and lay back down on his mat.

Chapter 5

"Wake up, kid, we're home." Sister Mary gave Mikey a push with her nose. "Come on, make way so they can get me out of here and I can get inside." Mikey looked around hesitantly before getting out of the car.

"What do you think, buddy? Pretty good, huh?" said Max, looking at Mikey as he helped Sister Mary out of the car. Ruth and Max both stretched and showed Mikey around the outside of the house. Even though it was dark, Mikey could tell that there were trees, lots of them. A backyard, not huge, but it looked adequate. The house, he thought, was of reasonable size. It looked pretty nice. Trees, space, house. We'll see, he thought.

Sister Mary shook, stretched, and ambled along behind Max, Ruth, and Mikey. She eyed her new friend fondly. It was nice to have another dog around again, she thought.

It was late. Ruth and Max were tired. They all were. "Let's just turn in for the night," yawned Ruth. With that, Max picked up Sister Mary and carried her upstairs.

Sister Mary settled into Max's arms as he carried her up the steps. Those steps were more than she could muster anymore and she welcomed the lift. Mikey bounded up the stairs behind them.

"Hey, Sis, where do we sleep? Where's your kennel?" Mikey asked.

"Kennel? No kennel here, I sleep on the floor where I want. You sleep where you want. Just don't sleep on his bed."

"Whose bed?" Said Mikey looking around the room in confusion.

"Boyo's. It's there at the foot of their bed. Just like he left it," sighed Sister Mary.

"But, Sis, where is he?" Mikey asked. He'd smelled another dog when he entered the house. It was clear that some other dog had been there. It was faint, but his scent was everywhere, inside and out, only Mikey hadn't heard or seen any sign of him so far.

"Boyo's not here anymore, kid. He passed away a month ago."

"What did they do to him?" Mikey asked, fear and buzzing starting to roll through his head. He remembered what "they" had done to Mamma.

"They did everything they could for him, kid. He was old. He got cancer. They tried to save him, but in the end, he just couldn't hold on any more. We all go sometime, you know. We're all trying to put his passing behind us. Max there took it really hard. He and Boyo were especially close. They used to go everywhere together, do everything together. Camping, hiking, eating, playing. They were best buds, right out of a story book. That man cried for days when he died. So did I."

Mikey studied Sister Mary's face. He could see that she was telling the truth. Her eyes were glassy and her breathing hard as she remembered her friend and his last days. "Hey, I'm sorry," he said. "How long were you together anyway?"

"Twelve years."

"Twelve years?! Wow; that's like forever!"

"Sure is, kid."

"And all that time with these people?"

"Umm'mm."

"Wow. I didn't think that could happen,"

"Well it does happen, kid. Now go on and go to sleep. We can talk all you want in the morning." Sister Mary had taken her spot on the floor near the heat vent and was ready to sleep.

Mikey looked around. The mats looked ok, but the ghostly echo of Boyo's presence was too much for him to claim Boyo's, which left the other mat and the floor. The floor looked hard and he thought he'd leave the other mat to Sister Mary in case she decided to move from the vent later on. Remembering the warmth of Ruth's lap on the ride home, Mikey looked up at the bed where the people were. Maybe Ruth and Max wouldn't mind if he joined them.

He mustered up his courage. "Don't get angry, don't panic, don't bite," he reminded himself as he jumped on the bed between Ruth and Max and braced himself for any hostile reaction. Ruth stirred and reached around to him softly, noticing his uncertainty. "Hey, buddy. No worries. You can sleep with us if you want," she said patting the spot next to her gently. The sheets were warm and the bed comfortable.

Max stirred and draped a hand softly across Mikey's back. "Hey, there fella," he said, "just leave a little room for me, ok?" he said as he shifted over in the bed.

Still worried that he'd make a mistake that would land him off the bed or back to the Shelter, Mikey played it safe and curled up at the end, making himself as small as he could and hoping they really would let him stay. "Hey, Sis. You awake?" Mikey whispered.

"What now, kid?"

"Do you miss Boyo?"

"Of course, every day," she sighed.

"Me too."

"What? You miss Boyo?" yawned Sister Mary.

"Yes. No. I mean, um, you miss Boyo. I miss Skeeter. Do you think we can go get her?"

"I hope so, kid. I hope so. Now get some sleep."

Mikey curled back up, put his head between his paws, shut his eyes tightly, and covered them with his tail. He tried to imagine Skeeter there with him, her small body curled up next to him like she did when they were at the Shelter, her head flopped across his back, snoring softly. But then he worried about what she was doing miles away at Shelter Lady's. Hopefully, she'd be okay without him and wouldn't get into trouble. This had been a very different journey than the last one. Certainly better than the journey from First House to the Impound. No banging, no crates, no shouting. Instead, French fries, pate, sausages, a warm soft lap, and a friendly old soul to pass the time with. But the ride had been so long, Skeeter and the Shelter were so far away. Mikey knew it was too far to make it back to her on his own. How could he convince these people that they have to go back for her? He got up quietly, turned, and found the warm crook of Ruth's legs. Settling in tightly next to her, he drifted off to sleep.

The next morning, Mikey awoke with surprise. At first, he thought he had dreamed of the long ride and nice people. Looking around, he realized he had not. The room was quiet, the bed large, soft, and warm. No kennel noise. Sister Mary was sound asleep on her mat in the corner of the floor. No buzzing in his head, no drum beats. None. No, this was not a dream, but maybe a dream come true?

Leaping off the bed with a joy he didn't know he had in him, Mikey exclaimed, "Hey, Ruth, hey, Sis, hey, Max! Let's do something!"

Ruth and Max just rolled over, still half asleep. Mikey bounded back on the bed, wagged his tail and pushed his nose under Ruth's still sleeping head. "C'mon Ruth, let's do something!" Mikey exclaimed again.

Sister Mary looked up at Mikey, yawned and stretched stiffly. "Hey, guys! come on, let's do something. I've got an idea! Let's go get Skeeter! She'd love this room!" Mikey tried again, bouncing from one prone form on the bed to the other.

"Alright Alright. Mikey, I hear you." Ruth stirred. "Come on, Sunny girl. Let's get you and Mikey outside." Ruth climbed sleepily out of bed and walked over toward Sister Mary, giving her a wake-up pat.

Mikey bounded down the stairs and turned to see where the others were. They were still in the room at the top of the stairs. Geez, they're slow, he thought. Let me go get them. Mikey ran back to the top of the stairs. "We're coming, we're coming," said Sister Mary as she shuffled stiffly out of the room.

"Hold on there, Sister Mary. Let me help you down those steps." Ruth picked up Sister Mary Sunshine and started down the stairs.

Mikey liked the stairs and decided to make a couple of laps on them for good measure while Ruth and Sister Mary made their way down. "Hey, Sis, watch this!" Mikey exclaimed. "I can go up the stairs and down the stairs; then I can go up the stairs and around the hall into the bedroom, jump over Max, and then back down the hall and back down the stairs! Whoo-hoo! Oh, wait, Sis, I can go up the stairs, down the stairs, into the living room, over the sofa and…"

"Hey, hey, hold on there, buddy, calm yourself!" Ruth interrupted. She was laughing, but he could tell she wasn't kidding. "Where are you going with all that energy? You're going to knock us over!" Mikey looked at Ruth and grinned. This place was cool, he decided. He was certain that Skeeter would be happy here.

Sister Mary was laughing too. "Kid, I remember when Boyo and I used to do that. I haven't seen stairs so thoroughly exercised in years! The way you banked around that turn? My, oh my. It took me back."

"Really?! You don't look like you could do that," exclaimed Mikey.

"Could I? Oh, you should have seen us. We were quite a team. When Max would come home at our old house, Boyo and I would run up the stairs and then race each other downstairs, around the hall, to the basement and back up again before Max got his coat off. Then, Boyo and I used to grab a toy, any toy, a rope usually. He would grab one end first and run through the house with it like it was the grand prize. Around and around he'd go. I'd chase him and eventually I'd grab it and try to take it away. Then, we'd pull and pull until finally, he'd let go. Sometimes he'd let go and I would still be pulling back so hard I'd fall over backwards. Other times, I'd be the one to let go and he'd fall over backwards. Then, we'd laugh and laugh and start the game all over."

Sister Mary sighed, remembering. "Anyway, we were a team. You're probably not ready for rope and I know I'm in no shape for it. But later tonight, let's see if we can get Ruth to throw some balls for us. That's another game we used to play. It's my game now. I'll show you. This old lady's still got some moves."

"Ball?" Mikey exclaimed, still in disbelief that Sister Mary could move out of a slow hobble. "You play Ball? What is this Ball game that you play?" he asked. She took forever to get up, had to be carried everywhere. How was she supposed to run?

"Yes, kid, Ball." Sister Mary looked at her friend with all seriousness, her ears pricked forward and her eyes shining brightly. "One is never too old for Ball. Ball is what keeps you young, boy. Alive!"

Ball was a sacred game to Sister Mary. Tug, or Rope as they sometimes had called it, had been Boyo's game. Ball was hers. She'd invented it, actually, and then taught Ruth to play. Max never learned, but Ruth was pretty good. Ruth kept the balls in a bag and every night when she came home, she would throw them for Sister Mary. Sister Mary was not a retriever though. Retrievers had their own game. She, being a herding dog had her own game. Balls were for chasing, pouncing, pushing, tossing, and then, well, chasing some more. The more balls in play the better. She could keep track of every single one.

Back in the day, Sister Mary, Boyo, and Ruth had all played Ball almost every night. Boyo had been bigger and stronger than Sister Mary, but she was quicker and more determined. So the match had been even. Ruth had kept enough balls in play that no one ever really got the upper hand.

In his final days, his strength sapped by his cancer, Boyo would lie in the yard and watch the two of them, Ruth throwing the balls to one end of the yard, Sister Mary stopping the balls and then pushing them with her paws, soccer style. Then Ruth would throw the balls back to the other side of the yard. Back and forth, back and forth. Sister Mary would eventually slow to a trot and walk back to Ruth, and the game would come to an end.

Sister Mary tried to put on a good show for her friend in those days. After the game, she would stretch out next to Boyo in the grass and they'd reminisce. Sister Mary would try to help Boyo remember the good times. "Hey, Boyo, remember when we used to play Chase with the plastic bottles? Remember how you and I used to grab the same bottle and run around the field with it? Sometimes the bottle would still have water in it and it would spill down our faces when we crinkled it as we ran?"

"Sure," Boyo'd say. "I also remember how you'd fake me out and run me into the storm pond every now and then," he'd mused, smiling.

"You didn't think it was funny then," she'd say.

"I was all wet, Sis, and it was cold that day."

"You think it's funny now?" Sister Mary had asked.

"Sure, Sis, sure."

"And remember when we first moved here and we played Stick?" Boyo's eyes had looked far off into the distance.

"Boyo, remember how you ran into the back yard and found the biggest, longest stick on the whole place? Then you tried to run through the woods with it but it kept getting caught on the trees? Remember, Boyo?" Sister Mary had noticed Boyo drifting and had tried to keep her friend with her.

"Of course, I do, Sis, Of course I do." Boyo had rested his chin on the ground and smiled. Those had been good times back then he thought.

Chapter 6

The first day flew by like a dream for Mikey. Ruth liked to work in her office on the top floor and the dogs were free to roam the house. Sister Mary, though, was not interested in roaming and was content to sleep at Ruth's feet. Mikey liked his freedom. It was new to him and there was plenty of exploring to do and games to invent. "Hey, Sister Mary. Check me out. I can run down the hall, jump on the bed and back into the office! Then I can run up the stairs and down the stairs again! I'm calling this game Loopty Loop!" Mikey exclaimed.

"Hey, Miss Ruth!" Mikey ran excitedly into the office and jumped into Ruth's lap. "You know what? This would be so much more fun if Skeeter were here! Can we go get her? Can we?"

Ruth put her hand on Mikey's head and gave his ears a gentle tug. "Having fun, buddy? How about you take it easy for a while?"

"Seriously, kid," said Sister Mary from her spot under Ruth's desk. "You're wearing me out just watching you. Besides, nagging Ruth about Skeeter isn't going to get you anywhere right now. Be patient. This will take a little time."

"Fine." Mikey slumped down next to Ruth's chair and quickly fell asleep, dreaming that his beloved sister was there to share the fun. He could almost see the small white patch on her belly and the twinkle in her eye as she rolled on her back in play, batting her paws at him. Maybe someday she'd be here and they could run up and down the stairs like Sister Mary and Boyo had, he thought.

At 6:00 p.m. on the dot, Sister Mary stood up, pushed her way out from her spot under the desk and announced, "Ball time!"

Mikey stirred, remembering their earlier conversation.

"What's the deal, Sis? You talked about it before, but how do we play?" Except for his and Skeeter's games of Chase and Clobber, where they took turns chasing and then jumping on each other, Mikey didn't know any games, much less ones involving people.

"Ok, kid. Here's how the game works. First, we have to get Ruth up to play the game. She always forgets the time and we need to remind her."

"How do we do that?" asked Mikey.

"It's easy, but sometimes she can be stubborn, or maybe just dense. So, stand in front of her and chant, *Play Ball. Play Ball. Ball. Ball.* Until she gets it. Sometimes, you have to herd her over to the cabinet where she keeps the balls because she gets distracted and forgets. And then you have to stick with her until she's outside with the balls. Once she gets outside and gets going though, she's pretty good and she will throw them for us."

Sister Mary was looking forward to playing her game again with another dog. Playing with Ruth alone was fine, but the game really did work better with another dog to contest possession and appreciate style.

"But the game, how do you play the game?" Mikey asked.

"Oh, well, you do whatever you want. That's the point. Once we get her outside, she'll throw the balls and we chase them."

"What do I do when I catch one?"

"Whatever you want. You can throw it, kick it, pounce on it, push it around. Sometimes I just grab it and run back to Ruth with it. I usually pick one and chew on it while I run and then she goes to another ball and throws that one for me to chase. The first ball, the one that I hold onto, keeps my mouth from getting dry," Sister Mary explained.

"Okay. She's standing up. Let's get her to play."

"Play Ball! Play Ball!" the dogs chanted at Ruth in unison.

"Come on Mikey, get your bark into it. She's almost ready to go to the cabinet!" cheered Sister Mary.

"Hold on, Sister Mary. We have to get you down the steps again," said Ruth scooping up her friend and heading for the stairway.

"Play Ball! Play Ball!" the chanting resumed as Ruth put Sister Mary down at the bottom of the stairs.

Ruth looked at her friends and laughed. She missed Boyo. The depression that had befallen the family in his final days and after had been crushing, but wow, was it nice to have some happy energy back in the house again, she thought. "Well, Mikey, I see Sister Mary has been tutoring you in her game. Let's see how you do." She grabbed the bag of balls and headed for the door. Opening the door, both dogs pushed and scrambled for position. Sister Mary seemed to magically transform from a stiff old dog to a fierce and able competitor.

"Play Ball! Play Ball! Ball! Ball! Ball!" she demanded of Ruth from the bottom of the backyard step.

And play they did. Mikey loved Ball. Back and forth and back and forth they went. Sister Mary, of course, couldn't keep up with Mikey, but it didn't matter. She still ran at her own speed, ball in mouth. Sometimes pushing, sometimes chewing, running, smiling, her grey ears flapping as she moved back and forth across the yard.

"Sister Mary, this is totally awesome!" Mikey shouted from across the yard. "I can run with the ball and then throw it and catch it again! Wow!"

Mikey ran at full speed, while Sister Mary loped along at quarter speed. Completely focused on the ball, Mikey ran full tilt for several laps around the yard, around the bushes, around the chairs, back to Ruth, back to Sister Mary. Ruth threw another ball.

Mikey didn't look around this time, just focused on the ball. It was magical. Flying through the air, orbiting, then bouncing, rolling. Amazing. Next ball. Throw, turn, run. Next ball. Throw, turn, run. And another. And another.

"Mikey, look out!" Ruth shouted. Mikey was so focused on the ball he didn't see Sister Mary right in front of him. Slam! Mikey plowed right into her, knocking her flat to the ground. He looked at his new old friend in terror and disbelief. Sister Mary's body was prone. Her legs stuck straight out and her head flopped around uselessly, struggling with the rest of her body. What had he done? Mikey had been so focused on the ball he hadn't even felt the impact. He approached his new friend cautiously.

"Sister Mary, are you okay?" Mikey whispered, pushing his nose at her gently.

"I'm all right, I'm all right," Sister Mary gasped. "Just give me a minute to catch my breath. You really knocked the wind out of me."

"I'm so sorry, Sis. I didn't see you."

"I know. Just watch where you're going next time." Still lying on her side, Sister Mary grabbed her game ball, pulled herself up and gave herself a good body shake.

"Come on Ruth, don't just stand there with your hand over your mouth, throw the next ball," Sister Mary commanded. Sister Mary was one tough cookie. Getting knocked down hurt, but it reminded her she was alive and that felt good.

It grew dark, the dogs were winded, and Ruth declared the game over. She returned the balls to their bag and the bag to the shelf. "Good job, Mikey. I think Sister Mary's taken a shine to you there kiddo," she said giving him an appreciative pat on the head.

Max, who had been watching the game from inside looked at Sister Mary with concern. "Next time, though, watch where you're going. Mikey, that was quite a wipe-out move. Do you think she's ok, Ruth?"

"I think she's fine. You saw her. She just grabbed her ball, shook herself off and kept on going. Just look at the way she looks at him, Max. It's the first time she's looked happy like that in a long time." Ruth gave Sister Mary's ears a gentle rub.

Sister Mary panted happily, and seated herself on the floor next to Mikey. After recovering her breath a bit she turned to him appreciatively. "Not bad for your first game," Sister Mary encouraged. "You've got some nice moves, kid."

"Thanks, Sis. I had no idea you could run like that. You came up behind me out of nowhere. I think that's why I didn't see you. I'm really sorry."

"Like I said, no worries, kid. Now it's time for dinner and Sofa Time."

Mikey cocked his head. Sofa Time? Like the Sofa Time the Shelter Dogs had so revered? They had told him and Skeeter about Sofa Time, endlessly chattering about pillows, blankets, and snuggling with their people, so much so that he thought it was just more of a dream than anything else, but here was Sister Mary declaring that it was about to begin.

It turned out that Sofa Time was Sister Mary's second favorite time of the day, well right after Ball and right after breakfast or dinner. In the warm months, Ruth and Max liked to sit outside and talk after work. That was fine, but the ground was hard and could get uncomfortable, not to mention the bugs. Now, though, it was too cold for Ruth and Max to sit outside, so they moved their conversation inside, down to their den, where the carpet was thick and the sofa was big and comfortable. Ruth sat there, while Max sat in his big, soft chair. When Boyo was alive, Sister Mary liked to lie on the sofa on one side of Ruth, with Boyo on the other side. They would lie there in the comfort of Ruth's lap under a big blanket, Ruth scratching their heads and bellies softly until both dogs were asleep. Sometimes Boyo would climb up into the chair with Max and keep him company for a while.

After Boyo died, Sister Mary hadn't felt much like sitting on the sofa. So she'd moved to a corner on the floor where she could think and remember the good times. But the ball game and her new friend had lifted her spirits, and besides, after that hit from Mikey, a massage from Ruth would be welcome.

But first, dinner. Sister Mary hadn't been hungry for a while, either. Food just hadn't smelled right after Boyo died, and besides, without Boyo racing with her to see who could finish eating the fastest, what was the point? She could take all day to eat her meal if she'd wanted to.

But now, the smells coming off of the counter were, well, just wonderful again. She pricked her ears as the aroma of beef, cheese, and liver all wafted down to her. Ruth put the bowl down in front of Sister Mary before giving Mikey his bowl. "Are you going to eat for me tonight, gal? No more hunger strike, right?" she said hopefully. No more hunger strike Sister Mary thought, and she cleaned up her bowl.

Ruth put away the bowls and declared, "Come on guys, let's go downstairs." Max picked up Sister Mary and carried her down the stairs. Mikey and Ruth followed. "Put her on the sofa?" asked Max.

"Sure, but I doubt she'll stay there. She never wants to anymore, but might as well give it a try," said Ruth.

Max eased Sister Mary onto the couch and Ruth moved in next to her, steadying Sister Mary as she situated herself.

"Sis, where do I sit?" Mikey asked, looking hopefully at the open spot on the sofa.

"Anywhere you want, kid. Just try not to knock into me, got it?" Sister Mary put her head on Ruth's lap and eased herself further into the soft cushions of the sofa.

"Come on, Mikey. You can sit up here if you like," urged Ruth, patting the empty spot on the sofa next to her. Hesitantly, Mikey took her up on her offer and Ruth pulled a blanket over everyone. The Shelter Dogs might have been on to something, Mikey thought. Sofa Time did exist after all.

Sofa Time was a quiet time for the most part. With the stillness and quiet, little sound but the television playing in the background, it was a time to reflect on the day's events and memories of the past. For Sister Mary, those memories were mostly good. She missed Boyo, with whom she'd shared many a Sofa Time, both with and without Ruth and Max. When the two of them had been alone in the house waiting for Ruth and Max to return, they often sat on the sofa together, watching out the window, keeping each other company and guarding the house.

In their first house, before they'd moved here, Boyo would spot the pizza guy on his delivery route and bark from the sofa to let him know where to find the house. Boyo had been good at giving directions, particularly for his favorite delivery man, the one who brought pizza *and* wings. The Indian food guy had gotten a special welcome as well. Wow, did that food smell wonderful! Smacking her lips appreciatively at the memory, Sister Mary snuggled her head deeply into Ruth's lap as Ruth massaged her back and shoulders gently.

Sister Mary gazed across the room at Max. Boyo and Max had been great friends. Boyo always said that Max played rope better than anybody, better even than Ruth. Many a night Boyo and Max played rope, each pulling and jumping and growling, grinning from ear to ear. Sometimes at the end of the game Boyo and Max rolled around on the rug together like a couple of puppies, giggling, tickling, one-upping the other as they wrestled. Sometimes, Ruth even grabbed the rope and pulled for Boyo's team. Those had been happy times, she thought. Her massage over, Sister Mary decided she'd had enough Sofa Time. It had felt good being up there for a while again, but it was time to get back on the floor.

For Mikey, the memories that came flooding back to him in the quiet of Sofa Time that evening were not all good. They were of the Before Time. Banging, banging, and more banging. Kicking, shouting, barking, running, chasing, Skeeter crying. Their First House had sofas, but no one could sit on them. Not even the people. There were too many boxes, books, toys, and the children never paused long enough to give a gentle belly rub. When they weren't running loose in the yard, Skeeter, Mamma and he had been in their crates, each in a separate room.

It was better for them at Shelter Lady's where they had a mat and blankets they could curl up on together, but still, life had been nothing like this. Today, he'd woken up in a soft bed, surrounded by warm covers. He'd played in the house, explored its rooms and wondered at the scents he found there. Then he'd played Ball with a fifteen-year-old ancient wonder. Then, there'd been dinner and now Sofa Time. Mikey pushed up into Ruth and curled up tight. Squeezing his eyes tightly, he tried hard to push away the bad memories and ghosts and to enjoy the comfort of the present.

Chapter 7

After the first few days, life settled into a predictable routine. Get up, go out, eat, go out, hang out with Ruth and Max, eat, go out, play Ball, eat, Sofa Time, bedtime. With Max and Ruth on holiday, they were home all of the time.

Mikey liked that routine. Mikey liked routine, period. It helped him push away the ghosts and shadows, the buzzing and drumming.

But then, one night came and Ruth and Max were upset. Mikey couldn't tell why. Neither could Sister Mary. "What's going on?" Mikey asked.

"Can't tell," said Sister Mary. "I think something's wrong with Max."

"Wrong? How wrong, what's wrong?" Mikey wanted to know.

"Can't tell." Sister Mary and Ruth looked worried. Max looked scared too. He was breathing hard and fast but didn't seem to be getting any air.

"Should I call the ambulance?" asked Ruth.

"No, but let's at least head toward the hospital. You drive. If it passes, fine. But if it doesn't pass, someone there can check me out," Max said. "Stay here guys. Hopefully, we won't be long."

"I'll leave a light on for you," said Ruth breathlessly to Sister Mary and Mikey as she grabbed her coat and hastily headed out the door.

And with that, Ruth and Max were gone.

The house was large. Full of strange noises Mikey hadn't heard while Ruth and Max were there. Windows creaked. Wind blew leaves outside and a branch scratched menacingly against a window. Except for the single light Ruth had left on in the living room, the house was dark. "Where did they go? When will they be back? Will Max be okay?" Mikey asked.

"Can't tell you, kid. I really don't know," said Sister Mary, looking out the window, equally worried.

"Should we go help them? I think we should go help them." Mikey was alarmed and paced nervously at the front door.

"I think we should sit here in the front room and wait. It might take time, but they'll be back. They always come back," Sister Mary said, relying on her experience to steady her nerves.

Mikey wasn't so sure. The last time people had left him abruptly was when things really started to go downhill at the First House. It was before Skeeter was born. The kids were annoying but tolerable then. The man kept them in order and protected Mikey and Mamma. But the man had gotten ill one night and went away, just like Max did. The man never came back, and the big lady cried for days. The kids ran wild. Things went bad. That was the beginning of the Before Time.

The buzzing in Mikey's head roared. His ghosts that he'd suppressed pulled out their drums and pounded wildly through his head. He panicked. Now racing from room to room, he panted, "Got to get out, got to get to the people, got to get out, got to get to the people. How to get out? How to get out?" Around and around the floor he went, pacing, pacing. "Got to get out, got to get to the people."

Mikey eyed a window. "How about this?" He tested it, pawing it with his front feet and pushing it with his nose. The window wouldn't budge. "I'll just pull off these sticks and it should open," he thought, grabbing the trim of the window with his teeth. He pulled the trim off and re-tested the window with his paws and nose. Nope. The window didn't budge. "Got to get out, got to get out."

Mikey ran to the next window. Same thing. "How about this door? Pull off the wood bars. Give the door a shove." Nothing. By now Mikey was frantic. He raced upstairs. "Maybe this way out."

Mikey pulled down the blinds, tore off the stick bars and pushed on the window. Still no luck. Mikey noticed a lever on the window. Maybe that would work. Pull off the blinds. Pull off the sticks. Pull off the lever. Shove the window…

"*Mikey! Stop!*" Sister Mary shouted from the bottom of the stairs. Mikey paused, Sister Mary's voice pulled him out of his state. "Mikey! Remember your phrases, Mikey! Tell them to me!" she barked as loudly as she could.

"Got to get out, got to help Max and Ruth, got . . ." Mikey resumed his chanting and pacing.

"No, no Mikey! Come on! Repeat your Mamma's lessons. What did your Mamma tell you to never forget?" Hearing Sister Mary's words, Mikey paused again.

Sister Mary kept trying, barking frantically to hold Mikey's attention. Now that he'd finally paused, she wasn't going to let up.

Mikey stopped. Sister Mary's last command brought him back to the present. What did Mamma say? Mikey looked down the stairs at Sister Mary.

"Come on, Mikey, what did your Mamma tell you?"

"Um, Don't panic," he said, eyes wide and sides heaving.

"And what exactly do you think you're doing now, Mikey?" Sister Mary said, her voice softening with kindness.

"Panicking," he whispered. Mikey lowered his head, caught his breath and looked around. His eyes cleared and the buzzing subsided. The drumbeats slowed. Oh, boy, had he panicked. The place was a mess, pieces of window trim shredded on the floor all around him. Curtains and blinds torn from their racks, demolished.

"What do I do, Sis? I blew it, didn't I? Now I'm going to have to leave. They'll take me back to the Impound and I'll never get Skeeter out of the Shelter. What do I do?" Mikey was shaking, panting, now with a different fear taking over.

Sister Mary shook her head, relieved he had finally stopped his tour of destruction. She'd been there before, too, of course. She'd torn her share of blinds down in the early days. The world hadn't come to an end then. It was a matter of handling the aftermath that counted. Boyo had taught her that. "Repeat your lessons, kid. Just repeat your lessons. When they come home, and they always do eventually come home, we'll just deal with it. But for goodness sake, get a hold of yourself and calm down. You're a mess."

Mikey looked at his new old friend. She'd moved into the living room by now and was lying on the floor next to the sofa, panting, exhausted after having followed him from room to room, imploring him to stop his panic. Maybe she was right. Maybe it was best to wait this one out on the sofa.

Hours passed. Eventually, headlights came up the driveway. "Sister Mary, they're here. What do I do? What do I do?" Mikey's fear swiftly returned.

"Let me handle it, kid. You remember your lessons. No matter what."

Ruth and Max came into the house. They were tired. It had been a long night for all of them. Whatever had been bothering Max when they left seemed to have stopped on its own.

Sister Mary knew what she had to do. She had to show them what had happened and she had to remain calm. She escorted her friends carefully toward the kitchen door, the first site of destruction. Max followed, thinking his friend needed to go outside.

"Oh, my God!" exclaimed Max as he looked at the door. "Ruth, look at this! It's destroyed!"

It was the first room where Mikey had tried to get out. Mikey's "sticks" lay in a pile on the floor. Pieces of trim were splintered all around.

Room by room they went. Finally, Ruth just shook her head in disbelief. Mikey followed nervously, head down, tail between his legs. Sister Mary tried to look calm.

"Don't get angry, don't panic, don't bite," Mikey repeated under his breath, trying to keep his head together.

"At least he didn't get the new windows," offered Max, trying to stay composed as he picked up the worst of the mess.

"What, Mikey? You don't like blinds? Or window panes?" Ruth said, her eyes soft and her voice kind. "You must have been pretty scared, huh. We're sorry, buddy. I didn't think you would miss us that much," she said giving her young friend a comforting scratch as she picked up some of the trim.

They were exhausted, all of them. Maybe that helped. Everyone was too tired to be angry. Mikey was too exhausted to run or panic. But, just like Sister Mary said, the world did not come to an end. Instead, they went to bed and closed the door.

They'd finish picking up the mess later. Mikey jumped up on the bed between Ruth and Max, relieved that Max was back and that he could curl up again at Ruth's feet. Ruth gave him a pat and stroked his back gently.

"Tomorrow, buddy, you get a crate," said Max as he drifted off to sleep.

"A crate? Sis, what's that mean? A crate to take me back to the Impound?" Mikey whispered.

"No, silly, it means you get a crate. You'll stay in it when they leave. Don't you ever just go to sleep?"

But Mikey was already in dreamland, bad dreams, good dreams and all.

Chapter 8

"Shelter Lady?" Skeeter looked up with her best face at Shelter Lady, eyes bright, ears up, head to one side. "Shelter Lady? When do you think Mikey's coming to get me?"

Shelter Lady looked down and gave Skeeter a pat on the head. "Don't worry little one, Mikey's working on it. Just give him time."

"But Shelter Lady, why he can't come get me now? I want to go to Forever Home. Buster went, Skittles went. Bubba too. Even that stupid cat, Otis. Why do I have to wait here?" Skeeter pouted and put a paw on Shelter Lady's lap.

"Hang in there, Skeeter. Your brother's doing his best right now. We have to be a little more patient."

Shelter Lady checked her email messages. Nothing from Ruth and Max. She worried that her decision to hold off putting Skeeter back on the available dogs list was not a good one. Just a little longer, she thought.

Chapter 9

Mikey was doing his best. It was hard, but he was determined. It seemed that every time something really good happened, it would remind Mikey of something bad. The ghosts and shadows of the Before Time would push forward in his memory and he'd have to stop having fun for a while and just sit by himself until they passed.

It was autumn and Ruth decided to rake leaves. They had a lot of them. The day was clear and the sun warm, so Ruth invited Sister Mary and Mikey to join her outside.

"What do we do?" asked Mikey.

"We watch," said Sister Mary.

"That's it? That doesn't sound like much fun."

"Well, sometimes I make sure that the cars driving on the road down there don't come up here and get in her way. But otherwise, yes, we just watch. You can look for bugs if you want or keep the squirrels in their trees."

Mikey thought for a while. That didn't sound like much fun either.

"Hey, I know. I'll help!" Mikey ran over to Ruth and pounced on the leaves she'd put in a pile. "Here, Ruth. I'll hold these ones down for you so they don't blow away!" he said, spreading himself out across the pile.

Sister Mary shook her head in amusement at Mikey's game, but decided the beetle making its way across the yard was more interesting.

"Wait. Wait, Miss Ruth! That thing you're holding looks like a dragon. Let me grab it! I'll save you!" Mikey plunged toward the rake and grabbed it with mock ferociousness, his tail wagging.

"Hey, Mikey! Don't do that!" Ruth said, suppressing a giggle.

"Okay. So, how about I run circles around you and then jump in the leaf pile?!" Mikey barked as he landed squarely on the pile in front of him.

"Way better idea, Mikey, way better."

Mikey liked helping Ruth with the leaves. She would rake them. He would jump on them and hold them down and then she'd rake them some more.

Max was out in the yard as well, on the driveway. Seeing Mikey and Ruth "working," as they were, he laughed. "It'll take you all day at that rate!"

"Oh, yeah, this one's a big help," Ruth exclaimed, giving Mikey a playful pat and throwing a stick across the pile for him to chase.

Sister Mary was enjoying her day out as well. The sun felt good on her back and it was nice to hear Ruth and Max laugh again.

That night, after Ball and dinner, Mikey snuggled up next to Ruth on the sofa and put his arms around her shoulders. Tucking his head just under her chin, Mikey gave Ruth a hug. It was nice being a house dog and living with these people, he thought, as Ruth returned the hug with a scratch on his belly.

Still, the ghosts of the Before Time continued to haunt and torment. Mamma, skateboards, jerky moving people, hovering, Impound Man, hands in his face, Skeeter. Skeeter, would he ever see her again? Mikey turned and sighed, trying to drive away the ghosts.

"Hey, Mikey." Ruth whispered, putting her face right next to his and giving him a gentle hug, "you're going to make it, buddy. You're going to make it. And, I know you miss your Skeeter. Just hang in there."

Snuggling into the sofa under the blanket and listening to Sister Mary's soft breathing next to them, Mikey drifted off to sleep.

Chapter 10

Sometimes, in a new situation, it takes a while to notice –
really notice – the surroundings. It was no different for Mikey. As
the days went on, Mikey started to hear and see things that he had
not noticed before. As the new man of the house, Mikey felt it
imperative that he alert Sister Mary, Max, and Ruth, who seemed
oblivious to these things. "Sound the alarm, sound the alarm!
There are people walking on the road!" Mikey barked, running
back and forth from the window to the kitchen where Ruth was
working.

Ruth walked to the window to find out what was troubling
Mikey, only to see her neighbors walking on the street, down the
hill, far below.

"Really, Mikey," said Ruth. "All the way down there? I'm
impressed you can see them from this distance, but seriously,
buddy, no worries." Ruth returned to her work in the kitchen.

"Sound the alarm, sound the alarm! The house is growling at
us!" Mikey ran from room to room, barking, trying to get Ruth to
follow him.

"Really, Mikey," said Ruth. "What is it this time?"

"It's the house! The house, it's growling at us!"

Mikey kept barking and ran toward the sound. Following him
into the living room, Ruth could hear the source of Mikey's
consternation. Ruth and Sister Mary both laughed.

"That? That's the heat coming on and yes, it is loud," smiled Ruth, scratching Mikey's chin. "It makes all kind of noises, but trust me, the house is not growling at you."

Mikey was skeptical but relieved that he did not have to take on the house.

"Sound the alarm!"

"What is it now, Mikey?" said an increasingly exasperated Ruth.

Mikey continued to bark and run around the family room this time. "It's an intruder! Don't you hear her? Intruder, come out from wherever you are! Show yourself!" he exclaimed, running from one corner of the room to the other, looking under the sofa and behind the chair.

"Mikey, that's not an intruder. That's someone singing on the CD I'm playing, silly boy. You sure have a lot of sounds to get used to, don't you?" said Ruth, giving Mikey a reassuring pat on the head.

"Sound the alarm, sound the alarm!" This time it was Sister Mary who sounded the alarm and she trotted toward the front window. Mikey hadn't heard anything, but felt he had to help, and ran over to inspect.

"What is it, Sis?"

"Nothing. Just messing with you, kid." Sister Mary had a sense of humor.

Mikey liked his new crate. Unlike the first one he'd had which had been too small and just had a plastic tray in it, this one was large and had a nice mat and a blanket inside. Max and Ruth put it in the living room where he could keep an eye on the front door and the window while they were away. It was also where Sister Mary stayed while she waited for Ruth and Max to come home.

Inside his crate was safe and Mikey enjoyed hanging out with Sister Mary while they waited. Her stories, The Amazing Adventures of Sister Mary and Boyo, as he called them to himself, were captivating. He wondered if they were true, but even if only half of them were, Sister Mary and Boyo had lived an awesome life.

"Did I ever tell you about the first time that Boyo and I went camping?" Sister Mary asked one day.

"What's camping?"

"You go someplace and hang out outside, go hiking all day, eat food by a warm fire, and everybody sleeps together on one big mat in a camper."

"Wow, that sounds fun," said Mikey settling in for Sister Mary's story to begin.

"I don't remember if it was the first time or not, but it was one of the first. Ruth and Max piled big pillows in the back of the car for Boyo and me and then we drove all day with the camper until we got there. We even stopped along the way for subs."

"What's a sub?"

"Big giant sandwiches piled with meat and cheese. Max shares. He gets chips and shares those too. Ruth shares, but not like Max. Anyway, we pulled into this campground and Ruth took me and Boyo for a hike while Max set up the camper. When we came back, the camper was all ready and Max had a fire going. Ruth made chicken and vegetables in this big giant pot that she put on the fire. That chicken was to die for. Boyo and I each got a whole plate full, on top of our regular meal! Even the vegetables were good; carrots, potatoes, celery, lip-smacking good. They laughed and talked all night. Boyo and I kept watch." Sister Mary's mouth watered at the memory.

"That night it was really cold so we all snuggled close to keep warm and the next morning we went for another hike. This one was a long one. Through the woods, over streams, all kinds of smells and things to look at. We walked a long time that day. Those two sure love to walk."

Sister Mary smiled wistfully. She could still remember those walks. Boyo and her running through the woods together, racing over logs, sniffing out mysteries, and then the warmth of him next to her on their ride home. Afterward, they'd talk about their walks for days, reminiscing over the sights, sounds, and smells of the places they'd been.

"Sister Mary, do you think I'll get to go camping?"

"Dunno, kid. They got rid of their camper just before you came. We hadn't used it since we moved here and it looked a bit of a wreck. They'll probably take you places if you're good, though. We always traveled with them, except for when they went on their long trips. Then we stayed with Mammaw and Pop Pop. You'll see. After you get settled, I bet they start going places again."

Mikey thought for a while. Camping sounded fun. "Hey, Sister Mary?"

"Yeah, kid?"

"Do you think Skeeter would be able to come camping with us?"

"I was wondering when you were going to bring her up again," said Sister Mary with a smile. "I bet she'd love camping, just like I did. Hopefully, her Forever Home people will take her with them."

Mikey put his head on his paws, his ears drooping and eyes sad. He didn't like Sister Mary's inference that Skeeter might have some other Forever Home people. He wanted her here, with him and these people. He knew his wish was a long shot. He hadn't heard the final word on the Skeeter decision, though. Until then, he would just work harder, fit in more with these people, and hope that one day they would go get her.

Chapter 11

Ruth was nervous. Happy, but nervous. Zipping around the house, putting things here, putting things there. Cooking. Cleaning. Cooking some more. Max was busy outside, clearing the leaves from the driveway and yard, generally tidying up. "What's going on?" asked Mikey.

"Looks like we're going to have visitors, probably Mammaw and Pop Pop from the looks of things. Lots of food. Lots of drinks and no candles," said Sister Mary with a wink.

"Why? Why visitors?" Mike was concerned. Visitors had never meant good news. Visitors only brought bad news, bad things.

"I dunno. They come sometimes. You met them once, remember? We stopped and visited them on the way from Shelter Lady's. They're nice. They always have good food and they give good head scratches and belly rubs."

Mikey thought for a moment. The trip from Shelter Lady's had been a blur, but he did vaguely remember stopping at a house full of food and strange people. "But why? Why do they have to come here? Can't they just stay where they are and we'll stay where we are?"

The buzzing of the Before Time started in Mikey's head. Sister Mary seemed unfazed, but he wasn't sure she was right about this whole visitor thing. He looked around the room at

Ruth. He couldn't read her expression. Was she happy? Worried? What? What should he do?

"Hey, Mikey," said Ruth, noticing her friend starting to curl up in a little ball on the floor, a posture she'd seen him take before. "Just be yourself, they'll love you," she said, bending down and giving him a gentle pat on the head, trying to reassure him.

"Why? Why do I want them to love me?" Mikey thought. Just when he thought things were going well and he was fitting in, Ruth starts talking about someone else loving him. The Before Time buzzing came back in full force and he tucked his head further under his paws and tail.

Also noticing Mikey's withdrawal, Sister Mary tried to pull him out of his gloom. "Come on, Mikey. Don't worry. Mammaw and Pop Pop love everybody."

"But Sister Mary, what if they take me away? I don't want to go away."

Sister Mary gave Mikey an exasperated poke as she settled herself down next to him. "Just because they love you doesn't mean they're going to take you. It just means that they love you. Haven't you noticed how much better things are for you when you're around people who love you? Do I really have to translate everything?"

Mikey put his head back on his paws and decided to take a wait-and-see approach.

The doorbell rang and Sister Mary sounded the alert. "They're here! They're here! Hi, Mammaw! Hey, Pop Pop!" She barked as she tottered toward the door to greet her old friends.

Sister Mary really did like Mammaw and Pop Pop. They'd always been kind to her, especially when she was scared and Ruth and Max were away. Pop Pop would always go looking for her at night, find her under her bush in the front yard and coax her back into the house. "Come on, Sister Mary," he say gently to her as he handed her a bit of treat, "you can wait for them inside tonight with Boyo."

Mikey wasn't so sure, but decided to at least make a good impression. "Don't get angry, don't panic, don't bite, don't get angry, don't panic. . . " he repeated to himself. But, that doesn't mean I shouldn't bark, and bark loud, he thought. Then, they'll know to leave me alone. Mikey barked as loud as he could and ran around the house for emphasis.

"Want me to take him outside?" Max asked Ruth.

"No, let's just keep him in here until he settles. You will settle, right Mikey?" asked Ruth, looking down at the increasingly agitated Mikey. Mikey wanted to settle, but the buzzing would not stop.

Pop Pop was tall and moved stiffly. Mammaw was smaller, but carried two large sticks that she used for walking. Those sticks could be used for other things, though, Mikey thought. Best to keep barking and running around the house.

Meanwhile, Sister Mary did her best to explain the problem to her human friends. "He doesn't trust you," she barked. "Kind of a nervous type if you know what I mean," she barked some more, tottering into the center of the kitchen where everyone was congregating. "Maybe you should give me some treats," she continued. "Do you hear me? He's nervous. It's just his way. You need to sit down and give me some treats."

Pop Pop and Mammaw stood in the kitchen, their coats still on, not sure of what they should do, while Ruth and Max tried to restrain their loud friends. People were dense, thought Sister Mary. "I said, he's nervous; you need to sit down," Sister Mary barked again.

75

"Sister Mary, *quiet!*" Ruth yelled.

"But they don't understand, Ruth, they don't understand," Sister Mary tried again.

"Sister Mary, quiet!" Ruth tried again.

"Don't say I didn't tell you," said Sister Mary and she lay down in the center of the kitchen in a huff.

Ruth suddenly remembered the first time she and Max met Mikey. "How about you both just come in and sit down? Just sit and I bet he'll calm down."

Mammaw and Pop Pop sat. Sister Mary looked at Ruth with mild approval. Finally, she thought, a good idea. Bravo, Ruth. Now maybe Mikey will stop acting like an idiot.

Mikey looked at Ruth. How'd she do that? She made Mammaw and Pop Pop sit. That was a help. Maybe he could stop barking and running around. Seeing him pause, Ruth dropped a treat for Mikey. "There you go, good boy. See, not so scary."

"Maybe not," thought Mikey. "We'll see."

The visit didn't last long, just a couple of hours. Mammaw and Pop Pop did seem nice, but Mikey didn't trust them. Occasionally, Pop Pop would drop Mikey a treat, which was fine. Ruth's cooking was good. Still, Mikey wanted to stay with Ruth and Max. If he got too friendly with Mammaw and Pop Pop, he thought, they might get ideas and take him away.

"Come on fella," Pop Pop said. "You can come up to me." Pop Pop's voice was soft, kind of like Ruth's. Mikey didn't care what Sister Mary said, though. He wasn't trusting them. No way. Last time he'd trusted people who looked like that, he'd ended up with a noose around his neck, thrown in a cage and hauled off to the Impound. He'd keep his distance, and worry about being liked some other time.

After a while, Mammaw stood up stiffly, extending her sticks for support. "Well, Pop Pop. Time to go," said Mammaw. "We've done enough visiting for one day," she said as she worked her way toward the front door.

Pop also got up, and tapped his leg with his hand. "Come on guy. You can at least come say goodbye."

Mikey's buzzing returned full force. The ghosts in his head pulled out their drums and pounded wildly. "See, I was right! He said it was time to go!" he exclaimed. "They are here for me!" Mikey looked frantically at Ruth, then at Max, then at Sister Mary, each of whom seemed perfectly fine with the situation. How could they be? What had he done wrong? Mikey panicked and charged the sticks. "*Hey*! You can't take me. I'm not going. I want to stay here with these people. I haven't done anything!" Mikey barked wildly as he lunged.

"Whoa, whoa, buddy! Take it easy!" Max grabbed Mikey's collar just before Mikey made contact with the sticks.

"*Mikey*! Remember your lessons. Come on, Mikey!" shouted Sister Mary.

Just in time. Mikey, his eyes wide and body braced for a fight, looked around. Everybody was looking at him with surprise and concern. "Let me get his leash," said Ruth. "Hang on."

Returning with the leash, Ruth snapped it on Mikey's collar and gave him a comforting pat on the head. "Come on guy, that's not how we say goodbye to our guests around here."

"Our guests? Did she say our guests? " Mikey asked Sister Mary.

"Of course. They're our guests. What did you think?"

"They're really not taking me away?"

"No, that's what I've been telling you. They're leaving; you're staying. That's the way 'guests' work."

By now, Mammaw and Pop Pop were out the door, so Mikey couldn't apologize to them for his outburst, but he wished that he could. Maybe he'd been just a little hard on them.

After they left and the dishes were cleared and put away, it was Sofa Time. Mikey pulled himself up gently into Ruth's lap, draped his arms around her shoulders, and buried his head in the crook of her neck. He liked it there. It felt safe. He sighed, long and deep. Ruth giggled at the sound of his sigh and rubbed his back. "Your sigh sounds just like Darth Vader!"

"What's Darth Vader?" Mikey asked Sister Mary on the other side of the sofa.

"No idea, kid." said Sister Mary. "Just go with it."

Mikey curled up on the sofa, put his tail over his nose, and closed his eyes as tightly as he could. He had a lot of processing to do. The shadows and ghosts of the Before Time still haunted him, but now they were getting mixed in with other images as well. Happier, calmer images, treats, quiet voices, play time, Sofa Time. But then the ghosts and shadows would push back at the happy images, and the battle continued.

Looking up, half asleep, Mikey said, "Sister Mary, one thing you said earlier confused me."

"What's that, kid?"

"Well, you said you thought it was Mammaw and Pop Pop coming over because there was lots of food and drinks but no candles. I get the food and drink part, but what's the deal with the candles?"

Sister Mary chuckled. "Oh that. It's a bit of family history. Anyway, years ago around Christmas time, Ruth and Max decided to invite Ruth's family over for a party. Their house was filled with food and drink, just like today, but also with candles and Christmas decorations. Everybody was eating and having fun opening packages. Ripping off ribbons, pulling out gifts, even some gifts for me and Boyo. Then, some little bit of paper drifted over a candle on the table and then kept drifting onto a pile of wrapping paper at Mammaw's feet. And, whoosh! Just like that. A fire started right in front of Mammaw. Pop Pop saw the fire and before it got out of hand, he jumped over Boyo and me and stomped it out."

Mikey's eyes grew wide at the thought. "Did anybody get hurt?"

"No, it ruined the carpet and the sofa Mammaw was sitting on, but nobody got hurt. Mammaw was pretty shook up, though, and as a result, Ruth doesn't light candles when they come over anymore."

Mikey got up, stretched, and moved to another spot on the sofa. Under the spell of the soft cushions, Sister Mary's storytelling, and Ruth stroking his ears and chest, the happy images in Mikey's head gained the upper hand over his ghosts. Mikey stretched out, uncurling his body, and dreamed of Skeeter. Perhaps, one day, she would share the sofa with him and Ruth and Sister Mary.

Chapter 12

A few nights later, well into Sofa Time, Mikey woke to hear Ruth and Max talking quietly. "I tell you Max. I think she can handle it. She's stronger than before. She's eating again, sleeping through the night. She clearly adores him. Mikey really seems to like her, too. I think we should go back up there and get her."

"Sister Mary, what's going on? What are they talking about? Who are they talking about?" Mikey asked.

"Shh. Just stay still and keep quiet, Mikey. I'm not sure, but I think they're talking about going back to get your sister."

"What?! Skeeter? Are we going back to get her? Is she coming?" Mikey whispered, hardly containing himself.

"Not sure yet. Just lie still and keep quiet," admonished Sister Mary.

"But Ruth, didn't you see the way he flattened her the other day? I mean, right into her. I don't think she even saw him coming." Max asked. "How is she supposed to handle two like that?"

"I saw it too, but she really didn't seem fazed by it, and he's learning to jump over. Did you see him when he came out of his crate last night? Sister Mary stood right in front of it and he just leaped over her. When they play ball, he tries to avoid her whenever he's running. Sometimes she just puts herself right in his path, almost like she does it on purpose. Maybe if Skeeter were here he'd have someone his own age to play with, and it might actually take pressure off of Sister Mary." Ruth was making her case for Skeeter as best she could.

"Sure, but why does he have to charge around like that? He's just…just…well, wild. I mean the guy is crazy. Can you imagine having two crazies in the house?" Max was worried about his old friend. She was tough, but how was she supposed to handle two young, out-of-control dogs?

"Boyo and Sister Mary used to run around the house, too. He's just young and feeling good. He's settling down, though. He's not barking at everything all the time any more. He's doing fine in his crate, and he only took two laps up and down the stairs when I got home today instead of the usual three or four. Look, if it's too soon for you, I understand, but we really do need to make a decision one way or the other. It's not fair to keep everyone in limbo this way. I don't know how much longer we can expect Shelter Lady to hang onto her, waiting for us to make up our minds. She emailed me a photo of her again just today."

"I know. Let me think about it," said Max.

"Ok, but we can't think too much longer. Christmas is almost here and we'll have a tough time making arrangements, if we do decide to get her, the more we wait." Ruth replied.

It sounded to Sister Mary like Ruth needed help. Sister Mary loved having the company of her young friend, but knew he wouldn't be fully settled or happy until he had his sister with him. She understood. That was how she'd come to feel about Boyo. It had taken them longer to reach that point, but she understood.

She decided to plead Skeeter's case to Max, as well. Sliding off of the sofa, Sister Mary gave herself a good shake, walked stiffly across the room and looked at Max squarely in the eye. Standing as steadily as she could muster on her tired arthritic legs, Sister Mary barked, "Look, Look! I'm fine. Get Skeet. Max, I'm fine. Get her. I'm fine." Sister Mary always found it more effective to say things more than once to her humans.

Max looked at his elderly friend, who had, indeed, seemed to have come out of her funk. Four weeks ago, he wasn't sure she'd make it on the long trip to the Shelter. She'd seemed disinterested, distant, stiff. The laser therapy she'd been getting at the time seemed to help some, but not much. She'd developed weird habits at night, wandering around the room, crashing into things, gulping water, panting. Nothing seemed to help. She wasn't even eating right. Sometimes she wouldn't eat at all, which, for a dog who at one time was known to eat an entire bowl of food in twenty seconds flat and then look around for more, was really disturbing.

But now, here she was, smiling after a game of Ball and a hearty dinner, standing in front of him demanding who knows what. She sure was back to her demanding, cheerful self. Ruth was right. Maybe Sister Mary could handle another friend.

But, could he? Getting Mikey so soon after Boyo's death had been the right thing to do for Ruth and Sister Mary, but it was hard on him. Boyo had been Max's first dog and it wasn't easy to let go. Every time Max turned around, something would remind him of Boyo. Sometimes he caught himself looking around for him, missing him, the feel of his fur, the sound of his bark. That big goofy smile he always had on his face. Would the sight of two young dogs playing in the same way that Boyo and Sister Mary had played bring back still more memories? Max looked at Mikey, curled up and quiet next to Ruth.

Mikey really had been making progress. He thought of Skeeter and what she and Mikey'd been through. Maybe, together, Skeeter and Mikey could finally be happy. Making the world right for them would be perfect a tribute to his lost friend, Boyo, and a gift for the old friend standing in front of him. It would be a nice gift for Ruth too. Max knew she'd been smitten by both dogs at the Shelter. He'd seen the tear in her eye when she looked at Skeeter being led away from them.

Deciding to put his doubts to the side in favor of his wife and friends, Max announced, "I can't go this weekend. I have to work and you and your sister are baking cookies. How about we go up next weekend?"

"Seriously?!" exclaimed Ruth. "You're sure?"

"Yes, I'm sure," Max smiled. Ruth grinned, got up and gave Max a hug. Having won her case, Sister Mary walked back over to the sofa and laid back down in front of Mikey. Returning to the sofa, Ruth paused and gave Sister Mary's belly a good scratch. "Good job, girl," she whispered. "Hear that guys? Skeeter will be home in time for Christmas!"

"Wait. What? Sister Mary, did I hear that right? We're going to get Skeeter? When's Christmas? What is Christmas anyway? But, Skeeter, we're getting Skeeter?!" Mikey's tail wagged in huge happy arcs.

"Yes. You heard right. It sounds like we're going to pick her up in two weeks, kid, two weeks. Christmas is when the people all eat lots of fun food, share it with us, listen to music, and get together for parties. We get extra treats and usually toys. Looks like you'll have a happy Christmas reunion!" Sister Mary confirmed cheerfully.

Mikey could hardly believe his ears. "Skeeter! Here! And in time for treats and toys! Oh, man! Oh, man!" Mikey jumped off the couch and jumped into Max's lap.

"Hey, hey there, buddy. There's a good boy!" Max laughed and gave Mikey a scratch behind his ears and a belly rub.

That night, the happy visions in Mikey's dreams defeated the ghosts and drove them back into the the shadows. Instead, Mikey dreamed of Skeeter, ears flopping as she ran happily around the house, barking, teasing, as he always hoped she would. Maybe she would like Ball and the three of them, Mikey, Sister Mary, and Skeeter could all play in the back yard with Ruth. Who was he kidding? Of course she'd like Ball. And Sofa Time. So happy were his dreams that night that Mikey forgot to curl up tightly as he had every other night and stretched out the full length of the bed.

The next two weeks were a complete blur for Mikey. It was Christmas time and Ruth and Max were happily making preparations. The tree went up in the living room, gaily decorated with lights, shiny ornaments and toys. The house was decorated, garland adorned the mantle, Ruth's Santa collection created scenes of good cheer throughout the house. Gifts started appearing and wrapping paper was strewn all over the dining room table. The house was filled with music and the smells of cookies and other baked things. It even snowed lightly, which made the happy house look like something off of a Christmas card. The snow made Ball playing more difficult, but Sister Mary always seemed to know where the balls were hidden beneath the soft frozen cover. Mikey couldn't wait to share with his sister.

In the meantime, Mikey invented a new game of his own, Race. "Watch this, Sis, I bet I can beat you and Ruth around the house!" Mikey pranced as Ruth and Sister Mary set out for a walk around the outside of the house. "Ready. Set. Go!" Mikey zoomed away, making a full circle around the outer perimeter of the house and back to Ruth and Sister Mary. "Sister Mary, you didn't even try!" Mikey grinned as he returned to the walking pair. "Come on Sister Mary. Try again. Ready. Set. Go!" Around he went again, racing as fast as he could, ears flopping, tail wagging with the joy of a good all out run. Sister Mary and Ruth were almost around the house and at the garage when he returned. "C'mon! Sis!" Mikey tried for a third time.

This time when he made his way back to them, Sister Mary and Ruth had managed to get from the garage door to the front door. "Whoa there, buddy! You've got the zoomies! Holy smokes, you're fast!" exclaimed Ruth looking with wonder at the happy face in front of her.

"Seriously, Mikey, you know I can't keep up with you in a race," said Sister Mary as they walked in the door.

"Well, you should see Skeeter run. She's amazing," said Mikey, panting happily. "She can totally keep up with me. She might even be faster. She lowers herself down to the ground and just tears it up!"

"Soon enough, kid. Soon enough," said Sister Mary with a smile. It would be good for Mikey to have someone his own age to play with she thought, and Skeeter did seem like a nice enough girl. It would be good to have the both of them around when Ruth and Max were away during the day. Yes, Sister Mary thought to herself, Christmas was shaping up nicely.

Chapter 13

"Skeeter, guess what!" Shelter Lady was beaming. Skeeter had been pouting in the corner of her kennel, but her ears pricked up when she heard Shelter Lady's voice. "It worked! Our patience worked! They're coming to get you this weekend!"

Shelter Lady gave Skeeter a scratch on the head. "Look, Skeet, I sent them your picture and told them you missed your brother. They just sent me an email asking if they could come to get you. See? It's right here on the screen. 'Dear Shelter Lady,' it says, 'Mikey misses his sister too. We wonder if we could pick her up in time for Christmas?' See, Skeet, right here?"

Shelter Lady was relieved. Given their past, she'd thought Mikey and Skeeter would become long-term residents, if not part of her lifer crowd, dogs whose pasts were just too troubled for people to take a chance on. At first, when Ruth and Max announced that they were only taking Mikey with them, she didn't really think they would make a second trip for Skeeter. The trip was just too far to make twice. But when she saw the look in Ruth's eye when she looked at Skeeter and the gentleness with which she responded to the dog, she decided to give it some time before actively trying to place Skeeter with another family. That gamble seemed to have paid off. "What am I doing, showing you the computer screen, Skeet? How silly!" Shelter Lady laughed giving Skeeter a playful push. "Anyway, it won't be long now and you'll be back with Mikey, living in your Forever Home."

Skeeter looked up at Shelter Lady quizzically, cocking her head to one side. She didn't understand everything Shelter Lady said, but she had caught a couple of words: Mikey and Forever Home. Skeeter decided to remain optimistic.

The next day, Shelter Lady was up early. "Come on Skeet, today's Adoption Day!"

Adoption Day? Skeeter knew that phrase. She'd heard it many times before. The other Shelter Dogs talked about it endlessly. "It's, Adoption Day," they'd go on as they tried to put on their best behavior and cutest expressions for the strange people who would show up at the Shelter. "Adoption Day!" they'd exclaim, certain that this would be the day they'd go to Forever Home. She never understood how it was decided which dog or how to be picked for Adoption Day. Shelter Lady and the strange people always seemed to pick someone other than her though. Skeeter blinked hard and studied Shelter Lady carefully.

"Come on, Skeet. Today's your Adoption Day. Let's get you some breakfast and a good run. Then you'll be in good shape for the long drive. Make sure you say hi to Mikey for me, okay?" Shelter Lady said, giving Skeeter a friendly scratch on the chin.

Skeeter was overjoyed. "Did you hear that?" she demanded of her kennel-mate.

"Hear what?" he yawned.

"Today's my Adoption Day! They're coming to get me! Mikey did it! He did it! See, I told you. You didn't believe me, but Mikey always keeps his word!" Skeeter bounced in front of her kennel-mate's face for extra emphasis.

"Good for you," he said, "good for you. I heard Shelter Lady say that somebody was coming for me this week, too. Maybe we'll both find Forever Homes."

"What? You're going, too? Wroo-wroo! That's awesome! Why didn't you tell me?"

"I dunno. You've been so gloomy, I didn't want to make it worse," he replied.

Skeeter dropped her head. Her kennel-mate was right. She had been gloomy. The time away from her brother had been hard, and she dreamed of him every night. What was he doing? Would he come get her as he had promised? It had been so long since she'd seen him, what if she didn't recognize him, or worse, what if he'd forgotten all about her?

Hours ticked by and Skeeter watched the door, willing it to open, willing herself to hear her brother's bark. Nothing. Could something have happened? Where were they? Had they changed their minds? Maybe she hadn't heard Shelter Lady correctly.

Skeeter fretted and paced nervously. The other Shelter Dogs tried their best to comfort their young friend, to no avail. "Come on, Skeet. Shelter Lady said they're coming, so they're coming. You're going to wear yourself out," they told her. But Skeeter couldn't sit still. Her yearning for a Forever Home and thoughts of reuniting with Mikey were just too powerful.

At last, the door opened and Shelter Lady appeared, leash in hand. "Come on Skeet. Max is here to pick you up. Be a good girl now and remember: don't get angry, don't panic, don't bite. There's a good girl, come on. Let's go see Max."

Skeeter was elated. Scared, but elated. But, she knew what she'd heard: Adoption Day, Mikey, Forever Home. Pushing her fears to one side, she burst into Shelter Lady's receiving room, where Max nervously waited. She looked anxiously around the room. Where was Mikey? Where was the old one? Where was the lady? It was just the man. She dropped her tail nervously.

"Hey, Skeeter, ready to go home with me?" Max asked quietly, handing her a piece of hot dog. "Mikey, Ruth and Sister Mary are all going to be so happy to see you," he said.

"Let me help you get her in your car. Are you sure you'll be alright riding with her like that?" Shelter Lady was skeptical of Max's car setup. No crate, just an open back with a divider between the front and back seats.

"We'll be fine. Mikey rides back there just fine." Max reassured her.

Skeeter hopped in the back of Max's car like she'd been there before, but once inside, seeing how close the quarters were, Skeeter had second thoughts. Maybe it would be better just to stay here, safe with Shelter Lady, she thought. What if Max really wasn't going to take her to live with Mikey? What if they were going someplace else? What if he was taking her back to Impound? Men had been known to be untrustworthy before. Doubts flooded her thoughts. Panicking, Skeeter tried to make a run for it. Shelter Lady snagged her leash as Skeeter tried to bolt from the car.

"Come on Skeet, hop back in here and be a good girl." Shelter Lady again looked skeptically at the set-up, but nothing could be done about it now. Summoning her courage, Skeeter tried again. This time, Max got the door closed before she changed her mind. "C'mon, girl, let's get home," said Max cheerfully as he got in the car. "We've got a long road ahead of us."

"You better keep that leash on her," said Shelter Lady.

"Don't worry, we'll be fine. I'm not making any stops until we get home," Max said as he shut the door.

As they headed out the driveway, Skeeter took one last look at Shelter Lady waving goodbye, and hoped for the best.

Chapter 14

The day was long, the wait interminable for Ruth, Mikey, and Sister Mary, too. Max had left the house early that morning and they expected him home with Skeeter around midnight. It would be a long trip for both of them, but Max and Ruth agreed it would be easier on everyone in the long run for Max to go alone. Ruth would continue Christmas preparations, take care of Mikey and Sister Mary, and Sister Mary would not have to endure another long car ride. Still, Shelter Lady lived nine hours away. Their eighteen-hour wait seemed like a lifetime.

"Where are they, Sister Mary?" Mikey fretted. "Are you sure you heard them say that Max was bringing Skeeter to live with us?"

"I'm telling you, kid, that's what I heard. Besides, look at Ruth, she's been flitting around happily all day, all week, really. I haven't seen her like this since the day before we met you. Good things are happening, I'm telling you."

Sister Mary knew her friend Ruth well. After thirteen years, a dog knows these things. But the day wore on and turned to night, and still no Max, still no Skeeter. Ruth was happy, though, so Sister Mary stayed confident.

Late into the night, Sister Mary, Ruth and Mikey were on the sofa when a call came. "What? You're here, as in here at the house?!" Ruth was ecstatic. "You guys must be exhausted. Okay. We're on our way up now. We'll meet you outside."

Ruth roused Sister Mary and Mikey off the sofa where they'd been sleeping. "Come on, Mikey. Come on, Sister Mary. Wake up. Skeeter's here."

Mikey's head filled with joy. "She's, wait, what? She's, Skeeter's here, really? Where, where?"

Hearing his sister's name and seeing Ruth's excitement, Mikey ran upstairs to the window and looked outside. He saw the car, but couldn't yet see who was inside. Mikey ran to the door, ran back to the window. Ruth, meanwhile, had scooped up Sister Mary and practically ran up the stairs with her. "Come on, Sister Mary, come on Ruth, hurry!" exclaimed Mikey, jumping over Sister Mary, then running back to the door.

"Stand still, Mikey. I need to get this leash on you so that we don't have any mishaps. We can't have the two of you dashing off on your first night together. Skeeter's right outside. Mikey, hold still!" Ruth said, laughing at their collective excitement and disorganization. Mikey tried to comply, but his feet, his tail, well his whole body just could not stand still.

"Hurry! Hurry! They might change their minds and go away!" said Mikey anxiously, bouncing back and forth on his feet.

Sister Mary was excited too, barking and standing at the door expectantly. "Open door! Open door!" she commanded.

Finally, leash firmly in hand, Ruth opened the door to a very tired Max and a very bewildered Skeeter standing in the driveway. Mikey charged full speed ahead toward the groggy Skeeter. *Hey, Skeet! Skeet! Welcome Home! Welcome Home!*

Skeet!" Mikey bellowed as he dragged poor Ruth across the snow to greet his sister.

"Hello, hello, welcome!" exclaimed Sister Mary, toddling up to Skeeter. "Geez, Mikey, take it easy. You'll knock everybody down!"

Ruth held on as best she could, but Mikey's joy was too great. There Skeeter was, almost two months after he'd taken a leap of faith with these people, almost five months after their ordeal of the Before Time had come to an end. There she was, his Skeeter, standing right in front of him, blinking bashfully in the light, but here, safe, finally safe. His joy was absolute. Play was definitely in order. "Come on Skeet, let's rumble!" Mikey bowed and pounced and gave his sister a playful nip and bark.

"Mikey? Is that really you?" Skeeter blinked. Skeeter had fallen asleep hours into the trip. She'd dreamed of her brother and Forever Home. In her dreams, Forever Home didn't really have a look to it so much as a feel. It felt warm, safe, right, and Mikey was always waiting there for her. But. But what if the Shelter Dogs had been wrong about Forever Home? What if Mikey didn't want to share it with her, after all? These people, were they good people like Shelter Lady and Shelter Man, or were they like Impound Man? Did they have kids? Were they bad kids? What if Sister what's-her-name, the old one, didn't like her?

Now, here she was, standing outside the car, the Shelter miles away, Max holding her leash firmly. Looking around, Skeeter could see that the house was lit brightly. Snow lay all around. The people were nervous, but seemed friendly, just like the first time she'd met them. Mikey seemed larger than she remembered. Sister Mary walked up and extended her a friendly welcome sniff.

"Where am I?" Skeeter blinked hard, trying to take in her new, strange surroundings. "Mikey? Is that really you?"

"Yes! Yes! It's me, Skeet, it's me! Yay, it's you! It's really you. You're home, you're home, you're home! Yay, you're home!" Mikey sang and ran circles around his sister with joy.

"Hey, kid. Tone it down. Can't you see she's had a long day? Contain yourself a bit. You have all night, heck, you'll have the rest of your lives to catch up. You need to chill," Sister Mary interceded, not so concerned about Skeeter as she was about Ruth, who kept getting tangled in Mikey's leash. Sister Mary knew Ruth was a bit clumsy. If she tripped and fell in the snow, who knew what would happen?

Mikey relented, but still couldn't help carrying on and bouncing into his sister. "Skeeter, Skeeter, we're here, you're here. This place is amazing. You've gotta see inside!"

Skeeter, still taking it all in, shook her head, flapping her ears hard. "Wow, Mikey, you look great! Hey, Sunshiny! I remember you. You came to visit us. I remember now. Is this where you live?"

"Skeeter, don't call her Sunshiny, that's not her name!" barked Mikey. "Show some respect; that's Sister Mary Sunshine. She is in charge here. Remember? When we first met her at Shelter Lady's? She was the one to say if we came here or not. You have to be nice to her or she might send you back." After all of his work to get Skeeter here, the last thing he wanted was for her to offend Sister Mary Sunshine.

Skeeter slunk to the ground, afraid she'd made a costly mistake. Mikey was always right. What if she'd messed it up in the first five minutes?

"It's fine, Mikey," Sister Mary Sunshine smiled. "Skeeter, I told you last time that you can call me Sister Sunshiny if you like. Mikey, I really don't mind. I answer to just about anything around here," she laughed.

Skeeter relaxed and blinked some more. Looking around, she liked what she saw. Nice house, big yard, lots of trees, lots to sniff, lots of room to stretch, Mikey, Sister Mary Sunshiny. "Hey, Mikey, Sister, are there other dogs here? And where are the kennels? What do they look like? Are there kids here?"

Mikey laughed while Sister Mary smiled. "No kennels. No other dogs. No kids," she said. "It's just us and Ruth and Max." Skeeter liked the sound of that. She was tired of sharing her space with lots of other dogs. It would be nice to be more the center of attention.

By now, the dogs had finished their tour around the outside of the house and Ruth and Max decided it was time to go inside and introduce Skeeter to her new quarters. They had planned to show Skeeter around gradually, let her take everything in.

Mikey had other ideas, however. As soon as the door closed and the leashes came off, Mikey took off around the house, determined to give his sister a tour of his own.

"Come on Skeet! Let me show you where the water is!" Mikey dashed into the kitchen for the water cooler and took a big slurping gulp. "Okay, let me show you the Christmas tree! Look here. Isn't it great! This is a Christmas tree. Lights and colors and toys! Right. Now, let me show you where I sleep when Ruth and Max aren't here."

Mikey tore into the next room and bounded into his crate. "Maybe they'll get you one too. It's like a house, but it's smaller. Sister Mary sleeps here on the rug next to me. Sometimes she sleeps next to the sofa, but she's always in here with me when they're not here. Oh, and let me show you the upstairs, it's where we all sleep at night."

Mikey flew up the stairs, with Skeeter in hot pursuit. "Let me show you where we have Sofa Time, it's downstairs, that's where Sister Mary, Ruth and I were waiting for you."

Mikey and Skeeter were now in full-throttle charge mode, racing upstairs and downstairs, ending in the family room.

"Wait. Where'd everybody go?" Mikey and Skeeter stopped at the bottom of the stairs. They'd lost track of Ruth, Max, and Sister Mary.

"C'mon, guys," Ruth laughed from the top of the stairs. "Enough play time. Let's go to bed."

Skeeter, blinked. Where was bed again? She'd forgotten. Mikey's tour had been rather fast and she'd lost track of where they were.

"C'mon, Skeet. You can share the bed with us." Mikey ran up the stairs, around the corner and leaped onto bed.

Looking around, Skeeter noticed Max carrying Sister Mary up the stairs. "Sister Sunny, why you don't come up the stairs on your own feet?" Skeeter asked.

"Because I can't," Sister Mary replied. "Too many steps, legs too tired, and the back just won't do it anymore."

"But why?" asked Skeeter.

"Because I'm old, child, that's why."

By now, Max had placed Sister Mary on the floor of the bedroom and Sister Mary looked around deciding where she would sleep for the night. Should she sleep on Boyo's mat tonight? Her own? Or over by the window where the floor was even and the heat from the vent warmed her belly and her aching bones?

Skeeter, seeing her brother on the bed with Ruth and Max, decided that the bed was definitely where she wanted to be and jumped up cautiously. Looking down at Sister Mary, who by now had chosen Boyo's old mat, Skeeter cocked her head in confusion. "Sister Sunny, why are you sleeping there? Why not up here with us? This feels nice!" Skeeter wiggled in next to her brother tightly, enjoying his closeness and the soft warm blankets.

Sister Mary Sunshine sighed. "I used to sleep where you are, child, but I don't anymore."

"But, why?" asked Skeeter.

"Because I don't want to, that's why." Sister Mary made a couple of turns on the mat as she settled in.

"But why?" Skeeter wasn't going to let Sister Mary off the hook. She needed an answer.

"Because, child. I'm old. I can't get there on my own and when they put me up there, it's too soft for me to move around on. Down here it's just more stable. You two sleep up there. I'll be fine down here."

"Ok, Sister Sunny. Have a good sleep." Skeeter said, happily snuggling in between her brother and Ruth.

"Good night, Child."

"Sister Sunny?"

"Yes."

"Thanks."

"Thanks for what?"

"Thanks for making them come get me."

"It wasn't just me, Child, we all worked hard."

By now, the sounds of Mikey, Ruth, and Max, sound asleep, filled the room, but Skeeter still couldn't sleep. "Mikey, too?" she whispered anxiously to the dog on the floor.

"Especially Mikey," whispered Sister Mary. "I've never seen a dog try harder."

Skeeter let out a long sigh. "I knew it, I just knew it. Those Shelter Dogs were wrong about him. I knew he wouldn't forget me. 'Night, Sister Sunny." Sister Mary's sleep sounds filled the room. Skeeter curled up tight, lodged safely among Max, her brother, and Ruth, and went to sleep.

Chapter 15

The next morning, everyone awoke to the quiet of gently falling snow. Ruth grabbed a coat, hat, and a pair of leashes, and took everyone outside before breakfast. Not needing a leash herself, Sister Mary followed along dotingly while her two young charges tried to see how much they could tangle themselves in theirs. She laughed at the threesome; Ruth stomping through snow, trying to keep the leashes untangled, Mikey showing Skeeter every last place he'd seen a ball, and Skeeter enjoying her first-ever snow, scooping up mouthfuls in giant gulps. Ruth, of course, was the funniest. She looked like a marionette, arms and legs flailing about.

"Hey, guys! Give Ruth a break, will you? You'll wear the poor girl out like that," Sister Mary laughed as she followed along behind them.

Back inside, Ruth got breakfast going while Skeeter and Mikey continued their reunion. "Hey, Mikey, catch me if you can!" Skeeter scampered from one sofa and one room to the next, and, like her brother, from one floor to the next. Mikey obliged, until, finally, Ruth had had enough.

"Guys, guys, this is not a freeway. Let's give it a break!"

Skeeter and Mikey paused. How could she be serious? Their game was way too much fun to stop now. Skeeter pounced on her brother and grabbed his collar.

"Hey! No fair! I wasn't playing!" Mikey exclaimed.

"Ha ha, too bad!" Skeeter rolled over laughing as Mikey grabbed her ear and then tickled her belly. Jumping up, Skeeter bolted for the next room. "Betcha can't catch me!"

"Bet I can!"

By now, both dogs had completely ignored Ruth's admonition, not to mention Sister Mary, who was monitoring them from the hallway. "Watch out, guys!"

Ruth saw the crash coming seconds before it happened. Too late. Skeeter plowed into Sister Mary and knocked her to the floor. Unable to stop, Mikey jumped over the Skeeter–Sister Mary pile on the floor and slid right into Ruth.

"Dang it, guys! I told you this house is not a freeway!" Ruth helped her old friend back to her feet. Seeing Sister Mary sprawled on the floor gave Skeeter a pause. "Sorry, Sister Mary.' We didn't see you there. Why didn't you move out of the way?"

Skeeter was contrite, but baffled by the old dog's apparent refusal to yield.

Sister Mary caught her breath and flapped her ears. "You two have to learn to look where you are going. When you're as old as I am, you just can't move like that."

"Sorry, Sis." Mikey was contrite too. "Skeeter will be more careful next time.

"Everybody, just chill! Stop zooming around like crazies." Ruth commanded from her place in the kitchen. She smiled. It had been a while since the house had been full of happy feet running from room to room and floor to floor. She remembered the days when Boyo and Sister Mary had romped at full speed in the townhouse, taking advantage of the carpeted stairs and floor for traction. But her old friend really had gotten clobbered by the two young dogs, and a slowdown in pace would be a good way for Sister Mary to catch her breath.

"Let me see, what do I have for you guys? Maybe this will take your minds off roughhousing." Ruth pulled three chew bones out of the closet. "One for each of you. Here you go." Ruth ceremoniously handed the first to Sister Mary, then one each to Skeeter and Mike.

Skeeter's eyes grew wide and she looked at her older friends. "Seriously?" she exclaimed.

"Yup. She hands these out on a regular basis. Go ahead and enjoy," Sister Mary explained.

Skeeter wasn't taking any chances that Ruth would change her mind. She grabbed the bone as quickly and firmly as she could and darted off to a corner of the kitchen. Soon all the dogs were munching quietly, while Ruth went back to her holiday preparations.

Chapter 16

It didn't take long for Skeeter to earn a crate of her own. A few hours after dispensing bones to everyone, Ruth decided it was time to finish gift and grocery shopping. Giving a quick shout down to Max, who was working in the basement, Ruth left the house with all three dogs loose upstairs.

"What do we do now?" Skeeter wondered out loud.

"We wait," Sister Mary answered.

"How long?"

"Don't know. Could be hours, judging by the number of bags she was carrying." Sister Mary replied.

"Well, can we play?" asked Skeeter.

"If you want to, go ahead. Just don't break anything," Sister Mary replied, remembering her own early-day escapades years before, escapades that resulted in bowls of tomatoes on the floor, broken vases and plant containers. Ruth had always seemed so disappointed when she came home to find things broken, so she and Boyo had curtailed their roughhousing while she was away as a result.

"What about Max?" Mikey asked. "Will he care?"

"Max? No. He usually just stays in his area working until Ruth gets home. He won't mind."

Sister Mary walked over to her waiting spot on the floor and laid down. "Me, I'm just going to wait here for Ruth. You kids do what you want. I recommend the sofa. I used to watch from there." she said with a nod.

Mikey and Skeeter weren't convinced they could do anything they wanted. That seemed risky. So, taking their cue from Sister Mary's actions instead of her words, both dogs decided to lie down. Looking around for a comfortable place of her own, Skeeter spied what she thought would work. "I'll just wait up here." This looks like a nice place to wait and watch. It's up off of the floor. The sun is keeping it warm, and I can see out the window," she thought to herself, leaping up onto a table in the room next to the living room. "Hmm. Look. This thingy has feathers. They're tasty. A nice snack while I wait."

Skeeter quietly chewed on the feather thingy for a while and then fell asleep. Meanwhile, Mikey settled in on the recommended sofa where he, too, quickly fell asleep.

The dogs' slumber was interrupted abruptly. *"Skeeter! Get off of the dining room table!"* Max roared. "And, look what you've done to the centerpiece!"

Max yelled, but inside he was laughing at the sight of his beautiful new puppy sprawled on the brand new dining room table with feathers poking out of her sleeping mouth. It was a funny enough sight to snap a photo and send it to Ruth before chasing Skeeter off the table. "Look where your dog is," he texted Ruth.

Skeeter bounded off the table in a panic. She hadn't meant to anger Max, and Sister Mary had said to sit anywhere she liked. Hiding behind her brother, Skeeter looked out meekly at Max who, for his part, was trying to look at the dogs as sternly as he could muster given the situation. "Mikey, Sister Sunny, what do I do now?" she implored cowering.

"Just sit still and be quiet," said Mikey, himself not certain what to make of the situation, but bracing for the worst. In the Before Time breaking random unknown human rules carried terrifying consequences.

From her post by the sofa, Sister Mary eyed her fearful young friends and Max with concern. She trusted Max, but knew the two of them had no idea how to handle the situation. "Remember your words, children," she admonished quietly. "Don't get angry, don't panic, don't bite."

Mikey glanced at Sister Mary and gulped, struggling to remember.

"Stay off the tables!" he commanded pointing forcefully at Skeeter, before turning around and leaving the room.

"That was it?" asked the bewildered Mikey, "that was it?"

"That was it," said Sister Mary resuming her post.

"Will he come back and beat us?" asked Skeeter, who was still trembling, remembering the consequences of her Before Time mistakes.

"Heavens no, child. Max gets mad, but he will never hurt you," said Sister Mary shaking her head for emphasis.

"So we just go back to waiting?" asked Skeeter looking around the room carefully for a human-approved place to lie down.

"Yes, child. We go back to waiting," said Sister Mary, shifting into a more comfortable position.

"C'mon, Skeet," said Mikey, "you can sit up here with me on the sofa. They don't seem to mind us up here."

Skeeter's crate arrived the next day, but where should it go? Neither Ruth nor Max were happy with the thought of crowding the living room with multiple crates, but they also weren't happy with the thought of reliving a housebreaking experience like they had had with Sister Mary years ago. Blinds ripped off of the wall, a set of ceramic mixing bowls broken, a set of steak knives with wooden handles ruined, carpet destroyed. The list went on and on. They hadn't crated Sister Mary back then because she had seemed claustrophobic, and they worried that a crate would make things worse. In hindsight, a crate would have probably helped considerably.

But, the past experience with Sister Mary, and the more recent experience with Mikey, not to mention Skeeter's foray on the dining room table, only reinforced Ruth's determination to avoid the housebreaking nightmare with Skeeter. So, the crates were definitely in order, as soon as they could determine the best location for them.

Finally, it was agreed that each crate would go in a separate corner of the living room, which would keep the drafts off both dogs and be as inconspicuous as possible. All the dogs would still be in the same room. Having long ago grown out of her home-wrecking, Sister Mary did not need a crate, but she generally stayed in the room where the crates were placed.

The room was a pretty one. It had two nice sofas. A nice rug, a new rug, was in the middle of the floor and a coffee table sat squarely in its center. Mikey's crate looked out a window into the front yard and driveway. On the wall between the crates stood another table.

Everything was brightly decorated for the season. Pots of poinsettias, stuffed dolls, and other toys from Christmases past filled the room and indeed, the house.

The following morning was a work day for Ruth and Max. Being the last out, Ruth put both dogs in their crates, gave them each a chew toy and a pat on the head and off to work she went. "Be good, be nice to each other, and have a good day! I won't be late, bye-bye." She said brightly as she closed the door behind her.

To say that Skeeter was dissatisfied with the location of her crate would be an understatement. Her buzzing started just about the minute the door closed. "Sister Mary? Sister Mary? Why am I way over here in this corner? Why can't I sit next to you and Mikey? Will you come sit next to me?" Skeeter complained.

"I don't know why they put your crate there, child. But, you're there because that's where they put you."

"But why? Why do I have to be here? In this stinky old corner? I can't see anything. Mikey? Mikey? You over there? You're so far away, I can only barely see you."

"I'm here, sis. I can see you. Stop exaggerating. There's only a table between us," Mikey admonished.

"But, Mikey, I'm scared over here. I don't like it." Skeeter pouted and squirmed in her crate.

Come on, child. We're all in this room together. Nobody's going anywhere. Just sit quiet." Sister Mary, hoping that would be the end of Skeeter's whining, returned to her post next to the sofa.

Skeeter thought for a while, and decided to try to follow Sister Mary's advice. As she sat, though, her ghosts continued to haunt her, ghosts that hadn't haunted her for a while, ones she thought she'd pushed away at Shelter Lady's and that she hadn't heard at all since reuniting with Mikey. Sitting in her crate, though, she remembered. The crate room at the First House. Its clutter. Its distance from Mikey. Alone. The boys. Banging on her crate. Toys flying. Boys jumping. Trying to cover her ears and eyes with her paws to shut out their noise and her terror. Mamma barking from her crate, urging both Mikey and Skeeter to keep calm and stay brave. Mikey shouting encouragement to her from the other room and finally drawing the boys away.

The memories flooded back in a torrent. No, she needed to get out of that crate and over to Mikey. Then, whatever happened, they could face it together.

"Must get to Mikey. Must get to Mikey," Skeeter said to herself over and over, spinning around in her crate, not hearing the admonishments from Mikey and Sister Mary who could see their young friend starting to fret herself into a frenzy. The crate was strong and well made, but no match for a panicked and determined dog. "Must get to Mikey, must get to Mikey," she thought as the ghosts raged through her head while she spun and squirmed in her crate.

Pushing at the bars on the crate with her nose and paws, the door, the corners, everywhere, Skeeter worked frantically to escape. "Must get to Mikey. Must get to Mikey," she repeated to herself as she worked against the enclosure. There. She'd managed to get her nose under the frame of one side and push, squeeze, there, out. Once out of the crate, Skeeter looked around the room. It was not nearly as cluttered as the First House, but toys were scattered here and there. They had to go. And it had plants. They had to go, too. The toys and plants were no match for a panicked and determined dog who, with her demons raging in her head, had forgotten entirely her first impulse to get to Mikey, and who in her panic could not hear her friends' barking, urging her to stop her panicked destruction. When the last potted plant hit the floor and was soundly crushed and stomped into the rug where it belonged, the roaring and banging in Skeeter's head stopped.

Looking around, she saw the horrified faces of her two friends, who were by now lying very still. "Skeeter," Mikey whispered, "look what you've done. You forgot."

"Forgot what? Where? I think I got everything. Well, I didn't get the sofas. Should I get those too?" said Skeeter, the drums in her head returning.

"No, No, Skeeter, No. You forgot Mamma's words. Don't get angry. Don't panic. Don't bite. Remember? Don't get angry, don't panic, don't bite."

Mikey tried to calm his sister and bring her out of her panic, as Sister Mary had for him only weeks before.

Still panting, but calmed by her brother's words, Skeeter looked around, saw the destruction around her, and hung her head. "I forgot one and two, didn't I?" she said.

"You sure did, sis," said Mikey, shaking his head at the destruction in front of him.

"But Mikey, those boys, that crate, those rooms, I couldn't ever get to you. I could hear you, but I couldn't ever get there," Skeeter cried.

"I know, Skeet. I heard you, too. But that was there. This is here. It's not like that here," Mikey cried a little too, remembering his own time in his crate at the First House.

"Skeeter, look, we're all together here, in the same room. No kids, no clutter. The room's brightly lit and we can see outside. We don't want to blow this, Skeet," said Mikey, trying again to reason with his sister.

"Mikey, Sister Sunny, what do I do now? First the feather thingy on the table and now this. What will they do? Will they send me back? I don't want to go back, Mikey, Sister Sunny, please? Don't let them send me back!" Skeeter implored her friends, her eyes wide and sides still heaving from her efforts and her fear.

Mikey looked around at the room thoughtfully. "Maybe it's not so bad, Skeet. It's just this one room and I made a mess of just about all of them. Maybe they'll go easy on you."

Sister Mary gave her young friends a long and kindly look. "Well, Skeet, you sure did a number on this room. That's for sure, but let me handle it. You two just remember your words. Mikey, why don't you practice them with your sister a while and help her calm down. Skeeter, come lie down next to your brother's crate a while and I'll lie down here with you, and we'll wait."

Skeeter did as she was told and lay down next to her brother's crate.

After a while, thinking maybe a story would help her friends, Sister Mary began, "Did I ever tell you guys about the time that Boyo and I trashed the bathroom?"

Mikey's ears pricked up. He hadn't heard this one. "Well, it began one day when Boyo and I were sitting on the sofa, bored. Boyo got this idea that he and I should pretend to be Ruth and Max getting ready for work in the morning. So, he and I ran upstairs and Boyo tried to put shaving cream on his face. I forget what I was doing pretending to be Ruth. I think I had her hair brush. No idea how she works that thing.

Anyway, Boyo couldn't figure out how to make the can work like Max made it work. He'd put his paw on it and push, and stuff would come out, but we couldn't get the stuff to squirt on his face instead of in the sink. In the end, we just emptied the whole can. We thought about eating it, but it didn't taste good. Just made bubbles come out of our mouths, which was pretty funny.

"So anyway, then, Boyo stood on his hind legs and stretched up as high as he could from the ground, but he couldn't see himself in the mirror. So I said, 'Why don't you just jump up there?' And he did. But when he did, he found out that the counter was slippery and he knocked everything, and I mean everything, toothbrushes, toothpaste, hair brushes, everything into the sink with the shaving cream. Man, Boyo just scrambled off that counter faster than you can say lickety split!

Well, I was doubled over laughing by then. So I said to him, 'Boyo, betcha can't touch the top of the mirror.'

'Bet I can',' he said. And he jumped back on the counter, this time more carefully, and he stretched himself all the way to the top of the mirror, where he left two paw prints for all to see. And then I said 'Boyo, betcha can't jump from the sink into the tub in one shot.'

'Betcha I can,' said Boyo. And he made a leap for it, which was hard because, well, like I said, the sink was slippery. He made it, though. He made it."

Sister Mary stopped and looked at her two friends, who by now had calmed down and were sitting in rapt attention.

"What happened then, Sister Sunny? What'd you make Boyo do then?"

"Well, Skeeter, I never really made Boyo do anything, I just gave him suggestions," Sister Mary said slyly with a wink. "But I will say that I won the race to the bottom of the stairs!"

At about that time, the dogs could hear the sound of Max's car coming up the driveway. Seeing her young charges' unease returning, Sister Mary admonished, "Remember, you two. Repeat your words and leave the rest to me."

Sister Mary intercepted Max at the front door hoping to explain, but before she could, Max saw the wreckage. His wife's childhood toys strewn on the floor, some of them ripped from limb to limb. The beautiful poinsettia plants he had bought for her only a week ago, dumped out onto the floor, shredded, their pots cracked, their dirt ground into the beautiful rug that he and Ruth had so admired when they'd purchased it. The crate, mangled in a heap in the corner.

This time, Max was not amused. No, this was truly a disastrous mess. What would Ruth think about her childhood toys? How had Skeeter gotten out of her crate? If she couldn't, or wouldn't, stay in there, what were they to do about keeping her from destroying their house?

Taking a breath and trying to stay calm, Max let out a long sigh. "Jeezus! What happened in here, Skeeter? What did you do? Why?" Max let Mikey out of his crate and walked out of the room in disbelief to call his wife.

"You will not believe what your dog did to the living room," he said to Ruth on the phone. "The place is beyond destroyed. I mean, it's a disaster. Everything is ruined. Should I punish her? She's going to have to go back if she won't stay in her crate. Otherwise, she's going to destroy the house and everything we have."

Ruth could hear the concern in her husband's voice and wondered herself what they were going to do if Skeeter would not stay in her crate, but she tried to stay calm, or at least sound that way. Maybe it wasn't as bad as it sounded. "No, no. Don't punish her. It's too late for that. She'll have no idea what she's being punished for at this point, anyway. Let's just talk about it when I get home," she said, "I'm almost there."

Max looked around the room. He turned to look at the dogs. Skeeter and Mikey sat quietly, trying to remember their words. "I'm sorry, Mr. Max. I'm really sorry," said Skeeter bashfully, looking up at Max's storm-filled expression.

"She won't do it again, Max. Give her a chance," pleaded Mikey, lowering his head and lifting a paw for emphasis. Max just shook his head and took another deep breath.

Sister Mary tried to intercede, pushing herself in front of Skeeter and Mikey. "Remember, Max. She's just a child. I was a child once, too and we all survived," she said, looking Max squarely in the eye. Where was Ruth anyway? I could really use her help right now, thought Sister Mary.

After a couple of minutes that seemed like hours to everyone, the lights of Ruth's car could be seen coming up the driveway. Finally. Sister Mary was more determined than ever to help diffuse the situation, if she could. This time, she met her friend at the door, and firmly pushed Ruth back outside. "Look, Ruth," Sister Mary said. "There was an incident this morning, but we have it under control."

"Come on Sister Mary, get out of the way and let me in," said Ruth as she opened the door.

Sister Mary pretended not to hear Ruth directing her back inside and instead walked Ruth back toward her car. "Let's just stay out here a bit until we're sure you're composed. You need to be composed, Ruth. It's important to all of us."

Ruth looked down at her old friend and took a deep breath. "You know, if I didn't know better, I'd think you didn't want me to go in there just now," she said.

"It's pretty bad in there, Ruth. It's really bad."

"Come on, old gal. Max already told me. It can't be as bad as all that. Let's go inside and face the mess. We'll work through it. We always do."

Giving her worried friend a scratch behind her ears, Ruth went through the door.

Looking around the room, Ruth could see the carnage. How could she miss it? But she could also see the uncertainty and fear in all of the dogs' eyes. The two young dogs were clearly nervous. Their heads were down, tails down, neither would really look

Ruth in the eye. They paced worriedly around her. Sister Mary, on the other hand, stood firm, looking her friend straight in the face, willing her to go easy on her young friends.

Ruth took a deep breath. "Well, that's special. What happened, Skeet? You don't like your crate? Or you just didn't like where we placed it? And what do you have against my old dolls? You know dirt goes outside, right? No need to spread it around in here. Come on, honey. Take it easy. Talk to me a minute," she said, sitting down on the stairway in front of the room and extending a friendly hand toward Skeeter.

Seeing Ruth sit, Skeeter lifted her head shyly and slunk over to Ruth, burying her head into Ruth's lap. "I'm so sorry, Miss Ruth. I didn't mean to break your dolls. I was scared," she cried.

Mikey was also grateful for Ruth's invitation. Pushing Skeeter out of the way, he put his head under Ruth's hand for reassurance and sat down on the stair next to her. "She's really sorry, Miss Ruth. She won't do it again. I just know she won't. Please don't send her back," he pleaded.

Sister Mary pushed her way into the crowd, too, gazing up at Ruth with relief and affection. Things were going to be alright, she thought. A bullet dodged.

Ruth shook her head and gave each of her friends a scratch on the head. No sense being angry, she thought to herself. Stay calm. Don't let things get blown out of proportion.

Apparently thinking the same thing, Max brought in the vacuum. Ruth reassembled her toys and moved them to higher ground, frankly glad that they were the only things that had been destroyed. The dirt could be vacuumed up. No furniture had been chewed. No one had gotten hurt. She'd wondered about the wisdom of leaving the poinsettias out with young dogs anyway. It looked as though they'd been torn apart, but not eaten, so at least she wouldn't have to add an emergency vet bill to the pile.

The next morning, Ruth looked at Skeeter sternly. "Okay, Skeet. Let's see how this will work. We really need you to stay put this time. Otherwise, I don't know what we're going to do with you," Ruth admonished as she headed out for work. "Hopefully, being closer to your brother will help."

After cleaning up the mess the night before, Ruth and Max had reinforced Skeeter's crate where it looked likely that she'd gotten out. They'd also moved it so that Skeeter was now positioned much closer to Mikey, with no furniture between them. Hopefully, the reinforcement and positioning would contain and calm their nervous friend. Skeeter looked over the new crate position skeptically. It was better. She would try again.

"You okay, Skeet?" Mikey asked from across the doorway.

"Yeah, I think so, Mikey." Skeeter put her head down on her pillow and tried to relax.

"Good, but just remember, if those ghosts start beating their drums in your head again, talk to us, okay?" Mikey said.

"I'll try, Mikey. I'll try."

"Good girl, Sis. I know it's hard. I hear them too, sometimes." Mikey put his head down on his pillow and tried to relax too.

"Seriously, guys. Let's try to talk it through next time, before things get out of hand." Sister Mary lay down on the rug between the two crates, preparing for her nap. "I'll be right here if anybody needs me," she said.

"Sister Sunny?"

"Yes, Skeet."

"Sister Sunny? Can you tell us another story about you and Boyo?"

Sister Mary smiled sleepily. Skeeter was always asking her something right as she was about to go to sleep. But Sister Mary liked telling stories, and if it helped her friends adjust to their new lives, she was happy to oblige.

"Did I ever tell you about the times Boyo and I chased the ocean?" she began. Skeeter and Mikey's eyes grew wide with anticipation. This sounded good. Settling down on their mats comfortably, they waited for Sister Mary to begin. "Well, there's this place far away, about three hours. It's called the ocean. Ruth and Max love to go there and they took Boyo and me with them lots of times. Often, we would stop on the drive and Ruth and Max would pick up subs and chips. Sometimes other things too, but always subs and chips."

"What are subs?" asked Skeeter.

Sister Mary's eyes shone brightly at the memory, but Mikey, eager to impress his sister jumped in. "Skeeter, subs are these huge sandwiches that people eat. They're packed full of meat and cheese and all kinds of things."

"Oh, my, they are delicious!" Sister Mary resumed, "Anyway, after subs, we'd arrive at the ocean and they'd let us out in this really big lot. There were almost always other dogs and their people walking around, out for an adventure just like us. We'd walk over a bridge and across a huge sand pit. I mean, this sand pit stretches for as far as you could see, and then you'd see the ocean."

"What's an ocean, Sister Sunny?" interrupted Skeeter.

"I was getting to that. An ocean is this enormous, moving lake-like thing. The water moves and crashes on the sand and when it does, it leaves little things on it, like bugs and shells, crabs, and other tasty stuff. The water also makes the sand hard and cool so you can run on it."

"Did you get to run on it?" interrupted Mikey.

"Oh, yes, many times. Max and Ruth would take off our leashes and Boyo and I would run and run. One time, the wind and the ocean made these foamy balls for us. They would bounce down the sand and I would catch them. We had to be careful, though, because if we got too close to the water it would knock into us."

"Did you ever get into the water?" asked Mikey.

"Well, one time we did. Max thought it would be fun to teach us to swim, so he and Ruth went into the water and took us with them. That was not a good idea. That water was deep!"

"So what'd you do?" asked Skeeter.

Sister Mary laughed, remembering. "We did what any sensible dog would do. We stood on Ruth and Max until they brought us back to shore! Balanced ourselves on their legs and shoulders until they got the point.

"Anyway, I'm not done. The ocean has lots of other fun things to do and see and smell, too. There are deer and ponies. You're not supposed to chase them, but you can always try. And, when you're done exploring, remember those subs and chips that I told you about?"

"I was wondering when you'd get back to them," said the always hungry Mikey.

"Well, Max and Ruth love to share. We would make out like bandits. We usually ate at a picnic table or bench and then we'd walk around a little more before heading home. Sometimes though, we actually camped there. Spent the whole night. That was great too, except that the ponies would wander into the site and we'd have to tell them to go away. And sometimes, it would be really cold, which was actually great, because then we would all sleep together under the blankets to keep warm."

"Wow, Sister Mary, you and Boyo sure had some fun times together," said Skeeter.

"I know, child. I know," said Sister Mary wistfully. Thinking back to those days, the days before Boyo's sickness and her arthritis, back to when they could run, ears flopping, mouths agape, snatching shells off the beach and then lying next to one another close and warm on the way home, Sister Mary knew Skeeter was most certainly right.

By the time Max and Ruth returned home, all three dogs were at ease. Skeeter and Mikey were safely in their crates and Sister Mary, who had managed to get her nap in after a couple of hours of storytelling, was comfortably lying next to the sofa. Everyone breathed a sigh of relief.

Chapter 17

Christmas Eve was a special time for Max and Ruth. Christmas day and night were spent traveling to visit their families, which, while enjoyable, could be a bit hectic. So, Christmas Eve was their time to enjoy each other's company and the holiday spirit at home.

Aware of the void caused by Boyo's loss, Ruth was determined that this Christmas Eve was to be no different than previous ones. She had trimmed the tree, baked cookies and Christmas stollen, and the house was filled with Christmas cheer. Even the living room that had been Skeeter's nemesis days before was restored to a happy, festive, and clean state. Ruth stayed home wrapping the last of her packages while Max finished his shopping.

As far as gifts were concerned, Max was in good shape this year. Only one gift left to find, but it was an important one; his brother's. Ruth chuckled as she tied the ribbon on the last of her packages. Why did it always come down to that one gift? Hopefully, Max would find it quickly and be home in time for dinner.

Skeeter, Mikey and Sister Mary watched the preparations with quiet interest. "What is she doing, anyway?" wondered Skeeter out loud.

"Remember what I told you about Christmas? Well this is part of it. This particular part is a strange tradition. The people put paper and ribbons around boxes filled with stuff, and then they give the boxes away and the paper gets ripped off, sometimes just shredded right there on the spot. It makes no sense. So, what you're watching now is Ruth putting on the paper, which will be taken off by somebody later on," informed Sister Mary.

"That seems like a waste of time," said Mikey.

"I know, but they seem to enjoy it. It's like a game to them, similar to when we hide our bones in plain sight where others can find them, I guess," said Sister Mary.

"Anyway, it gets better. Once Ruth finishes wrapping, she usually starts cooking. She fixes something special the night before Christmas and we always get some. Then she and Max will stay up most of the night eating, listening to music, maybe watching some TV. It's always fun."

"But what happens on Christmas?" asked the always curious Skeeter.

"Well, Christmas is different. Christmas can be a bit hectic. It usually works out, but it's … well," Sister Mary's voice wandered off, remembering her first Christmas.

Boyo had thought it was great. Music, people, endless food. Boyo loved a good party. Sister Mary, though, had been terrified at first. Nothing but legs, hands, and noise. Lots of noise. She could hear it as she, Ruth, and Boyo approached Mammaw and Pop Pop's house, and she had tried to convince Ruth and Boyo not to go. "Let's just stay here in the car," she had pleaded, pulling herself back away from Ruth, digging her paws into the rug of the car. Ruth and Boyo would hear none of it.

Snapping a leash on Sister Mary's collar, Ruth had declared brightly, "C'mon Sister, let's party!" and in they went. Boyo ran inside eagerly and announced his presence to everyone, particularly Pop Pop, who was always ready with a treat. Pop Pop loved a good party as much as Boyo. Nothing pleased the two of them more than lots of food and lots of laughs.

Clinging to Ruth's side, Sister Mary couldn't say that she agreed, at least not at first. But then, they entered the dining room. The table that year was laden with all sorts of meats and cheeses, ham, turkey, pate, venison, beef. Ruth sat down by the table with Sister Mary. Safe from her position under Ruth's seat, she had peered out from between Ruth's legs. And the treats had started coming. It was as though they were raining from the sky. Sister Mary had decided then that she'd keep an open mind.

Later that night, Sister Mary and Ruth had joined some of Ruth's family in singing carols by the piano. Ruth still held Sister Mary's leash, but sat with her, a bit apart from the crush of the crowd. She'd scratched her ear gently and rubbed her belly, offering a treat each time Sister Mary would peer out from behind Ruth's legs. Sister Mary had looked around at the tall people, singing merrily, and thought maybe she'd get to like parties after all.

Just then, Boyo had trotted by. He'd been making rounds. "Hey, Sister Mary," he'd said, helping himself to peanuts that were in a bowl on a table. "You should have come with me. Didn't I tell you this would be great? I go in the kitchen and Max gives me some cheese. I go in the dining room and Mammaw gives me some turkey and this other guy gives me some ham.

120

Then I come in here and help myself to peanuts! This is awesome! I'm going back for more cheese! See ya!"

Off he'd wagged, never missing a beat. Sister Mary could still almost feel the warmth of his back against hers as they'd slept on the way home that night.

"Sister Mary, Sister Mary, what happens at Christmas?" asked Skeeter again, interrupting Sister Mary's reverie.

"Oh, well, it's grand," she said, "Ruth and Max sleep in, and when they get up, Ruth makes a huge breakfast, usually steak and eggs. We all eat and then Ruth and Max visit their families. Boyo and I always went with them. We visit Max's family first. They're usually pretty quiet and there aren't too many of them, so it's a good warm-up. They're really nice. You'll like them."

"Wait, wait. Wait. Hold on. There's *more* people to meet? I don't like that. Nope, not one bit," exclaimed Mikey.

"Yeah, me neither, Sister Mary. I have enough people in my life. I don't need any more," chimed Skeeter.

"Oh, children, you're going to have to get over that if you're going to make it here," admonished Sister Mary. "Trust me, I had to get over it a long time ago. It was hard, but I did. Boyo helped me. I'll help you. Ruth and Max will help you, too. They won't put you in a situation you can't handle. Trust me on that."

"Anyway, after a while at Max's family's house, Ruth usually leaves and takes us to her family's house, Mammaw and Pop Pop's. Max usually comes later and joins in. You've met Mammaw and Pop Pop. Their house is where the party really gets going. Tons of food. Tons of people. All laughing, talking, eating, singing, and having a good time."

"That sounds horrible!" exclaimed Skeeter. "The food part's okay, but tons of people?! What do we do? Are they nice? What if someone tries to take us?"

"Nobody's going to take you, child. They're all nice. Some are a little odd, but I'll point them out to you and you can just leave them alone and they'll leave you alone," reassured Sister Mary.

"I dunno, sounds awful to me," said Mikey, shaking his head in dismay.

"Hey, guys, anybody interested in some salami?" Ruth interrupted the dogs' conversation.

Sister Mary was right. Christmas Eve had begun in earnest. And for Skeeter, Mikey, and Sister Mary, it was one for the record books. Food and treats flowed. Ruth had prepared a feast of small bites, salmon, smoked whitefish, and cheeses, which were followed by her homemade lasagne and salad. Max arrived in plenty of time, having quickly found the present for his brother, and soon got to wrapping his packages and joined in the festivities. Mikey and Skeeter played, prancing from one room to the next as Ruth finished up her preparations. Packages were put under the tree. Of course, Ball was played. Sister Mary would not hear of taking a night off from Ball! The music was merry, as were Ruth and Max.

Later that night, listening to the soft snore of Sister Mary, sound asleep on her mat, Skeeter put her head on her brother's shoulder. "Mikey? Mikey? You awake?"

Mikey stirred but kept quiet. "Mikey. Mikey. You awake?" Skeeter kicked her feet into her brother's back.

"I am now," Mikey said groggily, "What is it?"

"Mikey, do you think we've made it to Forever Home?"

Mikey stirred and stretched a little between Ruth and Max. "I dunno, Skeet. We haven't been here forever. We're going to have to wait and see. This Christmas thing sounds like it could be bad. Let's see if we get through it."

Skeeter got up, turned around, and lay back down next to Ruth. "I hope it's Forever Home, Mikey. And I'm pretty sure it is. I mean, we've got everything here, right? People, beds, sofas, snacks? We make mistakes and no bad stuff happens. It's just like the Shelter Dogs said it would be."

Mikey thought for a while, listening to Sister Mary's snores and the sounds of Ruth and Max breathing softly on either side of them. His sister, for the first time in her life, was lying comfortably next to a human. Only a few short months ago, he never would have imagined that would have been possible. It was something the Shelter Dogs had prattled on about during their time with Shelter Lady, but Mikey'd always scoffed at the notion, thinking the Shelter Dogs fools. But now, here, in the warmth of the room and companionship on the bed…Mikey stretched comfortably and worked his way closer to Ruth. "I hope you're right, sis. I really do."

"I'm pretty sure, Mikey. G'night."

"Good night, Skeet." Soon, the soft sounds of sleeping filled the room. No ghosts or nightmares tonight, no drums, just sweet dreams of hope and happy living.

Chapter 18

Christmas Day broke and, as Sister Mary predicted, Ruth prepared a feast of a breakfast, including steak, eggs, and toast, all of which she and Max shared with the three dogs. But, rather than packing a travel bag for her friends, Ruth tucked Skeeter and Mikey safely in their crates. "Guys, you're going to stay here today. I don't think you're quite ready for Christmas at Mammaw and Pop Pop's. Sister Mary, you stay here, too, and keep the kids company," said Ruth as she closed the crate doors and gave everyone a treat. "Be good. Be nice to each other, and have a nice day. We'll be late, but not too late," she said as she closed the door.

Whew! Mikey, Skeeter and even Sister Mary were relieved. That party really did sound like more than they were ready for. "But, guys," said Sister Mary with a wink, "you really do want to get to one. The food alone is worth it and Ruth and Max do watch out for you. The only party better is the Fourth of July party."

"The what?" asked Mikey, trying hard to imagine how a party with lots of strange people could be good, much less that there could be a better one. Sister Mary really did amaze.

"Ruth's family's Fourth of July Party. It's another party Boyo and I used to go to. Don't ask me why they call it that. The actual party is never on the Fourth of July, but it's what they call it."

Skeeter and Mike shook their heads in shared disbelief. "So what happens there? I guess you're going to tell us that it's just like Christmas, but in July?" said Mikey.

"Well kind of," chuckled Sister Mary. "Only it's different. For one thing, it's outside, which spreads out the people, so even though there are lots of them, it's less crowded. And sometimes it goes really late into the night. But the food, the food! Mounds of hamburgers, hot dogs, and crabs."

"Crabs, what are they?" exclaimed Skeeter.

"Crabs are spicy, salty, crunchy things filled with goodness. They come in large containers and humans will sit for hours eating them. They will pick and pick and then discard the shells, usually leaving something behind for us."

"Do we eat crabs?" asked Skeeter with wonder.

"Of course we do, dear. We eat everything, especially crabs. You just crunch through the shells and, my oh my! One year, Boyo figured out how to open the hamburger bin and I found where they were keeping the crabs. We had a feast before they caught us."

"So what's the catch? What's the *thing* about the Fourth of July Party?" asked the ever-skeptical Mikey.

"Ah, well, as the sun goes down and the last of the crabs are picked, the humans like to get loud, really loud. They start stomping around, flailing their arms and gyrating to really bad music, and then, to make matters worse, they light explosives. They think it's fun, but trust me, it's not. Well not to me, anyway. Boyo always thought it was great. He'd jump around and sing with them and never seemed to care about the explosives as long as Ruth or Max was nearby. But when the people started making all the noise, I usually found a quiet corner in the house and stayed there until it was over.

Skeeter and Mikey stared in wonder. Skeeter asked, "Splosives? They actually use 'splosives?" "What are 'splosives?"

"The people light them with fire. Sometimes they go far up in the air, make a really loud sound and then the whole sky fills with different colors. The colors are alright, but the sound is horrible," explained Sister Mary. "We had the party here last year and. . ."

"Wait, what?" interrupted Mikey, "We had the party here? As in here? At this house?"

"That sounds horrifying, Sister Mary," exclaimed Skeeter, putting her paws over her ears at the thought.

"Actually, this party wasn't horrifying at all," Sister Mary patiently. "It was quite wonderful. It was Boyo's last party. He'd always wanted to have a big outside party and there just wasn't enough room at our old place. Even though he was weak from the chemo, he absolutely loved it. You would have thought he was the mayor of the town, welcoming everybody, eating, drinking, lounging in the shade. It was great, a dream come true for him."

Skeeter interrupted, "But what about the stomping and flailing and – what did you call it – ry-rating?"

"And the explosives?" asked Mikey.

"Well, there was some stomping and gyrating but, this time, nobody brought explosives. So it was good."

Sister Mary had given Skeeter and Mikey a lot to think about. This Forever Home stuff was complicated, but for now, the dogs enjoyed each other's company and waited for Ruth and Max to return home.

Chapter 19

One morning, a few days later, Ruth awoke early and announced, "We're having company today! We're going to have a late Christmas celebration with Mammaw and Pop Pop, and Sister Stuff and Uncle Pete and Jake. Everybody has to be good, okay? No barking, no yelling, no jumping, no snapping," Ruth warned.

Mikey looked around, worried. Why did someone always have to come over when things were going well? The last two weeks had been awesome. Skeeter was here. Sister Mary was here. Max and Ruth were usually here and when they were, they were happily chatting about something or other well into the night. Ball had been played. Sofa time had been had. There had been one small incident involving Max's moving foot and Skeeter grabbing it—but that was it. Why would anyone want to add stress to the equation?

"Mikey and Skeeter, children, both of you, listen to me," Sister Mary commanded from the center of the kitchen. "Until they get here, practice what your Mamma taught you!"

"But, Sister Sunny? Why do those people have to come here?" Skeeter asked, echoing her brother's thoughts. "And who are they? Are they going to take us away?"

Skeeter blinked hard at that thought. The last thing she wanted was to be taken away. She liked it here, just like Mikey. Ruth always paid special attention to her, even making a spot for her on the sofa at night so that she could sit with the group instead of by herself. Nobody had ever done that for her before. Ruth also didn't mind if Skeeter slept curled up next to her at night, a comfort she'd never known.

Sister Mary looked at her young friends and smiled sweetly. "Skeeter, you worry too much, just like your brother. No, child, they're not going to take anybody away. They're part of Ruth's family, just like Mikey is part of yours. You've heard me talk about them before. They're nice people. You should like them."

"But what if they don't like me?" Skeeter replied, blinking hard.

"Don't worry, like I told your brother, these people like every dog they come across. They'll like you just fine. Go practice your Mamma's words now."

Ruth and Max's preparations reached a frenzied pitch. Cleaning, cooking, cleaning, more cooking. Music played in the background. Even the skeptical and nervous dogs got into the party mood. Skeeter began prancing around Mikey, inventing what she called her "party dance." "Watch me, Mikey. We're having a party, a party, a party!"

Skeeter bounced, pranced, and danced circles around her brother, around Ruth, around, well, everything.

This party sounded fun. Everything smelled good, too. From what the dogs could detect, Ruth had prepared a feast. Skeeter's youthful excitement was infectious, and by the time their guests arrived, the house was already full of merry bouncing, barking and prancing, "A truly happy chaos," Ruth declared.

Skeeter and Mikey immediately lost their nerve when the doorbell rang. The last time a doorbell rang, they'd been taken away from their First House and hauled to the Impound. The First House had its problems for sure, but the Impound was pure terror. The buzzing and drumming that had been pushed aside in the days before returned in their heads. "Mikey it's the bell. What do we do?"

Skeeter's happiness deflated. Her memories of the Before Time were coming back too strongly for her to continue in her party mood.

"I'm not sure, Skeet. Just stick with me, follow my lead." Mikey tried to look confident for his sister, but with his tail coiled tightly over his back and his eyes darting all around, he wasn't fooling anyone.

Ruth lost a little of her nerve as well. Seeing her young friends' distinct mood change, Ruth decided to put leashes on both young dogs as a safety precaution. "Max, can you let everyone in and I'll hang on to these guys in here?" she asked from the kitchen. "Let Sister Mary welcome everyone first," she said.

Max went to the door and, when he opened it, a torrent of noise, packages and people spilled into the house.

"Ho, Ho, Ho!" cheered Pop Pop. "Merry Christmas!"

"Merry Christmas," cheered Mammaw.

"Come in! Come in!" urged Sister Mary. "Come in! Come in!" she said again, wagging her tail with a smile. "Don't mind the children. They're a little nervous." Sister Mary barked out a caution as her human friends entered the house.

"Merry Christmas, Sister Mary. Merry Christmas, Max," said Mammaw, giving Sister Mary a scratch and Max a hug.

"Come on, Mammaw, get yourself inside," encouraged Sister Mary to the elderly woman with walking sticks. "If I can get my legs over that step, you can too."

Sister Mary urged her old human friend forward with a nudge.

Back in the kitchen, the sounds of people entering the house seemed anything but welcome. "We're being invaded!" hollered Mikey, "The stiff people are back! It's the big tall man, and he has boots!"

"Mikey! What do I do?" hollered Skeeter.

"Bark loudly!" he answered.

And they did. It was quite a scene. Mikey completely forgetting that he'd met Mammaw, Pop Pop, and Sister Stuff before, barking and pulling at his leash, with Skeeter joining her brother for effect. Sister Mary barking hellos and trying to explain to the people why Mikey and Skeeter were upset. And having no idea what they should do in response, Ruth and Max tried barking back. "*Quiet!* Sister Mary, Shush!" hollered Ruth.

"Mikey, Shush! Skeeter, Shush!" hollered Max. Now everyone except the guests was barking.

This was not how Ruth and Max envisioned their small party. Looking at her family in despair, Ruth hollered over the din, "I think if everybody sits, the dogs might calm down. So, everybody, please, just sit down!" Everyone did as they were told.

"Look, Skeet, it's working," Mikey said. "The people look uncomfortable, so maybe they'll go home. Let's keep barking."

Skeeter was happy to do as Mikey said and the house was now filled with a not-so-happy chaos: two young dogs barking in distress, one old dog barking directions at the people and at her young friends, and two people barking back, begging their dogs to stop. The guests sat uncomfortably with their packages in their laps, hands folded, ears ringing, mouths agape at the scene. They could smell the food cooking and see the drinks prepared on the counter for them across the room, but no one dared make a move. This was not good.

Seeing his wife in obvious distress, Max offered, "Should I take them out? You guys can have your visit and I'll bring them back when you're done."

"No, let's keep trying. Maybe you take one and I'll take one and then somehow I'll get dinner served," said Ruth, trying to maintain her composure. "Come on, Sister Mary, give me a break there, girl. At least you could set a good example for these guys and shush!"

"What?" said Sister Mary. "I was just telling these guys to settle and telling you that they were nervous and making sure everybody knew I was here, too."

"Sister Mary, please," begged Ruth.

Sister Mary decided to take pity on her human friend. "Guys, guys. Let's let the humans do some talking for a bit," she instructed her two young friends. "Besides, I think Ruth has dinner ready. We should start getting treats any moment now."

Mikey and Skeeter took a break from their barking, looked around and saw Ruth and Max and their obvious distress. Maybe they should give Ruth and Max a break. At least the strangers were sitting for now.

A long half hour into the visit Mikey, Skeeter and Sister Mary stopped barking. Max held firmly onto Skeeter's leash, Ruth onto Mikey's, and together they served their guests drinks, appetizers, and finally, dinner. The room relaxed. Conversation started. Gifts were opened. Treats, as Sister Mary predicted, were dispensed.

Skeeter looked around and liked what she saw. "So, Sister Mary, we're having a party, a Christmas party?" she said, relaxing a little.

"Yep," said Sister Mary, "this is a Christmas party."

"And we're getting treats!" Skeeter said, encouraged, munching on a peanut that had just come her way, courtesy of Max.

"Yup, treats," said Sister Mary, munching on a piece of cheese from Ruth.

"Hey, where's my treat?" demanded Mikey pushing his nose into Ruth's arm.

"Here you go, buddy," said Ruth handing Mikey a peanut of his own.

Feeling comfortable now that the dogs appeared relaxed, Sister Stuff decided to get up from the sofa and offer to help her sister with the food. "She's getting up! She's getting up! Get back here, Sister Stuff!" demanded Skeeter and Mikey, barking loudly again. "Get back here! You're supposed to stay where you were!" they barked.

"No, No, No, No!" barked Sister Mary. "Sister Stuff gets to move around during parties. It's the way they operate," she continued.

"Oh, didn't know that," Mikey said. "Okay, Sister Stuff, you can leave the room." Skeeter and Mikey sat back down with Ruth and Max.

"There you go, Mikey," said Max, handing him a bit of cheese and taking the leash from Ruth, "Just sit with me for a while, and see how things go."

Mikey liked the sound of that and appreciated the security of the leash. At least he didn't have to worry about losing track of where Max was.

When Pop Pop got up to refresh Mammaw's tea, Skeeter and Mikey protested again, leaping up from their spots on the floor and barking at Pop Pop. "Pop Pop, sit back down! You have to stay here!" they shouted in unison.

"No. No, guys," Sister Mary said. "Not just Sister Stuff, but all the people get to move around. It's what they do."

"Mikey, Skeeter, sit back down here," urged Max and Ruth, also in unison. "You guys need to stay with us," said Ruth, stroking Skeeter's head quietly.

Mikey shook his head. "How are we supposed to keep track?" he asked, bewildered.

"Just pay attention and keep your eyes on Ruth and Max. If they're okay, we're okay. Okay?" Mikey still wasn't sure about the whole disorganized plan.

"Wouldn't it be better if everyone just stayed in their seats?" he asked.

"Sure, but they won't. You have to get used to it. You got that, Skeet?" said Sister Mary, noticing that she, too, looked perplexed.

"Yeah. This party stuff is hard. Fun, I think, maybe, but hard."

"Just keep remembering your Mamma's words, child. You'll be alright."

"She's coming back! She's coming back!" announced Skeeter as Sister Stuff reentered the room.

Sister Stuff looked at her sister's dogs and grinned. "You guys are just like Boyo and Sister Mary used to be. I'm going to have to relocate my earplugs! Now, let's open gifts!"

It was Sister Mary's turn to shake her head. "Guys, letting them out of the room means we also let them back in. It took me a while to learn that one, too. Now, watch, and you'll see how they play the unwrapping game that I told you about. It's really something. All that work that Max and Ruth did to make those boxes look pretty, all torn up to bits in just a couple of minutes."

Skeeter and Mikey quickly decided that, although the game was strange, opening gifts was a good thing. "This one's from your cousins, L'il Bud and Sam," said Sister Stuff, handing a package to Ruth.

Smelling definite treats in the bag, Skeeter, Mikey, and Sister Mary all pressed Ruth. Shoving her nose in the bag, Skeeter took a deep breath and looked up, blinking her eyes and wagging her tail in large circular loops.

"Is that *all* for us?" she exclaimed in wonder. Mikey took a good smell too. He could hardly believe his nose.

"Wow! Really? Sister Mary, are you sure that there isn't some sort of trick going on here?" Mikey asked.

"Nope, no trick. Sister Stuff shows up with a bag of treats every year. It looks like this year, she's outdone herself."

Sister Mary could hardly wait for her Christmas treat. Ruth looked in the bag and pulled out one of the many items. "This should help you guys settle down. How about this? Everybody gets a rawhide!"

Ruth pulled out one for each dog, ceremonially handing Sister Mary hers first. In short order, the room was again filled with happy – this time quiet – dogs, people, laughing, talking, eating, and the music of Christmas. Working on his rawhide, Mikey looked around at the scene in front of him. Not bad, he thought. Not bad.

Skeeter looked at her brother and wiggled. "Hey, Mikey!" she said quietly.

"Yeah, Skeet?"

"This is some party, huh?"

"Sure is, Sis, sure is."

Later that night, after all the wrapping paper was picked up, and the dishes cleaned and put away, Ruth and Max sat in the living room relaxing after the long day. By now, the rawhides were a thing of Christmas past and the three dogs were fast asleep on the sofa next to Ruth. The lights of the tree bathed the room, and music softly played in the background. Her people content and relaxed and her new friends having survived their first regular party, Sister Mary stirred and looked up at the special tree that Ruth put out every year in addition to the regular Christmas tree. Ruth called it the "doggie tree." It was decorated with pictures of all of the dogs in Ruth's family, past and present, and small dog biscuits and rawhide bows. Sister Mary liked the look and smell of that tree.

This year, unlike the previous years, the tree stood next to a small wooden box. Atop the box was a toy dog from Max's youth and, next to the box, a trumpeter and a bugler, each bearing horns uplifted to the sky. Sister Mary had watched as Ruth put the box by the tree this year, tears running down her face at the time.

"You'd have been proud of them, Boyo," Sister Mary said softly, looking up at the box and the tree. "Your people did good. My two new friends managed to get through the day without a major issue. I tried to help them all, just like you always helped me. Sister Stuff brought her usual bag of treats, even a bit more this year. Mammaw and Pop Pop brought a bag of toys. Uncle Pete and Jake were quiet, as usual. Max tried hard not to see too many similarities between you and Mikey or me and Skeeter, but he did anyway. I saw him look your way a whole bunch of times. Ruth, well, you know Ruth. She cooked herself to death, but loved every minute of it. She looked your way many times, too. Anyway, Merry Christmas dear friend. Merry Christmas."

Sister Mary looked at the box and the tree a bit longer, sighed and went to sleep, using her friend Ruth as her ever-comfortable pillow.

An hour later, Ruth and Max decided it was time for them to turn in as well. Max picked Sister Mary up from the sofa and carried her upstairs to bed. Ruth turned off the lights, blew a kiss toward the box and the tree, and the two young dogs groggily followed her up to bed. Snuggled up together, safe and warm between Ruth and Max, Skeeter looked at Mikey, his head resting on Ruth's legs. "Hey, Mikey? Mikey? You awake?" she whispered.

"Yeah," he said.

"Mikey? Now do you think this is Forever Home? I really think this is it," Skeeter said hopefully.

"I dunno, Skeet. Things can still go wrong. You just never know. We really haven't been here that long."

"But, Mikey?" said Skeeter, her eyes tearing up. "This has to be Forever Home. I know it. These people, this house, this bed. Even the party. It was all good. Even the other people were nice. Why can't you believe this is Forever Home, Mikey? Sister Mary does. This is her Forever Home. She even said so."

Mikey thought hard. Skeeter had a point about Sister Mary. He wanted to believe as his sister did, but his Before Time had been too hard. Sister Mary, these people, the bed all on one hand. The Before Time on the other. It was tough to reconcile. Mikey looked at his sister. They had gone back for her, just like Sister Mary said they would. That had to count for something. "I dunno, Skeet. Maybe. Let's just keep behaving and see how it goes for a while, okay?"

Skeeter brightened. "Okay, Mikey. You'll see. Things are going to be just fine. We're in Forever Home. I just know it."

Just to be sure, Skeeter stretched herself between Mikey, Ruth, and Max and took a look down at Sister Mary, asleep on her mat below. She then fell soundly asleep; the ghosts in her head put their drums away, and the Before Time was firmly at bay for the night.

Chapter 20

At breakfast the next morning, Ruth had a surprise for her young friends. "Hey, guys, interested in these?" she said, pulling a couple of the toys out of the bag that Mammaw and Pop Pop had left the night before.

"Sister Mary," asked Skeeter. "What's that?"

"Take one and see," said Sister Mary with a smile. Skeeter and Mikey both tentatively accepted Ruth's offering. The toys were soft and light, and gave off the funniest sound when they were chewed.

Upon feeling her toy squish and hearing it squeak, Skeeter wriggled with glee. "Rroo Rroo!! Mikey! Toys! Have you ever seen anything as amazing as toys!?" Skeeter pranced and paraded her toy around the house. "Watch this, Mikey, I can throw it and catch it and then throw it again! Just like you do with the balls! Check this out. I can throw it and then pounce on it, catch it, and throw it!"

Skeeter bounced, growling playfully at the toy. "Ruh, Ruh, Ruh!" she said, tossing it in the air and catching it.

Mikey also delighted in the toys. "Hey, Skeet. Watch this. I can push it, chew it and then throw it. How about that move!"

"Really? Your toy pushes too? Does mine push? Oh, yes, there it goes. I can push mine too, Mikey. Watch."

"Betcha can't push yours as good as I can," taunted Mikey playfully.

"Can too."

"Can not."

By now both dogs were pushing, pouncing, throwing and catching all around the first floor. "Hey, Mikey, let me try yours," teased Skeeter.

"Try your own," said Mikey, slightly miffed.

"No, I want to try yours, it looks better than mine."

"Is not."

"Is too," Skeeter replied.

"Fine. Take it. I don't need the stupid toy," huffed Mikey as he dropped his toy and stomped away.

Skeeter immediately pounced on her brother's toy, careful to keep her own in the meantime. His toy was pretty good. Not as good as hers, frankly, but still a prize worth parading around the house. "Look at me, Ffister Mawy! I've got *two* toys! Bof in my mouf!"

"I see that, Skeeter. You look very stylish," laughed Sister Mary from her spot on the kitchen floor. "Are you planning to share those with your brother?"

"Nope," said Skeeter. "I'm piling these all right here on the rug next to Ruth and I'm going to top off my pile with one of yesterday's bones!"

Skeeter was feeling completely full of herself.

"C'mon, guys, time to go upstairs," announced Ruth. "Skeeter, you can bring those with you." By now, the dogs knew the morning routine. Get up, go out, come in, eat, go out, go upstairs and hang out with Ruth while she worked at her computer before going into the office for the day.

So, hearing Ruth's announcement, Skeeter grabbed her new favorite toy, the long floppy one with a squeaker in two spots, and ran upstairs. Mikey retrieved his toy and followed. Sister Mary stood patiently at the stair waiting for her lift.

Once in her office, Ruth took her place at the desk. Sister Mary took hers, right under the desk at Ruth's feet, and Mikey and Skeeter took theirs on either side of Ruth's chair. With her new toy, though, Skeeter was not about to just lie around like a bump on a log. No, the toy was too much fun to chew, toss, flop, and pounce. Rolling around on her back, toy in her mouth and between her paws, she rolled under Ruth's chair, which wasn't really a desk chair at all, but more like a dining room chair being used as a desk chair. It had no wheels and a long skirt that reached the floor. When she rolled under it, Skeeter discovered that not only could she fit entirely, but no one could see her.

The Chair of Invisibility! "Hey, Mikey," she teased, poking her brother with her nose. "Betcha didn't know where I was! Watch this! Now you see me, now you don't. Betcha can't get under here! Watch, now you see me, now you don't!"

"Hey, Skeet. Betcha I still know where you are," retorted Mikey, poking Skeeter back with his paw.

Seeing her friends about to knock Ruth's chair over with Ruth still in it, Sister Mary decided to intercede. "Did I ever tell you guys about the time I tricked Boyo into running into an invisible pond?"

Skeeter and Mike paused, both of their eyes drawing wide. "An invisible pond? What's that?" they asked in unison.

"Well, many, many years ago, Boyo and I lived in another place, the place that I've told you about before. Each morning, Ruth would walk with us around the neighborhood and in a big field behind where we lived. Sometimes, she would let Boyo and me play in the field, which was often littered with plastic bottles. We would grab the bottle toys and play keep-away with them. One day, it was raining really hard, and since no one else was around, Ruth decided it would be fun to let us play our game. I grabbed the first bottle toy I saw and took off running, just fast enough so Boyo couldn't catch me, but not so fast that he gave up. I was always faster than he was; I just never let him know. Anyway, about halfway around the field I spotted a pond, that had never been there before. Before the rain, it had just been a low area with some weeds and rocks, but with the rain, it had filled. Boyo was focused on catching me and grabbing the bottle toy. So I took a few quick rights and a few more quick lefts and then a dash forward toward the pond, making sure Boyo was right on my heels. I ran straight for the pond and right before it, I cut hard right. Boyo was running so hard and was so focused on me and the bottle that he ran, sploosh! Right into the pond!"

By now, Sister Mary was rolling on her back, laughing at the memory. It was one of her first truly happy memories with Boyo, happening just months after her adoption and weeks after her failed runaway attempt. The release of running in the field and playing with the bottles that day had been intoxicating. Getting one over on Boyo, then a first, was even more so.

"What happened then, Sister Mary?" Mikey asked, interrupting Sister Mary's reverie.

"Well, Boyo pulled himself out of that pond, and his whole face, his whole body, was drenched and muddy. I mean, his fur, his ears, even his eyes were wet! He was not happy, but Ruth and I were laughing so hard, he couldn't be mad. Ruth was laughing so hard she was almost crying. Anyway, she gave Boyo a good scratch on the chin and we all went inside and dried off before anybody got cold."

"Did the invisible pond ever appear again?" asked Skeeter

"Well, not really. The pond stayed a pond after that rain, but after Boyo ran into it, the pond lost its powers of invisibility," answered Sister Mary with a sly grin.

Chapter 21

"We're going to see Mammaw and Pop Pop," announced Ruth. Sister Mary's ears pricked up at the announcement. It had been a while since she'd taken a trip. Trips to Mammaw and Pop Pop's were usually good ones, especially when they were not preceded by lots of packing, which indicated that Ruth and Max were going away. No, judging from the small bag Ruth had assembled on the counter, just one can of food, kibble, leashes, treats, this would be a routine visit.

"We're going visiting, visiting, visiting," pranced Skeeter, catching Sister Mary's happy face at the announcement.

Mikey was suspicious. He knew things had been going too well. Maybe Sister Mary was happy because she knew "visiting" was code for something else, something like "going away." Maybe she was happy to get rid of them.

Seeing her brother's mood change, Skeeter paused her prancing. "What's the matter, Mikey? You don't want to go visiting? Sister Mary says it's fun," she said.

"Skeet, how do you know? Have you ever been 'visiting' before? It could be a setup."

Skeeter rolled her eyes. Mikey's constant mood changes and suspicions got on her nerves. Everything was always a setup to him. "Mikey, c'mon. Seriously? Sister Mary says it's okay, so it's okay."

Hearing the two, Sister Mary chimed in before an argument broke out. "Mikey, look around you. What do you see?"

"I dunno, just Ruth moving around the kitchen putting stuff in a bag," he replied.

"Sure, but look at what's going into that bag and look at Ruth. She has food enough for one meal for each of us in that bag, our leashes and enough treats for an army. She's a little anxious, but she's not upset, and she can look you in the eye without flinching. I might be able to pull off an invisible pond deception with Boyo and spin a good yarn for your entertainment, but Ruth can't fake anything. If she was going to get rid of you, you'd know."

Mikey paused to consider Sister Mary's counsel. "Maybe you're right," he said. "We'll see. Maybe Ruth is as gullible as Skeeter here is."

Sister Mary rolled her eyes. Sometimes it was hard to get through to that boy. "Just keep an open mind, kid, and remember your Mamma's words," she reminded. "Both of you," she added, looking sternly at Skeeter, who had again earlier that week nipped Max in misunderstanding.

Once in the car, Sister Mary took her spot braced securely against the back of the front seat, and Mikey and Skeeter situated themselves where they could get a good look at the scenery. Being in the back seat brought back memories for all the dogs: Sister Mary of trips gone by with her beloved Boyo, Skeeter of the last long drive she'd taken to this place with Max. For Mikey, being in the back seat with Skeeter and Sister Mary brought back memories of their trip to the Impound. He, his sister, and his mamma, all riding in the back of a truck, filled with other frightened dogs, all hoping for the best, but not really knowing what was going to happen. Bad things happened to him that time. Looking at his sister and Sister Mary, Mikey tried to put on a brave face for their sake.

Sister Mary looked up from her spot and noticed the tension in her young friend's face. "Relax, kid. It's going to be like I told you. We're just visiting. It will be fun. You'll see."

Mikey hoped so, but he could hear the buzzing in his head begin as the shadows and ghosts started to creep forward from the back of his mind where he'd pushed them.

A short way down the road, Ruth stopped the car. Looking out, Mikey could see a strange man standing on the side of the road. He knew it! This was a setup! His ghosts were beating their drums loudly now. Mikey was not about to let the strange man get close enough to separate him from Skeeter and Sister Mary. Mikey charged at the window with all the force he could muster. "Get away! Get away! You'll never take us!" Mikey barked. "Get away!" Mikey tore at the car's ceiling for extra emphasis.

"Hey, hey there, Mikey!" interrupted Ruth. "What's the matter with you? Never seen a person standing at a stop sign before?" she asked as she pulled the car out onto the next street and continued their journey.

Mikey looked at Ruth, remembering Sister Mary's words from earlier that morning. Ruth was looking him square in the face. Maybe he was wrong about the man. Sister Mary and Skeeter both rolled their eyes and settled in. This was going to be a long day.

As the car pulled into the driveway, Skeeter looked around and decided she liked what she saw,. Lots of trees, lots of room. It was quiet, no extra dogs around. "See Mikey, it's like Sister Mary said," Skeeter said brightly, hoping her brother would catch her mood.

"Maybe," replied Mikey.

Seeing her parents about to come outside to greet them, Ruth was quick to shout, "Let me get them out of the car and on leashes so nobody charges Mammaw."

"Sounds like a plan," Pop Pop said through the window. Ruth managed to get leashes on her young friends and picked up Sister Mary to help her out of the car. With the dogs seemingly in control, Mammaw and Pop Pop stepped outside, Pop Pop's hands bulging with treats. He wanted to make a good impression, too.

Seeing Mammaw and her sticks and Pop Pop looming at the top of the steps, Skeeter and Mikey's thoughts were immediately taken back to the First House and the Impound. Images of an elderly woman, steadying herself with canes, a tall man with boots, appearing to be friendly, but just when you let your guard down, bam! Out came the noose leash used by dog catchers everywhere. Then came the torment at the Impound called "temperament testing," where you were put in a situation you couldn't escape from, pushed and prodded, and people complained because you reacted poorly.

Skeeter slunk back, hiding behind Ruth and Sister Mary. "Don't let them take me, Miss Ruth, please don't let them take me," she implored. "Sister Sunny, please tell Miss Ruth not to let them take me," she cried.

"Don't worry sis, I got this. I'll take the lead." Mikey pushed himself forward to intercept Pop Pop, who was approaching, hand extended with a treat offering.

Sister Mary looked at her young friends with a mixture of sympathy and alarm. She remembered what it was like to be afraid of people approaching with treats. She never could understand why people thought that when in doubt, shove a treat in a dog's face, but over time, she grew to accept the treat or turn it down. It was her choice either way. Sister Mary could see that Pop Pop wasn't picking up on Mikey's fear and rather than backing off, he kept coming forward, the hand holding the treat extended toward Mikey, talking softly.

"Watch out, Pop Pop! Mikey, remember your Mamma's words!" Sister Mary barked. Ruth saw the apprehension, but didn't realize its likely outcome until a split second too late.

Mikey's buzzing was loud. His ghosts were in full fury, swirling through his head in a rage, banging their drums in full concert. Big Man. Fake friend. Big boots. Treat. One hand behind his back, likely hiding a noose with a pole. Lady next to him not comfortable. She knew what was going on and did nothing to stop it. She let the Big Man take Mamma away. She let the Big Man take him and Skeeter away. The Big Man pretended to be nice in front of the lady, but once inside the Impound kennel Mikey and Skeeter both learned why he had those big boots. No, Big Man/Impound Man was not going to do that again. Mikey snapped.

"*Ouch!*"

"Mikey, *no!*" screamed Ruth and Sister Mary simultaneously. "You don't do that!" screamed Ruth, shaking Mikey's collar and pulling both Mikey and Skeeter away from her father, who was holding the hand that had been bitten. "B*ad dog!*"

Ruth needed to make her point. When she looked at Mikey's eyes, however, she saw the fear. He was crouched back, leaning away from her, but ready to defend himself and his sister. Ruth could see that if she let herself get out of hand, so, too, would they. They'd backed off. She'd made her point. That was enough, she decided.

147

"Dad, are you alright?" she asked.

"I'm okay. That's only the second dog that ever bit me. You remember the first. It was when I stuck my hand down to break up the fight between Ebony and Elmo. Elmo got me instead of Ebony. Remember that?" he said.

"I sure do." Ruth responded, shaking her head, remembering scrappy Ebony, who never met a dog he liked, but who followed her, her sister, and her father on every trail ride they ever took.

"What do you think that was about, anyway?" Pop Pop asked.

"I'm not sure, but he really wasn't comfortable with you standing up and leaning over him. I saw him stiffen just before he snapped," Ruth said.

"I saw it, too. Next time, you should let him come to you instead of the other way around," Mammaw said.

Pop Pop shook his head in disbelief. "Never saw a dog that didn't want a treat. Oh, well. Tough for you, buddy."

"Let me get them some off leash exercise and see if that doesn't burn off some steam. We'll meet you back inside in a couple of minutes," said Ruth, needing some time to recompose herself as much as the dogs did.

"Sounds like a plan. Just let us get inside before you unleash them," said Mammaw, shaking her head.

Once Mammaw and Pop Pop were inside the house, Ruth took off their leashes and walked away. Looking around at the wide open woods and the lane in front of them, Skeeter's eyes grew wide. She and Mikey shook their heads, flapping their ears in relief. The Big Man, Pop Pop, hadn't done anything. No nooses, no sticks, no boots. He'd just received one of Mikey's best punches and did absolutely nothing. Ruth did, though. She'd made clear she was not happy with Mikey. But that was it. They'd survived. Skeeter again shook her ears in relief and disbelief.

Needing to blow off some steam, she looked at her unsettled brother. "Come on Mikey! I'll race you! Betcha can't catch me!" Skeeter exclaimed as she took off down the path.

Mikey might have been skeptical of the day's ultimate outcome, but knew that, no matter what, a run would do him good. Not to mention, Mikey was not about to let his sister get away from him!

Racing down the path and through the woods, Skeeter and Mikey stretched as hard and far as they could, each dog trying to outpace the other. The woods seemed endless and when they reached the fence at the end of the lane they turned and ran the other way, back toward the car, making a complete lap around the property. Sister Mary and Ruth were only a quarter of the way down the property lane, so Skeeter and Mikey decided to take another lap, or three. Shaking her head in disbelief at the dogs' speed and smiling at their obvious joy of running, Ruth looked at her old friend walking beside her. "Remember how you and Boyo used to do that, Sis? Only by now, you and Boyo'd be arguing over who was going to hold the stick one of you had found!"

Sister Mary remembered. It felt good to be on that path again. It had been months. The last time she'd been there, shortly after Boyo died, the memory of him had been too much to take and she had barely made the walk with Ruth. This time, watching the kids run brought back her happy memories. It was still hard walking the path instead of running it with Boyo, but at fifteen, she'd let the kids do the running for now.

A few moments and several laps around the property later, Ruth decided she could not put off entering the house any longer.

Hopefully, the run took the edge off of her young friends and she could get her visit in without any further incidents.

Getting inside Mammaw and Pop Pop's house, however, proved to be a bit of a challenge. Sister Mary insisted on entering first and announcing their presence. The two young dogs and Ruth were nervous, still anxious to make good first impressions, or at least to redeem themselves. Mikey and Skeeter remembered Mammaw and Pop Pop from the Christmas party, but it was different actually entering their house. The space was unfamiliar. The door was narrow and the hallway tight. The kitchen was large but crowded with furniture. Not much room for nervous dogs to make a quick exit if they felt the need. Determined to control the situation, Ruth snapped leashes on both of her young friends and stuffed her pockets full of treats.

Entering the house, Mikey and Skeeter looked around. Pop Pop was standing by the stove. Mammaw was seated, her two sticks propped in front of her like a fence, or perhaps weapons to use if anyone made the mistake of approaching her the wrong way, thought Mikey as he entered the room. Sister Mary was barking something or other. Mikey's and Skeeter's buzzing and drumming returned in full force. Forgetting to repeat their Mamma's words, they were determined to put on a united front. Best to be loud.

"Whoa, whoa! Easy guys, easy."

Ruth tried to steady her two nervous friends as they barked and strained at the end of their leashes. "Sister Mary, shush! You know better, now come on," she said. "Guys, let's try that again. Let's back up and get you some breathing room."

Ruth pulled her friends down the hall, away from Pop Pop and Mammaw.

Mikey's buzzing subsided a little and he looked around nervously. "Sister Mary, what do we do?" he asked.

"You don't have to *do* anything, Mikey. Just be yourself. You'll be alright. For me, I just bark. I bark. They tell me to shush, whatever that means. And I bark some more. After I'm sure they're all fine, I take a seat on the floor and wait for dinner," Sister Mary said reassuringly. "When it's time to leave, I stand up, bark and let Ruth know," she continued.

"So we should bark too?" Skeeter asked, her own drumming subsiding somewhat.

"Well, I don't know if we all need to bark. You see how Ruth reacts. If we all keep barking, we'll never get inside," replied Sister Mary.

By now, all three dogs had stopped barking and were seated in front of Ruth. "That's right. Good!" she declared and handed each dog a treat. "Let's get a little closer," she said and moved the dogs toward the kitchen door.

"Sister Mary, are you sure we shouldn't bark? I mean, look at Pop Pop. He's leaning over the counter just looking at us. What if he picks up something and throws it? Shouldn't we make him stop that?" asked Mikey.

"Well, I've never seen the man throw anything, but go ahead, kid. I'm pretty sure we've got all day," replied Sister Mary.

With the resumption of frantic barking, Ruth again retreated down the hall way with the three dogs in tow, but not as far this time. Turning around and looking at the kitchen, Mikey and Skeeter could see that their plan hadn't exactly worked. Pop Pop was still standing there, looking at them quizzically. He hadn't thrown anything, though, and he hadn't hollered at them. "Skeeter, Mikey, sit," Ruth said through the din of their buzzing.

Recognizing the command from their days with Shelter Lady, Skeeter and Mikey both sat and looked up at Ruth. "There. Good. At least you heard me this time," she said as she dropped a couple of treats down for each dog.

The entry process continued for about a half hour. Bark, retreat, sit, stop barking, treat, move forward, treat. Eventually, everyone was in the kitchen, more or less quiet. Mikey calmed down enough that Ruth took off his leash. Seeing that Skeeter still looked nervous, she kept her leash on for the time being. Pop Pop kept his distance and dinner was served with only a few outbursts that Ruth, in concert with Sister Mary and Pop Pop, managed to contain.

Later that night, Mikey and Skeeter both tried to process the day's events and reconcile them with the Before Time. Mikey curled up as tightly as he could by himself on the floor, eyes closed tight, paws over eyes, tail over paws. Mikey fought his shadows and ghosts alone. He knew Pop Pop wasn't the Big Man and Mammaw wasn't the lady, but they'd seemed so much like them. He knew his Mamma's words were right and that he should remember them, but it was so hard, especially when Skeeter was frightened. How could he count on Ruth to help? No person ever had before. Well, no person before Shelter Lady. She'd helped. Ruth seemed inclined to help, but she didn't always seem to know how. Why had she let Pop Pop get so close? But, after he snapped, Ruth had kept things from escalating out of control. Mikey peered out from under his tail to study Ruth sitting on the sofa with Sister Mary and Skeeter.

Curled up next to Sister Mary, who was snoring away on Ruth's lap, Skeeter tried to understand what she'd been through, too. Mikey, the Big Man, Pop Pop, the boot, but then Shelter Lady, Ruth, Sister Mary. "Sister Sunny?" Skeeter whispered.

"Sister Sunny? You ever forget your words? I mean, well, not your words, Mamma's words? Did you ever get angry or panic or bite?"

Sister Mary stirred and sighed. "Yes, child. I forgot my words sometimes when I was your age, too. I don't remember ever actually biting anyone, but I did get angry, mostly at Boyo, and I most certainly did panic."

"Sister Mary, how'd you learn to remember them, those words, that is?" Skeeter continued, working through her fears and memories.

"I just kept working, child, I just kept working. These people helped me too. You've got to learn to trust them."

Hearing Skeeter and Sister Mary Sunshine on the sofa comforted Mikey. He liked the sound of their voices. Opening one eye and uncurling just a little, Mikey looked up at the sofa. There was his sister, next to Sister Mary and Ruth. They'd left an open spot for him. Max sat in his chair to the right of the sofa. Everyone was watching the television. Getting up quietly, Mikey went up to Ruth, climbed gently into her lap and draped his paws around her shoulders, nestled his head next to hers, and sighed.

Putting her arms around him, Ruth comforted her friend. "Come on, buddy. You can do this. I know you can," she whispered. Mikey wanted to, in that moment more than ever before. He wanted to believe in Forever Home. He even was beginning to understand, really understand, what Forever Home meant. Mikey clung to Ruth as long as he could, sighing deeply as he let go of the past and the day's bad and holding on to the day's good. Finally, his hind legs and back tired, he climbed the rest of the way onto the sofa and went to sleep.

Chapter 22

The following week, Ruth decided to try visiting her parents again. After running and playing outside, and after repeating their loud and lengthy entrance, albeit with less barking than their first visit, the dogs found Mammaw and Pop Pop seated at the kitchen table. Pop Pop had an assortment of hot dogs, cheese, and nuts for everyone to enjoy. Determined to make friends with his daughters' new charges, Pop Pop knew, or thought he knew, the fastest way to their hearts. Food. Specifically, hot dogs. He'd heard about the piles of hot dogs at the initial pick up at the Shelter Lady's and witnessed Ruth manage the dogs' volatility using food. He remembered winning over the once very shy and frightened Sister Mary with peanuts and other dog treats. Boyo had definitely been a chow hound. He was sure that with enough hot dogs and other treats, he could win these young dogs' hearts.

Mikey seemed fine. Ruth had taken off his leash and was letting him wander around the kitchen, investigating odors and other interesting things. Skeeter, still nervous and growling, would stay on her leash for now.

Picking up a hot dog piece, Pop Pop leaned forward and gently held it out for Mikey. "Come on, fella. Have a piece. Come on," he encouraged. Mikey wasn't sure. The adrenaline from their entrance was still surging and the space Pop Pop was asking him to enter to get the hot dog was really tight. Hot dogs were among his favorites, but they'd also been used to lure him into traps before.

"Skeeter, what do you think?" Mikey asked.

"I dunno, Mikey. It could be a trap. I just don't trust that guy. He's big and he's tall. He talks quietly, but moves stiff. Just like the Impound Man. He had hot dogs, too. Sister Mary and Ruth like him, though. I'm just not sure," Skeeter replied.

"Come on Mikey, you can do it. Pop Pop's not going to bite you," Ruth urged, unaware of Mikey's past experience with tall, stiff men and hot dogs.

"I think you're pushing him too hard," said Mammaw watching from across the table. "Just give him time to come up to you on his own."

"Oh, Mammaw, he's fine. Come on fella, there you go," Pop Pop said as Mikey took a tentative step forward. Mikey had committed to try, but the closer he got to Pop Pop, the louder the buzzing got in his head and the harder it was to focus on the hot dog.

Hot dog, outstretched hand. Leaning man. Hot dog. "Come on fella." Hot dog, leaning man, stiff hand. Small space. Drums. Buzzing. Images flashed faster and faster. Hot dog. Stiff. Man. Leaning. Mikey snapped, trying to grab the hot dog as quickly as he could and then make a dash away. Only he'd snapped too far and too hard.

"*Ouch!*" screamed Pop Pop, grabbing his hand and leaping to his feet.

"Mikey! Watch out! He's going to get you!" screamed Skeeter, lunging at the end of her leash to try to assist her brother .

"Mikey, Skeeter, *no!*" screamed Ruth. Ruth grabbed frantically at Mikey's collar and pulled both dogs back away from her father while Sister Mary put herself between Pop Pop and the two now-panicked dogs. "Mikey! That's my dad. You don't bite him, *ever!*" hollered Ruth.

Seeing the situation likely to get worse before it got better, Sister Mary took control. Turning from Pop Pop to face her young friends, Sister Mary barked, "Mikey, Skeeter. Get hold of yourselves. Listen to me. You've forgotten your Mamma's words. Come on, remember your words. Say them with me, *now!*"

Sister Mary knew she, more than anyone in that room, needed to get Mikey and Skeeter back to reality. She needed to bring them into the present and then to help them move on. "Say them," she commanded again.

Through the cloud of their shared and remembered terror, Mikey and Skeeter looked at Sister Mary standing in front of them, her eyes focused evenly and her voice strong. "Say them."

Mikey looked up at Pop Pop, still holding his bleeding hand, smarting at the bite. He saw Ruth, her eyes wide and her face ashen. Her hands gripped his collar and Skeeter's leash. She was trembling. Mammaw was seated, looking from her husband to her daughter to the dogs, uncertain what to do or say. And Mikey looked at Skeeter, who was terrified but ready to come to his defense at the slightest provocation. No, this was not good. This was not good. At all.

Mikey dropped his head and lowered his tail. "Don't get angry, don't panic, don't bite," he whispered.

"I can't hear you," barked Sister Mary.

"Don't get angry, don't panic, don't bite," Mikey said.

"That's good. Skeeter, you repeat the words with us," Sister Mary commanded.

"Um, Don't, um, don't get, um, don't get, don't get angry," Skeeter swallowed, choking back her fears and looking at her brother and Sister Mary. "Don't get angry, don't panic, and don't bite," she said finally.

"Now, both of you, let him by so that he can put a bandage on that hand," Sister Mary instructed.

"Holy cow. Dad, are you okay?" said Ruth, snapping out of the grip of her own panic.

"I'm fine. The little twerp got the same finger he got last time. It had almost healed," Pop Pop said, trying to put on a brave face for his daughter. "Next time though, you give him the hot dogs. I'm done with that."

Ruth and Mammaw mustered smiles and a slight laugh at Pop Pop's effort to diffuse the tension. "I told you, you're pushing him too hard," quipped Mammaw. "It's better to just leave him alone. He'll come to you when he's ready."

Pop Pop looked at Mammaw. "But I can walk into a kennel of forty hounds and not a single one will bite me. I've done it for years. I'm good with dogs," he said.

Mammaw shook her head wryly, "Not this one, you're not." Pop Pop snorted and rolled his eyes.

Pop Pop knew Mammaw had a point, but still, forty dogs at one time and no problem. How could he be to blame? Looking down at the still frightened young dogs in front of him, Pop Pop flushed with anger. "You know the thing that really bothers me? We have no idea what really caused them to act this way. None. But if I ever figure out who the sucker is that did this to them, I'll kill him. I'm serious. Look at these two. How could you do this to a dog?"

Ruth and Mammaw looked at each other and then at Pop Pop. He was, by nature, a gentle man, and neither one of them had ever heard him say he wanted to kill anything, much less a person. He was right, though. The anger at the bite belonged with the Before Time, not with Mikey in the present. Not only had Mikey and Skeeter been abused, they clearly had never been socialized. Mikey was only trying to defend himself against a perceived threat. It wasn't his fault that he did not yet recognize that the perceived threat was not real.

Back on the leash and at Ruth's side, Mikey felt more secure. He knew the hand that was reaching for him, Ruth's hand never offered anything other than a treat or a scratch on the chin. That hand never brought back the drumming or buzzing of the past.

Ruth began to realize that hot dogs and treats offered by strangers would not erase Mikey and Skeeter's past. She hoped time and new, more positive, experiences might, if only she could get the dogs, and her family, safely through their transition.

Chapter 23

"C'mon, guys, time to play Ball," announced Ruth. "Skeeter, you'll have to leave those inside for later," she said, referencing the latest toy that Skeeter was chasing and throwing around the house.

Skeeter didn't yet really "get" Ball. She preferred to destroy her toys. There seemed to be an endless supply of them and the squeakers were fun to chew on once she got them out of the toy, even if Ruth did spoil her fun by taking the squeaker away. But, outside was outside and a chance to run around and play always sounded like a good idea to her. Besides, Ball seemed to make Mikey and Sister Mary happy. So Skeeter would run along with her brother and make up her own game with whatever ball she got.

Going out the front door and running around the side to the backyard meant Sister Mary and Ruth didn't have to navigate the still snow-covered steps from the back porch. It also gave the dogs an opportunity to get to know their yard better. Ruth picked up one ball and threw it. Everybody chased it, somebody grabbed it and took off, or returned it to Ruth; catcher's choice. Ruth picked up another ball, threw it, and the game continued until everyone was tired. Those rules worked for Mikey and Sister

Mary. Not so much for Skeeter. "Mikey, why don't we use the whole woods? Don't you see how big it is? This little yard stuff is for sissies," Skeeter sassed.

"Why do we need the whole woods?" Mikey replied. "Sister Mary couldn't go with us and Ruth is way too slow."

"Who needs them? This woods is bigger than Mammaw and Pop Pop's! Come on, catch me if you can!" Skeeter said, grabbing a ball and running with it into the woods.

As Skeeter took off, ball still in her mouth, she could barely hear Ruth's urgent voice calling her back to the yard. Instead, the sounds and smells of the woods opened up to her. The snow, the trees, the stream, all welcomed Skeeter like happy new friends. And then, she saw them. Standing right in front of her, tails flagged, heads alert, much taller than she, but clearly nervous to see her.

"Hi!" she wagged. "I'm Skeeter! Wanna run? I'm running." The deer lowered and raised their heads looking at her cautiously. "I said, hi! I'm Skeeter! What are your names? Wanna play with me?" she barked brightly. The deer paused for a moment, uncertain of what they should do. Most dogs didn't get this close this fast, but here was one right in front of them. Clearly this was a faster dog than the old ones who previously occupied the house. Playing it safe, they snorted, stomped and took off, scattering in all directions and into the moonlit night.

Skeeter looked around. "Where did everyone go? Where's Mikey? Oh well, guess I'll go tell him about it," she thought. She ran back to the yard where she found Sister Mary scowling for who knows what reason and Ruth hanging on to Mikey by a leash, about to go looking for her. "There you are, naughty girl! I was afraid we were going to lose you," said Ruth as she snapped a leash on Skeeter's collar.

"Wow! Mikey! It's amazing out there. You've gotta come next time. There are huge trees and a stream and a hill and these giant things with big long legs and tails. Some of them even have big long horns! I said hi but they just ran off. It was awesome!" Skeeter exclaimed.

"Yeah, I know. I've chased those things. They're called deer," said Mikey. I chased them a couple of times before you got here, but Ruth always got mad and interrupted me."

"But do you see what you've done, Skeeter?" admonished Sister Mary. "Ball is over. Mikey's on a leash, now you're on a leash, and now we're going inside. Nice work, Skeeter. Way to ruin it for everyone." Sister Mary was not happy.

"Well, maybe you and Mikey should have come with me, Sister Mary. Then we all could have had a good time," Skeeter said. She wasn't giving up on her new woods adventure.

"Skeeter, do you see me running around? There's no way that I can get these legs over those logs and through that snow. No way. I used to do that. Sure. Back in my day, I nearly caught a deer. Boyo and I used to chase them when we took walks in the park with Ruth. But now? No, dear, not anymore."

Skeeter shook her head as she walked in the house. She definitely wanted to know more about those deer. Stupid ball game. Who cared about that anyway?

Chapter 24

The next day, Ruth and Max announced that "school" was about to begin. "What's school, Sister Mary?" asked Mikey and Skeeter.

Sister Mary smiled. She remembered school fondly. "School," she said, "is where you and your people go to learn how to speak one another's language. It is where Boyo and I went with Ruth to learn the foundation of our communication skills. They learn some of our language and we learn theirs. We play games and get to talk to other dogs. Some of the dogs are very advanced students and know many, many words. Others, like you, just know what they've picked up around the house."

"Are you coming with us, Sister Mary?" Mikey asked, hoping that she would be with them in class, especially if lots of people were going to be there.

"No, you kids go along with Max and Ruth. I'll be here when you come back and you can tell me a story for a change," Sister Mary replied. "I could actually use a little peace and quiet," she continued as she tottered over to her spot in front of the sofa.

Nervous, but excited, Skeeter, Mikey, Ruth, and Max headed off to school. "Make sure you stay with me, Mikey," Skeeter said nervously.

"I will," he said as they headed into the school building.

Once inside, the two dogs were amazed at what they saw. The building was long and wide and filled with dogs and people, all doing something different. Some were walking in circles, others were jumping over bars, and still others were parading around in a group. Mikey could see puppies at the far end of the room, working with their people on something, but he could not tell what. A small group of people huddled around a table with their heads buried in books, which he later learned were records of admission and accomplishment for those who were present.

"Oh, are these the new dogs?" asked a strange man, as he started to walk toward Max and Ruth. Ruth had spoken with the school leadership the week before and told them about Mikey and Skeeter's troubled past. The man was one of the people with whom Ruth had spoken. He had offered Ruth much needed advice and resources for dealing with their issues and was eager to meet the two dogs.

"Mikey, here comes a strange person, what do we do?" Skeeter asked nervously.

"I don't know, Skeet. Let's bark. Tell him to keep his distance," Mikey responded.

"That's all right, that's all right," said the stranger kindly. "Most dogs do that when they start out. Remember your first two, Ruth? They were real barkers at first. Just stay positive with them and be alert, they'll come around," he continued.

Ruth did remember. Boyo's first tour through the school had started out with difficulty. Although he loved people, he was unaccustomed to strange dogs and found the class setting overwhelming. Sister Mary had the opposite problem: the dogs were fine, but the people terrified her. Either way, the solution had been the same for both dogs. Give them room and work them into the more pressured environment at their own pace, stay positive, keep them engaged.

"I'll just take her away a bit and see if she won't settle down. Come with me, Skeet. Let's give you a little bit of room," said Ruth as she pulled the now-growling Skeeter to a quieter part of the building. "There, now you can look around and see what's what. Is that better?" she asked, looking down at her nervous friend.

Taking his cue from Ruth, Max looked for a way to settle Mikey's nerves. "Come on, Mikey," said Max. "Let's you and me go exploring a bit." They began walking in the opposite direction.

"Mikey, where are you going?" called Skeeter from across the room.

"Don't know, Skeet, just stay with Ruth," said Mikey.

Kneeling down next to her, Ruth scratched Skeeter's chin. "There, you see, girl? It's just people and their dogs. Everybody here is here to help you and Mikey. Nobody's going to hurt you," soothed Ruth.

Skeeter looked up at Ruth's face and could see the kindness in her eyes. Feeling reassured, Skeeter put her head in Ruth's lap and took in the view. Not so bad, she thought. Maybe Sister Mary had been right about this place after all.

Soon, class started and Mikey and Skeeter found themselves trotting around in a circle with five other dogs; some big, some small, all nervous and anxious to make a good first impression. "Okay, everybody, let's see where everyone is and what they know. Forward!" commanded the man in the middle of the ring. And everyone went forward. "Circle-right!" commanded the man in the middle of the circle. And everyone marched around in a circle to the right. "Circle-left!" the man commanded. And everyone went around the other way. "Halt!" and everyone stopped.

Skeeter liked being in motion. The brisk pace of the class helped to settle her nerves. Looking over her shoulder at her brother, Skeeter exclaimed, "Hey, Mikey! This is pretty fun! I keep doing stuff and Ruth keeps giving me treats! Are you having fun, Mikey? I'm having fun!"

Mikey and Max were not having fun. "Skeeter, would you guys slow down and get back here? I keep trying to catch up with you and Max won't walk any faster. I don't know what the problem with the man is but he does not understand that I am supposed to be near you!" whined Mikey.

"Tell your dogs to stay and step out to the end of the leash," said the man in the center of the ring.

"See, look, Skeeter. I just tried to walk over to you and Max pulled me back here. What is wrong with this guy? And what's wrong with Ruth? Why is she totally ignoring me? Hey Ruth! Ruth! Will you talk to Max? I'm pretty sure this guy is thick-headed tonight," said Mikey, clearly exasperated.

"Return to your dog," said the man in the center of the ring.

"Hey, Mikey. I just got another treat!"

"Good for you, Skeeter, good for you. You get a treat and I get a jerk on the collar. Whoopie," huffed Mikey.

"Down your dog," said the man in the middle of the ring.

"Mikey, what's down? I don't know down," Skeeter asked.

Mikey wasn't going to help his sister. He was thoroughly annoyed. Shelter Lady taught him that word, but Max's accent was all wrong and he didn't do the hand signal right. Besides, Max was just being a jerk, so why should he lie down for him?

"Forward!" barked the man in the middle of the ring.

Heading back to the car after the class ended, Skeeter and Ruth were happy. Ruth was oblivious to Max's and Mikey's struggles in the class. She and Skeeter had a good time together. Skeeter had kept her cool with the other dogs and the people roaming around. She'd gotten treats and thought the other dogs looked nice. Obviously, Skeeter and Ruth had some work to do, but Ruth was confident that they were off to a good start.

Mikey and Max were another story. Max was tired. Mikey'd pulled and fretted for the whole hour. He'd refused every command and, from Max's perspective, was acting like a jerk. Mikey thought the same about Max. How could a person be as thick as all that?

With both dog and person lost in their own thoughts, Mikey and Max got to the car well ahead of Ruth and Skeeter. When Mikey jumped in the car and looked around, he suddenly realized that Skeeter was nowhere to be seen. "Stupid! Stupid! Stupid! You idiot, you're about to leave them both behind!" He thought as he tried to jump back out of the car.

"Mikey, stay in the car, stay in the car," coaxed Max, pushing Mikey back into the car.

"*No*! I'm not letting you leave them," Mikey declared, shoving himself back out.

"Mikey, get back!"

"No! You get out of my way!" said Mikey. Max pushed him again. That was one push too many. Mikey snapped.

"*Ouch!* Dammit, dog!" exclaimed Max, holding his hand. Seeing the rage welling up in Max's eyes, his arms and jaw tightening, Mikey immediately knew he'd made a mistake. He leaped out of the car to potential safety.

By now, Ruth and Skeeter had caught up with them and Ruth snagged Mikey's leash as he darted away. "Jeez, Max, what the heck's going on here?" she asked.

"That son of a bitch bit me!"

"Well, from what I saw, I would have bitten you too," said Ruth. "Why the heck were you arguing with him like that?"

That response surprised everyone, especially Max. People just didn't side with dogs in these matters. There was a rule somewhere, right? But Ruth pressed on. "I'm serious Max. You can't manhandle most dogs, but especially not these two, given what they've been through. Besides, how horrible would it have been to let him get back out of the car? He'd have gone back in once Skeeter got here."

Max took a deep breath. It had been a long night and he was tired. "Just get them in the car and let's go home," he said.

Back at the house, Sister Mary eagerly greeted her friends at the door. "How'd it go?" she asked.

"It was fun, Sister Mary, at least until Mikey and Max got in an argument. You were right. There were dogs, and treats, and Ruth and I had a real good time. What does down mean? I knew the other words mostly, but down? What's that all about?" Skeeter wagged.

"Not impressed," Mikey said grumpily as he sulked in the door and threw himself down on the floor in a corner.

Sister Mary looked at her four friends as they entered the house, a jumble of hope, confusion, and sorrow. She knew Max had never gone to school before, and she had had communication issues with him herself. She also knew he was still having a hard time getting over the loss of Boyo. She'd caught him looking at the box by the tree, lingering by the picture of Boyo and herself hanging on the hallway wall, and looking wistfully at Mikey many times over the past couple of weeks. But Mikey wasn't Boyo and he never would be. He and Max were going to have to make their way on their own terms.

Max taped up his hand and everyone moved downstairs for Sofa Time. Sister Mary, carried to her spot on the sofa, settled in comfortably. Skeeter found a spot next to Sister Mary and Mikey curled up on the floor, front paws covering his eyes, tail wrapped tightly around his body, in his processing mode. Ruth and Max were quiet, also processing. Eventually, Mikey got up, shook his head, walked quietly over to Max, and put his head on Max's lap.

Recognizing the apology for what it was, Max looked down at Mikey and gave him a scratch on the chin. "We'll get it next time, buddy. No worries," Max said. His voice sounded less than certain, but Mikey appreciated the effort. Looking at Ruth and the empty spot on the sofa next to her, he decided to take comfort there.

"Sister Mary, you awake?" Mikey said softly.

"Yeah, kid. What is it?"

"I just don't get it. One minute things are fine, the next they're not. One minute I'm happy and think I've got this whole Forever Home thing, and the next minute something reminds me of Before Time and I'm angry all over again. What if I never get it? What if I never get this whole home thing? What will happen? To me? To Skeeter? To you? Everybody? What if I don't get rid of these ghosts and shadows? I don't want live like this, Sister Mary, I really don't."

Mikey's eyes were red and brimming with tears. His sides heaved as he tried to control his sorrow and fears.

Before Sister Mary could answer, Ruth looked down and saw her friend working through his pain and stroked his chest softly. "Hey, Buddy, come on now. We all make mistakes. Just keep trying. You'll get this. I know. Sometimes, it's not all your fault," she said. "Just don't give up."

Sister Mary looked up at Ruth and Mikey. "Hear that, kid? There's your answer. Couldn't have said it better myself."

"Mikey? Mikey?" called Skeeter from her spot on the sofa.

"Yeah, Skeet?"

"Mikey, we'll get this together. I'll help ya, Mikey. Just like you help me. Like Sister Mary and Miss Ruth just said, we just have to keep trying." Mikey let out a long, deep sigh. He'd keep trying, but boy was it hard.

Chapter 25

"Miss Ruth? Miss Ruth?" Skeeter nudged Ruth, who was sound asleep. "Miss Ruth? I gotta go outside. Miss Ruth?" Skeeter again nudged the prone form on the bed.

Stirring, Ruth looked at the clock next to her. "Geez, Skeet, it's three o'clock in the morning. Are you sure?" she said.

"Miss Ruth, I gotta go now," Skeeter replied, bouncing from one foot to the other. Grabbing a housecoat and donning her slippers, Ruth picked up Sister Mary and headed for the stairs. Snapping leashes on her young friends, Ruth took the dogs outside. It was cold and quiet. The moon lit the snow and trees around them. After the dogs were finished, Ruth headed back to the front door, where she unsnapped both leashes before entering.

Mistake. Before she went into the house, Skeeter took one last look around at the scene before her. It was beautiful. The trees, the snow, the stars, the deer. "Wait, what?" she thought. "Deer? How did we miss them?"

Skeeter blinked once to be sure and then took off in a flash. Mikey'd seen the deer as well, but it was too early in the morning for him to commit to a chase on his own. But seeing his sister take off after them across the snow was too much to ignore. A split second after Skeeter sped off, so did Mikey, leaving the still-groggy Ruth at the door with Sister Mary, leashes in hand, jaw agape.

"Sister Mary, you stay here, inside," said Ruth as she hastily put Sister Mary in the house and closed the door.

Ruth tried calling, "Mikey, Skeeter, *come!*" Nothing. The dogs were gone. Nowhere to be seen. Trying to remain calm, Ruth started off in the last direction she'd seen the dogs heading. "Mikey, Skeeter, *come!*" she called again, straining desperately to hear some sound in the silent woods. Nothing. How could that be? The moon was so bright that Ruth could clearly see through the woods before her. She knew the snow would muffle the sound of the dogs, but she should be able to see or hear something. Unless. No, she would not let herself think the unthinkable, that they were too far away from her to see or hear. Lost. Gone.

Walking toward the last place she'd seen them, Ruth tried again. "Mikey, Skeeter, *come!*" Still nothing. Ruth pressed on forward, anxiously.

Being at large was intoxicating. As Mikey had predicted the week before, actually catching the deer was unlikely. They were just too fast. But giving chase was amazing. Running, jumping, smelling. The two dogs flew through the woods at top speed, each trying to outrun the other. "Mikey, Mikey! See! This is so cool! This is what I was talking about the other day when we were playing Ball. Hey, let's look over here!" Skeeter enthused.

"I'm checking something out over here, Skeet. Come this way! This way's awesome," Mikey said, nose to the ground and tail wagging.

"No, come this way. This way's awesomer," Skeeter said, running in an angle away from Mikey toward an interesting scent she'd found.

"Oh, hey, here it is. Look what I found, Mikey."

Having located the source of the scent she'd been following, an old shoe that someone had thrown in a trash pile, Skeeter looked around for her brother. She was alone. "Mikey?" Skeeter called. "Mikey?" she called again.

Nothing. Nervously, Skeeter circled the yard she'd just entered. No sign of Mikey. She'd have to make her circle bigger. "Mikey? Mikey?" Skeeter called again.

She stopped, listened, sniffed. "Don't get angry, don't panic, don't bite," she reminded herself. "Mikey?" she called again, heading toward the street in front of her.

"Skeeter! There you are!" exclaimed a very relieved Ruth. "You naughty girl! Where is your brother?"

Hearing her name, Skeeter looked around and recognized Ruth standing in the road in front of her. Relieved, Skeeter ran to her and allowed herself to be leashed. "C'mon Skeet, you can help me find Mikey," Ruth said. "Let's head back to where you came from and see if we can't pick up his trail from there."

Ruth was right. Once back in the woods and having the reassurance of a companion, Skeeter quickly picked up Mikey's scent and she and Ruth were able to catch up with him while he was still puzzling through a scent line of his own.

"What is this? What is this? Where does it go?" Mikey was muttering to himself, so thoroughly engrossed in his thoughts that he didn't hear Skeeter or Ruth approaching. "What is this? Where does it go?" he puzzled studiously.

"Hey, Mikey! This way!" said both Ruth and Skeeter.

Mikey continued working his line. Seeing that they were being ignored, Ruth tried again, "This way, Mikey!"

Ruth, still in her housecoat and slippers, struggled and puffed as she tried to keep up with Mikey through the snow. Mikey paused. He'd heard something. Looking around, he saw Ruth and Skeeter approaching.

"Oh, hey. It's you. Hey, Ruth. Check out this smell, Skeet. Tell me what you think." He wandered away from Ruth and Skeeter.

"Come on, Mikey," said Ruth, starting to wonder if she would be able to catch him, he was so focused.

"What?" said Mikey.

"She wants us to go back home with her, Mikey," said Skeeter. "I think we've worn her out. You were right, she is *slow*!"

Pausing to look at Ruth, huffing and puffing in front of him, hair tangled, cheeks red, feet soaked, Mikey laughed and shook his head. "Told you so. Let's give her a break. I'll puzzle that line out another time. When did you become Ruth's translator anyway?" A very relieved Ruth clasped the leash on him.

Once back home and inside the house, with the door closed before Ruth removed the leashes this time, Sister Mary looked at her two friends and winked. "Have fun? Feel better?" she asked.

"Oh, yeah!" both young dogs exclaimed. "Oh yeah."

Back upstairs and in bed, Sister Mary couldn't help but ask. "Did you make her run?" she said, pointing her nose toward Ruth.

"Yeah, but she couldn't keep up. She's really slow," whispered Skeeter.

"Boyo and I used to make her run, too. She'd get all out of breath," said Sister Mary.

"And her cheeks got all red!" exclaimed Mikey.

"Oh yes. Those cheeks. Did her eyes bulge too? One time we took off on her, ran clear around the neighborhood and back home three times before she caught up with us. By the time she did, her face was all red, her eyes were all bulgy. We were sitting on the front step waiting for her for ten whole minutes. We got tired of running laps around her!"

All three dogs were now rolling on their backs laughing at the image of Ruth chasing them in the dark, housecoat flying, cheeks puffing.

"What happened when she caught you guys, Sister Mary?" asked Mikey.

"Nothing, really. Poor dear was probably too exhausted to do anything, she just put our leashes on and took us inside with her. It was a while before we were off leash again though, I can tell you that much."

"What about him? You and Boyo ever run off on him?" asked Mikey, looking at Max.

"Yes, but it's not a good idea to run off on him. Max gets too upset and sometimes gets mad. He forgets his words sometimes just like you two do," said Sister Mary.

"Hey, guys. Quit rolling around and let me get back to sleep, okay? Haven't you had enough fun for one night?"

Ruth, who was pinned between two laughing dogs on the bed, could hear the third laughing dog on the floor next to her and leaned over to give Sister Mary a scratch.

Shifting to make more room for Ruth, Skeeter had one more comment for the night. "You know, Sister Mary, it was kinda nice when she did find me, though. I was a little scared when I lost Mikey and when she got there, I wasn't scared anymore. I liked that."

Sister Mary smiled. Her young friend was starting to get it. "That's right, child. It's like that with me, too."

Mikey looked up. "Was it like that with Boyo, too?" he asked.

"Absolutely," said Sister Mary.

Snuggling closer to Ruth, both young dogs – finally – went back to sleep.

Chapter 26

Max, Ruth, Mikey, Skeeter, and Sister Mary developed a new evening routine. Max usually got home before Ruth, so he let Mikey and Skeeter out of their crates when he got home. They'd exercise and then wait for Ruth. Right before Ruth came home, she'd call Max and he would put Mikey and Skeeter back in their crates. Ruth's arrival caused too much excitement for Mikey and Skeeter to handle without toppling Ruth and knocking Sister Mary over in the process. So upon her arrival, Sister Mary would meet Ruth at the door, leading a rousing chorus of "Hello! Hello! Treats! Treats!"

After duly acknowledging her old friend and upon her new friends quieting sufficiently, Ruth doled out treats, let Mikey out first, and then Skeeter. Then everyone scrambled into the kitchen.

Sister Mary led the next song of the night: "*Ball! Ball! Play Ball!*" Ruth eventually capitulated and the game ensued, followed by a cool-down, and dinner.

After the first day of school, though, Ruth added another element to their nightly routine: Lesson Time. Ruth knew that the best way to make certain her friends recovered from their past and had a bright future was for them to learn communication skills. Ball, walks, and Sofa Time are all great, she thought, but her friends really did need a basic education. Besides, who knew? Maybe one day they would actually be able to compete.

Lessons usually started with Skeeter and Ruth working together, and Mikey watching from his crate. When Skeeter's turn was over, she watched from her crate while Mikey worked. Sister

Mary accompanied whichever dog was working and offered helpful pointers. When Lesson Time ended, Sofa Time began.

One such night, after completing the exercises of the evening – heel, sit, stay, heel, down, stay, heel – Skeeter and Mikey happily paraded downstairs with Ruth and Sister Mary for Sofa Time. Hearing them come down, Max, who had been working in his office, joined them in the family room. Not very tired or ready to join her friends on the sofa, Skeeter eyed a large rope toy on the floor. Bouncing over to it, she pounced on it and tossed and flipped it in the air. "Hey, look, Mikey! I found a new toy! Check this out, I can flip it in the air, catch it and then run around the floor! Whoo-hoo!" exclaimed Skeeter, thoroughly enjoying herself while the others watched from the sofa.

Seeing Skeeter playing with the toy that he and Boyo had so enjoyed, Max decided to join Skeeter in her game. Perhaps he could rekindle some of the joy he had felt when playing rope with Boyo. Picking up the rope from the loose end, Max gave it a tug. "Come on, Skeet, let's play!" he said.

Skeeter misunderstood Max's friendly gesture and took offense instead. "Hey! You can't have my rope! You let that go!" she barked through her clenched teeth, pulling hard.

Boyo had also often barked and growled when they played, and, thinking Skeeter understood the game, Max pulled harder.

"*No! It's mine!*" Skeeter yelled, fighting back.

"Max, look out! She doesn't understand you are playing. Max, Max!" barked Sister Mary from her spot on the floor.

Seeing the struggle unfold from his post on the sofa, Mikey felt the buzzing starting in full force. He knew nothing about playing tug with people. He was only just starting to figure out how to play it with Skeeter. He had no idea why Max was so animated.

"Mikey, help me! He's taking my toy!" shouted Skeeter. Mikey was undecided, trying to remember his words above the buzzing.

"Mikey, help me!" Mikey moved to the stair behind Max for a better view. It looked to him like Max was unfairly trying to take the toy from Skeeter.

"Hey, stop trying to take her toy!" Mikey chimed in.

"Max, look out, you don't know what you are getting into, Max!" barked Sister Mary.

"Max, look out, watch out!" Ruth hollered from the sofa.

Still unaware that Skeeter and Mikey did not know this was a game, Max continued to pull. Sister Mary had often barked in happy accompaniment to his and Boyo's games.

"*Ouch!*"

Skeeter had snapped and grabbed Max's hand. "I told you to let go!" she exclaimed.

"God dammit, dog!" Max roared, grabbing a shoe and holding it high above his head.

Seeing his sister in trouble, Mikey bolted from the stair. He ran at Max and grabbed him by the heel. "Hey! Nobody strikes my sister!"

Whirling around in pain, Max turned his fury to Mikey.

Max lunged toward Mikey, shoe in hand. Skeeter grabbed for Max's leg but mostly missed.

"*Hey! Everybody stand down!*" shouted Ruth leaping from sofa toward the fray.

The entire incident had happened before her eyes in a matter of seconds. A quiet, comfortable night turned into a nightmare. "*Stop it, everybody! Stop it!*" she pleaded.

Hearing her voice and not wanting further trouble, Skeeter and Mikey retreated. Skeeter ran to Ruth and cowered in front of her. Mikey ran behind the sofa to a corner. Max, still enraged, hurt, and confused, pursued Mikey, shoe still in hand. "Don't do it, Max. Let him go. He has retreated. You can see he is frightened," Ruth begged.

"He ought to be frightened. Do you see what he did?" said the enraged Max, still waving the shoe over his head. "My pants are ripped, my hand is bleeding, my leg is swiss cheese! These dogs are out of control!"

"Max, don't. Just stop. You touch either of these dogs right now and you will ruin any chance we have at bringing them back into the world. Please!"

Max's chest was heaving, his face red, eyes blazing with fire. He looked at Mikey, now curled tightly into a ball on the floor in the corner of the family room, watching him. Skeeter had wedged herself between Sister Mary and Ruth, who had her hand firmly on Skeeter's collar. Skeeter and Ruth were both trembling, holding their breath at what would happen next. Sister Mary held his gaze steadily, willing Max to regain control. Max took a deep breath. Ruth's words made sense. "I just wanted to play with the dog," he said quietly, dropping his arm back to his side, trying to compose himself.

"I know. I just don't think they know, or know how," said Ruth. "They just don't know anything. Are you okay?" she asked.

"Yeah, I'm fine. My pants are shredded, and it hurts like bloody hell, but I'm all right," Max replied. "Let me bandage up these wounds."

When he returned moments later, Skeeter and Mikey were exactly where he'd left them. No one had dared move. Everyone needed to calm down.

"Sister Mary?" Mikey called from his corner. "Sister Mary?"

"Yes, kid."

"I thought he was going to hurt her. I mean, I saw him lunge. I saw his eyes. I saw everything. Wasn't he going to hurt her?"

"I doubt it, kid. Especially at first. He was just trying to play with her at first."

"But, Sister Mary, what kind of game is that anyway? It makes no sense. It's our toy, right? So why'd he try to take it away?" Mikey was genuinely confused.

"You have a lot to learn, kid. Rope is a game he and Boyo played endlessly. Boyo loved it. Max wasn't trying to take the rope away. Skeeter was supposed to pull it with him. More to the point, what you guys did was wrong. These people are your best chance at a normal life, or life at all for that matter. You have to remember your words or they will give up on you."

Mikey pulled his tail tightly around his body and covered his eyes, closing them tightly, trying to shut out the ghosts in his head, the drumming in his ears. "Closing your eyes is not going to help the problem, Mikey. Go apologize," admonished Sister Mary.

Mikey looked up, startled at the thought of approaching Max just then. "I can't," he gasped. "I mean, I thought he was going to kill me. I thought he was going to kill Skeet. Shouldn't he be apologizing to me?"

Sister Mary scowled. "Kid, you broke the number one rule; you bit him. Frankly you broke all three rules. It doesn't matter why or whose fault it was, you must apologize."

"Really?"

"Really. Just remember your words this time and keep your head."

Mikey knew Sister Mary was right. Standing up quietly, Mikey nervously approached Max in his chair. "Go away, Mikey. Leave me alone. I'm not talking to you right now," said Max.

"He's trying to apologize," said Ruth, recognizing the act for what it was.

"I don't care. Go away, Mikey." Max pushed Mikey away, but it was a gentle push. "Leave me alone."

Mikey hung his head, uncertain what to do next. "What do I do now, Sister Mary? He wouldn't take my apology. I don't want them to send me away. I like it here. I like these people. I just get upset sometimes. Please. Help me."

"You have to try harder, Mikey. Keep trying. Leave him alone for now, though. I think he got your message," replied Sister Mary softly.

Seeing an open spot on the sofa next to Ruth, Mikey walked over to her. "Come on, fella," said Ruth quietly, patting the sofa next to her. "You can join us up here."

Grateful for the invitation, Mikey climbed up and curled up next to Ruth. "Don't give up, Mikey. You can do this. Just keep trying," said Ruth, stroking Mikey's head gently, unknowingly echoing her old friend's advice.

"Sister Sunny? Should I try? Should I apologize to Max?" asked Skeeter bashfully.

"No, Child. Let's leave the man alone for a while. From what I've just seen, you'd be better off staying put."

The rest of the evening passed uneventfully. The following day was a school day, however. At the allotted time, Ruth and Max packed Mikey and Skeeter into the car and headed to class. "Have a good time!" cheered Sister Mary as they headed out the front door.

"How's everybody doing?" asked the Instructor. "Before we begin, any problems? Any issues?" Ruth held her tongue on that one. The last thing she wanted was to announce that, yes, they were having issues with Mr. and Mrs. Snappy, with their backgrounds. She'd spoken at length with the Instructor previously about the dogs' history, so he knew there were issues they were working on, but she really wanted both dogs to have a fresh start.

Hearing no reports, the Instructor began the class. "OK, everybody in a circle and Forward!" commanded the Instructor.

"Skeeter, heel!" commanded Ruth brightly, and the pair bounced off happily.

"Mikey, heel," said Max sternly, and they stomped off. "Stop pulling, Mikey," said Max, giving Mikey a tug on the collar.

"Stop pulling, Max. I'm trying to catch up with Skeeter. Can't you see they're getting away?"

"About Turn," commanded the Instructor.

"Skeeter, heel!" said Ruth and around they went.

"Mikey, heel," commanded Max, and around they went.

"Hey, Mikey, this is really fun!" said Skeeter from behind. "We can play this game all night!"

"Fun? You call this fun? Where are you? I can't see you!"

"Mikey, stop trying to turn around. Just keep going," said an exasperated Max.

And so the night went. Driving home, Ruth, again oblivious to Max and Mikey's problems, was eager to talk about the day's successes. Max cut her short. "I think Mikey and I need to pull out of class," he said. "All we are doing is tugging and pulling one another. He's a complete pain. I can't hear half the time, and I don't have time to work with him at home right now."

Ruth knew better than to argue. Max had been through a lot with Mikey and pushing him to do something that didn't make him happy was not going to improve anything. Still, she did believe that the professional guidance of the class would be good for both Max and Mikey. "That's fine, but I really think you guys should go through this training together. It will help you both," she said.

"Oh, I know. I fully intend to go through the class with him, just not now. Can't we pick up the next session?"

"Sure, and I can work with him in the meantime," said Ruth, relieved.

Back at the house, Sister Mary greeted her friends in her usual happy way. "Hello! Hello! How'd it go this time guys?" she asked.

"It was great, Sister Mary," said Skeeter. "We did turns, and stops and downs. Well I'm still not really sure what down is, but we did stays and more turns, and I got treats!"

Sister Mary was pleased with Skeeter's report. She seemed to have dispelled the problems of the night before. "And you, Mikey? No biting this time, I hope? How'd you do?"

Mikey sulked. "No. I didn't bite anybody, but geez, that guy is dense. Pulled on me the whole time. Never let me catch up with Skeeter and Ruth. I mean, what's the point of going somewhere together if you don't get to stay together? He really doesn't get it." Sister Mary chuckled. At least they'd gotten through the night without an incident.

Chapter 27

As winter loosened its grip, spring began to assert itself with a thaw. Snow began melting and Ruth and the dogs were able to play longer games of Ball and began taking walks in the woods. Ball was always fraught with the risk of running off, but Ruth played the game in the evening hours, after most of the neighborhood had gone in for the night, which minimized the possibility of neighbor contact in the event of an unscheduled excursion. She knew that exercise was an important tool in helping her friends manage their issues.

Ruth had one rule for dealing with a run-off. It ended the game of Ball for everyone. Usually, it was Skeeter who instigated the run-off. If Ruth could catch Mikey before he decided to give chase, Skeeter would quickly tire of being alone and come back to see where he was. But even if she did, Ruth's rule still stood. Leashes on. Game over. Back inside.

"Why do you keep doing that, child?" asked an exasperated Sister Mary one evening.

"I know, seriously, Skeet. You've ruined it for everybody," said an equally exasperated Mikey.

"I dunno. I just like to run. That's all. Stupid yard's not big enough for me. Besides, I think I'm making friends with the deer," huffed Skeeter.

"No, you're not. They're just messing with you," snapped Mikey in retort.

"Am too. The one with the horns lowered his head and motioned toward me tonight."

Sister Mary piped in, "Gracious, child, but you have a lot to learn. The 'one with the horns,' as you call him, is a buck. They do that when they're threatened and he's warning you to stay away or he'll use those horns on you."

Skeeter didn't want to give up her position, "Well, I think he did it very nicely, and I think he likes me," she sulked.

"Either way, Skeet, look where it got us. On a leash and going back inside. Thanks a lot," huffed Mikey.

Not wanting her friends to quarrel, Sister Mary thought a story was in order to entertain them on their walk home. "Did I ever tell you about the time Boyo and I tried to make friends with a skunk?"

"A skunk? What's a skunk?" asked Skeeter.

"Yeah, I've never heard of a skunk," added Mikey.

"Well, I didn't know either at first, but it is a very strange creature. It's furry and black with white stripes. It moves kind of slowly, and is pretty fun except for one thing." Sister Mary paused, carefully stepping over the branch in front of her.

"What's the one thing?" Mikey asked.

"The tail. It has a blaster tail."

"A what?" asked Skeeter.

"A blaster tail."

Sister Mary paused for effect and to catch her breath. "Boyo and I were out one night and we came across this skunk. We didn't know what it was at the time, but it looked friendly enough, so we thought we'd introduce ourselves and then take it to Max and show him. We figured he might let us keep it.

At first, the skunk cooperated. It gave us a play bow. We bowed back. It bowed again and smacked its feet on the ground. We bowed back and tapped our feet, too. Then, Boyo and I got behind it and pushed it along toward Max, and it went along, wagging its tail. We wagged ours. Then, the darndest thing happened." Sister Mary paused again as she lumbered over a log.

"What happened, Sister Mary, what happened?" asked Skeeter, caught up in Sister Mary's tale.

"Well, we were all going along at a pretty decent clip, but when it saw Max, that thing turned his tail and fired! One blast at Boyo, right in the face, another at me, and another in Max's direction. Missed my face, but I still got this godawful smell all over me. Boyo's eyes were stinging, Max was hollering, 'Leave it, leave it, that's a skunk!' And that thing just kept spraying until he was out of sight."

"What'd you do?" asked Mikey.

"Well, we went inside, and oh, my, did we smell. Everybody's eyes were watering, it was so bad. At first, Ruth tried to wash me off in the shower with tomato juice. No clue where she got that idea, but it didn't work. Then, she went to the store and got peroxide, baking soda and dog shampoo. Back in the shower we went. The stench came off that time, but it lingered in the air for hours."

"Did you ever see a Blaster Tail again?" asked Skeeter.

Sister Mary laughed and tripped over a log. Picking herself up, she smiled sheepishly. "Yes we did, two nights later. It was another skunk. Different stripes. Boyo thought that the first one was a mutant, so we tested his theory." Sister Mary paused to catch her breath as they turned for home up the hill. "Bad theory. Same Blaster Tail. At least this time, we avoided the tomato juice!"

"Did it at least taste good?" asked Mikey.

"The skunk or tomato juice?" asked Sister Mary laughing.

"Well, both I guess," said Mikey.

"Well, the skunk, we left alone. After that blast, who could stand to eat it? And the tomato juice? Not really. Tomatoes are only good on pizza and spaghetti, and sometimes with chicken."

They continued along, Sister Mary lost in her memories and Skeeter and Mikey contemplating this new creature with the Blaster Tail. The occasional unauthorized excursion notwithstanding, Sister Mary was in her glory, chasing her balls during their game and pointing out familiar smells and places to her friends on their walks. "See here, this is where we always stop and get treats," she'd say.

She would stop and look up expectantly at Ruth, who did not disappoint, dispensing a treat to everyone at the prescribed location. "Ooh, guys, check this out, here is where a hawk had a fight," she'd say, poking her nose at a pile of feathers on the ground. "Oh, and here, hmm, wait, no, here is a deer leg!" she'd exclaim when she found a large bone on the ground.

"Where?" "Where?" asked Skeeter and Mikey.

"Right here, under your noses," said Sister Mary, pawing at the leg to judge its heft.

"Nah, nah, nah, guys. Leave that," said Ruth, belatedly realizing where Sister Mary had led her, and pulling everyone away.

Sister Mary huffed. "Spoil sport. But watch, guys, I bet she forgets tomorrow."

"Sister Mary, where'd you learn all this stuff?" asked Skeeter in wonder.

"Yeah, seriously, you always seem to know stuff," said Mikey.

"Live to be my age and you'll learn a thing or two yourself," said Sister Mary, doing her best to keep up with her younger friends.

Chapter 28

"Everybody ready? Okay, here we go. Forward!" said the Instructor. Skeeter and Ruth were in the last week of their basic obedience class. It was graduation test night, and both of them were happy. Skeeter loved going to class, loved everything about it. She loved the time alone with Ruth especially. She'd never had alone time with a human before. She loved the rhythm of the class. The warm-up exercises, followed by harder exercises, and the camaraderie of the other dogs.

"Left about turn," commanded the Instructor.

"Skeeter, heel!" said Ruth, and around they went.

"Down your dogs!" said the Instructor.

"Skeeter. Down!" and down she went. Ruth beamed.

"Leave your dog," commanded the Instructor.

"Stay!" said Ruth as she confidently walked away from her friend. The Instructor walked around the room, weaving through the dogs and their handlers.

Skeeter looked up at her from the floor and smiled; she wasn't going to budge. "Good stay, Skeet. Good stay!" said Ruth, smiling back at her.

"Return to your dog and exercise finish," commanded the Instructor.

"Good girl!" said Ruth, giving Skeeter a treat and a big hug. Skeeter loved that part, too. Treats and hugs, treats and hugs.

"Stand your dog."

"Skeeter, stand," said Ruth. Skeeter was still working on this one, but she stood, mostly.

"Good girl!" said Ruth. The Instructor walked closer. Ruth could see Skeeter getting nervous. They'd made lots of progress in the last several weeks. No more barking or low growling when the Instructor came by. The Instructor and Ruth had worked together to increase Skeeter's comfort level. Looking at the Instructor, Ruth reminded, "Watch her."

"Just take her collar and brace under her belly. Just like that. Good," said the Instructor. "I'll keep it to a minimum."

The Instructor walked up, and touched Skeeter gently on the back of her head and then stepped away. Skeeter's knees shook, but she held her ground, repeating her mantra to herself.

"Good girl!" exclaimed Ruth and the Instructor simultaneously.

"Ruth, give me a treat to give to her," said the Instructor. "There you go, Skeet. Good girl!" Skeeter took the treat timidly from his hand.

"Good girl, Skeet!" said Ruth, giving her another treat. Yup, that's what she liked about school. Treats and hugs and good girl!

When she and Ruth returned that night, they were greeted by Sister Mary and Mikey at the door. "Did you pass? Did you pass?" they both asked.

"We did!" Skeeter exclaimed. "The end was scary but I remembered Mamma's words like you told me to, Sister Mary, and we passed! We get to go with the big dogs next week and go to heeling class! That looks so fun!"

"Oh, I remember heeling class," said Sister Mary with a grin. "That was fun. Everybody going in all different directions, the Instructor trying to get people mixed up. Then, we would all sit or lie down while all the people walked around us in a circle. We had to stay where we were and watch. Ruth was so proud the day we did that. Not to mention, we would stop on the way home after class and get chicken tenders."

"Did Boyo go to heeling class?" asked Mikey, still not sure this whole class thing was a good idea. Maybe it was just for girls.

"He sure did. He and Ruth actually won an award the first year as the most improved rookie team. After I started, Ruth took both of us on alternating weeks. He went until his knees got bad and then it was hard for him to do all the moves, but he went. It was the same for me. I went until my hips and elbows got too sore for me to get up and down easily."

Sister Mary paused while Ruth gave her a scratch on the head. "But, Boyo was good at it, too. One time, Ruth and her nephew, Jake, took us to a dog fair that was just for our breed. She took Boyo in the obedience class challenge and he came in second. Beat every dog in the place save one, and that was because they tricked him."

"Tricked him?!" exclaimed Skeeter.

"They played a game called Simon Says. Whenever a dog or handler would make a mistake, they'd get eliminated. Boyo and one other dog were the last remaining dogs doing a down stay. One minute passed, two, then three. No dog would budge. So they started trying to distract the dogs into moving. First, a lady went by banging a pan, right behind them. Next, they fired off a starting pistol. Not even a flinch. Then, two men went by clapping their hands. Still, neither dog moved a muscle.

Finally, a little girl walked into the ring and stood in front of them. Her hair was long and brown, tied back with a pretty little ribbon. She just stood there in front of the dogs and leaned over and said 'Here, doggie,' in the sweetest little voice. Well, Boyo was such a softie for kids. It was all over. He just couldn't resist and got up and walked right up to her. Game over."

"Wow, he learned all that in heeling class?" asked Mikey.

"Well, not all. We practiced a lot like you two do here, but he learned a lot there. That's for sure," said Sister Mary.

Mikey thought for a while. Skeeter did seem to be having a good time at her classes. She always came back bouncing and with a belly full of treats. And, he enjoyed practicing with Ruth around the house at night.

"Maybe I'll give it another try," he said.

"Try harder, Mikey. Try harder," said Sister Mary. "If you get this stuff down, maybe they'll take you to a dog fair. It was fun. They had this other game there that I remember. It was bobbing for hot dogs."

"Wait. What? No way!" exclaimed Mikey. "A game devoted to hot dogs?"

"Yup, all you had to do was stick your head in the water and eat as many hot dogs as you could before they called time." Mikey was amazed.

"Did you get to play that game, Sister Mary?" asked Skeeter, also incredulous at the idea of a game about hot dogs.

"I did, but frankly I didn't like it. I can get hot dogs without getting my face wet. Boyo on the other hand, won the game, paws down! So you see, Mikey, there's more to this obedience stuff than you thought."

The following week was to be Mikey and Max's return to class. Ruth was determined that their relaunch would go better than their first effort. Max was still unable to work with Mikey because of his work schedule, so Ruth had been practicing with both dogs at night. Mikey liked working. He enjoyed interacting with Ruth as they puzzled out moves together.

Class night arrived. Ruth and Skeeter's class started about an hour before Max and Mikey's, so Ruth arrived home first and took everyone out to play a quick game of Ball. On finishing their game and their dinner, Ruth had Mikey go to his crate and snapped the leash on Skeeter. "Now, you be good for Max tonight, okay? No pulling, and remember what we've been working on these last few weeks. You can do it. I know you can. Just keep trying," she said as she headed for the door.

"Good luck, Mikey!" said Skeeter.

"Have fun, Skeet. Learn a new game for us to play this week," encouraged Mikey. As the door closed behind them, Mikey looked at Sister Mary.

"You've got this, kid. You can do it," she said before he could get the question out.

Minutes later, Max arrived. He was nervous, rushed. His day at work had not gone well, but he was determined to give the class with Mikey another try. Maybe it would be different without Skeeter and Ruth in the ring, he thought. "So, Mikey, here we go. Let's give this another shot."

Max optimistically snapped the leash on Mikey's collar and they headed for the door. "Stay here, Sister Mary. We'll be back soon," he said, giving Sister Mary a snack and a pat on the head.

"Good luck, Mikey!" cheered Sister Mary. "Remember your words and remember your lessons!"

With the house empty for the first time in a month, Sister Mary returned to the living room to wait, hoping for the best. She'd modified her story about Boyo and his class successes for the benefit of her friends, but only a little. The stories about his award and the dog fair were definitely true. But, Boyo had struggled in class. He had loved people, but did not get along with most other dogs. It was true that he had worked through most of those issues. In the end, he was no longer jumping, lunging, or barking at other dogs in class.

And it was true that he had managed to achieve a high level of obedience knowledge, but he was never really comfortable with the disorder of heeling class. Indeed, much to Ruth's dismay, more than once Boyo had broken from his stay to correct another dog.

The kids didn't need to know all that, though. They had enough worries on their minds. Better to stick with the positive, she thought as she settled in for her nap.

About an hour after Max and Mikey left, Sister Mary awoke to the sound of Skeeter and Ruth bounding through the door. They were upbeat, as usual, about their adventure. "Hey, Sister Mary, guess what?" exclaimed Skeeter. "We had a whole new group in our class tonight. There were big dogs, teeny tiny dogs, all kinds. It was cool. And then, we did heeling class. I love heeling class. The man in the middle of the ring though, boy is he loud! I was kinda scared of him at first, but, I think he's just loud, that's all. I guess some people are like that, huh?"

Sister Mary smiled. "Big, really tall guy? Kinda walks around with an attitude?" she asked.

"That's him! How'd you know? Boy, Sister Mary, you do know everything."

"I remember that guy. He ran heeling class sometimes when I was there. Yeah, he's really loud, but he's okay," Sister Mary said, chuckling and remembering her own initial fear of the man.

Their conversation was interrupted by the sound of Max and Mikey bursting through the door. "Easy, easy, easy, boy. Let me just get the leash off of you," said Max with a laugh.

"Hurry! I have to tell them!" said Mikey impatiently, pulling on the leash. Finally free, Mikey bounded into the kitchen to greet his eagerly waiting friends.

"Well, how did it go?" Ruth, Sister Mary, and Skeeter said simultaneously.

"Much better," said Max, both he and Mikey smiling with relief. "He was a completely different dog. No more pulling, no straining, no whining; much better," he said.

Ruth beamed. "And did he down? How did he do with that one?"

"He was fine. He didn't want to do it at first, but rather than trying to push him down and muscle him, I just used the treat and he went down. Not too good at staying there, but we can work on that," Max said, looking kindly at Mikey.

Sister Mary walked up to Mikey with a knowing smile. "Hey, kid. Is that chicken I smell on your breath? Did you guys stop for chicken?"

"Oh, and we stopped for chicken on the way home. I saved some for you guys." Max put a box on the counter. "You know we had to stop for chicken!" he said, laughing.

Skeeter looked at Sister Mary in complete wonder. She was beginning to think the old dog had super powers. Sister Mary knew everything there was to know about Ruth and Max!

Later that evening, after a quiet but contented Sofa Time was had by all, Ruth announced that she was off to bed, and asked Max to bring Sister Mary up when he was ready. Max gently carried his old friend upstairs and put her to bed, while the two young dogs bounded ahead. Before going to sleep, Ruth sat on the edge of the bed looking at her old friend on her mat, already asleep, snoring softly. She reminisced about Sister Mary's tour through obedience school. Like Skeeter, Sister Mary always seemed to enjoy meeting the other dogs and playing the obedience school games, at least until her arthritis interfered with her ability to get up and down easily. Now, her old friend doddered along during their practice sessions, but no longer had the strength to make the old moves as she used to. At least she was sleeping well these days and appeared happy. At Sister Mary's age, that was a lot.

Mikey hopped up on the bed and sat next to Ruth. Looking at their reflection in the window, Mikey did not know what to make of himself. He could still see ghosts and shadows behind his eyes, but on the other hand, he liked his image sitting next to Ruth, the cozy bedroom in the background. If only he could chase those ghosts away for good, he thought. He glared at the ghosts reflected in the window, willing them to go away.

Catching her friend's hard look into the window, Ruth put her arm around Mikey's shoulders and pulled him toward her. "Hey, buddy. You done good tonight. You're getting there." She pet him softly. Mikey barely heard her, he was so lost in his own thoughts, transfixed by the image in the window.

Seeing the internal struggle going on in his eyes, Ruth tried again. "Look over there. You see Sister Mary sleeping? You guys have done wonders for her. She adores you, clearly. Her face lights up every time she looks at you. And look here, Mikey. Look at Skeeter sprawled out sound asleep on the bed next to us. She doesn't even bother to ball herself up any more. You saved her, buddy. You did that. So come on, give yourself a break. You're a really good guy. You just need to keep working. Don't give up on yourself. You'll push through those demons and ghosts. I know you will." She hugged him to her gently and put her head next to his.

Mikey reflected on the evening with Max. Tonight had been a good night. He and Max had worked well together, and even the Instructor remarked how much better a team they'd become. He'd loved getting the chicken. That had been a neat surprise. It was just that every time he thought he could let go of the past and enjoy the present, a memory would trigger and create doubt, distrust, fear. Mikey glared at the ghosts reflected in his face in the window. They had to go, once and for all, he thought.

Ruth gave him a pat, got up and shut the blinds, eliminating the reflection and breaking his focus on his demons. "There you go, Mikey. Let's give it a rest." She got into bed and pulled the blankets up to her chin. "Here you go, buddy. Lie down here and I'll tell you a bedtime story."

Mikey blinked and shook the thoughts from his head. Stretching out next to Ruth, he put his paws around her neck and his head on her shoulder and sighed, a deep long exhale that seemed to release one or two ghosts. He knew there were plenty of others, but he'd keep trying.

Chapter 29

"I just think that if we had a fence it would be so much better, and safer for everybody," argued Ruth to Max. "Every time Skeeter gets a scent up her nose, off she goes and I have to go chasing after her. Nothing's happened yet, but given their past, I don't want to risk an accident. God forbid they get on the road and get hit."

It had been another rough evening for Ruth. Ball was going well until Skeeter and Mikey spied a deer in the distance and off they went, with Ruth huffing and puffing behind them, trying to catch up. They had developed a "usual" route, so she was able to head them off at the pass instead of chasing them from behind, which helped, but still she worried.

"I have to play Ball with these guys. Sister Mary will drive me nuts and Mikey and Skeeter will be nuts if we don't. They really need the outlet after being cooped up all day. I walk them, but I can't get enough of a walk in to burn off their steam."

"What are they talking about, Sister Mary?" asked Skeeter, sure that her all-knowing friend would provide a translation.

"I'm not really sure," said Sister Mary, "but I bet it has something to do with your little excursion today. That had Ruth really worried."

"Are they talking about sending us back?" exclaimed Mikey in alarm, standing up and pulling his tail tightly over the top of his body.

"Geez, you're quick to jump to conclusions, Mikey. No, that's not the tone they're taking. I'm sure there'd be more volume to that conversation. I think they are just trying to figure out how to get you guys to stop running off the property."

"Easy, Mikey," said Ruth, noticing Mikey's sudden change in posture, "we're just talking, not fighting. Everything is okay."

Reassured, Mikey sat back down and continued to listen to the conversation.

Two days later, Ruth announced, "We're getting a fence tomorrow!" Uncle Pete, Aunt Stuff, Mammaw, and Pop Pop are all coming over and helping us put it up. No more running off!" she grinned.

The next morning, Uncle Pete arrived at the crack of dawn, before Ruth had taken her friends out for their morning exercise. Scrambling down the stairs to greet her brother-in-law, Ruth discovered her sister and mother at the door. Knowing she could not simply "release the hounds," Ruth scrambled to get leashes on everyone.

"People are at the door! People are at the door!" hollered Sister Mary.

"What should we do? What should we do?" yelled Mikey and Skeeter in reply.

"Keep barking so they know we're here!" yelled Sister Mary.

"Sister Mary, SHUSH!" hollered Ruth.

"See, Ruth agrees. She's barking too," said Sister Mary. "She always tells me *Shush* when I bark, just like she tells you guys Heel when you follow her around. Same thing."

Eventually, Ruth managed to get Mikey and Skeeter leashed, the door opened, and her amused mother and sister welcomed.

"Well, hi! That's quite a greeting!" exclaimed Mammaw.

"Ruth, it's the leashes, you need to let them off the leashes," offered Sister Stuff.

"No. They will stay on their leashes until they calm down," said Ruth, pulling the dogs back away from Stuff and Mammaw. "Guys, didn't we go through this the last time everybody was here? When are you going to learn there is no reason to carry on like this?" she asked in exasperation.

"Sister Mary, how do we know when to stop barking?" asked Skeeter, getting a little tired of the game. "Will Ruth tell us?"

"Sometimes she does. Stop barking and see what happens." Skeeter, Mikey and Sister Mary all stopped barking.

"Good!" said Ruth, and handed each dog a treat.

After getting their mother situated with some hot tea and a comfortable chair where she could see what was going on outside, Ruth and Stuff decided to investigate Max and Pete's progress.

They found that Max and Uncle Pete were already loading posts onto Pete's tractor, and the two were preparing to drill the first holes. Seeing the opportunity to get in some socialization training, Ruth decided to work with the dogs on their people-approaching skills. Approach quietly, pause, get treats. React, retract, no treats.

Being only the third time they'd had guests, Skeeter and Mikey were understandably nervous. It was a noisy morning, but they got through it.

"They're fine. Why don't you just let them loose?" Sister Stuff inquired a couple of hours later.

"No, they're not fine and I'm not having them run off chasing things while we're putting up a fence," Ruth retorted.

"You need to relax," chimed Sister Stuff. "You're too hard on them. They're not going to go anywhere or do anything."

"Stuff, you have no idea what you're talking about. They're staying on their leashes. Unless you want to put on your track shoes and help me retrieve them when Skeeter decides to chase the squirrel and then the other squirrel and then the deer," huffed Ruth.

Sister Stuff rolled her eyes. Her sister needed to relax, she thought, but she knew there was no point in arguing with her.

"Sister Mary, what are they doing anyway? I'm not sure I like the look of this," asked Mikey anxiously.

"Well, I'm not entirely sure, but it looks like they're putting up a fence," responded Sister Mary.

"A fence? What kind of fence? Me and Skeet don't like fences." Mikey's anxiety was returning to the surface. He could hear the drums starting to beat in his head.

Skeeter cocked her head to one side and looked at Mikey. "Why don't we like fences, Mikey?"

"Don't you remember, Skeet? The fence at the First House. Sometimes those kids on skateboards would come up to it and even those kids on bicycles, remember? And then one day somebody knocked it over and came into our yard to chase us. Remember?"

It was Sister Mary's turn to be perplexed. "So, what was the problem with the fence?"

Mikey's eyes grew wide and his face tensed. "When it was there, we couldn't make them go away! When it came down they came even closer! And we got stuck out there all the time with nobody to help us!"

"But, Mikey, we had a fence at Shelter Lady's house. Remember that fence? Nobody ever hurt us there and she always kept an eye on us. So maybe it wasn't the fence's fault," offered Skeeter.

"So how am I supposed to know which way it will be this time? Good fence? Bad fence?" worried Mikey. "Besides, good or bad fence I still don't see that it will do us any good. How are we supposed to chase away the bad guys? And how are we supposed to check on those trails we've been tracking? I don't know, Skeet. I tell you, no good will come of this fence."

Skeeter rolled and blinked her eyes. "Sister Sunshiny, would you please tell my brother that he worries too much?"

"Seriously, kid, your sister is right. You are really over thinking this one. Let's get the fence up and see what happens. I can tell you what won't happen though. Ruth and Max won't leave us outside on our own, not in a million years. And, they're not going to let anyone in here to bother us. No way. That I can tell you. C'mon, haven't you learned anything about these people in the last eight months? Let's just play the rest by ear."

Mikey sat down to give that some thought. "I don't know guys, I hear you, but I just don't like this whole fence idea."

Mikey and Skeeter also worried over whether Pete and Stuff, and later Pop Pop, who arrived later in the morning, were standing too close to them. "Why does Ruth keep walking up to them, Sister Mary? And, why do they just ignore us when we bark at them?" fretted Mikey.

"Yeah, Sister Mary, I don't get that either. Are they deaf? We bark and they just ignore us. We walk back and stop barking, then we walk forward again. I'm confused," said Skeeter.

"I think she's trying to teach us something," said Sister Mary. "I'm not quite sure what, but she's done this before."

Skeeter sat down and cocked her head inquisitively at Ruth. She liked learning and figuring out puzzles. This one though was tricky. "Hmm," she thought. "Sort of like when we're in school. I bark or rumble at the teacher and she walks away with me. I stop barking and rumbling, I get a treat and we go back to playing games with the class. I wonder."

Given the lack of fence and the dogs' evident nervousness, Ruth kept them tethered to her all day. It was a long day, but at the end of it the post and rails were up and in. All that remained was to install the wire, which Max completed two days later.

"Check it out, guys! Now, we can play ball or just hang out in the yard," Ruth announced brightly the evening the wire was completed. "Dinner's on the grill and while it cooks, let the ball game begin!"

She threw out the first pitch. Running with her ball in her mouth, Skeeter called over to her brother, "See, Mikey, thith ith fun! The fenf is not a problem!"

Sister Mary agreed, grabbing her ball firmly and taking off after her friends, "Righ! Shee, Mikey! No worwies."

Mikey was too busy chasing and catching the ball to respond to his two friends. He had to admit that being able to focus on Ball and not worry about Skeeter spoiling the game by running off was an improvement. He also liked the backyard barbecue, with its intoxicating aromas that floated by as they played. With the fence in place, maybe they could do this more often. Maybe the fence was not such a bad idea after all.

The weekend arrived and Ruth was eager to work in the backyard, accompanied by her friends. She had loved working in the yard in years past, after Boyo and Sister Mary had passed the age where they would run off. But she had given up most of her gardening in the months following Skeeter's arrival. By himself,

Mikey mostly minded her, but it was simply too challenging to keep both dogs in check off leash and loose in the woods. They were too young, too fast, too curious. The fence afforded a welcome opportunity for everyone, including Ruth, to get outdoors and simply relax.

The afternoon started off as splendidly as Ruth imagined. She worked around the yard, pulling weeds, straightening beds and generally tidying up, and her friends tagged along with her and kept tabs on her progress.

Sister Mary used the time as teaching moments for her young charges. "Hey, Mikey, check this out. A most interesting smell here on this plant."

"What do you think it is? Is it a skunk?" asked Mikey, joining Sister Mary at the interesting smelling plant.

"No, I don't think so. It's not nearly strong enough. Maybe a chipmunk. They like to sneak out in the afternoon when no one is around and pick up the bird seed that is on the ground."

"Hey, Sister Mary, what's this smell?" asked Skeeter, investigating a nearby bush.

Sister Mary walked over and gave the bush a good smell. "Well that, Skeeter, is definitely a chipmunk. There must be a hole nearby. Let's see if we can find it."

"Sister Mary, what's this?" asked Mikey, putting his paw on a jumpy thing on the ground.

"That, Mikey, is a toad. Push it with your nose and it will jump for you. It tastes bad though, so I wouldn't try to eat it."

Mikey pushed it. The toad jumped as predicted, but Mikey decided to give it a lick just to confirm Sister Mary's prediction. "Yuck! That's nasty," he exclaimed.

"What's nasty, Mikey?" asked Skeeter, coming over to investigate. "That, the toad thing. Taste it."

Mikey gave the toad a nudge toward Skeeter. "Yuck, that's gross," she sputtered, licking the toad before it hopped off in puffed indignation.

The dogs continued their investigation of the yard, examining and cataloguing plants, insects, and animal smells that they hadn't taken the time to examine while playing Ball. "Ooh, Sister Mary, I've got a hot one!" exclaimed Skeeter, following her nose toward the fence.

"What do you have, Skeet?" asked Mikey, trotting up to her.

"I think it's a deer or a squirrel or something," said Skeeter, increasing her pace. "Yup, it went right through here! If I can just get my shoulders, yup, right here."

"Oh, I've got it, too, right through here." Mikey followed Skeeter through the hole she'd found in the corner of the fence.

Ruth managed to spot the escape, but as usual, she was a half second too late. "Skeeter! Mikey! *No!*" she cried. "Skeeter, Mikey! Come!"

Ignoring Ruth entirely, Skeeter and Mikey took off, determined to find the source of the scent.

"Mikey, it's over here," said Skeeter, running through the woods.

"I've got it, I've got it! It goes up this way," said Mikey, picking up speed and passing Skeeter.

"Is Sister Mary coming?"

"No, I don't think so, but I can hear her. She's still at the house. She's barking something, but I can't hear what she's saying."

"Over here, Mikey, this way!"

The dogs ran happily through the woods, making a wide arc that put them right back in the neighbor's yard, almost the exact same place that Mikey had lost the scent the last time. "Darn, it Skeet. I think we've lost it again. Same place too," said Mikey.

"Mikey, Skeeter! Come!" heard Skeeter. Lifting her head and seeing Ruth, Skeeter was happy to comply. "Hey! Ruth! It's you. Yay! You've decided to come with us! Look, Mikey! It's Ruth!"

Skeeter wagged her tail as she bounded over. Relieved, Ruth snapped a leash on Skeeter. "Good girl, Skeet. Good girl."

"Skeet, are you and Ruth coming?" asked Mikey, still puzzling out the trail.

"No, I don't think so, Mikey. We're just standing over here. I think Ruth wants to go."

"Mikey, come," said Ruth.

Mikey looked up at her. He couldn't read her expression. A mixture of relief, anger, and hope seemed to be working their way through her eyes.

Max, however, was clearly furious. He had seen the dogs take off and was driving around the neighborhood looking for them. Mikey could hear him bellowing angrily on the street, still several yards away.

"Mikey, come!" Ruth repeated softly as she approached. Mikey was undecided. Hearing the anger in Max's voice from the street, Mikey wasn't sure what was going to happen when they returned home. "It's okay, boy. Nobody's going to hurt you," said Ruth walking up to him.

He decided to put his faith in Ruth. Lowering his head and blinking cautiously up at her as she snapped on the leash, Mikey reminded himself, "Don't get angry, don't panic, don't bite."

By now he could hear Sister Mary, who was barking her warning from the driveway. "Guys! You better come home! Come home! Max is really mad!"

Ruth had heard Max on the street as well, and although she'd called back that everything was under control, she, too, knew that Max was furious with the escape. All of his time, his effort, and their money to build the fence and it had lasted all of one week. Hoping to give Max some time to cool off, Ruth took the road home in lieu of the direct route through the woods.

Sister Mary met the three on the driveway. "Boy, oh boy, are you two in big trouble," she said. "Max is furious that you went through his fence. I haven't seen him like this in a very long time. Ruth, you and I have a lot of work to do on this one," she said, nudging Ruth as they walked toward the door.

"I know Sister Mary. I know," answered Ruth, grimly scratching her friend's chin. "Thanks for not trying to catch up with us. At least there's that."

"Ruth! Put them in their cages! I don't want to see those dogs outside for the rest of the day! Or ever!" roared Max when they walked in the door.

He slammed the door behind him. He was not just angry, he was enraged. Hurt, betrayed, furious. "I don't want them loose in the house. I don't want them loose in the yard. I don't want them loose anywhere, ever! I want them in their cages, now!" he bellowed, face red, neck veins bulging.

Being strong-willed herself, Ruth hated capitulating to Max when he overreacted. However, under these circumstances, she thought that it probably was best for everyone if her friends spent a little time in their crates. Cooling off seemed like a smart idea. "C'mon guys. Skeeter, Kennel. Mikey, Kennel." "Good girl. Good boy," she said, closing the crate doors gently behind her.

Taking a few deep breaths, Ruth returned outside, hoping to calm Max down and resume what had been a picture-perfect day.

Taking a few deep breaths herself, Sister Mary turned to follow Ruth out the door.

"Sister Mary, wait! Are you just leaving us here?" called Skeeter. "Sister Mary, what were we supposed to do? The scent was there, the opening was there!"

"What did we do wrong?" asked Mikey.

Sister Mary shook her head and turned briefly in exasperation. "Yes, I am walking out with Ruth. Thanks to you and your little prank, I am going to have to look out for her by myself today. For smart kids, sometimes you amaze me. Mikey, you knew the fence was put up to keep you in the yard. You broke the rules, both of you. Wait for me, Ruth. I'm coming too." Sister Mary turned away and Skeeter and Mikey were alone in their crates.

The buzzing and the drumming began in earnest. As the ghosts started their dancing and drum-rolling through their heads Skeeter tried hard to push her ghosts and their drums aside. She noticed her brother, struggling with his own, start to bark, spin and pace in his crate. "It's not like First House, Mikey. We screwed up this time. We screwed up, just like Sister Mary said. Mikey, remember, don't get angry, don't..."

"I know, I know," said Mikey, slowing down somewhat. "Don't panic, don't bite. I guess I should have stopped you, Skeet. I really let us down this time."

"No, you didn't, Mikey. It was my fault. I was the one who found the stupid hole."

"Yeah, but..."

"No buts, Mikey. You can't always be the one to take the blame for things that I do. I'm old enough to stand on my own."

Mikey sighed. He knew his sister was growing up, but he also knew he still had a lot of looking after her to do. "Maybe if we just called them back and explained that we are sorry," said Skeeter, determined to resurrect the day.

"Good idea, Skeet. Let's give it a try."

"Miss Ruth! Mr. Max!" the two dogs barked in unison.

Outside, Ruth and Sister Mary got to work, trying to restore the family harmony with Max. Ruth had resumed planting and weeding, an activity that helped steady her nerves and clear her head. Sister Mary lay down quietly in the grass nearby to observe. "I think we should get those radio collars and set up a perimeter around the fence," Ruth mused.

"What!? We just paid all this money and spent all this time putting up this fence and now we need another one?" steamed Max.

Ruth could hear her friends barking and crying in their crates indoors, but knew she needed to focus on Max for the time being. She continued her weeding. "You have to keep an eye on these dogs every second of every freaking moment or, bam! They're gone! Where did they get out? I don't see any place where a dog could get out."

Ruth was relieved by this last statement. Max was working through his anger, focusing on the real problem, the hole in the fence. "Right here, right in this corner. It was almost like we all saw it at once," she explained, gesturing toward the hole. "I've looked at the rest of the wire, Max, and it looks pretty good. There's only a couple of other weak places."

"What other places? Are you telling me we are going to have to rewire the entire fence?" Max exclaimed.

"No, but we will need to fortify it in some spots."

"Have they been digging?"

"No, Max, but the squirrels do. See, right here."

Ruth showed Max a depression where a small creature had clearly worked a tunnel under the fence. It was not yet big enough for a dog, but in time, it would be.

The sound of Skeeter and Mikey complaining inside the house intensified. Max's anger flared. "Tell them to shut up!"

"I'll do no such thing," said Ruth. "We can't keep them in there all day. They won't understand…"

"Oh, they understand, all right!" interrupted Max angrily, his frustration returning, "they know what they did."

"No, Max. All they know is that they're inside alone and we're out here. They want to be with us. That's all."

"Well, I don't want them with us right now. They're going to stay in there for the rest of the day," he grumbled half-heartedly.

Ruth resumed her weeding and left Max to his own thoughts for a while. Hoping to move the conversation along, Sister Mary got up and walked over to the porch step. Max watched his old friend, her stiff arthritic gait and her soft eyes. He'd once had a difficult relationship with her too, but they'd become good friends over the years and, knowing the fears she'd conquered, he had a particularly soft spot in his heart for her. "Let me see if I can add some wire to that fence," he said. "That was one of the first corners I did. The rest look secure."

"Miss Roooth, Roooth, pleeeze, can't we pleeeze come out?" Skeeter and Mikey cried from inside. "Sister Mary, tell him we'll be good, we promise!" they continued. "Maaax, Maaax, we're soorry!"

"It's no use, Skeet. We're stuck in here," said Mikey, sulking down in his mat.

"I'm going to keep trying, Mikey. I'm not giving up on us, brother."

Skeeter continued her crying, using her most plaintive voice.

Finally, Mikey and Skeeter heard the soft swish, swish of Sister Mary's feet on the floor. "Fine. You let them out. I'm going downstairs. Don't let them downstairs," huffed Max as he closed the basement door behind him. Ruth and Sister Mary entered the room and quietly opened up the crates.

"Come on guys. Come on. Let's get you back outside. The fence is all fixed now. For goodness sake, stay in it this time."

"We will, Ruth, we will. Promise, extra promise!" said Skeeter, understanding the tone if not the literal words of Ruth's message.

"Mikey, that goes for you, too. You have no idea what we went through to get you two out of here today," admonished Sister Mary.

"I know, I know," said Mikey glumly. "We'll try harder."

"Good. Now, let's get Ruth to throw some balls. Then, we'll all feel better."

Of course, Sister Mary was right. After the game was over, Ruth sat with her friends outside for the evening, relaxing in the backyard as she had hoped to do all day.

Just before sundown, Max quietly joined them. "No more escapes?" he asked.

"None," said Ruth.

Chapter 30

The next week was uneventful. The dogs and humans settled into their morning, daytime, and evening routines. Sister Mary entertained her friends with stories during the day and Ruth entertained them with Ball and Obedience Practice at night. This was followed, of course, by dinner and either Sofa Time or Porch Time, both of which had their benefits. Obedience Practice continued to be particularly fun for Skeeter, who enjoyed the special attention that Ruth gave her during her turn. She also liked to tease her brother from the sidelines when he got confused by one of Ruth's commands.

Even in class, things went well for Skeeter. She improved her stand for examination, where she had to stand quietly as the Instructor approached and then touched her head and shoulders, and her Down Stay while the Instructor walked around the room trying to distract everyone. And, with Max's help, Mikey also learned to Down and Stay.

Indeed, by Friday, the aggravation of the weekend escape seemed a thing of the distant past. Sitting outside under an awning, Ruth and Max were happily chatting about the advantages of having the fence and reviewing the week's events.

Their canine friends were doing the same, lying around Ruth's feet.

"Sister Mary, you and Boyo ever sit outside like this?" asked Skeeter as she pawed inquisitively at a beetle that happened by.

"Oh yes, dear. Many times. We sat out here almost every night in the summertime. Wait until autumn comes, though. Then, the bugs won't be so annoying, and the air will be much cooler."

"Yeah, I know," yawned Mikey, stretching himself out on the grass. "Stupid bugs keep landing on me."

"I think they're funny," chimed Skeeter. "Watch, I can pounce on this one and make it squish!" She jumped playfully onto the unfortunate beetle.

"See, this is what I'm talking about," said Ruth contentedly. "Everybody outside, relaxed, enjoying the view."

"I know, it's great. I'm glad we put the fence in now that it's up. And the kids don't seem to be trying to escape all the time. We need to be careful with this awning, though. It looks like some water is collecting in the pockets up there," said Max, reaching down and giving Skeeter a scratch on the chin.

"We really should just put the awning away. We don't need it out here anymore and it will just get ruined in the weather," remarked Ruth.

"True, but it needs to be cleaned and dried out first. Let me see if I can get the water out and I'll put it away tomorrow." He stood up and walked toward one corner of the awning. "Shoot, it is too high to reach. Maybe I can poke it out this way." He stretched and jumped up and down to bump the awning.

And that's when it happened. Seeing Max jumping up and down, being goofy, Skeeter decided to join the action, and she grabbed Max playfully by the ankle.

"Max! Watch out! Your ankles!" hollered Ruth, again, as usual, a split second too late.

"Skeeter! No!" barked Mikey, rushing across the yard to intercept his sister and prevent her from doing more damage.

"Goddammit!" Max screamed in pain and surprise as Skeeter landed her ankle bite. "Get these goddam dogs out of my sight. Get them out! They are going back to Shelter Lady's tomorrow. First the escapes, then the constant barking, and now I can't even do anything without that one biting at me! I will take them myself. They are not to come out of their cages until we load them up tomorrow!" he roared. The seeming unpredictability and randomness of the act completely shattered the confidence that Max had begun to have around the dogs. At the sound of Max's roar and seeing that he was fully enraged, the dogs backed away and braced for what was to come next.

Shaken, Ruth knew there could be no arguing, at least not now, and it would be better for everyone to cool off. She quietly called the dogs to her and put Skeeter and Mike in their crates and left the room. "Hey, why am I going in the crate? I didn't do anything. I tried to stop her," complained Mikey as the door to his crate closed.

"Oh, Mr. Max, I am sooo sorry. I thought we were playing," cried Skeeter from her mat in the crate.

"Hey, Ms. Ruth, please don't lock us up in here, please don't take us back, pleeese!" cried both dogs. They'd heard Max loud and clear. They knew what Shelter Lady meant.

Max was adamant. After putting yet another bandage on his ankle, he fumed to Ruth and Sister Mary, who were sitting very still and quiet having returned to the porch outside. "I mean, this is crazy, Ruth. I can't walk, I can't talk, I can't do anything without somebody taking a bite out of me. It's almost every week.

214

I can't live like this, Ruth. I've tried; I just can't." Max paced, hurt and angry, but mostly hurt, around the porch.

"I know," Ruth whispered, "but you have…"

"*No!* I don't have to do anything. These dogs have to go. I've had it. I can't take it anymore. They have to go."

Ruth could hear Skeeter and Mikey crying in the background and the sound broke her heart. She knew it had been an accident. Skeeter's leap had been playful, not defensive or aggressive. She saw Mikey try to intercept and correct his sister. The dogs really had come so far, she thought. But, the house had become a combat zone and she could not bear to watch her beloved husband get bitten, either, regardless of the reason. That was intolerable.

Glancing down at Sister Mary, who was looking up at her expectantly, Ruth saw the concern in her old friend's eyes. "I know, Sis, I know. We're in a mess and I have no idea how to get out of it," she said. "I just don't know what to do."

Mikey and Skeeter's cries grew louder in the background. Looking angrily at his wife, Max declared, "Do not let them out. They will stay put tonight. I don't care what they do."

Ruth sat quietly, not looking at her husband. The cries in the living room continued. "Jesus Christ! Shut Up!" bellowed Max, storming into the living room and pounding on the crates to make his point. "Shut Up! Shut Up!" he screamed.

Mikey and Skeeter were now thoroughly confused and frightened. Inside their crates, both dogs cowered, remembering the crate pounding of the First House. The ghosts inside their heads pulled out their drums and started beating wildly. Afraid, both dogs crouched as far away from Max as they could. Seeing the dogs' reaction, Max came to his senses and left the room.

Outside on the porch, Ruth cried. Everything they had worked for seemed to be falling apart. "Sister Mary, what do I do?" she cried, stroking the soft folds of Sister Mary's neck and throat. "I am lost. What do I do?"

Sister Mary looked first at Ruth and then at Max, now standing some distance away, composing himself. She could hear her young friends crying again, albeit softly this time. Ruth was right. This was a bad mess. Sister Mary knew she had to get to work.

"Stay here, Ruth. Let me see if I can get things settled down." Sister Mary turned from Ruth and walked into the living room.

"Sister Mary! Sister Mary! What is going on? Why was Max pounding on our crates? Why does Max hate us? Is he really going to send us away? We don't want to go away, Sister Mary!" cried Mikey.

"Sister Mary, I'm scared," whimpered Skeeter from a corner in her crate.

"You guys are in a lot of trouble. More than last week. You know that. I've never seen Max this mad, and I have no idea whether he's just mad for now or whether he really does intend to send you away this time. I do know that this is probably the last straw. Skeeter, child, what on earth were you thinking?"

Skeeter bit her lip and lowered her head. "I thought we was playin'. Jes' like me and Mikey do sometimes. You know, he jumps on me and I nip his ear or grab his neck or his paw. I didn't mean to hurt him."

Sister Mary shook her head. "Child, you should know by now that people can't play the way we do. They don't have any fur and their skin breaks. You might have been able to do that when you were a puppy, but you're an adult now. You just can't do those things," she admonished.

"But what about Mikey? Why's he in trouble, Sister Mary? He didn't do anything bad. He told me to stop." Skeeter pleaded her brother's case to Sister Mary.

"I'm not sure about that one either. Sometimes people don't see things very clearly."

"Sister Mary, can't we get another chance? I really want this to be Forever Home," cried Mikey. He was truly convinced that this time, Max meant business.

"Sister Mary, please! You have to help us. We want to live here with you forever," cried Skeeter plaintively.

Sister Mary looked at her anguished friends with kindness. She wanted them to stay, too, but she sympathized with Max's plight. Living in constant fear of random bites could not be fun. "I know, and I hope it works out, kids. Let me go back and work on it. You two sit here quietly."

Sister Mary turned and left the room. Heading back outside Sister Mary found Ruth and Max sitting apart, Ruth on the porch, Max standing in the yard, each keeping carefully to themselves. She could see that Ruth was still crying, so she went to her first and nuzzled her hand gently. "Come on Ruth. We have to hold it together and work as a team here if we are going to figure this out. You can't fall apart on us now."

Ruth bit her lip and hung her head, giving her friend's ears a gentle tug. "I don't know, Sister Mary. I love those guys and really want to help them get through this, but I am at a complete loss of how to do it. And, I can't just stand by while they jump and bite at Max every time he makes a quick move. I think they'll probably get over it with time, but I can't be sure, and how long does Max have to keep living like this? What do I do?" Ruth whispered through her tears.

"Let me keep working on it, Ruth. I'm not ready to give up on them and I don't think you should either," said Sister Mary, pushing her head into Ruth's hand. "Let me go talk to Max."

Sister Mary eased her way down the steps and across the yard to Max, approaching him softly but firmly. Max was still seething. His jaw was set. His eyes blazed. But when he saw Sister Mary standing in front of him, quietly demanding his attention, Max's eyes softened. He loved Sister Mary. He admired her struggle to become the confident dog she now was and he knew how important her two young friends were to her continued health. He also knew that he could not continue to be a target, regardless of the trigger. Max bent down and scratched Sister Mary's head gently, "Sister Mary, what do you think I should do?"

Sister Mary sympathized with Max but thought the answer was obvious, and she said so. "Work. Try harder." She barked commandingly. Max gave her a half smile. "Hmmpf, so you're siding with them too, huh? I'll think about it," he said.

Having received the answer she wanted, a softening of Max's position, an opening, Sister Mary turned and walked away, pulled herself back up the steps and walked through the house, back to her anxious young friends. "Sister Mary, what's going on? How did it go?" asked Mikey.

"We have a long way to go, but it might be okay. We all have to work hard. Just sit tight for now." I have to go back out and talk to Ruth," she said, turning to leave so that she could continue her negotiations.

"Sister Mary?"

"Yes, Mikey."

"Sister Mary, thank you," he said quietly.

"Don't thank me yet, kid. It's not over."

"I know, Sister Mary. But whatever happens, thank you."

Sister Mary bit her lip and turned. She knew she had to make this work.

"You're back? Working your shuttle diplomacy, eh, old girl?" said Ruth, giving her friend a grateful pat on the head. Absolutely, thought Sister Mary, easing herself down next to Ruth's feet. She needed Ruth to break her silence toward Max and speak up for her friends. But it was Max who broke the silence first. Seeing Sister Mary and Ruth sitting apart from him, he looked at them defensively and said, "Oh, so you guys are siding against me? Great. I get bitten and you two take sides with the crazies."

"No, I'm not taking sides, Max. But I don't understand why you thought banging on the crates would do any good. And, Mikey, he was trying to help you."

"Trying to help me!?" he exclaimed.

"Yes, he tried to intercept Skeeter. He wasn't piling on at all. But you insisted that I dump him in the crate and then you went in yelled at him," said Ruth firmly. "That's not fair to him."

Sister Mary's ears pricked up. So Ruth had seen Mikey's effort and recognized it for what it was. There might be hope that they would resolve this mess after all.

Max looked at his wife, his temper subsiding along with the ache in his ankle. He could see that she was not making up her observation. She believed what she thought she saw. It had happened so fast, Max wasn't sure she was wrong. Maybe Mikey should be given the benefit of the doubt this time. "But what about Skeeter? Why did she do that? I wasn't directing anything at her at all! Everything with that dog is completely random," he lamented.

"It's not random, Max. You just don't pay attention and she – they – don't know anything. I think she meant to play with you, like a puppy would play. She just doesn't know. If she was a puppy, an ankle bite would be normal. Annoying, and something we'd correct, but normal. It's because she's full grown that the ankle bite is a problem," answered Ruth.

Max shook his head. "I don't know, Ruth. I just can't take it anymore."

"I know, Max. I don't know how much more I can take either. I feel that every time we move forward, we have to go back three steps."

"All I know is I don't want anything more to do with them. If you want to let them out tonight, go ahead, but just keep them away from me."

Max retreated to the downstairs sofa, leaving Ruth with Sister Mary.

Ruth sat for a moment and gathered her thoughts before entering the living room to release her friends. "Sister Mary, we've got to get this right. I just wish I knew how."

Upon seeing Ruth and Sister Mary enter the living room, Mikey and Skeeter sat up alertly. "Miss Ruth, Sister Mary, what's going on? Are we okay?"

Ruth dejectedly opened up their crates and let out her two friends. "Come on guys, out you go. Let's sit outside a bit longer and give Max his space."

Skeeter and Mike were glad to comply. They'd had enough of Max and enough of the crates for one night.

A couple of hours later, Max returned to the backyard to find his wife and the dogs sitting quietly. Ruth was perusing one of the many dog training books she'd been reading lately. He noticed her bristle when Mikey approached him and he pushed him aside. "What?" he said.

"Nothing," Ruth said, tears welling in her eyes. "Max, are you really giving up on these two?"

The night grew silent and, hearing the question, all of the dogs looked up expectantly at Max.

"I don't know. I guess not. I don't know. I mean, the bites hurt, but they're not the only problem. It's just that everything is so random with these guys and I never know what to expect."

Ruth sighed. "What if we had a rule that whenever you're around I will have Skeeter on a leash. I know that both dogs have bitten at different times, but I think she really is the one who is starting the problems and Mikey's just getting caught up in the mix. He's either coming to defend her or joining with her. If I leash Skeeter, I can correct her before she reacts, or at least prevent her from getting to you. If I'm wrong and it's Mikey who's starting things, at least you'll only have one dog to deal with if he rushes you."

Max looked around at his family sadly. "The thing is, I really do love these guys. I don't want to get rid of them. I just don't want to keep living this way."

"I know, Max. Let's give my plan a try. If that doesn't work, we might have to get a professional in to help us."

Sitting in the corner with Ruth, Skeeter looked at Sister Mary, her eyes big and blinking hard, she tried to understand what Max and Ruth were saying. "Sister Mary? What are they saying? They're awfully quiet the way they're talking now. Are we done for? Is it over for us?"

"Yeah, Sister Mary, what's going on? Are we staying? I want to stay; I don't want to go back to Shelter Lady's. It doesn't sound like it but I can't tell," asked Mikey, hoping he understood the tone if not the words of Ruth and Max's conversation.

"For now, kids. For now. No more mistakes, not like that one," said Sister Mary gently, relieved to hear the conversation move from anger to problem solving. "From now on, you must remember your Mamma's words."

The next night, after playing Ball and having dinner, Ruth implemented her plan. She snapped a leash onto Skeeter and held on as she and Max discussed the day's events. "Just sit here with me, Skeet," Ruth said gently as she took a chair at the counter.

"Sister Mary," Skeeter asked, fretting at the restraint. "Why do I gotta have this leash on? How come I can't sit with Mikey and help him keep an eye on Max? Mikey's on the rug over there and I'm over here. I don't get the point."

"She's trying to teach you, child," said Sister Mary patiently.

"Teach me what? She's just sitting there." Skeeter squirmed as she took her place next to Ruth.

"Well, just watch her and watch Max as they interact. You can learn a lot just watching people."

"That sounds stupid," complained Skeeter slumping onto the floor next to Ruth's feet and putting her chin between her paws "Did you ever have to just watch?"

"Oh yes, dear. I spent many an hour watching from the end of a leash. Ruth took Boyo and me everywhere when I first came to live with them. We'd go to her sister's house, or her parents' house, and Boyo, well now, he'd just trot right in like he owned the place. But me, I didn't want to go at first. So, she'd snap on a leash, drag me in, and sit me down next to her. Then, at home, when Max's voice got loud or his feet stomped, I'd try to leave the room and hide in Ruth's closet under her clothes. Ruth would walk upstairs and snap on that leash…"

"You'd hide? Under her clothes?" Mikey interrupted in disbelief, "I can't see you hiding from anything! You're so confident. You're not afraid of anything!"

Sister Mary smiled. "See? Exactly my point. Ruth's leash worked. Like I said, she'd come upstairs where I was hiding, snap on that old leash, and back downstairs we'd go. She almost never said a word when she snapped on that leash. Never did anything other than keep me with her and hand me a nibble of something every now and then. That was her rule. Where she went, I went. Period."

"Kinda like me and Mikey! Right?" exclaimed Skeeter.

"Kind of. The point is, when you're tethered to Ruth you know a couple of things. One, you know nothing bad will happen to you because Ruth won't let it. And two, you know that you can sort things out on your own because you're safe with Ruth."

Sister Mary paused, seeing her friends' heads cocked inquisitively. "Make sense?" she asked.

Skeeter blinked. "Sister Mary, I'm confused. What do I sort out exactly?"

"Ah, well, you sort out whether or not there is a threat to you. See, when I first moved in with them, I thought just about everything Max did was a threat."

"Me too!" exclaimed Skeeter, lifting her head off of her paws, eyes wide.

"Yes, but it isn't. If you watch him, you'll understand he is loud and moves around a lot, but that's just how he is. Kind of like us when we run and bark. When you sit or lie down at the end of the leash and watch, you'll see. And, if you decide Max is threatening and you need to react by jumping or running at him, Ruth will let you know that there is nothing to worry about. You will learn to sort things out and keep yourself out of trouble."

"But, Sister Mary," interrupted Mikey, "why not put me on a leash, too? Maybe I could use a leash."

"She does put you on a leash, kid. When she thinks she needs to. Remember that party we had a while back, or remember Fence Day? My guess is that she doesn't think you need a leash in the house now because she's seen you exercise better judgment lately."

"Sister Mary, did Boyo need a leash with Max?" asked Skeeter.

"Never," said Sister Mary emphatically. "Boyo adored and trusted Max and Max him almost from the start. Boyo loved people, all people, all the time. The more people the better. He'd say to me, 'Sis, more people means more food! What can possibly be wrong with that?' Eventually, I mostly agreed with him."

"But, why?" asked Mikey. "I like Max, and I love and trust Ruth, but how can you like and trust all people? Was Boyo just a fool?"

"Oh, no. Nothing foolish about Boyo, but he didn't have a rough start like you did. And, everybody was always nice to him."

"So, did he ever have to have a leash?" asked Mikey with mixed wonderment and jealousy.

"Oh yes, absolutely. As much as Boyo loved people, he never did get comfortable with dogs he didn't know. He and I got along just fine, and he got along with Stuff's dogs, but with strange dogs and the other dogs in our neighborhood?" Sister Mary paused, remembering Boyo's encounters. "Well, let's just say he needed a leash."

"But, why?" asked Skeeter. "Why did he have problems with other dogs?"

"Boyo had a rough start with dogs. And he never got over it. He tried. He tried really hard. Went to school like you two. He learned all of the games and we practiced for years. He got to where he could manage his fears, but he never really conquered them."

Mikey put his head on his paws in thought. "I can understand that. I'm just hoping one day, I can conquer mine. Except for last week and last night, I haven't felt them lately, but the drumming is horrible when it starts, and those ghosts are the worst."

"Me too! Do you think I will conquer my fears, Sister Mary?" asked Skeeter, putting her head on her paws like her brother.

"I don't know. It really is up to you both. I got over mine. Boyo had to learn to manage his. Everybody's different," said Sister Mary. "What I do know," she continued, shifting her position on the floor to get a better vantage point of Max and Ruth, "is that, for now, you both should watch and learn."

That sounded like good advice to both Skeeter and Mikey and for the next few hours they observed as Ruth and Max talked, then laughed, then argued, then laughed again about their day.

Ruth's leash initiative paid dividends. Over the course of about a week, she faithfully tethered Skeeter every time Max was in the same room. Skeeter watched and learned, becoming a student of Max's movements.

Ruth soon noticed that Skeeter had begun to relax more often. She started to take the leash off after a few minutes and put her hand on Skeeter's collar when she noticed her tense up. And, for his part, Max became a student of Skeeter and Mikey, taking his cue from Ruth and observing when his actions caused them concern and moderating his movements to alleviate their fears. A couple of weeks passed, and there were no panic attacks. The weeks stretched into months. Max's wounds healed. Skeeter and Mikey's did, too.

Chapter 31

"Are you sure you can't take him? It's the last night of class and it's Mikey's final exam night."

Ruth knew how important and helpful Mikey and Max's classes had been to both of them. She could see the difference in Mikey every time he came home from school with Max. He was calmer, more focused. His threat/non-threat judgment continued to improve. She also saw the tension that Max had around both dogs lowering as each day passed without an incident. He had learned to better read the dogs through the school's training exercises. So she really wanted both Max and Mikey to have the satisfaction of having passed their first basic obedience class together.

"I'm really sorry, Ruth, but I just can't. I have to attend this meeting. If you took him, would it still count?"

Max wanted Mikey to complete the course, too. Despite his misgivings and their initial difficulties, Max enjoyed working with Mikey in school and, like Ruth, he recognized the milestone that graduation represented for both of them.

"Well, I could. Don't see any reason why they should care. Besides, it will give me a chance to see how he's doing in a group situation," Ruth replied.

"Great. The Instructor said to bring his favorite toy to class for the final. I guess you'll have to take one of the balls."

That gave Ruth pause. After the rope incident, toys had been limited to the bag of balls that was used to play Ball. Mikey had learned to play Ball well in recent months, but it had not been entirely smooth. On occasion, he had gotten overly excited and grabbed Ruth's hand before she'd had a chance to throw the ball. It hadn't taken Mikey long to learn that mistakes like that immediately ended the game, but recently another problem had developed at the end of the game. Mikey had begun guarding the last ball of the game, determined to keep that ball for himself, rather than returning it to Ruth. So far, Mikey's ball guarding hadn't escalated into a real problem, but Ruth knew she had to nip that issue in the bud before it turned into something serious. As a result, Ruth was not so sure she wanted to set Mikey up for an incident in class the very evening he was supposed to be graduating.

But she decided a little optimism was in order, so after hanging up the phone and wishing Max success with his meeting, she packed up Mikey, stuffed her pockets full of treats, and brought one of the balls with her just in case. "Come on, Buddy," she said brightly as she loaded him into the car. "Let's see what kind of team we can be."

"Good luck, Mikey!" cheered Skeeter as they headed off to class.

"Have fun and remember your words," cheered Sister Mary.

Mikey was pleased. What an opportunity to show Ruth how much he'd learned, he thought.

Arriving at the school grounds, Ruth nervously fidgeted with the leash and treat bag before getting out of the car. "Mikey, wait," said Ruth as she opened the door. Mikey sat calmly in the seat next to her. "Good boy. Nice wait. Good. Come on out," she said. Mikey hopped out of the car and Ruth carefully switched leads from his regular collar to his training collar. "Ok, here we go!"

Entering the school, Ruth was struck immediately by the difference in her friend. She hadn't seen him in the school setting since their first two classes, months ago. Back then, he'd been edgy and nervous, tugging, barking, and tugging some more. Tonight, he entered the school quietly, no tension on the leash, his relaxed tail wagging happily. Mikey got his first treat for the night.

"Okay, everybody, let's form a circle, and get started. Forward!" called the Instructor. Mikey and Ruth fell in line with the other dogs in class. They were truly a mixed lot. A tiny reactive terrier. A large Dogue du Bordeaux, who took every opportunity to lie down and take a nap. A very alert Airedale. A ding-batty young Doberman who bounced and spun at the end of her leash.

"Wow, Mikey, you have a lot to deal with here. Being a herding dog, this group must really tax your patience. Good boy," said Ruth chuckling to herself as Mikey walked along next to her. She remembered Boyo's reaction to the apparent disorder of the class and was pleased that it didn't seem to faze Mikey, confidently trotting by her side.

"About turn," directed the Instructor.

"Mikey, heel." Ruth wheeled around to go in the other direction. "Good boy," she praised, pleased that Mikey kept right with her and ignored the Doberman bouncing around next to him.

"Halt," said the Instructor.

"Mikey, sit," said Ruth brightly. "Good boy!"

"Everybody, step away from your dogs. Tell them to stay and step right out to the end of their leads."

"Stay!" Mikey sat confidently at the end of the leash, focusing all of his attention on Ruth. "Good boy! Mikey, good boy!" Ruth was beaming.

"Down your dogs."

"Mikey, down!" Ruth knew what was coming next in the routine and had reached in her pocket for a treat. Mikey immediately lay down. But, confused by commotion going on next to him, Mikey stood up again. "Oops. Mikey, down." Down he went.

"Step out to the end of your lead."

"Mikey, stay! Good boy." Ruth kept an eye on the other dogs. Some were doing better than others. It was a beginner class, after all. She noticed that the Instructor was gradually moving the dogs closer and closer to one another with each exercise, increasing the level of difficulty for everyone. So far, the dogs had maintained their cool, but she knew that cool could be blown in a split second. Noticing that the Doberman's owner was not paying attention to her dog's playfulness, Ruth moved Mikey out of harm's way. Just in time.

"Hey, hey, watch your dog. Don't let her do that," said the Instructor to the Doberman's owner. The dog had just pounced at the spot of light where Mikey had been lying down. Mikey held his ground confidently. Sister Mary had been right, he thought. Ruth did work to protect him when he was on a leash.

Mikey and Ruth worked well as a team. He trusted her and she was starting to trust him. Weaving through the other dogs, no problem. Letting other dogs weave around Mikey and Ruth, no problem. Reactive terrier barking next to him. Whatever! With each exercise completed, Ruth was more and more confident that Mikey would pass.

"Handlers, stand your dogs. Examine your own dog, and then step out to the end of the lead."

"Stay." Ruth went through the routine. Mikey stayed.

The Instructor then walked around the room, stopping at each dog for an examination. Ruth took a deep breath. She knew this would probably be the most difficult exercise for Mikey. So did the Instructor. "Alright, Ruth. I'm just going to walk up and stand next to you. Just keep him where he is and we'll take it one step at a time."

The Instructor angled over to Ruth, keeping his eye on Mikey, who stood quietly, but at attention. "How's he doing? Everything okay?" he asked Ruth.

"He's doing great. I'm really pleased," she said, watching Mikey for signs of discomfort.

"He has been doing well with Max, too. As long as you and Skeeter aren't around, he's great," joked the Instructor.

"Don't get angry, don't panic, don't bite," Mikey repeated softly to himself as the Instructor approached and then entered his space. After quietly showing the back of his hand to Mikey and then stepping away, the Instructor said "Good. We'll leave it at that for tonight. Do you have any treats? Let me have a treat to give him."

"Don't get angry, don't panic, don't bite," thought Mikey as the Instructor extended his hand toward him.

"Here you go, buddy. Good boy!"

"Good boy, Mikey," beamed Ruth as Mikey gently took the treat and the Instructor moved on to the next student. Another milestone.

"Really good job, guys. So, now, everybody, we're going to learn the game of Take it, Drop it, Leave it. Did everybody bring your dog's favorite toy?"

Ruth, still on the fence about playing the game with Mikey, had left the ball in the car. The night had been wonderful. Should she push Mikey further? Seeing his student without a toy, the Instructor walked up to Ruth and Mikey. "Where's his toy?"

"I don't know if this is a good idea," said Ruth. "At home he tends to resource-guard with his toys. We're working on it, but I don't know."

The Instructor shrugged. "Well, as long as you're working with him. Never let him win that game. It can turn into a real problem. He's not that way with his food or anything else, is he?"

"No, it's just his toys. We play the trade game with him and he is getting better, but tonight, I'm just not sure I want to push him any further."

"Ok. Then just watch the others, and you guys can teach this game to him at home."

As Ruth watched the Instructor work with the other dog and handler teams, she reconsidered. "Maybe I'm letting us both down here," she thought looking down at the happy, confident dog next to her. "We should at least try. This Instructor has been training dogs his whole life. What better opportunity do we have to get some real help with this?"

With a fresh bout of determination, Ruth mobilized quickly. "Hey, come on, buddy, let's go get that ball out of the car."

Returning to the class moments later, ball in hand, Ruth motioned to the Instructor. "I've changed my mind. Let's give this a try and see how it goes." She took a deep breath.

"Good! Ok, show him the ball and see if you can get him to take it."

Ruth showed Mikey the ball. "Mikey, take it!" she said brightly.

Mikey looked up at her in confusion. "Take it? What's that mean? Ruth, throw it," he thought, looking hopefully at the ball in Ruth's hand.

"Mikey, take it!"

"Ruth, throw it!" Mikey willed Ruth to throw the ball, looking first at the ball then at Ruth and back at the ball again.

"Oh, yeah, a real resource guarder that one," the Instructor laughed. "Try one more time, Ruth," said the Instructor, still chuckling.

"Mikey, take it!" She offered the ball once more to Mikey.

Sniffing it, Mikey took the ball out of Ruth's hand, then immediately dropped it. "Maybe she'll get the idea," he thought looking up at Ruth expectantly and then back at the ball and then at Ruth.

It was Ruth's turn to laugh. "Good drop it, Mikey," she said.

"Now, tell him to leave it and reach down and pick up the ball. Keep your eye on him and don't make any snatching moves," said the Instructor.

"Mikey, leave it," said Ruth, picking up the ball.

"Now, give him a treat and tell him he was a good boy. Try the exercise two or three more times. I see what you mean though, he really is focused on that ball," said the Instructor before moving on to the next student.

"So before we end tonight, anybody having any problems, questions?" The Instructor was finishing up with the last dog. Ruth stood next to Mikey, contentedly scratching his head as he sat quietly next to her. Hearing no questions, the Instructor continued. "In the next couple of weeks we will be mailing out graduation certificates for those dogs who graduated, and if you do, you are welcome to join the next class when we start back up in September. Not all of the dogs are ready to graduate and for those dogs, you are invited to rejoin this class next time. Have a great summer, everybody."

Ruth and Mikey were on cloud nine. They didn't need to see the certificate. They both knew Mikey'd passed. The spacey Doberman? The reactive terrier? Who knew. But Mikey? Absolutely. Ruth and Mikey couldn't wait to get home and share the news with their friends.

"Mikey, wait," said Ruth as she opened the car door after arriving home.

"Wait?! Are you kidding me? Wait? I've got to tell Skeeter the news!" said Mikey as he bolted past Ruth to the front door.

Ruth laughed. "Buddy, you deserved that one. Go tell the girls and Max how you well did."

"Mikey, how'd you do? Wasn't it fun playing with Ruth?" Skeeter jumped over Sister Mary as Mikey burst into the house.

"How'd you guys do?" asked Max from the kitchen.

"It was great!" said Mikey and Ruth in unison. Mikey ran over to Max, tail and tongue wagging.

"Oh, buddy, you've caught me!" said Max laughing. "Here you go, I brought home chicken and fries!"

"Chicken and fries! Hey, Skeet, there's chicken and fries!" exclaimed Mikey.

Sister Mary laughed as Skeeter scrambled past her into the kitchen. "Hey, Skeet," she said with a conspiratorial wink, "Don't tell him that we've already had some!"

"So, did you guys pass?" asked Max, somewhat anxiously.

"He did great, Max. He really did. I'm sure he passed. You know they don't give out the certificates in class, but I have no doubt. We even did the Take It, Drop It, Leave It game and there was no problem. I'm going to work that into Ball next time we play."

"All right! Good boy, Mikey!" exclaimed Max as he handed Mikey a piece of chicken.

"Speaking of Ball, how about we play?" barked Sister Mary cheerfully from her spot on the kitchen floor. "Have you forgotten, Ruth? We have not played Ball tonight! The night would just be perfect if we could only play Ball!" Sister Mary moved toward the Ball cabinet to make her point more clearly.

"Yeah, let's play Ball, Ruth! Sister Mary'n me have been here all night and haven't played a single Ball!" chimed Skeeter wagging her tail in big circles.

Ruth shook her head in amusement. "Well, Max. I guess it's time to play Ball!"

A week later, the official news came: Mikey passed.

Chapter 32

"You go first."

"No, you go first."

"You go first."

"No, you go first!"

Skeeter and Mikey stood at the top of the stairs arguing over who would go downstairs first.

"Guys, just *go!*" Ruth was also at the top of the stairs, holding Sister Mary in her arms.

"Would someone just go first!" barked Sister Mary.

"You go first."

"No you go first."

"Let's go together."

"No, you go first." The debate continued.

"Go!" hollered Ruth.

"For God's sake, shut *up!*" yelled Max from the bedroom. It was 5:00 a.m., after all, and the morning debate about who would go first had gotten old. Max's command had the desired, if unpleasant effect, and Mikey and Skeeter both bounced down the stairs and raced into the kitchen without further discussion.

Ruth and Sister Mary followed, Ruth shaking her head in bemusement. Things had continued to improve in the past few weeks. There was, however, the small matter of all of the barking. Barking at the top of the stairs, barking when she and Max came home, barking at Max when he entered a room, barking when they entered Mammaw and Pop Pop's house. Although having Skeeter leashed and tethered to Ruth during most evening hours seemed to have helped prevent it from escalating to an incident, the barking needed to stop. Given that Sister Mary was probably the biggest barker of all, Ruth wondered how and whether that would be possible.

Then one day, while browsing in the training aisle of her local pet food store, Ruth discovered what became affectionately called "the Canister of Calm." It was a small orange canister filled mostly with compressed air and what the manufacturer claimed was a "calming pheromone." Ruth was not one for gimmicks, but she was intrigued by the label, which claimed that it would help stop excessive barking, charging, and general nuttiness. What did she have to lose?

Opening the front door, she found her three friends in their typical state of frenzy. "Ruth, Ruth, Ruth!" they all exclaimed. Sister Mary, ever the greeter, ambled over to Ruth and gave her a friendly bark and nip on the leg. "Ruth, Ruth!" Skeeter and Mikey eagerly exclaimed from their crates. Mikey grabbed his mat and gave it a good shake for emphasis.

Ruth, deciding that now was as good as a time as ever, pulled out the canister, showed it to her friends and demanded "Stop that!"

Of course, they didn't. So, she pulled the trigger, unleashing a loud hiss and strange orange smell. Skeeter and Mikey stopped dead in their tracks. Sister Mary literally fell to the floor.

Looking up in surprise, all of the dogs demanded, "Ruth, what the heck is that?"

Seeing that she finally had their attention, Ruth countered, "Good dogs! Nice quiet!"

"What'd we do? Sister Mary?" asked Skeeter. She blinked her eyes in total disbelief. How did such a noise came from that tiny little canister?

"I have no idea, guys. That thing is totally new to me. Damn! That hurt my ears!" said Sister Mary, still regrouping from the sound of the spray.

"Smells kinda nice though," said Mikey, also regaining his composure.

"I think we give it some space," said Skeeter, now sitting quietly in her crate.

"Me too," said Mikey

Ruth couldn't help but giggle as she watched her friends try and figure out what had happened. "Great! Good job, guys!" she praised, handing each dog a treat and opening Mikey's crate.

"Whoopee! My crate's open!" Mikey whooped as he bounded out of his crate toward Ruth.

"Ah, ah, Stop that Mikey," demanded Ruth, showing Mikey the canister. Remembering the noise, Mikey sat. "Good Boy!" she said, handing him a treat. "Here you go, Sister Mary. Here you go Skeet. Treats for you, too. Thanks for being patient."

Next, Ruth opened Skeeter's crate. Skeeter sat tight, looking up at Ruth expectantly. "Nice job! Good girl! Okay. Come on out."

"Who-hoo! C'mon Mikey! Let's run!" barked Skeeter as she released some of the energy that she'd been building up all day.

"Race ya to the kitchen!"

"Pssst!" blasted the canister.

"Oops!" Both dogs startled and stopped in the doorway. "What now?" asked Skeeter, turning to Ruth.

"Yeah, Ruth, what'd ya do that for?" exclaimed Mikey.

"Thank you. I don't want you doing that. This house is not a race course. Now, let's try again. Have some manners this time."

"Manners? What's manners, Sister Mary?" asked Skeeter.

Sister Mary shook her head in exasperation. "Oh, she gets this idea in her head every now and then that we're not supposed to bark at her, not supposed to run through her, not supposed to do a whole bunch of things. It will pass. It always does." Sister Mary looked at Ruth and eyed the canister suspiciously. "Maybe we can figure out how to get that thing away from her before she ruins all of the rest of my hearing."

"But this manners thing, will she give us treats? I like treats. I don't mind manners if they come with treats," said the ever-hungry Mikey.

"Yeah, probably, but this whole thing she has against us barking really gets on my nerves. You've heard her bark and we all know how Max barks. Why can't we bark? After 13 years, I just don't get it. I might just bark anyway just to make a point."

"Well, yeah, but we get treats, right?" Mikey wanted to be sure before he committed to Ruth's quiet dog approach.

"You'll get treats, you'll get treats," said Sister Mary, now as exasperated with Mikey as she was with Ruth.

For the next few days, "Canister of Calm," ruled supreme. Ruth discovered that there were many annoying traits that the canister could interrupt: rowdy behavior when she entered the house, barking at the top of the stairs, barking at the bottom of the stairs, barking at the commencement of Ball. A quick spray of the can interrupted all of them. Sometimes just the threat of the spray did the trick

True to her words, Sister Mary ignored the spray, or she squeezed up her eyes and took it. Nobody was going to tell her she couldn't bark!

Pleased with the peace that was evolving in the house, Ruth decided to test the Canister of Calm's effects elsewhere. "C'mon Skeet, let's you and me go visit Mammaw and Pop Pop," Ruth announced one afternoon. "You guys will stay here with Max. Next time, you'll go, Mikey. And if all goes well, we'll add you back into the mix on the third time, Sister Mary."

Ruth snapped a leash on Skeeter, stuffed her pockets full of treats and grabbed her Canister of Calm. Happy to be going on a trip with Ruth, Skeeter trotted out the door and hopped into the car.

"Bye, Mikey! Bye, Sister Mary!" she exclaimed.

"Bye Skeet! Have fun," called Mikey back to her.

"Remember your words, Skeeter," reminded Sister Mary.

Skeeter was pretty sure she had that part covered, but she practiced them a couple of times just in case.

Pulling into Mammaw and Pop Pop's driveway, Ruth spoke firmly to her friend. "Now, Skeet. We're going to Mammaw and Pop Pop's. So just remember your lessons and you'll be fine."

Skeeter swallowed and blinked hard. "Don't get angry, don't panic, don't bite," she repeated to herself nervously. The last couple of trips out to Mammaw and Pop Pop's hadn't gone so well. Either she or Mikey had gotten nervous and poor Pop Pop had borne the brunt of it, causing everyone to stay on edge during their visits. Now, without her brother's support and Sister Mary's interpretive skills, Skeeter wasn't sure how she and Ruth would manage. But Ruth seemed determined and there was a whole pocket full of treats to earn, so she'd try.

"C'mon, Skeet, let's have you take a run first. Burn off some steam before we go inside," said Ruth as she opened the car door for her.

"Good idea," thought Skeeter, bounding out of the car.

Seeing Skeeter barreling down the driveway and through the woods caught Ruth by surprise. She remembered the days when Sister Mary and Boyo used to run down the same path, side by side, pushing each other, laughing, usually finding a stick to play with as they ran. Sister Mary's running days were over, and the previous year, Boyo couldn't so much as walk the distance back to the barn where the driveway led. Cancer had just sapped all of the strength from her once vital and vigorous friend. But watching Skeeter as she arced around the corner behind the barn and raced back to her, Ruth was reminded of the joy her old friends had once shared.

Ruth's reverie was broken by the sight of her youthful friend, bounding back to her at full tilt, mouth agape, ears flapping happily in the wind. "Hey, Ruth!" Skeeter exclaimed, "let's go around again, ok?"

She jumped up on Ruth and gave her a full face grin. Having Ruth to herself had advantages. All the treats to herself, no big brother telling her to slow down or do this or that. "C'mon, Ruth! Let's do it again!"

Brushing aside the nostalgic tear that had started to make its way down her cheek, Ruth gave her pup a smile and a scratch behind the ear. "Good idea, girl. One more trip around the property will do us both good."

A few minutes later, with Skeeter relaxed and confident and feeling composed herself, Ruth snapped on Skeeter's leash and collar, refilled the treat bag and, Canister of Calm firmly in hand, entered Mammaw and Pop Pop's house. Her parents were seated in the kitchen, a bowl of peanuts on the table. "Hey, look, Skeet, a start-over peace offering from Mammaw and Pop Pop," said Ruth quietly, but hopefully.

Skeeter looked around cautiously and then looked up at Ruth. "What do I do now?" she asked.

Seeing her friend's confusion in the absence of Mikey and Sister Mary's influence, Ruth smiled. "Good girl. I can help you. All you have to do is come in quietly like you learned in school. Just be a good girl and everybody will give you treats."

"I think I'll leave the treat giving to you for now, Ruth," said Pop Pop, smiling ruefully. "My fingers have just about healed from the last go-round."

"Ruth, what's happened? No barking, no lunging – what have you done to her?" asked Mammaw incredulously.

Ruth put the Canister of Calm on the table in front of them. "I think I've found magic. We've been using this stuff for a few days and it really seems to work. The sound seems to disrupt them from misbehaving just long enough to reorient to me and then I can tell them what they should be doing instead of yelling at them all the time. I do think it has brought the decibel level in the house down by twenty points!"

Seeing that all of the people in the room were calm, especially Ruth, Skeeter relaxed and walked over to sniff Mammaw. Extending her head cautiously, she reminded herself, "Don't panic. Don't bite. Don't panic. Don't bite."

Mammaw looked down at her kindly and slowly reached out under Skeeter's chin. "There, there girl. That's a good puppy."

"Good girl, Skeeter!" said Ruth, offering Skeeter a peanut. Hmm, that wasn't too bad, thought Skeeter as she took the peanut quietly from Ruth's extended hand. Maybe I'll just lie down and take a nap. That running wore me out. And without further ado, without a bark, growl, grumble or comment, Skeeter plopped down next to Ruth.

"Well, that's a new one," exclaimed Pop Pop. "Think I can get up and get dinner on the table without her making a big fuss?"

"Just don't make any sudden moves. You don't want to try your luck," said Ruth, smiling broadly at the improvement of her friend since their last visit. "I think we are going to try this for a while. Let them each visit you guys separately and sort things out on their own. Then we'll reintroduce Sister Mary to the equation and hopefully go back to bringing all three. This way is easier on me," she said, "not to mention, on Pop Pop!"

The phone rang. It was Sister Stuff. She, Uncle Pete, L'il Bud, and Sam were on their way to join in for dinner. In fact, they were at the front gate. "C'mon, Skeet. Let's go meet them," said Ruth brightly.

Snapping the leash back on Skeeter's collar, refilling the treat bag and grabbing the Canister of Calm, Ruth quickly moved operations outside. One thing she'd learned was that more room meant more calm. Tight places created by having three dogs and five people in the kitchen made for too much stress for friendly greetings.

Once inside the gate, Sister Stuff's dogs, Sammy and L'il Bud, hopped out of the car and reintroduced themselves to Skeeter.

"Hey, you're L'il Bud, right?" asked Skeeter, giving the diminutive LB a thorough smell over. L'il Bud lowered his head and backed away.

"Back off there, young lady. Watch your manners around LB. He's my friend." Sammy pushed her large frame between LB and Skeeter, giving her a glare.

Reassured by the presence of his hundred- pound friend, LB made himself as tall as a ten-inch dog can and looked Skeeter right in the eye. "Yes, that's my name. You're Skeeter or something, right?"

"Yeah, that's me. I've been playing. Wanna play? I can chase you if you want." Skeeter bounced around LB and Sammy hopefully.

Sammy shook her head. "We don't play with strangers and nobody chases LB," she said scornfully.

"Well, Sister Mary says that sometimes she chases, LB, and that you guys used to play all the time."

Standing stiffly next to his body guard friend, Sammy, LB gave Skeeter a snort. "First, it's Mister LB to you. Sister Mary and I go way back. I might play with her sometimes, or at least I used to, but that was a long time ago, and I don't do that anymore." LB looked at Skeeter with all of the haughty disdain that he could muster.

"Whatever, Mr. Little Britches Bossy Boss. Just askin'. Geez," sassed Skeeter from the end of her leash.

"Hey, I said have some respect, young lady." Sammy glared at Skeeter and again pushed her way between the two dogs.

Seeing she was getting nowhere, but still hopeful of having some fun, Skeeter ducked around the imposing Sammy and tried once more. "Well, I know what, you can chase me first and then I can chase you." She hoped her enthusiasm would entice the older dogs to play with her.

L'il Bud looked at the bouncing Skeeter and sighed. She did remind him of Sister Mary, the love of his life. Bouncing, sassing, teasing, all good-natured. He remembered how Sister Mary and he used to play tag. Around the house they'd run, him ducking under a sofa when Sister Mary got too close for comfort, but then poking his head out and nipping at her when she least expected it and starting the game over again. He knew Skeeter just wanted to play, but he was older now and he could see that Skeeter was much quicker and stronger than he. One thing he'd learned as a little dog was that it did not take much for a friendly game of chase to turn into a too-real game of hunt and hunted. "Nah, not today. Let's just see what Pop Pop has cooking."

"OK, we can do that too. I've been in there already and it smells really good."

Seeing that she was not going to have to rescue LB from a game of chase, Sammy relaxed. "It always smells good in there," she said with a dreamy look toward the kitchen door.

Noticing that the three dogs had relaxed, Ruth unsnapped the leash and headed inside.

The three dogs trotted into the kitchen and, after an obligatory inspection of the cooking area, everyone settled down on the floor. "Wow, what's happened to her?" asked Sister Stuff looking at Skeeter incredulously. "She's so, well, normal. What did you do to her? Drugs? Swap her for another look-alike dog?" she said only half-jokingly.

Skeeter shyly approached Sister Stuff, who was seated at the table. "Hey, baby. How are you?" Sister Stuff asked, giving Skeeter a gentle pat. "Seriously, Ruth, what did you do?"

Ruth grinned. She knew the Canister was really a prop, and no substitute for the hours of work that she and Max had put into Skeeter's training and retraining, but it did seem to help. Ruth was pretty certain that having Skeeter find her way on her own, without the influence of Mikey, helped keep her focused on Ruth when she needed guidance.

Later, after dinner, Sister Stuff had an idea. "Let's do a pack walk! Let's take everyone for a walk together. It will be fun!"

"What's a pack walk, Miss Sammy?" asked Skeeter.

"Oh, it's this dumb thing that they do. We all get on leashes and then we walk, sometimes for a whole mile. It's exhausting."

Sammy slumped onto the floor and put her head between her paws. Maybe if she laid really still they'd leave her there with Mammaw.

"Don't listen to her, Skeeter," interjected LB. "She's just grouchy because she had a knee operation a few months ago and it still hurts a little. Come on, Sam. The walk will do both you and me good."

"A walk? That's it? I love walks!" exclaimed Skeeter.

"Of course you do. Why does that not surprise me," sulked Sam, rolling her eyes with a yawn.

Everyone went on the walk except for Mammaw, who stayed behind to wash the dishes.

Heading out the driveway, trotting contentedly with her new friends, Skeeter was happy. "Hey, Mr. LB, this is cool. Check those out, what are they?" Skeeter pointed a field full of horses. "Hey, Ms. Sammy, check this out; what is it?" She sniffed the scent of something interesting. "Hey, Pop Pop, I'm in front walking right next to you and I don't even care!" LB and Sam couldn't help but laugh. It really had been a long time since they'd seen the world through a young dog's eyes.

And that's the way it went. For the next few months, Ruth alternatively took Skeeter, Mikey and Sister Mary to her parents' house for dinner, but never Skeeter and Mikey together. Without the need to worry about one another, both dogs learned to enter the house quietly and they enjoyed their trips.

Chapter 33

"One early summer morning, Ruth announced a new plan. "Today, we are going on your first official road trip. Just you two and me. Let's see how you both do. Sister Mary, you'll stay here and watch the house."

Max was away for the weekend scuba diving, and Ruth was anxious to get outdoors herself.

Mikey's ears pricked up, remembering Sister Mary's stories about road trips to the ocean. "Do you think we're going to the ocean, Sister Mary?" he asked hopefully.

"Or maybe camping?" asked Skeeter, wagging her tail excitedly at the thought.

"Can't tell, kids. She has her book out, so probably not the ocean. She only pulls out the book when she's looking for something different or trying to remember how to get somewhere. It's just basically one road to the ocean. So the book isn't necessary. And she never goes camping by herself."

"But, she's not taking us back, right?" Mikey was still concerned that something would trigger Ruth or Max to send them back to the First Home or Shelter Lady's.

This time, Skeeter jumped in and answered before Sister Mary could paw the exasperation off her face. "Mikey, you have to stop saying that! Ruth loves us. After all we've been through? No way. We haven't forgotten our words in a month and besides, look at Ruth. She looks happy. I don't think she'd be happy if she was going to take us back."

Sister Mary looked at Skeeter with approval. "Good job, Skeeter. You're absolutely right. Everything about Ruth says she's happy to be doing what she's doing. She wouldn't be that way if she were taking you somewhere bad."

Mikey gave their comments some thought. They were probably right. He sure hoped so.

Sister Mary *was* right, of course. Ruth did plan to take Mikey and Skeeter hiking. She'd thought about going to the ocean, but decided to save that trip for a time when Max could come, too. For now, she just needed a trail that was broad, shaded, and, hopefully, uncrowded. Something that would challenge her friends, but not over-challenge them.

Unable to decide where exactly to take them and fearing that the morning was slipping away from her, she decided, "We'll just get in the car and go west. I'll decide exactly where when we stop for breakfast."

After throwing some water bottles and snacks into a bag with leashes and the Canister, Ruth loaded Skeeter and Mikey into the car, said goodbye to Sister Mary, and off they went.

Riding in the back of the car as Ruth sped down the highway toward their unknown destination, with the radio on, coffee still hot, and the sun barely up over the horizon was invigorating. Skeeter and Mikey looked out the back window with eager anticipation as the miles stretched on and the view grew wider, less crowded by houses and traffic.

Eventually, Ruth pulled into a convenience store. "Wait here, guys. I need some breakfast. Then we'll decide where we're going to end up today." Returning moments later with a sandwich for herself and one to share with her friends, Ruth consulted her trail book again.

"Where do you think it will be, Mikey?" wondered Skeeter as she munched on a piece of egg and sausage.

"I have no idea, Skeet, but with food like this, who cares?" Mikey enthusiastically downed his piece of the sandwich.

Back on the road again, Ruth drove for another hour or so before pulling off the highway. "The sign says it's just a ways down here." Her plan was to find a quiet part of a canal trail. The local one ran for miles and provided a good, mostly flat, well-maintained trail that would give her lots of room to maneuver if she had a problem with the dogs. This being their first excursion, Ruth was hopeful of success, but really had no idea how the dogs would react to running children, bicycles, joggers, and anything else they might encounter. Her goal was to have a successful outing, get some air and some exercise, all incident-free.

Although she had not been to this particular portion of the trail before, the spot she selected looked perfect. It was busy, but not crowded. The path was shaded and the view was spectacular. Leaping out of the car almost before Ruth could grab their leashes, Mikey and Skeeter were ecstatic. "Check this out, Mikey! Look, there's water and woods and…"

"Whoa! Look over here," interrupted Mikey. "There's an amazing smelling pile of something."

"Mikey, get out of that," interrupted Ruth, laughing, pulling him away from the amazing pile of something. "Ok, guys, let's go." And off they went.

The trail was a young, inexperienced dog's delight. It was full of smells, full of things to investigate and it was long. They would not walk the entire length in the time they had, but it didn't matter to Skeeter and Mikey.

After the first fifteen minutes of crossing each other's leashes and pulling in different directions, Skeeter and Mikey settled into a comfortable pace, sometimes in front of and sometimes right next to Ruth.

"Mikey, isn't this just great? The three of us, walking at a normal pace instead of that slow pace we have to walk at home?" exclaimed Skeeter.

"It is, Skeet. I don't mind walking slow at home because I know Sister Mary can't keep up, but it really feels good to stretch like this."

Then Skeeter noticed a pack of bicyclists approaching. "Wait, what's that? Oh, no. Mikey. Bicyclists. Remember them from before?"

Mikey saw them, too and stiffened. Still, he didn't want to ruin the happy mood. "I think it's going to be alright, Skeet. Ruth is with us this time. Let's see what happens. Maybe we should say Mamma's words."

Noticing her friends' mood change and the approaching bicyclists, Ruth reined the dogs in to her a little more closely. "It's okay, guys. Just heel. Mikey, heel. Skeeter, heel." the bicyclists rolled closer.

Skeeter and Mikey exchanged glances. "Did she just say heel?" said Mikey.

"I, I, I think so," said Skeeter nervously.

"Well, we can do that, Skeet. You take the inside next to Ruth and I'll take the outside. If they give us any trouble, I've got us covered."

Skeeter gulped. Bicycles had been used at the First House by the neighborhood kids to chase her. Some of the neighborhood children had tried to run her down. "C'mon, guys. Just keep going. You'll be okay. I promise. Mikey, heel. Skeeter, heel." Ruth interrupted Skeeter's train of thought.

"Don't get angry, don't panic, don't bite," Skeeter chanted, nestled safely between her brother and Ruth.

"Good job, guys, good job!" Ruth exclaimed as the bicycles passed, both dogs managing to maintain their cool.

"Wow, Mikey, that was close, but did you see how Ruth handled those bikers? She just looked at them and they kept on going, right past us. They didn't turn and chase us or anything."

That was pretty cool," said Mikey. "Skeeter, check out this smell. Don't you wish Sister Mary was here to tell us what it is?" Mikey mused.

"That'd be nice, but maybe we can just remember it and ask her when we get home. Stick your paw on it so we can show her later. This trail is fun," said Skeeter.

"Here we go again, guys. More bicycles," interrupted Ruth. "Mikey, heel, Skeeter, heel. Just like before."

"C'mon, Skeet. We got this," said Mikey, trying to be confident. He ducked a little as the bikes went by this time. They were too close for his comfort but he held his ground.

The trail stretched on like that for hours. With every passing bicycle, runner, or hiker, their confidence increased, and the threesome's collective joy of the moment was magnified tenfold. By the time they returned to the truck, hot, hungry, and tired, all three friends were elated. They'd done it – a quiet, long, uneventful walk in the park, completely incident-free.

Riding home in the back of the car together, Skeeter put her head over her brother's shoulders sleepily, enjoying the comfort of his support. "Do you think this is how Boyo and Sister Mary felt after they went hiking, Mikey?"

"I dunno. Probably. It was awesome walking with you today, Sis. I'm really glad we did this."

"Mikey, did you see Ruth stare down those runners when they went by?"

Mikey laughed, "I had planned to just let them go, but I think Ruth thought they were too close!"

"I know, and Mikey, did you get a good pawful of the that stuff we smelled on the trail? We have to run that by Sister Mary. I bet she'll know exactly what it was."

Mikey was starting to fall asleep, happily listening to his younger sister. It had been a perfect day, filled with exercise, sunshine, companionship, adventure. Riding in the car, with Ruth at the wheel and Skeeter by his side, was heaven. The only thing that would have made it better, he thought, would be if Sister Mary and Max had shared their fun. He knew Sister Mary could not have made the hike, but maybe one day Max would join them too, just like he had with Boyo and Sister Mary.

It had been one year to the day since their ordeal had begun. Mikey hadn't mentioned it to Skeeter. Why ruin her perfect day by bringing up the past? Back then, he could only imagine a day like today. When Impound Man showed up at their First House and forcibly removed him, Mamma and Skeeter, he had yearned for a day like this for his sister. He had had no expectation of such a day for himself.

Funny, riding in the car now, thinking about the Before Time didn't summon the usual ghosts, just sad and fading memories. Yawning contentedly, Mikey looked up at his reflection in the window with satisfaction before looking over at Skeeter. Mikey smiled sleepily. "Hey, Skeet."

"Yeah, Mikey?"

"I'm pretty sure now," he said yawning.

"Sure about what?"

"I'm pretty sure…" and with that he drifted off to sleep, stretching out the full length of the car bed, back to back with his sister. Skeeter cocked her head and wondered at Mikey's unfinished thought. Oh, well, she thought, as she too drifted off to sleep. Sure was a better day today than it was last year.

Chapter 34

"Sister Mary? Sister Mary? Were you and Boyo ever scared about anything?" asked Skeeter one day as she sat in her crate waiting for Ruth and Max to return home. "You told us all about the Fourth of July and Christmas parties but, I'm talking about other stuff, like, people, feet, bicycles, crowds, you know."

"Yeah, Sister Mary, was Boyo ever afraid of anything?" asked Mikey, putting his head on his paws thoughtfully. Sister Mary smiled at her young charges, who were clearly fishing for a story.

Settling into her spot comfortably and knowing the point they were driving at, Sister Mary replied, "Boyo, not so much. I've told you before, that guy loved people. Never met a person he didn't like, and he certainly wasn't afraid of any human being. Come to think of it, I don't think he was afraid of anything except the occasional strange dog, but I've told you about that. Me? Now, that's a different story. Like you two, I didn't exactly come to this family knowing how to deal with people and it took me a while to figure them out, especially men."

Skeeter blinked her eyes in appreciation of that thought. "Sister Mary, I know. I just don't get how human men operate. They wear these big shoes and walk really heavy and they talk so loud and growly, and that's when they're not even mad or anything."

"So how'd you stop being afraid of them, Sister Mary? What's the trick?" interrupted the impatient Mikey.

"You know, there really wasn't a trick. It just became the sum of all things. One day they scared the heck out of me and then, well they just didn't."

Mikey wasn't satisfied with that answer, "Oh, c'mon, Sister Mary, that can't be it."

"Really, it's true. Think about it Mikey, when you and I first met, every time something would happen, you'd think it was a threat. Or you thought Ruth and Max were going to send you back. Now you don't. Skeeter, you used to think every time Max lifted his foot he was going to kick you. Now you don't."

Mikey had to think about that one. Sister Mary had a point. The ghosts with their drums and buzzing of months past had significantly subsided. They weren't gone, but they no longer took over his mind on such a routine basis. Still, he wasn't satisfied with Sister Mary's explanation. "But Sister Mary," he pressed, "how did you know? Was there a time, a moment, when you knew?"

"Knew what?" asked Sister Mary who, having momentarily forgotten the story, had been nodding off to sleep.

"Knew that you weren't afraid?" asked the exasperated Mikey.

Sister Mary looked at her friends. She really didn't have an answer for them. For her, the journey from fearful to confident had been long and slow, and her fears had seemed to dissipate slowly, imperceptibly, melt away. Thinking back on it, though, maybe it had not been as random a journey as she thought. Maybe there was something she could offer that would be of use to

Mikey and Skeeter on their journey. Looking up and stirring herself to her feet, Sister Mary looked around at both of her friends and declared, "Ruth. Yes. Ruth and Boyo. No, actually, Ruth, Boyo, and Max."

Skeeter flapped her ears in exasperation. "No, Sister Mary, we're not afraid of Ruth. We've got that one. And Boyo's not here and we all know you're not afraid of Max. We're talking about other men and other stuff. And when, how, did you know not to be afraid?"

After giving herself a full body shake and a stretch, Sister Mary settled back down into her waiting spot. "I know, child, but the answer to getting over your fears of men lies with Ruth and Max and, now, me, the same way for me it once began with Ruth and Max and Boyo, and being afraid was just something that got lost, forgotten almost over time."

Skeeter cocked her head inquisitively. "What d'you mean?"

"It's like this. Years ago when Boyo and I were Mikey's age, we lived in a townhouse in the city..."

"We know, we know," interrupted Skeeter, striking her paw at her crate with impatience.

"Well, what you don't know is that for the first two months I did everything I could go get out of there and go back to my First Place."

Skeeter and Mikey blinked in amazement. "But why?" Mikey exclaimed.

"Seriously, Sister Mary, what were you thinking?" asked Skeeter incredulously.

Sister Mary smiled knowingly. "Remember, my First Place was not so bad: I lived in the country, lots of room, my family all around, and I never had to deal with men before. Suddenly, I was living in a cramped space with the ever-boisterous Boyo and the loud Max. The city life was too much. Too many people, too many strange dogs, cars, and every time we went for a walk, everyone and everything on the path seemed to jump out at me. Kids, skateboards, cooing strangers with outstretched hands. No, at first I liked Ruth just fine, but not enough to stay with her. Max I liked, but only from a distance. Boyo just got on my nerves. No, I wanted to go home, period."

"So what'd you do?" asked Skeeter, still not believing anyone would want to leave Ruth.

"Well, one day, as Max was leaving the house to go to work, I pushed through the door past him and went for it. I just ran, as hard and fast as I could."

"Wow! How'd you know where to go?" asked Mikey.

"Mikey, do you remember how you watched out the window on the drive home from Shelter Lady's, trying to memorize the way? I watched you that day. Well, I did the same thing on my first ride home. I thought I had it memorized, every road, intersection, and waypoint home. I thought it would be a snap."

"So what happened, Sister Mary?" asked Skeeter, squirming in her crate anxiously, hoping Sister Mary would get on with her story and to the point.

"At first it started out just as I imagined. I ran down the road, straight for home. I ran hard and fast at first, hoping to put as much distance as I could between me and Max and Boyo. I kept to the sidewalk and then found the power lines where I could just keep going. Once I got off the road and knew I was out of Max's sight, I slowed to a jog and really enjoyed myself. Oh, the sounds and smells of freedom. It was wonderful. But, as the miles went on, I got tired. I started thinking about Ruth and Boyo and Max, and then I thought about my family who I supposed was waiting for me back at my First Place. My thoughts kept flipping back and forth between them as I trotted along.

Eventually, I got to a really big highway with an endless stream of cars and trucks, four lanes of them going in each direction. I knew that if I was going to get back to my First Place I had to get across that road. I'd made a mental note of it on the ride to Ruth and Max's. I just had to get my timing right, I figured. But the lights of the cars and trucks were dizzying. Boy, they were fast. So, I decided I'd wait it out and see whether they would slack off with time. Night came. As I paced back and forth on the side of the road, a couple of cars came screeching to a stop right behind me. Another car came stopped in front of me. I had ducked under a fence to get out on to the road, but I couldn't remember where the hole was, so I was trapped.

"A really big, but kind-looking man jumped out of his truck and held out a piece of hot dog. I hadn't eaten anything all day and it smelled really good."

"I love hot dogs," said Mikey thoughtfully, putting his head between his paws.

"I know. I'm a sucker for them too," said Sister Mary, remembering the man on the side of the road.

"The point, Sister Mary, get to the point," said Skeeter impatiently. She was looking for wisdom and so far she'd only gotten a story with a man and a hot dog on the side of a busy highway.

"Right. Anyway, as soon as I stuck out my head to get the hot dog, he took ahold of my collar and wouldn't let go. He wasn't mean or anything, but he was not letting go. By then, the people from the other cars had gotten out and had me surrounded. I was tired and decided I'd figure out the road crossing some other day, so I gave up and let him catch me."

"Why didn't you bite him?" asked Mikey.

"I don't know. Unlike some dogs I know, I never really saw the point in biting someone who was handing me a hot dog, I guess." Sister Mary took the opportunity to make a gentle poke at her friend.

"But then what happened, Sister Mary? We were talking about how you aren't afraid anymore," interrupted Skeeter. "Stop talking about hot dogs and get to the point!"

"Well, a couple of things. First, the man took me back to his house. I didn't like it there. Nothing wrong with him, but I just didn't like the smell of it. I started thinking about Ruth and Max and Boyo's house and it didn't seem so bad. I thought of their sofa, Ruth's cooking, the nice mat that I slept on next to Boyo at night. It all seemed pretty good, now that I'd had some time to think about it. So I paced and whined all night to let the man know that I didn't want to stay. The next morning, he took me home to Max and Ruth."

"What happened then?" asked Mikey, curious about Max's reaction in particular. "Were you in trouble?"

"Well, it was the strangest thing. When I got back to the house, I found Max on the phone, pacing, his face and his eyes all red, and when he saw me, he caught his breath and hugged me. He was so relieved to see me. He said so. He thanked and thanked the man, and held on to me for all he was worth. I was still pretty tired and scared…"

"Why were you scared, Sister Mary?" interrupted Skeeter, hoping that Sister Mary would finally get to the point.

"Riding in the strange man's car on the way home, I realized that I had no idea where he was taking me. I was afraid we would end up at the Impound, I'd heard stories about that from other dogs. I was afraid that I'd never see either of my families again. I got to thinking about the road and the night before. I could have been killed on that road. And the more I thought of it, the more I realized that running away had been a huge mistake. If the man took me back to Max and Ruth's, would they still want me? I had been pretty awful, to Max especially. I wouldn't even let him feed me. I'd destroyed things, hidden from him, and now I'd run away. What if he and Ruth just got rid of me?"

Mikey and Skeeter trembled, remembering the Impound of their past.

"So, anyway," continued Sister Mary, "seeing Max and the way he greeted me, I didn't know what to think, and I had no idea where Ruth and Boyo were. The doors to the townhouse were all open, in the middle of the winter. So after the man left, I went upstairs into Ruth's closet, where she kept her laundry in a big pile. It looked and smelled warm and nice so I decided to wait there for whatever was going to happen next. I could hear Max shutting the doors downstairs and pacing for a while. He checked on me from time to time, and after about an hour, I could hear Ruth and Boyo come in."

"What happened then? Were you in trouble then?" asked Skeeter.

"No. Not even close. When I heard Ruth gasp when she learned that I was home, and when she called my name, so softly and gently, in that moment, I just knew."

"Knew what?" asked Mikey, shifting in his crate and studying his old friend's face for its customary joke or punch line. But there was no joke or punch line this time.

Sister Mary continued, not hearing her friends' questions, lost in her own train of thought. "I heard her voice calling my name, so gentle and kind, so I crept down the stairs and saw Ruth standing with her back to the door facing me. Her face and her

259

eyes were as red as Max's had been. She melted to the floor when she saw me, so I ran to her. We must have sat there for an hour. She held me, crying, shaking. I was crying and shaking. Oh, we were a mess. I think even Max and Boyo cried. Boyo was so glad to see me. He was bouncing all over, knocking into me and Ruth, running back to Max, then back to me and Ruth. It was quite a scene. We were all so relieved.

And in that moment, I got it. I knew right then that these people and Boyo were my family, my Forever Home. I knew that I would probably never see my first family again. Somehow, they'd have to make it without me. Somehow, I would have to make it with my new family, my Forever Family. How could I leave Ruth with her holding me like that? And how could I do that to Max again? And you know, I think Ruth and Max must have decided the same thing. That day, we all decided to try harder."

"You see, to overcome your fear, you and your people have to decide that you've found Forever Home. Once you've done that, you've started. I won't pretend it was easy, but once you've decided and started, then you know it's worth it."

Mikey put his head back on his paws in thought, remembering the ride home from the recent hike. Sister Mary was on to something, he thought.

"So what happened next, Sister Mary?" asked Skeeter.

"Ruth, helped me see the world through her eyes. Remember your first day in school, Skeeter? Remember how overwhelming that was?"

"Sure do!" gulped Skeeter.

"Well, it was for me, too. I didn't want to go in. Ruth had to convince me it was safe. And Boyo, he became my friend. I'd been hard on him too. But he was always there for me. There I'd be, hiding behind Ruth's legs when we'd go on a walk and a stranger would approach and he'd say, 'Don't worry Sis, I'll take this treat for you.' When we went on walks, he always stayed next to me. I could go anywhere safely between Boyo and Ruth."

"Just like you and Ruth on our walk, right Mikey?" piped Skeeter from her spot on the floor.

"But, Sister Mary, you also said Max. How did Max help you?" asked Mikey, now focusing more on the point of Sister Mary's story than his distracting sister.

Sister Mary smiled, remembering. "Max never gave up on me, and boy, did I give him lots of reasons. I tried that poor man about as much as you two have. He'd come into a room. I'd leave. For a while he'd come onto the floor and I'd leave. He was upstairs, I was downstairs. Ruth would go away and I'd go on a hunger strike."

"Funny thing is, I actually liked him. I would watch him from under a table or from the top of the stairs and think, 'What is wrong with me?' Boyo thought the world of him and I'd watch them play and really wanted to join in, but the minute he looked at me I'd tuck my tail and skedaddle. Usually he'd try to make friends with me, but he never did it quite right. Something always set me off. I'd see the pain in his face and I'd vow to try again, and I did. Again and again. Eventually, I just got used to his ways and realized they were just different from Ruth's. Not bad, just different."

Skeeter sat up and looked at her ancient friend thoughtfully. Scratching her head again, she asked, "When he wasn't acting right, why didn't you just bite him?"

Sister Mary shook her head in exasperation, "Child, have you learned nothing? Biting only gets you put in your crate, or worse."

"Oh yeah, I forgot," said Skeeter contritely and laying back down to think.

"Do not ever forget that lesson, Skeeter. It is one of the most important ones you've learned. And another thing. For all of the stuff that I put that man through, he never once, not once, not ever laid a hand – or foot – on me in anger. That counts for a lot, children. He can bellow with the best of them. We all know that. Everyone has to have a way to express themselves. But he never ever struck, or kicked."

Mikey and Skeeter lay back down in their crates. Sister Mary had given them a lot to think about.

Chapter 35

"C'mon, guys. It's time to take another hike," Ruth announced one morning.

"Where we going, Sister Mary? Are you coming with us this time?" asked Skeeter.

"No idea where, Skeet. But, judging from her preparations, one bottle of water, dog snacks but no people snacks, not far. I think she just wants to get some air. I'll stay here. You guys can keep her company just fine." Sister Mary adjusted herself into her usual spot in the center of the kitchen.

Skeeter and Mikey laid down on either side of her. "You sure, Sister Mary?" asked Mikey, looking fondly at his old mentor, and giving her an affectionate nuzzle on her head.

"I'm sure. You guys go on without me. Tell me all about it when you come back."

"C'mon, guys. Let's go. Bye-bye, Sister Mary. We'll see you in a while," said Ruth as she gave Sister Mary a pat, snapped on her young friends' leashes and headed out the door. "We're going someplace new," she said, "not too far away this time."

After about an hour, Ruth pulled the car into a parking spot and out spilled Skeeter and Mikey. It was a hot summer morning. The park was one of Ruth's favorites, but this particular spot was new to her. The map indicated that the trail went along the river for a few miles and then crossed the river and returned on the other side. A perfect loop, she thought.

The trail was spectacular, one of the area's best unknown gems. It rambled along the river and was filled with green. Lots of green. Ruth, Mikey, and Skeeter breathed deeply, enjoying the fresh, clean air. "Wow, Mikey, this is awesome!" exclaimed Skeeter as they walked through the welcoming woods.

"C'mon guys, we need to cross this stream," interrupted Ruth. They'd come to a wide crossing where the stream ran swiftly. It was something Mikey and Skeeter had never seen before.

"What do we do, Mikey?" asked Skeeter, peering at the stream curiously.

"I dunno," said Mikey, dipping his paw in the water and giving it a good sniff. "It seems okay."

I say we follow Ruth," said Skeeter, putting both feet in the water. Seeing no real problem, Mikey did the same.

A few minutes later into the walk, the trio heard barking and yelling ahead. "What's going on, Mikey?" asked Skeeter.

"I dunno. Let's see what Ruth thinks." Mikey looked expectantly at Ruth, who had also heard the barking and yelling.

Seeing her friends looking up at her questioningly, Ruth answered, "I don't know either, guys. The cover is too dense in here to tell for sure. Let's just keep going and see what happens." The threesome continued walking, enjoying the scenery, but right as the trail narrowed to single file, out burst a single loose dog, followed by a stream of people in hot pursuit.

"Hey! Hi!" exclaimed the dog. "I'm exercising my people through the woods! We've been in the river and over the hill and, well, everywhere!" He danced and wiggled on the path in front of them.

Skeeter and Mikey stared at the strange dog in wonder. Where had he come from? What should they do? One thing was for certain – they were staying with Ruth.

The people came pouring up the trail after the errant dog. He jumped into Skeeter and Mikey's pack. "Can I hang out with you? I might be in trouble," he asked, tucking his tail.

"No way! Stick with your own humans!" exclaimed Mikey, pushing the dog back onto the trail with his nose.

"Yeah, you should go back to your people. They look tired," said Skeeter, seeing the concerned faces approaching.

"Oh, we're so sorry. We had no idea you guys were here," said one of the people to Ruth as they emerged from the brush onto the trail. "Let us just get our buddy here and we'll be on our way. Hey, you, where were you going anyway?" they exclaimed with relief as they retrieved their exuberant dog.

"Well, see ya, bye!" he wagged as he brushed past Skeeter and Mikey and headed back down the trail in the opposite direction.

"Bye!" said Skeeter, relieved that the people had left and the dog was out of her way. "Whew! Mikey, that was close," she said later as they trotted down the path.

"I know, Skeet, but did you see Ruth? She never batted an eye and just pulled us out of the way. Those people never could have touched us. Did you see that?"

"Yup. And she gave us treats, Mikey, treats!"

Hours later, cooling off in the back of the car, Skeeter snuggled up next to her brother contentedly. "Hey, Mikey, did you see how I jumped over that big log today?"

"Yeah, sure, of course. Did you see how I pointed Ruth to the right path when she got lost?"

Skeeter laughed, "Thank goodness you did, Mikey. I was beginning to think we were going to keep going in circles for hours!"

"I know. Sister Mary warned me about that as we walked out the door. Apparently, Ruth doesn't have a great sense of direction."

"Speaking of Sister Mary, do you remember the smell of that thing we smelled?"

"You mean the thing in the bush that we couldn't figure out? Yeah, I remember that. Let's ask her when we get home," said Mikey, cleaning some of the mud off of his paws.

Chapter 36

September came, and with it the return of school. With Mikey having graduated from the beginner basic class to the advanced basic class, and Max unable to take off work in time to attend the earlier evening session, the two dogs had to alternate school nights with Ruth.

As Mikey jumped in the car for his first night of heeling class, he could hear Skeeter and Sister Mary wishing him luck and he hoped to have a good story to tell them when he returned. "C'mon, Mikey, let's get in there and show them how much you've learned over the summer," said Ruth as she clipped on Mikey's leash.

Entering the school, Mikey took in the quiet cadence of the advanced classes, already in session at either end of the building. Dogs and their handlers were all working together, no barking, no fussing, everyone practicing their communication skills at increasingly sophisticated levels.

Looking up at Ruth, Mikey hoped that one day they would be able to work together like that, in rhythm, seamlessly. It looked so orderly, he thought. Catching her friend's look, Ruth gave Mikey a pat on the head and a scratch on the chin. "C'mon, Mikey, let's

267

get warmed up," she said, and the two began working the basic patterns of obedience work: heel, sit, stay, heel, down, and so on.

Soon, Mikey's other class members arrived. Some he recognized, like the ditzy Doberman, and the hardworking retriever. Others he did not. But like he and Ruth, each team earnestly wanted to attain that level of communication that would send them on to the next group.

"Okay, everybody. Before we get started, any problems or concerns? Everybody doing okay?" The Instructor started the class as he always did. "All right, let's get going. Forward!"

"Mikey, heel," said Ruth, briskly taking off in the direction of the other dogs. Mikey liked her pace. Trotting along next to her, he looked up from time to time to confirm that Ruth was satisfied with it as well. "Good, boy, Mikey, good heel." She said as they marched around the ring.

"Halt. Leave your dogs."

"Mikey, Sit. Stay. Good stay," Ruth stepped out to the end of the leash and faced Mikey.

The Instructor walked around the room as the dogs sat, weaving between and among the dogs and pausing from time to time to chat with the handler. Mikey held Ruth's gaze as the Instructor walked by, invading the space that previously would have caused Mikey's head to buzz. Ruth smiled as the Instructor passed. Mikey didn't move a muscle. "Good stay, Mikey, good stay."

"Return to your dogs."

Ruth gave Mikey a pat on his head and a gentle squeeze as she returned to the heel position. "Good boy!" she said. Mikey loved the sound of Ruth's voice.

"Everybody just relax and we'll do the stand for examination exercise one at a time. Let's start with you, Ruth," said the Instructor.

"Mikey stand, good, stay." Ruth took a tentative step backwards.

"That's far enough for now. Just stay where you are." The Instructor approached Mikey. "How's he doing? How's he getting along with Max these days?"

"He's doing much better. They both are," answered Ruth, keeping a careful eye on Mikey.

Mikey studied the Instructor carefully. He wanted to like him, but he still wasn't sure. Focusing on the exercise and shifting his gaze back to Ruth, Mikey quietly repeated to himself, "Don't get angry, don't panic, don't bite."

Having respectfully entered his space, the Instructor offered Mikey the back of his hand to sniff and walked casually past him. Staying focused on Ruth and seeing her eyes fill with approval, Mikey held his ground and his nerve. "Don't get angry, don't panic, don't bite."

"That's great, Ruth. Give me a treat and let me see if I can give it to him without losing my fingers," joked the Instructor. "There you go, good boy." Mikey quietly accepted the treat.

"Good boy! That's a good boy, Mikey!" effused Ruth. Mikey relaxed. That exercise was finished for the night, he thought.

The energy in the room changed suddenly. A loud, shrill whistle, followed by "H*eeling class in two minutes! Two minutes, everybody!*" filled the space. Both noises came from a very loud and very tall man at the other end of the room. Ruth suppressed a giggle as Mikey broke his stay in alarm. "No worries, Mikey.

That's just his way. You'll get used to him, too. He won't hurt you."

"Yeah, right," thought Mikey. Just as long as he keeps his distance. Sure enough, two minutes later, here was Mr. Loud Man, banging a chair and pushing himself into the center of the ring where Mikey's class had been working quietly. No one seemed to care, not even Ruth. Other dogs from other classes came into the circle and joined them, stepping smartly around Mr. Loud Man. Glancing up at Ruth, Mikey couldn't believe what he saw. She looked happy! Almost everyone, dogs and people, looked happy! Hmm, he wondered, was this the guy Sister Mary and Skeeter were talking about?

"Left about turn! Circle *right!*" fired Mr. Loud Man.

"Mikey, heel! Good boy, Mikey. Good boy!"

"Circle *left!*"

"Mikey heel, good boy."

"H*alt! Leave your dog!*"

"Stay," said Ruth as she stepped away from Mikey confidently. Mr. Loud Man walked through the dogs as had the Instructor, only faster and louder. He carried a bottle filled with pebbles that he shook and tossed around like a toy. Mikey was mystified. No one, not a single person or dog seemed to think there was anything strange or inappropriate with Mr. Loud Man's behavior. "Good stay, Mikey, good stay," beamed Ruth as Mr. Loud Man passed behind Mikey.

"R*eturn to your dogs and give them lots of praise,*" ordered Mr. Loud Man. Ruth didn't need to be told that last bit. She was already giving Mikey a hug for hanging in there on his stay.

"*Forward!*"

"Mikey, heel."

"*Fast!*"

"Mikey, heel."

"D*own your dog!*"

"Mikey…"

"*Forward!*"

"Oops, Mikey, Mikey, heel!" said Ruth, laughing as she missed the command.

"S*tand your dogs!*"

"Mikey, stand."

"T*ell your dogs to stay and step out the full length of the lead. Do not let them move!*"

As Mr. Loud Man approached Mikey, Ruth reminded him, "Just watch him. Remember, he's a bit nervous with strange men."

Mr. Loud Man understood and slowed his pace down so that Mikey could take it all in. Don't get angry, don't panic, don't bite, Mikey thought, steeling his nerves as Mr. Loud Man approached. "Good dog," Loud Man said quietly as he showed Mikey the back of his hand. He then moved on. "We'll do the full exam some other time. That was good for now." Give him lots of praise, Ruth, lots of praise."

"Way to go, Mikey! Good boy!" effused Ruth. Mikey exhaled and accepted Ruth's applause and the treat she had at the ready.

"*Forward!*" and the class continued the drill.

Trotting around the room next to her, weaving between other dog and handler teams Mikey looked up at Ruth. She seemed to be having a good time. Maybe she was right. Mr. Loud Man was just, well, loud. He'd reserve judgment.

Max, Skeeter, and Sister Mary eagerly greeted Mikey and Ruth when they returned. "How'd it go, Mikey?" asked Sister Mary as he bounded into the room.

"Did you meet Mr. Loud Man?" Skeeter teased her brother, jumping playfully at him as he came through the door.

"Wow! Did I ever! You guys were right! What a voice!"

"I know!" said Skeeter, jumping over Sister Mary and giving Mikey a shove, "and he's tall!"

"I know!" said Mikey, returning the shove.

"Did you bite him?" asked Sister Mary with a smile, ducking as Mikey jumped over her. She was sure she knew the answer already, seeing Ruth's grin when she walked in the door, but she wanted to be certain that both dogs understood that lesson.

"Nope. I just kept repeating Mamma's words, Sister Mary, and before I knew it, the whole thing was over and Ruth was giving me another treat."

"Even on the stand for examination, Mikey? Did you stand?" asked Skeeter, her eyes wide with wonder.

"Even on the stand for examination. It was really hard. He came right up to us, but I did it, Skeet, and nothing bad happened and Ruth was really, really happy. I could tell."

Later that night, with all dogs tucked into their positions on the sofa next to Ruth, Sister Mary smiled. She remembered the days she and Boyo had swapped tales from their obedience school classes. Boyo had had another name for Mr. Loud Man though. What was it? Oh yeah, Funny Dave. Boyo had enjoyed his boisterousness. Sister Mary shook her head, remembering. Sometimes her old friend had been a mystery.

Chapter 37

Mikey got up from the floor by Ruth's chair, stretched, and yawned. Ruth had been at her desk most of the day. Skeeter was under her Chair of Invisibility, sound asleep. Sister Mary was stretched out at Ruth's feet, also sleeping. It was far too quiet he thought; time to play Ball. Leaping up onto Ruth's lap and pushing her hands away from the keyboard with his nose, Mikey gave Ruth a friendly nuzzle. "C'mon, Ruth. Let's get going," he said, wagging his tail softly.

Ruth looked at the clock and smiled. "It looks like you are taking over the timekeeping job, huh, boy?" she said, scratching his belly.

Mikey leaned into her and tried again. "Let's go, Ruth. I'm bored!"

"All right, all right, Mikey. Let's go." Ruth got up from her chair and headed for the door.

"Wake up, ladies! It's time to play Ball!" announced Mikey as he headed toward the stairway. Skeeter immediately jumped up, practically knocking over the Chair of Invisibility.

"I didn't think the time would ever get here!"

Hearing her two young friends bouncing and barking, Sister Mary was roused from her slumber. She had been dreaming about splashing in a stream with Boyo years ago. "What time is it?" she asked, looking around, still not quite awake.

"Sister Mary, it's Ball time!" exclaimed Skeeter.

"Yeah, Sis, hurry up, let's go!" barked Mikey, wagging his tail and bowing in front of her.

"Oh, yes, yes, Ball. Good. Let's play Ball." Sister Mary pulled herself up stiffly and headed for the doorway.

"C'mon Sister Mary, let me give you a lift down the stairs," said Ruth, picking up her friend gently and carrying her. Of course, by the time Ruth got to the bottom, Mikey and Skeeter had been up the stairs and down the stairs and to the ball cabinet several times.

Once she was put back on the floor, Sister Mary was fully awake and ready for Ball too, and joined her friends in their cheerful chant as Ruth made her way to the cabinet.

"Play Ball! Play Ball!" they all cheered.

Ball had changed over the last couple of months. After Mikey's introduction to the take-it-bring-it-drop-it-leave-it game, Ball became more simplified, more structured. Three balls, not twenty, were in play. Sister Mary, who always recovered and claimed the second ball thrown, was now the referee. She took the inner circle track and monitored Skeeter and Mikey for missed balls and personal fouls. Mikey was the catcher and lead runner. Skeeter was the seeker and second runner, finding balls for everyone if a ball bounced where it could not be found. Skeeter also was the backstop, stopping the ball Mikey dropped and informing Ruth with her nose and paw as to which ball was to be thrown.

"C'mon, Ruth, throw ball! Throw ball! Throw ball!" chanted the three dogs from the top of the porch steps.

"I'm coming, I'm coming! You guys have to make way!"
Ruth pushed her way forward through the excited pack. "Here
you go. Ball one!"

The ball flew and everybody pursued. Sister Mary did her
best to get to the scrum before any fouls were committed. Skeeter
arrested the ball, left it in place and returned to Ruth with Mikey
hot on her heels. "Ball two!" The second ball flew. This time,
Mikey returned with the ball, dropping it at Ruth's feet. "Ball
three!" Skeeter and Mikey took off full speed after ball three and
Sister Mary grabbed the second ball before heading out to referee
Mikey and Skeeter.

Next ball. "I got it! I got it!" exclaimed Mikey as he and
Skeeter thundered across the yard.

"Good catch, Mikey!" said Skeeter, catching up to him.

"Way to go, kid, right on the first bounce!" cheered Sister
Mary.

"I got it!" charged Mikey as he powered across the yard.
"Watch this! I can put some swizzle on it!" he said as he leaped
into the air, caught the ball and then tossed it back for another
bounce.

"Wow, Mikey!" cheered the girls. Mikey ran back to Ruth
and dropped the ball somewhere near her feet.

"I got it!" said Skeeter as the ball started to roll away.
"There you go, Ruth. I stopped it right here for you," she said as
she bumped the ball with her nose.

"Wait, wait. I'm not sure you gave her the right one, Skeet,"
said Sister Mary, ambling up to her friends. "Let me check and
make sure." She put her ball down to investigate. "Is it this one?
Or that one? Yep. It's this one." She pushed the proper ball in
Ruth's direction and backed away to give her two young friends
room to spin and run.

And so the game went, back and forth, back and forth, until the dogs were happy and spent. After the throwing came the game of tricks, or as Sister Mary called it, "Steal-it."

"Sister Mary, Sister Mary! Watch me run around with my ball!" bounced Skeeter, circling Sister Mary playfully.

"Oh, child, you do cut a fine form like that. I'm just going to lie down here and chew my ball. You go on, run and play if you like," said Sister Mary lowering herself to the ground.

"But Sister Mary, let me have your ball and then I can run around with two balls!"

"No, one ball's enough for you. Mind your own business."

"How about if I take your ball, Sister Mary," said Mikey.

"How about you guys leave Sister Mary alone," said Ruth, who had seen a steal setting up and walked over to give Sister Mary some backup.

"Hey, Ruth, how about you take my ball and give me a biscuit?" said Sister Mary, looking up at Ruth hopefully. It was part of her plan. Ruth reached down and put her hand out for Sister Mary, who gently but firmly deposited her ball into Ruth's outstretched hand, careful that one of the two youngsters didn't make a surprise steal and end up with two balls. "There, now you two kids don't pay any attention to me." She munched on her biscuit with a sly smile on her face.

"Hey, Mikey, betcha can't catch me with my ball," sassed Skeeter.

"Bet I can," said Mikey, taking off after Skeeter.

"Betcha can't." Skeeter circled back around toward Sister Mary.

"Bet I can. Hold on, I gotta put my ball here," said Mikey, getting ready to give serious chase. Sister Mary went in for the steal. "Hey! Sister Mary! No fair!" exclaimed Mikey, realizing he'd been had. Sister Mary had stolen his ball.

"Good teamwork, Skeet. Maybe I'll share my biscuit with you next time," laughed Sister Mary as she quickly handed the stolen ball off to Ruth in return for another biscuit.

Seeing that her brother was not amused, Skeeter put her ball down and pushed it toward him, "Oh, Mikey, don't pout. Here, you can have my ball."

"Funny trick, ladies. Real funny." Mikey grabbed Skeeter's ball and trotted off with it.

"All right, come on Mikey. Time to give up that ball too," said Ruth.

"But I don't want to give up this ball. I won it fair and square," "Besides, if I put it down, one of the girls will just steal it again."

Seeing her friend's conundrum, Ruth offered him a way out. "C'mon Mikey. Let's you and I go inside. You can give me the ball there. Let's go." Mikey thought that sounded fair, so in he went. "Skeeter, you stay outside," said Ruth closing the door behind them.

"Thanks Ruth," said Mikey dropping the ball at her feet and looking up at her for his biscuit.

"There you go. Ok, let's go back outside and cool off a bit before dinner."

Once outside, Mikey dropped into the cool grass. "Ahh, that was another great game, ladies!" he said as he rubbed his back into the grass, grinning ear to ear.

Skeeter took a couple more turns around the yard, playfully bouncing and pouncing on sticks and bugs, giggling. "Hey, Sister Mar Mar, that was a good call you made earlier, and did you see how I did the fake with Mikey? That was some fun, huh?"

"Sure was, child, sure was. You're really getting some moves." She enjoyed watching "the kids" play. Sure, it brought back memories, but seeing Skeeter and Mikey laughing and enjoying themselves, relaxed and happy, really warmed her heart. They'd come a long way over the last nine months. What adventures they would have together, she thought contentedly.

Chapter 38

Sister Mary woke with a cough. The morning was still young and she could see the prone forms of Ruth, Skeeter and Max fast asleep on the bed. Looking across the floor, she could see Mikey, stretched out full body style on the mat next to her. She liked his company there. She coughed again, clearing her lungs of the fluid that had accumulated there overnight. "You okay, Sis?" asked Mikey sleepily.

"Ahh-hem, ah-hem, yes, dear, I'm fine. Just need to clear my throat a bit," She raised herself up to see if that would help. "Maybe I should get a drink of water."

Watching Sister Mary struggle to her feet, Mikey worried. "You sure, Sis? You don't look so fine."

"Ahh-hem, ahh-hem, cough, yes. Really, I'm fine. A drink of water is all I need," Sister Mary insisted.

Listening carefully from their spots in bed, Ruth, Max and Skeeter were worried too. Sister Mary had been having coughing bouts frequently in the morning. They never lasted long, but their growing frequency, every morning and again before she went to sleep at night, seemed ominous.

Checking her calendar that morning, Ruth decided that a trip to the vet was in order for everyone. The kids needed their annual shots and she would have Sister Mary given extra attention. Unwisely, she scheduled all three dogs for the same time the same day. Luckily, Max volunteered to help handle them.

Entering the vet's office, Skeeter and Mikey were immediately on alert. Other dogs in the waiting room, anxiously waiting their turns, looked at them expectantly. The smell of disinfectant and medications permeated the air, mixing with the smell of frightened cats and dogs.

"Oh, no Mikey! It's *that* place," exclaimed Skeeter in alarm.

"I know, Skeet. Why are we here? We haven't done anything wrong," questioned Mikey, the drums starting to roll in his head. He hadn't heard them in weeks, but the strange yet familiar look and smell of the office brought back memories for him. Memories of pinching, pulling, struggling.

Mikey looked around to Sister Mary for guidance and to his utter astonishment found her completely serene. Sister Mary entered the building as if she owned the place, smiling, confident, even happy. To her, the welcome sound of the friendly and gentle staff calling out to her from behind their posts, the smell of candles, the kind people who always took care of her all gave her a reason to smile and offer a welcome bark. "Hello, people; hello other dogs," she wagged.

"But Sister Mary, don't you know where you are?" asked Mikey, mouth agape and panting nervously.

Sister Mary looked at her friends quizzically. "Of course I do. I'm at the spa."

"The what?" exclaimed Skeeter, looking around the room for an escape exit.

"The spa, the spa. Ruth brings me here from time to time. Nice people look over me and if there's something wrong they fix it. Before you guys came along they brought me here a lot. A nice lady would sit on the floor with me and wave a magic wand around my body. Oh, boy, did that feel good. I hope that is what we're here for today. I could use a good wanding."

Mikey and Skeeter looked at each other in disbelief. "A magic wand, Mikey, really? Do you believe that?" whispered Skeeter.

"Not for a minute, Skeet. I think the old girl is off her rocker. You and I both know what this place is. I don't care what you call it. We've been in places like this before and there sure weren't any magic wands, and especially not ones that made you feel better."

Overhearing her friends' conversation and seeing their anxiety, Sister Mary tried again. "Look guys, look at Max and Ruth. They're not angry or mad and they have never done anything to hurt you, even when they were really mad. Why would they let someone else hurt you? Come on, kids, use your heads. I'm telling you, there's this lady here and she has a magic wand. The people put on special glasses and then the lady waves her wand over me, first, my back, ooh that feels good, and then my legs, that tingles. When she finishes, I feel like a million bucks. You never know what they're going to do here, but whatever it is I promise you it won't hurt."

Skeeter and Mikey weren't convinced, but had to admit that Sister Mary made an interesting point about Max and Ruth. They clearly weren't angry and seemed perfectly at ease.

"Well! Here are the new kids and Sister Mary. It's so nice to meet you all," said a young technician as she entered the room.

"Let's get everybody weighed and into the examining room. Ruth and Max, do you want to take them all in together?"

Thinking that maybe Sister Mary would provide a good example for their friends, Ruth and Max agreed they should go in together. Sister Mary did provide a good example. She stood quietly while the vet took her vitals, gave her her shots, took her blood sample and listened to her lungs. "See, guys? Piece of cake," said Sister Mary as her examination concluded.

"So, who's next?" asked the vet.

"Let's start with Mikey here. He looks ready," said Max hopefully. "I'll hold him and Ruth can hang on to Skeeter and Sister Mary."

"Just remember your words, Mikey. They're not going to hurt you," urged Sister Mary gently. Mikey swallowed hard and tried to remember Mamma's words as he felt Max gently but firmly take hold of him.

"Mikey, watch out! That person is going to stick something in you!" Skeeter barked and lunged from across the room, her own drums pounding loudly in her head.

"Oh, for goodness sake, Skeeter, that's a thermometer. It doesn't hurt," barked Sister Mary sharply.

"Sister Mary, are you completely nuts? Do you see what she's doing? Get out of my way. Mikey, I'm coming to help you! Ruth, let go of me!" Skeeter barked and pulled furiously, trying to get to her brother.

Seeing his sister so alarmed, Mikey's drums began to pound wildly as well. "Hey, Max, let go of me! Why are you letting that man approach me like that?" Mikey barked and squirmed, trying to get away.

"Well, *that's* not what we had in mind," said the vet calmly, backing away from Mikey before he could land a bite. "Let's try another approach. How about we get Sister Mary back in your car and then we'll examine Skeeter and Mikey in separate rooms? Maybe they won't feed off of each other that way."

Bewildered at Skeeter's outburst and determined that the first vet visit would not end in disaster, Max and Ruth agreed.

"Hey! Where are you taking Sister Mary? Where are you taking my brother?" Skeeter watched as Ruth and Max went in different directions. "Max! You get back here with Mikey! Ruth, what is your problem? Can't you see what's going on?" Skeeter barked frantically, completely forgetting all of the good experiences she had been having recently.

Minutes later, sitting alone in the room with Ruth, Skeeter had calmed down somewhat. Ruth was doing her best to redirect her frightened friend's energies, but with little success. The vet entered the room again. Skeeter glared at her defiantly and growled.

"Wow, Ruth. We have a lot of work to do here," said the vet. "Let me see if I can get close to her without an outburst."

Skeeter growled some more. "You stay away."

"C'mon, Skeet. It's not so bad," said Ruth, softly taking ahold of Skeeter's collar. Skeeter's eyes rolled nervously, darting from Ruth to the vet and back again.

"You know what? I think we need to start again. I'm not going to push her," said the vet. "How about you take her home for now and then bring her back in later this afternoon? Just give her an hour or so to settle down." Appreciating the wisdom of that thought, Ruth agreed.

Leaving the examination room, Skeeter was sure she'd dodged a bullet, but she worried about Mikey. Where was he and what had they done to him? She dragged Ruth out of the building to the car, where her friends were waiting.

"What the heck was that about, Skeeter?" demanded Sister Mary with a scornful snort.

"Yeah, seriously Skeet, you really lost it," said Mikey who had quickly recovered his composure after Skeeter left the room.

Skeeter blinked hard. There was Sister Mary and Mikey and they were both fine— and they were angry with her? "But Sister Mary, that lady poked you and hovered all over you," she said, biting her trembling lip.

"So? She didn't hurt me at all, Skeeter. Just like I told you. And, she gave Ruth a bottle of something that should help my coughing. What's wrong with that?"

Skeeter hung her head. "Nothing. But Mikey, they took you away! What did they do to you?"

"Same thing, Sis. It was the darndest thing. The man looked at me, took a little blood, and then I got a cookie. Totally different from the other place."

Skeeter had to think about that for a while. It sure smelled the same. But riding home with both of her friends comfortably lying next to her, clearly no worse for wear, Skeeter wondered if maybe she should reconsider her alarm.

A couple of hours later, she got her opportunity. "C'mon Skeet, let's try again," said Ruth kindly as she clipped on Skeeter's leash.

"Good luck Skeet!" cheered Mikey.

"Good luck, child. Remember your words," urged Sister Mary. You forgot them last time."

"How do you think she'll do, Sister Mary?" asked Mikey as the car pulled out of the driveway.

"I don't know. What do you think, Mikey?"

Mikey scratched his head and thought a moment. "I think she'll hold it together this time. Yeah, I think she'll be all right."

"I sure hope so, kid. That scene was over the top."

About an hour later, the door opened and Skeeter burst into the room. "How'd it go, Skeet?" asked Mikey.

"Did you remember your words?" asked Sister Mary.

"I did, Sister Mary. I did. It was really scary, but Ruth was there and she kept talking to me and the lady held onto me, but didn't hurt me. It didn't hurt at all." Skeeter bounded across the room and gave her brother a relieved, playful punch.

"Hey! Let's see if we can get Ruth to play Ball," pronounced Sister Mary, also relieved.

Later that evening, as the dogs sat comfortably on the sofa with Ruth, Mikey looked at Sister Mary with wonder. "Sister Mary, did you always think that place was a spa? The last time we went into a place like that, it was very scary. A spa was the last thing I would have called it."

Sister Mary thought back and remembered. "That place, yes, but not all are like that. Oh, yes. I do remember the early days. The first time Ruth took Boyo and me to a vet it was definitely not a spa. I nearly took the room apart, and so did Boyo. Those people were not nice. Not at all. They were all about putting you in a strangle hold. They pinched you and if you even flinched they would bring out the muzzle. It was awful. I tried to get away and hide under the bench, but they yanked me right out."

Mikey raised his head and looked at Sister Mary with focused interest. "What happened? What about Ruth, didn't she help?"

Sister Mary smiled. "Oh, she helped alright. She tried her best, but more importantly, she never took us back there. The next time, we went to another place, a lot like the place we went today. The people were nice. It took a couple more visits to convince us, but we kept going there and we all became good friends. After we moved, Ruth found this place."

Weeks later, Ruth clipped the leash on Sister Mary's collar and headed for the door. "C'mon Sis, let's go get you a spa treatment," she said. "It's time to get those joints of yours some relief." Sister Mary liked the sound of that and happily followed her out the door.

"Going to the spa, kids. See you in a bit," she said as she left.

Entering the vet's office, she was greeted by familiar sights, smells and sounds.

An elderly woman walked out of the examination area and approached Sister Mary and Ruth. "Well hello, old friend! How have you been? Back for some more laser therapy?" Sister Mary gave her a friendly nuzzle. It was Magic Wand Lady! Settling into the floor comfortably between the technician and Ruth, Sister Mary welcomed the pulse along her back, relieving her aches and pains. That lady and her wand always had the right touch, she thought. Ooh, that felt good!

Chapter 39

"Hold on, I'm coming. Just let me get my legs under me." Sister Mary looked steadily at Ruth as she struggled to get over the log and up the hill on their morning walk. Sister Mary still enjoyed their walks, but they were getting harder for her to handle. The hills seemed steeper. Logs were difficult to negotiate. Ruth cleared the path of branches and logs as best she could for her friend, and let her set the pace, but Sister Mary and Ruth both knew that there would come a time when Sister Mary could no longer make the walk.

Sister Mary was determined to make the most of the days that she could still pull herself around the trail, down the hill, to the stream and then back up the hill. "Hold on there, Ruth," she said, stopping for a minute to look around and catch her breath.

"Look at those trees. My, they are pretty. What d'ya think, Sister Mary? Aren't the leaves pretty this year?" Ruth gave her friend a sympathetic look.

Sister Mary looked around the woods before her. They were beautiful. She recalled running through them with Boyo, finding deer antlers and other wonders to bring home to Ruth and Max. They never went far, like Skeeter and Mikey did. They always stayed within Ruth's sight. Running through the woods with Boyo had always made Sister Mary happy.

Listening to the sound of the stream gurgling next to her, she could almost hear Boyo's voice, laughing as they bumped and bounced off of each other. "Come on, Sis!" he'd say. "Race you over that log!" And off they'd go, laughing and joking through the woods. "Check this out, Sis!" Boyo'd continue as they made their way through the woods together. Sometimes, he'd find something that he'd share just with her. That Boyo had some nose. He once smelled a buried rawhide from half a mile away. Yes, looking up the hill, across the stream, it seemed to Sister Mary like it was only yesterday.

"Sister Mary, Sister Mary," Ruth tugged gently on the leash, interrupting Sister Mary's thoughts. "Come on, girl. You ok? Let's get going. The kids are getting impatient."

"Oh, sure. Sorry, guys. I was just looking around is all." Sister Mary's thoughts returned to the present.

"Hey, Sister Mary, smell this," said Skeeter, who, like Ruth, had caught Sister Mary's faraway look. "Sister Mary, what do you think it is?"

Sister Mary ambled up to the spot her friend had marked and gave it a good hard sniff. "Probably a turtle went through here," she said. "You remember, that guy that hides in his hard shell. That's what he smells like. Probably looking for a place to hibernate for the winter."

Sister Mary continued along the path, carefully picking her way through the sticks and logs. "Hold on a minute, guys," she said, stopping. Mikey looked at his friend with concern. She was panting hard and they'd only been walking, slowly.

"You okay, Sister Mary?" he asked.

"I'm fine, son. Just fine. Sometimes, I just need to pause and look around. Look at the beauty in front of you. The stream. The hill. The way the light filters through the trees. The smells of all the woodland creatures. Every now and then, stop and take it all in."

Mikey wasn't sure he believed what Sister Mary was saying, but decided to go along with it anyway. Looking at the hillside before them, he was surprised to see deer lying in the woods, keeping very still, looking at them intently. "Hey, Sister Mary!" he exclaimed, returning the deers' intent gaze. "Did you know they were there? Do you see them, Skeet? They're right there in front of us."

"What, what?" asked Skeeter who had been investigating the turtle trail.

"Deer, deer, right there."

Skeeter looked up in surprise. "Wow, I've never been this close before! Should we chase them? Come on Ruth, let's chase them!" Skeeter pulled on her leash, aiming for the deer that were now beginning to stir, uncertain whether they needed to move or continue their statue like stillness.

"C'mon guys. No chasing today. Let's get Sister Mary up the hill," said Ruth.

"Aw, man, Ruth, you can be such a spoil sport. Well, I'll just give them a bark," grumbled Skeeter. "Woof. Woo-woof!" To the dogs' delight the whole floor of the woods erupted with deer, many of whom they hadn't seen, leaping and scattering like leaves on a windy Fall day.

Sister Mary pulled herself forward, up the last hill of their walk, but her legs just would not cooperate. Each step grew smaller. Each effort greater. Turning around, Ruth looked at her friend with sorrow. "Can't make it, huh? Need a lift?" "Cooperate with me guys. We don't have that far to go," said Ruth as she gathered her friend up in her arms, holding onto her young friends' leashes tightly for good measure. Sister Mary looked up at Ruth gratefully.

Once up the hill, Ruth put Sister Mary down inside the fence where the ground was flat and uncluttered by leaves and sticks.

"You okay, Sis?" asked Mikey, giving Sister Mary a cautious nudge.

"I'm fine, Mikey. Just got a little tangled up back there, that's all. I think next time, I'll let you kids take the trail without me. I don't think Ruth will mind, and you can tell me all about it when you get back."

Later that day, as the dogs sat waiting for Ruth and Max to return home, Skeeter looked at Sister Mary in her spot, sleeping by the sofa. "Sister Mary? Sister Mary?" she asked quietly.

Stirring, Sister Mary looked around to see Skeeter looking at her, her face full of thoughtful concern. "Yes, child, what's bothering you?"

"Well, I was just wondering. Remember today, when we were back by the stream? Remember?"

"Yes, what about it?"

Skeeter squirmed a little in her crate, not quite sure she should ask. "Well, Mikey and I were looking at stuff and smelling stuff, but you, well, you didn't look like you were looking at what we were looking at and you weren't really smelling what we were smelling. I don't know, well, you just . . . ," Skeeter's voice trailed off with uncertainty.

"Yeah, Sis, and then later, you stopped again and I looked at you and you looked at me, but it was like you just looked right through me. What was going on?" asked Mikey.

Sister Mary's eyes were soft and she smiled at her young friends. "Nothing was wrong. Watching the two of you ahead of me, looking at this, exploring that, tangling yourselves in your leashes, Ruth trying to keep up with you and back with me, I just got to thinking about Boyo and how he and I used to run through the woods together on days like today. We'd run up that hill across the stream. One of us would find an antler or a bone or a stick and the other would try to take it. Just like you two do. We'd run through the woods with it, growling and laughing and bumping each other. And looking up that hill, I could almost see him. It was like he was there, barking, tail wagging, calling me. Only with the leash on, and these legs I couldn't go to him ..." Sister Mary's voice trailed off to a whisper.

Mikey didn't like where this was going. "Sister Mary," he interrupted, "you guys got to run around without a leash?"

Sister Mary looked at Mikey, snapping out of her reverie. "Oh, yes. All the time. We never ran as far as you two and we actually came back when we were called, so we were off the leash quite a bit. Did I ever tell you about the first off-leash hike that Ruth took me on?" Sister Mary's voice had lost that dreamy quality it had just moments ago and she returned to her normal story telling voice; strong, wisecracking, yarn-spinning.

Mikey relaxed a bit. "No, Sister Mary. I don't think we've heard that one."

"Tell us Sister Mary, tell us!" said Skeeter, also relieved that the spell over Sister Mary seemed to be broken.

"Keep in mind that by the time I met Boyo, he'd been with Ruth and Max for several months and he'd already had off-leash hikes. My, oh my, he kept telling me about them. Sometimes, it was all he could talk about. 'The cornfield, Sister Mary,' he'd say. 'You should see the cornfield, it's huge!' That boy would carry on and on about the cornfield until I couldn't stand it. After I ran off I didn't think I'd ever get to see that cornfield, much less see it off-leash, but Boyo kept encouraging me to keep working and maybe we'd go one day. Sure enough, one day, a day just like today, the air was cool and crisp, the leaves were off the trees, and as we would soon find out, the corn was cut. After about an hour's drive we pulled into a parking lot. Boyo was bouncing all over the back of the car, he was so excited. 'The cornfield, the cornfield! We're going to the cornfield!' We tumbled out of the car, Boyo was so excited. At that moment, Ruth looked me square in the face, and I'll never forget this, she said, 'Girl, I hope you're ready for this. Sister Mary, I'm really trusting you.' And then she looked at Boyo and said, 'Boyo, it's your job to show her the ropes and make sure she comes back. I'm counting on you, Boyo.' Boyo looked right back up at her with a huge smile, his whole body wagging." Sister Mary's eyes shone brightly as she remembered that day.

"What happened, next Sister Mary?" asked Mikey eagerly.

"Ruth unsnapped our leashes and walked into this enormous field. This field is bigger than anything you've ever seen. And Boyo, looked at me with his big ol' grin, and barked, 'catch me if you can, Sister!' and took off. He ran half way around the field and back, and when he returned, he looked at me and asked 'Aren't you coming?' Well, I didn't have to be asked again!

Boyo and I ran and ran, all the way around the first field, through the corn stubble, without a care in the world, wind under our ears, oh my! It's like nothing you've ever seen, fields stretching as far as you can imagine. Nothing in our way. No cars, no roads, just fields. Boyo said it was always important to make a big circle so that we would never lose track of Ruth and he was right. Sure enough, we circled and there she was, with a big smile on her face and a handful of treats. It was magical."

Sister Mary took a breath. "The rest of the day was unbelievable. Boyo showed me the trails and holes he'd found on past walks and together we found others. We raced each other down the trails, jumped logs, splashed through streams, rolled in dirt. By the time we got back to the car, we were a muddy mess! Ruth packed us up with plenty of blankets and towels and drove us to Mammaw and Pop Pop's for dinner. I'm pretty sure it was steak night and we each got a big share."

"So, this corn field. How big was it, exactly?" asked Mikey skeptically.

"Remember how far you guys would run through the woods before the fence got put up? Each field was about four times the size of your loop." Sister Mary paused for effect, enjoying the look of her friends' astonished faces.

"Oh, come on, Sister Mary. There's no place like that. What about the roads? The houses? You're telling us it was just field?"

"That's right. Just fields. Fields and woods for as far as you could go. Boyo was right. It is a magical place. It's filled with birds, and squirrels, and deer, rabbits, fox, and all kinds of smells and things to chase. Just incredible."

Sister Mary looked at her friends and could see that they still did not really believe her. Shrugging her shoulders and settling back down into her waiting spot, she smiled. She knew the truth. Hikes in those fields with Ruth and Boyo were among her fondest memories. "Maybe one day you'll get to go there. You'll see. You all are faster than Boyo and I were, even back then. You'd absolutely love it. Play your cards right and I bet Ruth takes you there one day."

Skeeter shrugged, "You know, Sister Mary, if it's only half as big and half as fun as you say it is …"

"You have no idea, child. No idea."

"Sister Mary? Did you ever go back there?" asked Skeeter.

"Oh, yes, many times. Sometimes Ruth would pack a lunch and we'd go. We'd walk for a while and she'd find a nice log or rock by a stream. Boyo and I'd play in the stream while she ate and then she'd share part of her lunch with us. One time we walked so far that she got lost and Boyo and I had to help her find her way back. We didn't even care that we were lost. It was just me and Ruth and Boyo and the woods. I was almost sad when we found the car again that day."

Mikey thought for a moment, remembering the hike that Skeeter and he took with Ruth the week before. "You know, Sis, I understand what you're saying. Last week Ruth got turned around on the path too. Skeeter and I knew she was lost, but it didn't matter. It was just us and her and the woods. We really didn't care about anything else."

"Yeah, and it was nice, 'cause when we got back me and Mikey curled up in the back and remembered everything we smelled and did," said Skeeter.

"That was one of my favorite parts, too, Skeet. Boyo usually didn't like to curl up together with me at home. Said he got too hot and he needed his space. But whenever we traveled, we would curl up back to back and swap stories or sleep all the way home."

Sister Mary paused and bit her lip a little. Then, standing up she gave her ears a good flap. "Enough reminiscing about Boyo this afternoon. What did you think about breakfast? I told you last night that the dinner gravy would be good this morning!"

Following Sister Mary's cue, Skeeter and Mikey changed the topic to every dog's favorite, food, and soon the room was filled with laughing, drooling dogs recounting stories of meals gone by, food found on the trail, and snacks stolen from the counter.

"Hey, Sister Mary, what was your all-time best counter steal?" asked Mikey.

"Oh, let me see. It could be the time I stole a whole boneless ham off the counter, or maybe it was the time I took the half-eaten Thanksgiving turkey off the counter. Yours?"

"I thought that apple pie I took down last week was pretty good."

"Yeah, and I stole a whole bunch of bananas!" Skeeter chimed in.

Sister Mary shook her head in amused disbelief. "I tell you about a whole ham and a half a turkey and the best you can do is pie and fruit? What kind of dogs are you guys, anyway?" she laughed.

"Give us time, Sister Mary," laughed Mikey. "You guys trained Ruth and Max too well and made it harder for us!"

"I know. Did you see how fast Ruth cleared off the counters yesterday? I didn't even get a chance to get a good noseful of what they were eating," giggled Skeeter.

"Besides, what's wrong with pie? I like pie."

"Oh, Mikey, you and that sweet tooth of yours. Go for some meat or some cheese, boy. Something worth the effort."

"But I like pie," said Mikey, still proud of his steal.

Sister Mary shook her head, "I know, and you like raw vegetables, too. That still doesn't make it right. Now pizza. That's a food worth stealing. That's proper dog food. Pizza usually comes with meat. Or a steak." Skeeter and Mikey looked at each other and giggled. Sister Mary was on a tear now. It would be hours before she got off the topic of food.

Chapter 40

Sister Mary looked expectantly up at the kitchen counter. She liked what she saw. Water bottles, binoculars, soft water dish, treats, leashes, and collars. Ruth and Max were busy assembling the gear for an outing. They hadn't been for an outing since before Boyo got sick and she couldn't remember how long it had been. Sister Mary watched as Max put a mat in the back of the car. Yup, she thought, an outing. Far enough away for a mat. This could be good.

"What's going on, Sister Mary?" asked Mikey, who also saw the pile assembled on the counter.

Looks like we're going on an outing. Maybe the ocean," said Sister Mary brightly.

"The ocean? You mean the one you told us about?" said Skeeter.

"With the ponies and the big water?" asked Mikey.

"Could be. You never know until you actually get there, but it could be. I sure hope so. I haven't been there in ages. It would be good to feel the sand between my paws again. See the ocean. Taste the treats."

Sister Mary was right. An outing was in the making and it was to the ocean. However, Ruth and Max were not sure that

296

Sister Mary should go. "I just don't think she can handle it, Max. The drive is so long and the kids will be all over her in the back of the car. As much as she loves the ocean, I don't think she'll be able to manage the walk. It's just too much, I'm afraid," Ruth fretted.

Max gave his old friend's ear a gentle pull. "What d'ya say, girl? Can you handle the trip?" Sister Mary looked up at Max from her spot on the floor. "I don't know, Ruth. It's just been so long for her. I think she'd really like it. If we don't take her, she'll be here by herself all day."

Ruth smiled wistfully at her old friend still lying on the floor. "It's up to you, Max, but I think she'll be fine here alone for a few hours and the kids could use a nice long walk."

Max was torn. He really wanted Sister Mary to have what he thought would probably be her last walk on the beach. He loved watching her play with the waves lapping on the shore. He remembered the time the wind blew the water into little balls of foam that Sister Mary and Boyo chased down the shore for hours. Inevitably, they would find a stick and then they'd run with it, jaw to jaw, down the shore. He missed that, and he missed picnicking with them when their walk was through. Sharing his sandwich and chips with his friends on the beach was a simple joy. But Max knew Ruth was right. The ride and the hike would be too much for her now. His spunky friend was simply too frail. "I guess. If we get going now we can be back in time for dinner. That shouldn't be too long for her to stay by herself," he said, giving Sister Mary's back a gentle rub.

Sister Mary didn't like the tone and looks she was getting. She'd been around long enough to know what they meant. "Hey," she commanded from her spot on the floor. "I can make it. Don't leave me here."

"Sister Mary, what's going on?" asked Mikey, still not quite gifted in the art of reading Ruth and Max.

"Well, it looks like they plan to take you two on a trip to the ocean and leave me here," said Sister Mary indignantly.

"Why, Sister Mary? How come?" asked Skeeter.

"Oh, I don't know. Something about it being 'too much' for me to handle. I can 'handle' the trip just fine."

Mikey cocked his ears skeptically at Sister Mary. "Are you sure, Sister? I mean no disrespect, but didn't Ruth have to carry you up the hill just yesterday? From what you've described, that ocean place sounds longer and harder than the hill."

Sister Mary thought for a moment. She knew Mikey had a point. She would like to see the ocean again, she thought, but maybe it was better to remember it the way it was, the way it had been, with Boyo. Running on the beach when she was able to run, really run. Pulling herself up, she looked at Mikey and Skeeter firmly. "Well, I *can* handle it. It's just that I don't want to go today. You two go and have a good time. Come home and tell me a story for a change."

"But, Sister Mar…"

"Let it go, Skeet," Mikey said sharply. "Sister Mary said she doesn't want to come. That's her choice."

Mikey looked back at Sister Mary, kindly. No need to rub her nose in it, he thought. "Maybe we can bring back some good smells too, Sis."

"You better. There's a lot there that you guys haven't smelled. Bring me back something interesting." She tried her best to conceal her disappointment.

"C'mon guys, let's go," said Max snapping the leashes on Mikey and Skeeter.

"Sister Mary, you stay here and watch the house for us, okay?" said Ruth as she headed for the door.

"I'll just see you guys to the car. Have fun." Sister Mary pushed through the door and ambled toward the car.

"Come on, Sister Mary. We need for you to go inside." Sister Mary dropped her head as she turned away from the car and headed back toward the house. It had been worth a try, she thought. Able or not, she really did want to go. "Sorry, Sis. We'll be back in time for Ball." Ruth scratched her friend's head before closing the door.

Ball, thought Sister Mary dejectedly as the door closed in front of her. They're going to the beach and I've got to stay here all day. They probably won't want to play Ball when they get back.

As the car pulled out of the driveway, Sister Mary eased herself down onto her spot in front of the sofa to wait. Her back was stiff. Her elbows hurt. The house was quiet. It was going to be a long day. A long, quiet day. Soon, Sister Mary was sound asleep, dreaming of her days past at the beach with her Boyo and Ruth and Max. She could almost taste the subs and chips and feel the breeze of the ocean.

Hours later, as the last of the day's light faded, the door opened. Skeeter and Mikey bounded into the hallway.

"Sister Mary! Sister Mary!" exclaimed Skeeter.

"Sister Mary!" exclaimed Mikey.

Sister Mary awoke with a start. She could see from the expressions on her friends' faces that the day had been a good one. Toddling over to meet them, Sister Mary tried to keep clear of the two bouncing dogs. "Watch out, guys!" exclaimed Max as he tried to catch Sister Mary before Mikey knocked her over.

"I'm okay, I'm okay, Max," said Sister Mary.

"Sister Mar-Mar! Guess what?" exclaimed Skeeter as she dashed through the house with glee. "We went to the ocean! It was awesome!"

"Yeah, Sis, it was great! Bigger and wider even than you said! There was sand and there was more sand and then there was all this water and it was all back and forth and back and forth! We were jumping at it and it jumped back at us and…"

"Did you see the ponies?" asked Sister Mary, catching her friends' enthusiasm.

"Yup. Sure did. We watched one pony rubbing his butt on the fence. He looked so funny. And then you know what?" wagged Skeeter.

"What?"

"Then he turned around and jumped right over that fence."

"Just like that?" asked Sister Mary.

"Just like that," said Mikey.

"And oh, Sister Mary. The beach. It had little birds all over it. They kept running in front of us. First they'd run to the water and then they'd run from the water. They were cool!" Skeeter laughed as she remembered the funny little birds running in the surf.

"Sister Mary, smell this. Smell my paw," said Mikey. "What's that? I ate some but it was kinda squishy and really salty."

Sister Mary gave Mikey's paw a good long sniff. "Ah, well. Did you find big brown crunchy things on the beach? Weird looking, dead creatures?" she asked.

"Yeah, yeah, lots of them," said Mikey.

"I'm thinking it was probably just some guts from one of those things. Boyo and I ate ourselves sick on those things one time. You didn't eat too many of them, did you? 'Cause if you did, we're in for a long night," she laughed.

"No, we only got a little. It tasted funny, so we left it alone."

"Sister Mary, Sister Mary, now smell my paw," said Skeeter. "What's that, Sister Mary? What did I step in?"

Sister Mary took a long, deep smell of Skeeter's paw. "Ummm. Now that, that is what you call pony poop. It's everywhere there. Sometimes if you find some that is particularly right, you can throw yourself on it and use it to polish your coat. Ruth and Max don't like the smell, but ..." Sister Mary paused remembering the sweet smell of her coat on those occasions she'd managed to get a good rub in before Ruth or Max intervened.

"Hey, Sister Mary, did you ever step on these little pointy things that get stuck in your feet?" asked Skeeter.

"Oh, those things. They're called burrs. I hate them. Did you step on one?"

"One!" exclaimed Skeeter. "I had three paws full at once. It was awful!"

"Yeah, but Sister Mary, you should have seen the show Skeeter put on. All ooch, ouch, poor me, ouch," teased Mikey.

Sister Mary looked at Mikey sternly. "Mikey, those are no laughing matter. Get them stuck in your pad too far and you'll hurt for days. They might even have to cut your paw off."

Taken aback by Sister Mary's somber pronouncement, Mikey blinked hard. Skeeter sat down and examined her paws carefully. "No way, Sister Mary. Take off your paw?" she said cocking her head to one side.

Sister Mary couldn't repress her giggle. "Nah, I'm just messing with you. They do hurt, though. I remember that."

Relaxed now that she wasn't worried about losing her paw, Skeeter looked up. "Mikey, did you see? I didn't even flinch when Ruth pulled them out."

"Yes, you did!" said Mikey. "Sister Mary, they put on quite a show. You should have seen them. Ruth would lean over and try to pick up Skeeter's paw. Skeeter would look at her Ruth would try to take it out, and Skeeter would pull away. But then she'd step on it and she'd …"

"I get it, I get it," laughed Sister Mary.

"So tell me about the subs. Did you get good snacks?" she asked.

Mikey and Skeeter thought for a moment. "You know what? I think they forgot those, Sis," said Mikey.

"No, Mikey, they didn't forget. Remember? They were going to get them on the way home but they decided to come home to hang out with Sister Mary."

"That's right, Skeet. I think I must have been sleeping when they were talking about that."

"You guys came back to be with me?" asked Sister Mary.

"That's what I heard Max say," said Skeeter. "He said we needed to be home before dark so that you could play Ball today."

Sister Mary was surprised. "You guys want to play Ball after all that?" she asked, half expecting them to say no. Any time she and Boyo had gone to the ocean they'd been too tired to play Ball when they got home.

"Man, oh man, Sister Mary, that would be great! First the ocean and now Ball!" Skeeter bounced around the kitchen.

Drawing on her friends' youthful engergy, Sister Mary decided a game definitely was in order. "Hey, Ruth!" barked Sister Mary as she ambled up to the Ball cabinet. "Play Ball! Play

Ball!" Of course, in no time the house was filled with the happy chaos of three dogs demanding their favorite game.

That night, Ruth made Ball extra special fun, throwing the balls back and forth across the yard, making sure that her old friend kept up with the game. Later that night, tucked snugly into her corner of the sofa, her head in Ruth's lap, Sister Mary sighed contentedly. Being left behind had been hard, but listening to the kids carrying on, she knew Ruth and Max had made the right decision. Besides, she thought, she'd had the whole day to dream about being on the beach with Boyo, rolling in the sand, rolling in everything, eating strange stuff, running, running, laughing. In her mind, she had spent the day at the ocean, too.

"Sister Mary?" asked Mikey from his side of the sofa. "Sister Mary? Can you tell if they're going to take us back there, back to the ocean? I'd really like to go back there. Do you know? We were really good, Skeet and me. But something didn't seem right with them all day."

Sister Mary looked across the room at Max, sitting quietly in his chair, and then at Ruth, who was quietly rubbing Sister Mary's chin. They hadn't said anything about him all day, but she could see the sadness in their eyes. "Oh, I think they'll take you back, guys," she said quietly. "This was probably a tough day for them. Boyo's been gone for a year now and they were probably thinking of him a lot. That's got nothing to do with you. The good thing is that, since you were good, you made it easier for them to move on. Good job, guys, good job." Sister Mary eased herself off of the sofa to her spot on the floor. Yes, she thought, it had been a long but good day.

Chapter 41

"Sister Mary. What's going on?" asked Skeeter from her spot on the kitchen floor. She had been watching Ruth carefully cut strips of something that smelled wonderful into little bits and then shove them into a case. A training leash was on the counter and Ruth's nervous energy infected the room.

Sister Mary studied Ruth and the situation carefully. "You need to learn to figure these things out for yourselves. I'm not going to be around forever, you know. What do you see, Skeet? Look first at Ruth. Happy or sad?"

Skeeter studied Ruth intently. "I'd say…"

"Happy," piped Mikey.

"Right. Good. Now, is she coming or going?"

Both young dogs looked at the growing pile on the counter. "Going," they said in unison.

"Right! Very good. How many leashes?"

"One," said Skeeter.

"Regular leash or training?"

"Training," said Mikey.

"Whose?"

"Mine. Hey, it's mine! Ooh! I got it. I got it!" bounced Skeeter. "I'm going to school!"

"Very good, Skeet!" Sister Mary beamed at her pupil.

"Wait a minute," said Mikey. "It's the wrong day and time. Everybody knows we go to school in the middle of the week and after dark. The timing's all wrong."

Sister Mary thought a moment. "You've got a point there, kid. But I do think Skeeter's right. Maybe she's going to a different kind of school."

Mikey and Skeeter looked perplexed. "But what kind of other school is there, Sister Mary?" asked Mikey.

"Well, there's herding school for one."

"Hurting school? What kind of school is that? I don't think I want to go to hurting school."

Sister Mary giggled, "No, child, I said herding school, not hurting school."

"Hearding school? Sister Mary, I heard really good. I can even hear the moles as they wander around under the yard. I don't think I need to go to school for that," said Skeeter confidently.

"No, no, Skeet, not hearing school, herding school. Herding school is where you learn how to chase things without getting in trouble." Skeeter's eyes brightened. "You mean they teach these things?" she exclaimed in wonder.

"Sister Mary, did you ever go to herding school?" asked Mikey.

"Oh, yes. Ruth took Boyo and me there once. We also went to an event where they had herding. Both were fun."

"What'd you do there, Sister Mary?" asked Skeeter.

"There are a bunch of other dogs there and a guy with some sheep. The guy stands in a ring with the sheep. Ruth takes you in and lets you go. Then, you just chase around whatever sheep you want until the guy says to stop."

Mikey was incredulous. "No way. You get to chase as much as you want? Why is that a school? I already know how to do that!"

"Yeah, Sister Mary. I'm really good at chasing stuff already. Do they teach you how to catch it? Why don't they call it catching school?" asked Skeeter.

Sister Mary scratched her head a moment. "I tell you, I have no idea. Every time we went, Boyo would shake his head at me and say I was missing the point. He would go in the ring and get all looky with the sheep, drop his head and move real slow, get them all in a big tight group, and then they'd march around the ring like they were in a parade. Me, I would go in, find me a fast one and chase it. So much more fun, but that's just me."

"I think I'm with you, Sister Mary," said Skeeter. "If that's where we're going I hope I can find me a fast sheep, too!"

Mikey shook his head. "No, I think if I was going I'd go with Boyo's approach. It sounds more controlled."

"Well, Mikey, you're a big ol' control freak," sassed Skeeter.

Discussion about the relative merits of herding versus chasing were still going on when Ruth finished her preparations. "C'mon Skeet. Time for your first agility class!"

Perking her ears at the sound of a new word, Skeeter blinked. "Agility? Sister Mary, what's that?"

"Child, I have no idea about that one. Maybe they'll teach you how to open the cabinets or something. Either way, from the look on Ruth's face and the smell of those treats she's shoved in her bag, I bet you're going to have fun. Whatever you do, remember your Mamma's words. That is always the key to having a good time, even if you start off scared. Now, off you go." Sister Mary escorted her young friend to the door.

"But why can't I go to agility? I wanna go too. Why's she get to go and not me?" pouted Mikey.

As if hearing his question, Ruth looked down at her friend and gave his head a good scratch. "Don't worry, Mikey, you'll get fun classes too. Skeeter's just more ready for this kind of excitement than you are. Give us a couple of weeks and we'll get you going too."

Mikey didn't get most of her words, but he liked her tone, so he hopped in his crate, accepted his treat and decided to wait for Skeeter's return patiently. Well, kind of patiently.

Skeeter watched Ruth as she drove. She studied the lines on her face, the angle of her shoulders, the pace of her breathing. Catching her focused look, Ruth gave Skeeter a friendly scratch on the chin. "Here's the deal. I think you will really like this and have a lot of fun. It might be scary at first, but no one's going to hurt you and you'll get to run and jump and climb on things. Let's try it for six lessons, just six times, and if you don't like it after that, we won't go back. Deal?" Skeeter laid down on the seat next to Ruth and continued her study.

They pulled into the school yard. Hopping out of the car, Skeeter was immediately confronted with unfamiliar smells, other anxious dogs and people milling about, all new objects that she needed to study from a distance. She gave a few barks to the group for good measure.

"Hello guys! Everybody come on over and into the ring!" The Instructor's voice sang out cheerfully. "Come on in, come on in, everybody," she greeted as they entered.

"Skeeter, heel," said Ruth, stepping into the ring at the brisk pace that Skeeter liked. Walking around the ring, Skeeter could see a vast array of … things, things she'd never seen before.

Wonder what those are, she thought as she passed each one, looking at them with curiosity.

"The first thing we're going to do is to have each dog hop up on this table here. When your dog hops up, ask him or her to sit, then introduce yourself and your dog to the rest of the class," directed the Instructor.

Looking down at her young friend, Ruth said, "We can do that, right, Skeet? No worries!"

"Ok, let's start with you," said the Instructor, motioning to Ruth and Skeeter.

"Come on Skeet, heel. Skeet, table. Skeet, sit!" Skeeter hopped up on the table. Looking at the other dogs watching from their positions on the floor, Skeeter thought they looked like a pretty fun bunch. A couple of Border Collies lying in focused earnestness next to their people; a Chesapeake sitting with a huge grin on her face, ready for whatever came next; a Corgi standing commandingly next to his owner; a very young Golden Retriever, anxiously working the dog and human crowd, tail wagging furiously; and an Australian Blue Heeler clearly ready for work or play, whichever came first. Well, she thought, so far so good.

After hopping off the table, Skeeter and Ruth went back to their place in line and the other dogs took their turns. Skeeter sniffed toward the Chesapeake standing happily in front of her. "Hi! I'm Skeeter. What's your name?"

"I'm Bay, hi! Can you believe it? It's finally here. Our first day of agility. OMG. I am so excited. Wait till we get to the tunnel. Do you think we'll get to the tunnel? I really hope so because I love the tunnel. Do you love the tunnel? I love, love, love the tunnel!" she wagged with her whole body.

Skeeter blinked shyly, overcome by Bay's outward energy, but intrigued by her apparent knowledge of this agility thing. "So you know about this stuff? What is it anyway?"

"Oh, you don't know?" asked the Border Collie from behind her. "You've never heard of agility? Everybody knows about agility. Who's never heard about agility? What kind of dog are you anyway? some sort of Beagle mix or something?"

Skeeter dropped her head in embarrassment. "I haven't heard of it, either," said the Corgi, two dogs back.

"Just ignore him, Skeeter," said the Chesapeake warmly. "BC's think they own the agility space, which they do not. Just watch, two exercises in and he'll get distracted by something and, boom, off he'll go. Just watch, you'll see."

Skeeter perked up at her new friend's reassurance. "But, what is it?" she said.

Hearing the conversation, the Australian Heeler chimed in. "It's really cool. I've heard about it from dogs in my dog park. See all those things in here? They teach us to go up them, down them, over them, whatever. We get to do it really fast and our people dispense tons of treats," he said.

"Really? So basically, we're just here to run and play with our people?" Skeeter liked the sound of this agility thing more and more.

"Yup, and we get to go through tunnels. I love, love, love tunnels!" wagged the Chesapeake.

"Tunnels are for terriers," groused the Corgi, "and I'm no terrier. What am I supposed to go through that thing for?"

The class began practicing the first obstacle, the table. Skeeter liked the pace of it. Trot to the table, hop on it, sit or down and hop off again, followed by a treat and a scratch.

"Now we're going to introduce your dogs to the tunnel," said the Instructor. "So just bring your dog to the tunnel, hand her leash to me and go call her from the other end. I will send her through. Lots of praise, everybody. Lots of praise."

Skeeter watched as the Australian Heeler approached the tunnel and noticed that the tunnel moved as he bolted through. "How was it? The thing moved. Did it bite?" she asked as he got back in line behind her.

"No, no. It didn't bite and going through was no big deal," he shrugged.

"Rroo! Rroo! I'm next! I'm next!" wagged the Bay the Chesapeake as she pulled her person toward the tunnel.

"Wow! she's really strong," laughed the Instructor, holding on to her just long enough for her owner to get to the end of the tunnel before Bay burst through the other side.

"Here we go, Skeet. It's our turn," said Ruth as she walked up to the Instructor. "She's a little frightened of strangers, so watch her," cautioned Ruth as she handed over the leash.

"I've got her. Hand me some of your treats and I'll take it from here."

Seeing Ruth quickly moving away from her, Skeeter lost her nerve. But, she remembered her words. Don't get angry, don't panic, don't bite, she said to herself. "Here you go, girl," said the Instructor, offering her a treat. "Right this way."

Ignoring the treat, Skeeter looked around frantically. Where was Ruth? What was going on? "Right this way, girl," coaxed the Instructor, trying to aim Skeeter into the tunnel. "Look through the tunnel to the other side, Skeet!" cheered Bay and the Australian Heeler.

"Just hurry up! I'm next!" barked the Border Collie. Hearing him helped her focus, and right before she forgot her words,

Skeeter looked through the tunnel and saw Ruth kneeling down and calling her on the other side.

"Skeet, Come!" said Ruth, louder than she had the previous times. Seeing Ruth's outstretched hand and holding her breath, Skeeter bolted through the tunnel like a shot, right into Ruth's arms. "Way to go, Skeet!" cheered Ruth, handing her a jackpot of treats.

"Way to go!" cheered the Instructor and Skeeter's new friends.

"Out of my way! You took too long. I'm coming through!" hollered the Border Collie as he barreled through the tunnel, hot on Skeeter's heels.

"Oh, don't mind him," said the other Border Collie in line. "We're not all like that. It's just his way. I'm Polly, by the way. Nice to meet you. I think I heard your person say you were some sort of cattle dog, right? Never met one of you guys before. What did you say your name was again?"

"My name's Skeeter. Nice to meet you, too. What did you think of the tunnel?"

"Me? I thought it was kind of dumb, but I went through anyway. They keep saying because I'm a Border, I'll like this. Frankly, I don't know what this has to do with herding sheep, which is what I do for a living, or I would do for a living if they let me. But going through the tunnel made my people happy. So that's fine." Polly sat down next to her person and looked up at her with affection.

"You know about herding, too? My friend Sister Mary says it's the best." asked Skeeter, looking at her new friend with wonder.

"Well sure. It's amazing…"

"Come on Skeet, our turn again," interrupted Ruth.

"We'll talk later, Skeet," said Ruby as Skeeter and Ruth trotted toward their second tunnel attempt.

"Give me some more treats, Ruth," said the Instructor as Ruth handed Skeeter's leash to her. "I think she will learn this pretty quickly."

As Ruth ran to the end of the tunnel, Skeeter watched anxiously, hoping she had this figured out. Through the tunnel to Ruth. Get treats. "Skeeter come!" she heard Ruth call from the far end of the tunnel. She peered in. Yup. There was Ruth. Zoom! Treats!

"Outta my way! I'm coming through!" barreled the Border Collie right after her. Back in line, most of the dogs were exuberant.

"We did the tunnel, the tunnel!" bounced the Chesapeake. "Isn't it the most fun ever?"

"I know!" Skeeter barked back. "Let's do it again!" And they did.

The class worked with the tunnel for a while, making it longer and adding some jumps. Sure enough, just as Ruby predicted, the male Border Collie proved distractible, running through the tunnel and around the jumps, through the tunnel and over to Ruby, through the tunnel and over to investigate something he thought he smelled. Skeeter always took the shortest route to Ruth and her ever-available treats. She was having fun.

Eventually, the Instructor announced, "Everybody's doing so well, we're going to add one more obstacle today. The A-Frame."

"What's an A-Frame?" asked Skeeter of her new friends.

"See that thing over there? The two boards, one going up the other going down?" said the Border Collie.

"Over there? That thing?" said Skeeter, looking skeptically at the A-Frame.

"Yup. That's the one. You climb up it and then back down it. Easy peezy."

"Well, I can do that," said Skeeter, sizing up the obstacle.

"Who's first? Polly, let's start with you," said the Instructor.

"Oh, Lord, here we go," grumped Polly. "I'm a sheep dog, not a bloody mountain dog." But she moved off anyway to try her paws at the obstacle.

"Skeeter, your turn!" the Instructor called. "Ruth, guide her up with the treat and then right back down. We'll spot from the sides so that she doesn't fall off."

"Skeeter, A-Frame!" said Ruth brightly as she urged her friend up the first side.

Well this is a cinch, thought Skeeter as she climbed up the frame. "Hey, look at me guys! I'm on top! And I am a mountain dog! Whoa! It's a long way down there!" Skeeter paused at the top and took a look around.

"Keep her moving, Ruth. Don't let her stop!" urged the Instructor, noticing the pause.

"Skeeter, target!" said Ruth, driving down the back side of the frame. Skeeter motored down the board and saw the target, a tray full of treats. Treats! Ruth! Yay!

"Hey, girl. Nice work," said the Border Collie as he ran up behind her. "What did you say your name was again?"

"Skeeter. Thanks. What's yours?"

"Oh, I'm Rocky, nice to meet ya. Sorry about the beagle crack a while ago. I just get impatient sometimes."

"No biggie," Skeeter said, hoping to have found a new friend, "my brother and I get that all the time. Nothing against beagles, but we're not them. We're Entles."

"You're wha's?" asked the Border Collie.

"We're Entles," Skeeter said brightly, buoyed her new experiences and embracing herself and her personality for the first time. "You've probably never heard of us, but you will." Rocky the Border Collie looked at her skeptically.

"Nope, can't say I've ever heard of that before. Sure you're not a mix of something?"

"Rocky, mind your manners!" admonished Polly.

"It's ok, Polly. I can handle myself. Just cause Rocky here's never heard of my breed doesn't mean anything. Just means he's got more to learn than me, that's all." Skeeter looked back at her new friends with newfound confidence.

"Hey, look at me, I got the target!" bounced the Chesapeake as she raced by the group with the target in her mouth.

"Your turn again, Skeet. Bet you can't go as fast as me," Rocky challenged on their next run over the A-Frame.

"Bet I can. Watch this. Come on Ruth! Let's go!"

Seeing her friend's enthusiasm, Ruth ran with her towards the obstacle. "Skeet, A-Frame! Skeet Target! Good girl! Way to go!"

"Top that, Rocky!" said Skeet as she pranced back to line.

"Rocky, scramble," commanded Rocky's owner as they charged toward the A-Frame.

"Hey, guys did you know there are cows outside?" said Rocky as he paused on the top of the frame.

"Rocky, target," commanded Rocky's owner, and down the back-side of the A-Frame Rocky went to his waiting treat.

"I was so much faster than you," teased Skeeter when Rocky got back in line.

"Yeah, but did you see those cows?" said Rocky. "There were so many of them and they were spread out all over the place."

After a few more turns at the A-Frame, the Instructor
wrapped up the class. Back in the car on their way home, Skeeter
curled up in a happy, tired ball in the seat next to Ruth, her chin
resting on Ruth's hand. So that was agility, she thought. Wow.
For once she would have stories to tell Mikey and Sister Mary.

"Sister Mary, Mikey, Sister Mary, Mikey! I did it! I did
agility!" Skeeter burst into the house. "We did jumps and tunnels
and the A-Frame. There were other dogs and people and we all
got treats and Ruth and I did all of it together and it was, it was …
Wow!" Skeeter zoomed through the house, bouncing and jumping
over her brother and barking with glee.

"Well, I got to play frisbee with Max and we walked through
the woods and ate hot dogs," said Mikey.

"Yes, and your brother is quite good with the frisbee,
Skeeter. You should see him. He gets right under it and catches it
before it lands. Very fun to watch," said Sister Mary who had
enjoyed sunning herself in the backyard while Max and Mikey
played.

Max and Mikey had themselves had a good afternoon, Max
seizing the opportunity to build some play time in with Mikey
while Skeeter was away. "Yeah, Skeet, you should see Max throw
that frisbee. It really sails."

"Tell us about this agility thing, Skeet. What is it?" asked
Mikey curiously.

"Was it fun?" asked Sister Mary.

"Oh, man was it ever!" Skeeter enthused as she settled in to
recount the day's activities.

Over the next several days, the dogs would analyze each
move, each handler and each of other dogs with great care, but for
now, Skeeter held forth on the virtues of proper timing on the A-

Frame and the importance of taking the most direct path to Ruth through the tunnel.

Chapter 42

Sister Mary awoke with a start. She had been dreaming, recalling the day she jumped off of the balcony because she incorrectly thought that Ruth was in danger from the neighbor's dog. That landing had hurt. Even remembering it hurt. It had nearly knocked her out, and when she dreamed of it, the landing always woke her to aching joints, still complaining over the insult.

Looking around the room at the prone forms, snug in bed, she smiled. Sister Mary was pleased with her family. The "kids" were shaping up into good packmates, not just for each other, but for Ruth and Max as well. They were still haunted from time to time by memories of the Before Time, but Sister Mary could see that those memories were growing dim as they were overcome by the good memories Ruth and Max were building for them. Yes, she thought, the kids were going to be just fine. Ruth and Max, too. They'd all worked hard over the past year to move forward after Boyo's passing and to help Skeeter and Mikey recover from their trauma.

Today, though, was a special day for Sister Mary. She coughed and cleared her throat to awaken the slumbering pile on the bed above her. "Ahem, ahem. Cough. Cough." She looked expectantly upward, hoping to see some movement. Nothing. Not even an eye opening or a twitch of an ear. "Ahem, ahem. Cough. Cough. Cough," she tried again. Still nothing. Fine, she thought. Maybe I'll get a drink of water and then wake them. Easing her way over to the water bowl, she heard Ruth stir ever so slightly. Good. That should get the ball rolling. She hoped Ruth would remember.

Ruth looked at the clock, turned on the light and quietly got out of bed. Walking over to Sister Mary, she knelt down and gave her head and belly a good scratch. "Happy birthday, Sister Mary Sunshine. How does it feel to be sixteen? What would you like to do today?" Sister Mary grinned. She had remembered!

Sister Mary was the oldest and sweetest dog Ruth had ever known. She, too, had struggled through the years to conquer her own demons. Despite her late start, she'd learned to stand her own ground, make her own way, and meet each day with joy and a smile. Losing Boyo, her best friend and constant companion of 13 years, nearly cost Sister Mary her life, so profound was her grief. But now, looking at the smiling face blinking back up at her from her mat on the floor, Ruth could see that her plucky, cheerful personality was back.

Of course Ruth had remembered her birthday. So had Max. Ruth saw the package of treats that he had quietly placed in the refrigerator last night. They would be dispensed and shared later with much fanfare. Max was always very particular about the disposal of treats. Sister Mary got hers first, every time.

"Sister Mary, what's up?!" Skeeter bounced off the bed with the exuberance of youth, front paws and tail swatting and wagging in every different direction, eager for a game, any game, not waiting for Sister Mary's answer.

"Hey, Ruth! Let's go!" Mikey jumped off the bed with equal glee.

"C'mon guys. Let's get Sister Mary downstairs and outside. It's her birthday today, you know," said Ruth as she scooped up Sister Mary from her place on the floor.

"Today's your birthday? Sister Mary? What's that?" asked Skeeter as she raced down the stairs.

Once downstairs herself, Sister Mary made her way outside to greet her friends. "A birthday is a day that happens every year and it is special, just for you. You get extra pieces of meat, sometimes a new toy, extra walks and scratches. Sometimes there's pizza. It's nice. That's all."

"That sounds great," said Mikey as he inspected the backyard, making sure that it was clear of squirrels, birds and any other errant wildlife. This was his yard now. He made certain that the other animals were aware of that fact.

The day went by quickly for Sister Mary. Ruth had arranged a "spa treatment" for her in the morning and the staff met Sister Mary with lots of good wishes and treats. Sister Mary's special friend, the lady with the magic wand, gave her an extra-long wand workover and then a massage. The spa was followed by a nap on her mat next to Ruth, who had decided to work from home that day. Of course, there was Ball. After Ball, Max's treat stash turned out to be more than just treats; it was dinner, as well. Steak, which was cooked to perfection, cooled and then sliced. Delivered just the way Sister Mary liked it.

Later that evening, Sister Mary lay on the sofa and enjoyed the gentle rub of Ruth's hands, massaging her back, stroking her ears and chin. She resumed her musings from the morning. Skeeter and Mikey were on the sofa next to Ruth, curled up next to each other. Sister Mary noticed that Mikey had spent a little time on the chair with Max before returning to the sofa, but she bet that he'd start to spend more and more time there. She'd overheard talk of Max and Mikey taking classes with the frisbee. That would be a good thing, she thought, as she drifted off to sleep.

"Sister Mary," whispered Skeeter from her spot on the sofa.

"Shh, Skeet, she's sleeping," said Mikey quietly, watching as Sister Mary, her feet flickering as she ran with Boyo in her dreams.

"Sister Mary," said Skeeter, still whispering, "Happy birthday, Sister Mary. Sweet dreams."

"Yeah, sweet dreams, Sister Mary," echoed Mikey.

And, indeed, Sister Mary dreams were sweet, happily playing keep-away with Boyo.

Chapter 43

Following Sister Mary's birthday, the holidays came with a rush and passed with a blur. On Thanksgiving, Mikey spent the day with Max and Max's family while Sister Mary, Skeeter, and Ruth spent the evening with Ruth's family. Then came the obedience school Christmas party followed by the final agility class, and Christmas baking at Mammaw and Pop Pop's.

By the time Christmas Eve arrived, Skeeter and Mikey had completed the year-long socialization course that Ruth had constructed for them months before. They had been "incident free" for six months. Both dogs were confidently managing their obedience classes, taking walks in different parks and in the neighborhood. They all enjoyed nightly Ball games.

And Sister Mary? Sister Mary adored both of her young friends. Sure, she got knocked over occasionally as they exuberantly bounded from one room to the next, but thanks to Skeeter and Mikey, Sister Mary had a purpose again, a job to do. She had become their ambassador to the world of living with humans. In return, they dispelled her sorrow over the loss of her long-time friend and broke the isolation that had befallen her. Sister Mary had returned to her hale and hearty, wisecracking self.

As she put the last of the ornaments on the tree, Ruth looked at her friends and smiled. Yes, she thought. It was time to take them to the next level. How would Mikey and Skeeter handle a full-scale Christmas party? Didn't Sister Mary deserve one as well?

The invitation to Christmas Eve dinner at Mammaw and Pop Pop's seemed to afford the perfect opportunity. The three dogs hadn't traveled to a party together for almost a year. The house would be crowded, but not too crowded. It would be merry and loud. Only family would be involved so they would be safe in the event a mistake was made. Also, Ruth thought with a chuckle, there would be plenty of food, positive reinforcement for her friends.

So, with leashes in hand, treats packed and hearts filled with hope, Max and Ruth piled gifts, dogs, and baked goods into the car and off they went. Riding in the back of the car, Skeeter and Mikey quizzed Sister Mary. "Sister Mary, which party is this one?" asked Skeeter. "Will there be explosions?"

"No, no dear, no explosions at this one. Just food and laughter.

"Is this the party where all the people are?" asked Mikey.

"I'm not sure. It's definitely a party, but I don't think it's quite Christmas yet. Ruth and Max usually travel separately on that day."

"So, Sister Mary…"

"Guys," Sister Mary interrupted Skeeter with a chuckle, "you're ready for this. Just remember your Mamma's words and remember all that you've learned. You'll be fine. Skeeter, you told me all about how much fun you had at the obedience school party last week. Mikey, you had a really good time with Max at his family's Thanksgiving party. Just enjoy yourselves." Sister

Mary settled in for the long drive and, taking their cue from her, so did Skeeter and Mikey.

The dogs could see Mammaw and Pop Pop's house, brightly lit with Christmas lights, the doorway festooned with garland and wreaths, and, as always, wonderful smells wafted out the door to greet them. "Here we go, kids. Showtime," announced Sister Mary as Max lifted her out of the car.

"Do you think we should put leashes on them?" asked Max as they approached the front door.

"No, let's just let them settle a bit outside and then take them in off-leash. We can always put one or both on later if we need it. Let's see how they do," said Ruth as she helped Sister Mary up the steps.

Mikey peered into the kitchen window and liked what he saw. Pop Pop was at the stove. Sister Stuff was helping. Mammaw and Uncle Pete were seated at the table. The kitchen itself was brightly lit. Food and good cheer overflowed. Mikey was beginning to see what Sister Mary and Boyo saw in these party things. "Come on, Skeet," he said. "Let's go inside. It's cold out here!"

"Hello! Hello!" announced Sister Mary as she entered the kitchen.

"Well hello, Sister Mary!" exclaimed Mammaw with a smile. Mikey and Skeeter joined Sister Mary in the kitchen.

Mikey had his sights on Pop Pop. Trotting up to him with a wag to his tail, Mikey looked up at him expectantly. "Pop Pop, what is that you are cooking? It smells amazing!" he exclaimed with a hopeful smile.

Skeeter kept her sights on Ruth. Skeeter knew Ruth would help her navigate things if and when they got scary.

The people in the room looked at one another with wonder, and Max and Ruth grinned from ear to ear. Sister Stuff broke the silence with a laugh. "Well! Merry Christmas, guys! It's so nice to see you all!"

From her spot in the center of the kitchen, Sister Mary also smiled. The transformation was remarkable. No fussing, no barking, no biting. Just confident, happy dogs enjoying their pack's company.

Later that evening by the fire, they were joined by Jake and his girlfriend. As gifts were exchanged, wrapping paper wadded and thrown playfully around the room and into the fire, Sister Stuff pulled out her famous dog gifts—rawhides for all!

Chewing on her rawhide contentedly at Max's feet, Skeeter looked at her brother and announced, "This party thing is pretty great."

Munching on his own rawhide, Mikey looked around at the scene in front of him with approval. His sister, happy. His people, happy. Yes, even he was happy. "Sure is Sis, Sure is," he said, giving the rawhide a good pull.

For her part, Sister Mary was content. She hadn't seen Mammaw and PopPop in ages it seemed and she'd always enjoyed their company. PopPop always had a ready treat for her and he did not disappoint this year.

Chapter 44

Ruth had one more test up her sleeve for Mikey. Christmas. The full day, the full party. Ruth thought that the full party day would be too exhausting for Sister Mary and maybe still a little overwhelming for Skeeter, but Mikey had been shortchanged on the holiday social scene. He'd missed the obedience school party and hadn't had a chance to go to Mammaw and PopPop's for Thanksgiving like Skeeter had. So Ruth determined that he would be her "wingman" on Christmas day, accompanying her to Max's family's party in the morning and traveling with her to the extended family's party Christmas night. It would be a long day for both of them but, she thought as she packed his bags for the day, it would be a good one if she managed it just right.

"Come on, buddy, let's get this show on the road!" Mikey, now accustomed to fun times traveling with Ruth, eagerly jumped in and assumed his post in the passenger seat.

"Have fun, Mikey!" Mikey could hear the girls cheering him on as he and Ruth sped down the driveway. Ruth was happy. Max seemed happy too. All signs pointed to a good day.

And it was. Arriving at Max's family's house, Mikey could smell dinner cooking and see the cheerfully decorated house he remembered from Thanksgiving. Trotting through the entry, he located Max and said hello to Max's mom. Everything was as it should be: friendly, warm, predictable. A perfect warmup for what lay ahead.

After the gifts were opened, jokes exchanged, and music played, Ruth decided it was time for her and her wingman to move on. Max would stay awhile longer and enjoy time with his family and then return home to take care of the girls. He and Ruth would enjoy their Christmas together late that evening and the next day.

"Are you ready, buddy?" asked Ruth as she gave Mikey's head a friendly scratch. "It's going to get crowded and loud in there, but just stick with me and you'll be fine." She opened the door to her family's house.

She needn't have worried. Entering the house, Mikey was on familiar ground. Moving past the strange people and finding Pop Pop at the kitchen counter, Mikey gave him a friendly nudge.

"Hey, buddy!" exclaimed Pop Pop. "Would you like a bit of ham? Or maybe some turkey?" Of course, Mikey did!

"Why, who is this here?" asked strange man standing at the counter.

"That's Ruth and Max's new dog, Mikey," said Pop Pop with a smile. "He's a bit wary of strangers. Let him come to you. Don't you go to him. Just give him some space and he should be fine."

The man, Pop Pop's brother, looked at Mikey standing confidently at Pop Pop's feet. "He looks pretty friendly to me," he said. Pop Pop grinned. "Well, he does, doesn't he? He's come a long way. But, let's everyone give him room tonight, okay?" Like Ruth, PopPop was anxious that Mikey's first party go well and he didn't want his guests to make some of the same mistakes he'd made.

Ruth's extended family and their close friends were all dog people. They all spread the word to the other guests to give Mikey his space as much as possible so that he had every chance for a successful night.

Arriving home late that night, hours later, Mikey could hardly wait to tell the girls about his first big party. "Skeeter! Sister Mary!" he exclaimed as he burst through the door. "Oh, my gosh! There was food, and there was food and there were people and food and …"

"Slow down, big guy!" said Sister Mary, picking herself off the floor where Mikey had knocked her over. "Take a breath and tell us about it."

Mikey was still bouncing but managed to collect his thoughts. "There was a room, with a table full of all kinds of meat and cheese, and I don't know what else. Ruth went in there a lot and she would give me stuff from the table. Then, she'd walk away and sometimes I'd follow her and other times I didn't. Sometimes there were other people in the room and they'd give me stuff from the meat table. Skeet. There was ham. There was beef. There was turkey. Cheese. Sausages. Peanuts. I mean, it just kept coming!"

Sister Mary grinned. "Let me guess, were there cheese and nuts in the kitchen?"

"Oh, absolutely!" Mikey gushed, "and the people kept dropping the food!"

Skeeter shook her head in amazement. "What about all the people? Were they nice?"

Mikey paused to take a scratch. "They were all nice. Nobody gave me any trouble. It was awesome, Skeet. You have to come next year!"

And the chatting went on long into the night and through the next morning.

Ruth and Max continued to marvel at the change in their friends. "You should have seen him, Max. He never once wavered, the whole night. Just amazing. And you should have heard Pop Pop backing him up as people came in. Nothing short of awesome," said Ruth as she fell asleep.

From his spot on the bed, curled up snuggly between Ruth and Max, Mikey flopped his head over Skeeter's shoulders. "Hey, Skeet. You awake?" he whispered. Skeeter stirred sleepily. "Are you awake?" Mikey gave her a nudge.

Yawning, Skeeter stretched and looked at her brother. "I am now."

"I just wanted to tell you. Remember you are all the time asking me about this whole Forever Home stuff? Remember?" Skeeter turned to look at her brother. She could see the earnestness in his face.

"Yeah, sure. Of course, Mikey. What about it?"

"Well, I just wanted to tell you, I know now. I get it. This is it. This is really it, Skeet. These people. You. Me. Sister Mary. This is it."

Skeeter caught her breath, and lay back down, closer to her brother.

"I know, Mikey. I know." From her mat on the floor below, Sister Mary smiled. She knew, too.

Snapshots

Sister Mary Sunshine, My Sasha.

Colby and Sasha loving their time in Assateague.

Getting Home

Bonnie, Sasha and Atari supervising yard
work.

Below, Colby and Sasha enjoying their
game of Ball.

Acknowledgements

First, to my husband, Tim, he who has borne the brunt of each of our dogs' fears, aggressions, and misunderstandings through torn skin and clothes, all the while never giving in to the thought of giving up on them. More than anyone else, he represents the personal human strength needed by our troubled pack mates.

Then to my father, Tom Pardoe, who like Tim bore his fair share of snaps, snarls, and panic attacks, but always managed to drop a well-timed peanut on the floor in response to a flicker of friendliness shown by our canine charges.

To my mother, Frankie Pardoe, who endured endless hours of my prattling on about the dogs, their problems, their triumphs and nuances and who then endured my whacky request to paint a cover for my book, made up right out of my imagination, and the cover is exactly what I imagined.

To my Sister, Stephanie Stull, and her family, who with their dogs made the journey with us.

Then, to my best friends of so many years, my Sasha and my Colby. She, who gave me a window into her dog's heart and who taught me what it takes to conquer her fears so that she could express the happy soulmate she so wanted to be. And he, who patiently guided his fearful friend as she tried to find her way in the world. He, who never met a human he didn't like, but who always stood ready to protect me.

To Third Thyme Rescue, Vilma and Ron Briggs, and to Sandi Guillemette and Jan Vincent, who had the insight, strength and kindness to pull and shelter Bonnie and Atari when they needed it.

To Dog Owners Training Club of Maryland and instructors, Adam Willie, David Cramer and Gail Phillips, who provided me training resources, encouragement, and whose instructors each made individual effort to help me train each of my dogs to remain calm in the face of distractions and stranger's approaching hands.

To Home Grown Dog Sports and Sally Zinkhan, who through their agility classes have shown Bonnie and Atari that it can be fun and safe to play with people and other dogs.

To my first round editors, Joan Eberhart and Anne Moe, who shared with me the roughest of drafts and encouraged me to see it through.

To Bonnie and Atari, two dogs who got off to a rough start but are determined to "get" home.

ABOUT THE AUTHOR

Kim Manuelides grew up in rural western Howard County, Maryland, where she, her sister and father spent countless hours riding their ponies through the back woods with their Cocker Spaniel, Ebony, who always seemed to find the shortcut home. When she was not riding her pony, and later her horse, Kim could always be found in the family's backyard, tending the family's horses, and 4-H projects, their sheep, chickens, rabbits and the family dog. Kim graduated from the University of Maryland, College Park with a degree in Animal Science, and later from the University of Baltimore School of Law. Now a practicing attorney, Kim and her husband, Tim, rescued their first dog, an Entlebucher Mountain Dog, 15 years ago. Following their adoption of their first dog, Colby, the couple adopted Colby's half-sister, Sasha, and much later Bonnie and Atari.

ABOUT THE EDITOR

Lauren Lowther, formerly a web designer, is currently a stay at home mom. She resides in Florida with her husband, children, and two dogs, Ribs and Paddy. Lauren's interests range from history, politics, and religion to fitness and sports.

Made in the USA
Middletown, DE
27 March 2016